DEUS EX
MACHINA

HAMARTIA, BOOK 2

RAQUEL RICH

Edited by Victoria Bell

DEUS EX MACHINA

Sequel to: Hamartia

Copyright © 2022 Raquel Rich

First printing

Paperback ISBN: 978-1-7771105-2-9
E-book ISBN: 978-1-7771105-3-6

Author photo by Christine Albee
Visit the author: www.raquelrich.com

For Gregory and Liam.

"Don't stop, believin'…" ♪♫

CHAPTER 1 - GRACE

Oh, what I wouldn't do for another day to digest life-travelling from Toronto, 2080, to 1930s Germany. It took everything in me not to pee myself or cry when air traffic control announced this flight was a go. It seemed golf-ball-sized hail wasn't a good enough reason to ground an aircraft. Now my brother, Charlie; my best friend, Kay; my husband, (new) Marc; and I are unregistered guests stumbling our way through the underbelly of an aircraft to meet Adalia, and all I can think is that I wish I had called in an anonymous bomb threat. It would've solved two problems: my fear of this turbulent flight and my growing angst over setting off a deadly chain of events—again.

Even though this mission was my idea—and I have valid reasons (preventing a holocaust, undoing another, guilt)—I'm not fully on board. The trouble is, until now, I've never stopped to think about what will happen if we fail. Or what if succeeding will be worse? It's true that the contents of a single pink vial could save millions of lives and stop the suffering of even more. But if we alter the timeline by using the vial to remove Dr. Messie's past life—Adolf Hitler—who's to say another villain won't fill his shoes? Hitler didn't work alone. What if whoever steps in wins the war instead of loses it?

I keep thinking about what Kay said when we first found out Dr. Messie was Hitler reincarnated. "Why couldn't he have been Johan Vaaler in his last life?" I couldn't puzzle out who this Johan person was and Kay said, "That's exactly my point." Then she sighed and told us that Johan invented the paperclip. I told her I would understand if she chose not to come; killing Hitler's a big ask. It was a stupid suggestion, and she made sure I knew it by way of shooting daggers at me with her eyes. "After what Dr. Messie did to my brother," she said, "it wouldn't matter if he'd been Charlie Brown in his last life." If only Hitler had been that insignificant.

But there's no going back now, which means there is no room for my self-doubt, my fear, and certainly not my guilt. For the sake of the people with me, I have to be strong. After all, they're only here because of me, including Kay, regardless of what she says. If I hadn't killed Leo, the human race wouldn't be spiralling toward extinction. Killing Leo to save Jordan, my nine-year-old son's life, triggered widespread Metagenesis: people lost their souls and their reincarnation cycles halted. So responsibility for this voyage lies squarely on my shoulders, weighing as heavy as a hippo.

Charlie kills the flashlight now that Adalia and the glass room are in sight. Soundless heat lightning illuminates the rest of the journey. I'm not claustrophobic or anything, but the glass room seems smaller than I recall. It's cylindrical in shape, six by six, and I already can't breathe just thinking about how tight a fit it's going to be with all five of us crammed in there.

Adalia is dressed in her usual all-white pantsuit, waiting at the entrance with an unreadable expression. Charlie gives me a reassuring nod and I'm reminded of how lucky I am to have my brother by my side. This makes me sad for Adalia. Dr. Messie is a monster to us, but to her, he's her big brother. She works as his assistant, so she must've believed in him once. He couldn't have always been evil, could he? Then again, he is Hitler reincarnated...

Kay nudges me. "You OK?" she whispers.

This isn't the first time she and I have been thrown from a plane, life-travelling. Last time, it was a bright and sunny day and the flight was smooth as butter. We were heading to Las Vegas, back eighty years to the year 2000, taking part in an illegal clinical trial to save Jordan from Metagenesis before he lost his soul for good. If the current flight and weather serve as omens, Vegas will seem like a visit to an amusement park compared with a country on the verge of a Nazi-led war. I wish we hadn't graduated from "let's stop Dr. Messie" to "let's kill Hitler."

"Fine. You?" I reply. What am I supposed to say?

"Doing better than him," Kay mutters, tilting her head toward Marc on my left. Her big blue eyes say, *Grace, distract your hubby.*

I let out a deep sigh and switch my focus to my petrified husband, (new) Marc. He isn't blinking. He's clenching his jaw and staring at the glass room the way Kay and I did only two short months ago. I'm caught off guard by his fear—will I ever get used to this new version of him? My Marc would've been pumped about being terrified, not frozen: he was a thrill-seeker.

I can't decide which is worse; that my soulmate is a complete stranger, that this stranger-soulmate has appropriated my husband's body, or that I sometimes can't tell the difference. One thing I know for sure is that if I hadn't killed Leo, my Marc would've been here, not this new... I give my head a good hard shake, ridding the circular thoughts from my mind. First off, I need to stop comparing new Marc to my Marc: it isn't fair. Second, what's the sense in obsessing? My Marc lost his soul when I killed his past life, Leo. This new Marc—new soul, same body—is here to stay, and step one on my journey to atonement is to make him feel like he belongs.

Ignoring my stomach, which flips with each dive the plane takes, I plant a fake courageous smile on my face and lead Marc by the hand. I almost lose my footing but still offer a reassuring squeeze and pull him along the last few metres to Adalia at the doorway. He releases my hand to raise his arms above his head so Adalia can strap bricks of money under his shirt, wrapping them around his torso with thick blue tape.

"I'll keep the papers and the vial with me. You hold on to the money," she tells him, her tone suited more to addressing a child than a man. It's clear to everyone but him that she's giving him something to be responsible for, to keep his mind off his fear of heights.

I poke my head into the glass room and try not to let my apprehension show, for Marc's sake. This trip would strike terror into even the bravest thrill-seekers, *which he no longer is*, the relentless little voice in my head reminds me. My stomach flips at the sight of those intra-cloud flashes and I have to force myself to take the first step across the threshold into the glass room. I thrust my chin up to give the appearance of bravery while keeping the looming billow beneath my feet out of sight, though not out of mind. In my head, I envision thick, smoke-like clouds waiting to swallow me whole. It doesn't help that when I look at Kay, her face says what I'm thinking: is this plane going to crash before or after we escape it?

As if in response to our question, the engines shut off, and for a heart-stopping moment it feels like we're on a tilting bobsled instead of an airplane. Seconds later, the power resumes, as does my heartbeat.

Adalia hands everyone a glass containing that foggy liquid. "Drink every last drop, quickly, and all at once."

What she doesn't say is, if we don't finish before the glass shatters away from our feet, we'll be plunging to our deaths instead of free-falling (up) to the 1930s.

She doesn't lift her glass to drink yet. Her eyes dart around without meeting ours. She seems pensive, like she wants to say something important and is searching for the right words, so we all wait. A moment later, she tucks her hair behind her ear and then speaks.

"You know, my parents thought they'd done mankind a favour by proving that reincarnation was a fact. I'm glad they've passed on so they don't have to live through what my brother has done with their discovery," she says, and pauses as if to rein in her emotions before adding: "or to watch him pay for his crimes against humanity. He is already dead to me." Then she holds her glass up and looks at each of us. "Our mission is to stop two genocides. We will kill Dr. Messie, creator of Metagenesis, by ensuring he contracts his own disease in his past life as Hitler. If we're successful, he will lose his soul and die, and will never be reincarnated again." She pauses, tucks her hair behind her ear again, then locks eyes with me. "Ending one life will save the lives of many. It's the right thing to do."

Guilt heats my cheeks. I did the very opposite of what she's just said—if I had let Jordan die, I would've saved the lives of many. Jordan's full recovery from Metagenesis is the reason the clinical trial was fast-tracked despite the legalities, and cloning souls from past lives was approved for the masses. I don't need Adalia's subliminal shaming to remind me that I share the blame with Dr. Messie for triggering human extinction. Sure, he started Metagenesis, but I could've ended it. To prove how damn sorry I am, I've agreed to change world history. I live with so much guilt that I won't voice my unpopular opinion: maybe we shouldn't kill Hitler?

Eager to leave before we lose an engine and nosedive, I hold up my glass to clink with Charlie, Kay, and Marc as they file into the glass room one by one. Thank goodness the liquid sloshing around my glass can be explained away by turbulence, so it doesn't call attention to my shaky hands.

Adalia joins us in the little room at last but doesn't shut the door. She seems to be the most nervous of us all, moistening her lips and over-tucking her hair. It's unsettling, as she's the one who organized our trip. She had our papers made up so we won't get accused of being spies; she stole the vial we'll need to inject into Hitler (so we halt his reincarnation cycle); and apparently, she even speaks German. Though I must say, I'm more worried about Charlie and me not looking European than I am about a language barrier.

Without meeting my glass, Adalia holds hers up high for another toast. "Thanks for trusting me. I wish everyone success." She doesn't smile, something we've grown accustomed to, but her eyes are kind as always. She looks at each of us, holding Marc's gaze a beat longer than the rest of us, and though I find it strange, I have no reason to mistrust her. She doesn't know I killed Leo, who will one day be her grandson, so I chalk it up to her fascination that Marc isn't dead. We didn't tell her that *this* Marc is a *new* Marc from another life, far in the future. My Marc lost his soul the moment I shoved his past life, Leo, to his death.

I meet Adalia's glass with a clumsy clink. We all chug. Charlie gags like I did the first time I drank this stuff. It leaves the kind of aftertaste you'd get from licking a rotten tree stump.

When white lightning flashes and shakes the plane, my empty stomach almost rejects the liquid. I salivate and cool sweat runs from my hairline. Marc has only half finished his drink and is backing up into a corner, his face pale as a thinning sheet. Afraid he may faint, I follow, bumping into Charlie on my way, who grabs my elbow to steady me. My brother's hand is strong, betraying his eyes wide with fear. Marc hits the wall and slumps to the ground; his empty hand makes like a squeegee against the glass wall.

I take a seat beside him. "Marc. Your drink. Finish it," I urge, using simple vocabulary for our mutual benefit. His fear is fogging his comprehension, and mine is making the task of putting a simple sentence together impossible. I don't think I'd be able to recite the alphabet right now if I tried.

A woman's voice comes over the intercom. "Ladies and gentlemen, the captain has left the seat-belt sign on." *No shit*. She speaks at auctioneer speed about remaining seated with seat belts fastened—seat belts I wish we had on. I want her to announce that the captain is turning the plane around. That way, we could come up with a better, less ambitious plan: a way to stop Dr. Messie in this life, not his past life.

The plane drops and shakes hard, the engines struggling. Kay fumbles her glass, almost drops it, then places one hand on a wall and opens her feet into a better stance.

Again we drop in altitude.

"Ladies and gentlemen, this is your captain speaking. We're encountering a little storm cell, not unusual when flying over a tornado zone."

"A *what* zone?" Marc cries out.

"This aircraft is equipped to fly through all weather, but the plan is to get above it. Things may get a bit hairy. I'll do my best to turn the seat-belt sign off in a jiffy. Bear with me."

The pilot's announcement, although light in tone, just makes me feel worse. And Marc too, judging by his ashen face. For his sake, it's a good thing my inability to speak, scream, cry, or even breathe makes me appear calm on the outside. Sweat dampens my back yet I'm frozen as my mind spins up worst-case scenarios: what if we crash before the glass shatters? What exactly does the pilot mean by "hairy"?

"Adalia, close the door before the right turbulence hits," I urge.

She tucks her hair behind her ear and nods in agreement but doesn't shut the door. She looks terrified and I wish she'd snap out of it. She's making me edgier by stalling at the doorway.

"Adalia," I plead, and then I notice her glass is still full.

"I'm sorry," she says and takes a quick step back, then another—right out of the glass room.

I stare hard at her and tilt my head. The door closes and latches shut before it hits me that she's changed her mind about coming with us. I'm left speechless.

"Adalia?" Kay says and then begins repeatedly screaming her name when she realizes it, too. "Adaliaaa!"

"I'm sorry," Adalia's lips move to say. I'm not sure if she says it out loud or just mouths it. Can she hear us through the glass wall? Is it soundproof?

"What the heck are you doing?" Kay shouts at her.

"What's going on?" Marc asks me like I'm in on it. He's plastered on the floor as still as a statue and he hasn't yet finished his drink.

The plane rocks again.

"We can't do this without her, Grace!" Kay shouts, and glares at me as if it's my fault Adalia is bailing on us.

"But... but I don't know what to do," I respond in a small voice, palms up, helpless. I want to cry.

Kay pounds her fists on the glass wall and screams the assistant's name.

"Marc." I zoom in on him. "Marc, please, you have to finish that drink." I don't know how to get Adalia back into this room, but I do know that without that drink, Marc will be heading in a downward death drop when the turbulence hits. He'd better get a grip on himself or this ride will be his last ever. My mission for the moment isn't about Germany and Hitler, or Dr. Messie and Metagenesis. I only need to make Marc—

"Drink," I beg, threading my fingers through his, his hand clammy as a piece of raw meat.

"The vial." Charlie breaks his silence. I can barely hear him over Kay's screaming but I immediately understand. "The vial!" He raises his voice to overpower Kay's and she spins around.

She glances from me to him, and we all come to the same conclusion. We're going to Germany without the damn syringe that will kill Hitler's soul, and thus Dr. Messie. This will all be for nothing. Charlie joins Kay and pounds on the glass wall. I'd join them if my legs weren't jelly. I wave my hand in front of Marc's face; his eyes are glossed over and glued to the glass floor. Charlie screams obscenities I've never heard come from him before, and Kay pleads frantically for Adalia to open the door, using her usual idioms.

"The game won't be worth the candle, Adalia! Give us the vial! *Please!*" Kay screeches, her voice cracking.

I have no idea what that expression means, but I feel Kay's panic all the same.

Adalia stares at us like a nurse observing unhinged patients in an old insane asylum. She's even wearing white and we're literally locked inside a glass room, at her mercy.

Desperate, I grab Marc's arm and give him a good shake. "Damn it, Marc! Snap out of it and drink up or you're a dead man!"

Between Marc's silent fear and Charlie and Kay's screams and incessant thumping on the wall, it's complete chaos in here. My chest is going to implode if I can't get control of something in this situation.

I shake Marc's arm harder. He finally looks up at me—a small victory—and brings the glass to his lips, downing the drink just as the airplane seems to drop out of the sky. We're airborne a few inches, our butts off the ground as if we've hit an actual bump in a real road. The lights flicker and go out but not before I watch in horror as some of that drink spills over on Marc's lap. Blood-red lightning snaps, followed by the first crack of thunder at the exact moment the glass floor and ceiling shatter into pieces.

"Oh shit," I mutter and squeeze Marc's hand tighter and my eyes shut; I vow to keep them closed until this ordeal is over. I've done this before. I know what's coming. I hold my breath and brace for it.

A wild twister sucks us out of the glass room and tosses us into the blustery atmosphere, telling me we haven't made it over the tornado zone as the pilot promised. *Liar!* The feeling is familiar but intensified by the violent storm. It doesn't matter that I tied my hair back in preparation: strands come loose and scratch like a wire brush up my nose. The world swirls around us and the cold rain thrashes like mini razors at my face and exposed torso, my shirt now untucked.

I'm desperate to hold onto Marc's hand, to keep him close, but it proves impossible. I should've wrapped my whole body around his. I wasn't thinking. *Don't let go, don't let go.* I struggle to bring my arm in, defy the g-force, and pull us together. The task is futile. I'd have a better time doing a curl-up with a thousand-pound dumbbell. My shoulder is at the brink of snapping out of its socket when Marc purposefully untangles his fingers from mine and lets go. *No!*

Screams and the sound of rain and wind all fuse together and I try to pick out Marc's voice, but I can't. In my mind's eye, bodies and airplane scraps whip around in a tornado, and I replay Marc's drink spilling onto his lap. What if he's hurtling *down* to the earth and not *up* with the rest of us? My eyes are iron-clad shut, but fear for Marc's whereabouts gets the better of me and I chance a squint, peeping my lids open just a slit.

Terror pumps through my veins. There is nothing but storm around me and I'm right in the eye of it. An eerie green ocean of clouds threatens to swallow me whole in its giant tsunami wave. I force both eyes open, wide as an owl, wishing I had their night vision. I whip my head around; not only is there no Marc, but there is no Charlie, there is no Kay, there is no plane. I am utterly alone. A new panic consumes me and the momentum of my hysteria sends me spinning and spiralling. I can't tell which way is up and which way is down, left nor right.

"Marc! Marc!" I scream his name but the wind snatches the words away.

I scream and screech until my throat burns and my chest aches and I lose the ability to breathe. The storm is having its way with me, throwing me around like a plaything. Lightning strikes, followed by thunder so loud my eardrums vibrate and tremble, electricity raises the tiny hairs.

The desire to suck in air vanishes the instant the white light penetrates the world around me, and then that unwanted calm pulls me under its spell. It no longer bothers me that Adalia just screwed us over, that we're going to Germany alone, with no papers and no vial. I could care less that Kay, Charlie, and Marc have disappeared into thin air. The fact that Marc spilled his drink and is crashing along with the plane is a fleeting thought. And just like the last time I travelled back to another life and time, I let the nothingness take me and I lose sense of myself and everything around me. Gone are my best friend, my brother, my husband… then my consciousness.

CHAPTER 2 - GRACE

A cold wind blowing dirt on my face wakes me, but it's not strong enough to be the storm and definitely not the tornado that damn near killed us when it sucked us out of the plane. I'm on solid ground—cold, solid ground. My head throbs as if equipped with its own heartbeat, but eventually, the buzzing in my ears fades and gives way to voices swirling around me. I rub the sand and grit out of my eyes until they unglue, and I squint into the twilight. That's when I spot Charlie, his clothes tattered and torn, on one knee, bent over a pile of something. Is it Marc? Kay is further away, behind them. She's on all fours, vomiting. I squeeze my eyes shut and turn my face away. Even on a good day, I don't have the stomach to watch others losing theirs. I wait a minute and then try to sit up, but my body is surfboard stiff, leaving me no choice but to rest.

In a nutshell, my biggest worry up to this point has been: who the hell are we to change world history? And now... No vial. No Adalia. No plan. We have to turn around and go right back home to Toronto, 2080. At least I got my unspoken wish: History will remain untouched. But at what price?

A memory surfaces of twelve-year-old Walt, Jordan's friend who had a bed next to him at Dr. Messie's clinic, Recycled Souls. I think of the first time we met Walt. His cheeks were gaunt, blue veins zigzagging through his sickly pale skin, yet he introduced himself to us with a big, confident smile as if he were the grownup whose job it was to make newcomers feel at home. He was a charismatic, beautiful child who withered away and died. A lot of people I've known have lost their souls and succumbed to Metagenesis, including Kay's little brother. But Walt always stood out to me because that day, it could just as easily have been Jordan. So, yes, history will remain untouched, but the consequence is that Dr. Messie will live and the Metagenesis plague will spread until every soul on earth is lost. The effects won't be immediate. We know it'll take a few generations, but when people lose their souls, like Walt did, they won't be reincarnated again.

"Marc?" Charlie says and I turn my attention back to him.

When I realize the pile he's bent over hasn't moved, I jump right up. *Marc!* I make it two feet from my spot but then give in to vertigo. Tumbling to the ground, I stick my hands out in front of me to brace my fall and wince when little stones cut into my palms. The world twirls like I've consumed a giant bottle of vodka rather than a small, foggy drink, and I'm immediately nauseated. I flip over flat on my back and let a wave of heat ripple through me. My mouth salivates. With my eyes closed, I beg the world to stop spinning. It doesn't help that I can hear Kay retching, even if I can't see her. If I move one more inch, I'll be just like her.

"Marc!" Charlie repeats more urgently.

Remembering Marc spilling some of that drink on his lap renews my motivation. *Please be OK, Marc.* I draw a big breath in through my nose and release it slowly through my mouth before trying once again, at the speed of a sea cow, to rise. Using my arms the same way a tightrope walker would a balance pole, I teeter my way toward Charlie, who is hunched over my unconscious husband. I can't tell if the sun is setting or rising; it's either dusk or dawn, but the pinkish-orange light is enough for me to see the blood sunk into the earth around him. Charlie has removed his sweater and tucked it under Marc's head.

"What can I do?" My voice comes out crackly.

"Good, you're up." Charlie looks me up and down. "Your ribbon—give me your hair ribbon."

"Huh?" I tilt my head at him.

"He's got a fat lump on his head like he whacked it pretty hard. But the blood, that's from his arm. Something took a good gouge out of it."

Relief washes over me. Unconscious is better than dead. I remove my hair tie, ripping a wad of tangled curls with it, clean it off, and hand it to Charlie, who ties it tight around Marc's arm.

"Gracie?" Charlie's tone is one of unease. He keeps shifting his gaze back and forth from Marc to me and then to whatever is over my shoulder, worry creasing deep between his eyes.

"What's the matter?" I'd turn my head to see what he's looking at if I weren't so dizzy. Like me, I'm sure he's wondering where in Germany we've landed. From my vantage point, it seems to be a desert: there are cacti in the distance. I didn't know Europe had deserts. That gnawing fear that I don't know enough about Germany or the 1930s washes over me again. We have no business being here and I can't wait to leave.

Charlie shakes his head, dismissing whatever he was about to say, and instead asks me to go check on my friend. I don't budge and his worry melts into a smirk at my yuck-face. "Never mind," he says. "I'll go. Stay with Marc, try to get him to wake up, talk to him until he does."

Charlie leaves to tend to Kay, moving quick and nimble. As a kid, he loved the spinny rides. He must feel as adrenalized as we do dizzy. I suppose one out of four is better than none.

"Marc?" I take his hand and bring it to my lips, kiss his fingers. I brush his hair off his forehead and run my thumb along his cheekbone. Tears sting my eyes and I don't hold them back. I don't do that anymore. I let my tears run freely down my face and drip off my chin. I will be open and honest from now on. That was my promise to myself and to those I betrayed: topping that list, by a long shot, are Marc (both versions) and Leo.

I'm not reckless with my honesty, though. For instance, I don't volunteer details that I know will hurt Marc—including anything about Leo—but if he asked me, I'd answer. I wish that openness was a two-way street. I'll never know this Marc the way Rachel will, his wife from his next life, but I'd settle for knowing his real name. Each time I ask him, he won't tell me. Other than that he comes from the 2190s, I know nothing about him. In the days leading up to our departure to Germany, he flip-flopped between warm and cold, becoming distant even toward Jordan. His aloofness has forced me to be patient and give him space. If he would only tell me something, anything… it might ease my guilt. But guilt isn't synonymous with regret.

Dr. Messie told me only what he thought I'd agree to: to save Jordan's life, I had to travel back in time, find the right subject (Marc's past life, Leo), clone his soul with the vial, then bring the data back to repair Jordan's before he died of Metagenesis. He didn't tell me that the subject, Leo, would have to complete a life cycle right after being injected, meaning someone had to kill him. He didn't tell me that once Leo died, it could mess with his reincarnation cycle, which meant I risked losing my Marc. But Adalia told me. She intercepted me in Vegas. Sometimes I'm convinced that I ignored her because by the time she told me, I was too invested to turn back. Other times I admit that just because I'm sorry for my mistake doesn't mean I wouldn't repeat it, even with 20/20 hindsight. And that knowledge makes the guilt that much worse.

My mood lifts the instant Marc's lips twitch and he lets out a low groan. His lids flutter and I make sure I'm the first thing his hazel eyes see when they open. I dry my face with my sleeve.

"Marc, can you hear me? Wake up."

And he does. He looks at me, and then past me. His eyes widen and his face contorts into an expression of horror. He tries to prop himself up into a sitting position.

"No, no, relax. You've hit your head and have an open wound on your arm."

Marc's face doesn't show an ounce of pain. Instead, his mouth is agape and he glances back at me for a second, as though he wants to say something but he's in too much shock to utter even one word. I know how he feels. I remember when Kay and I arrived in Las Vegas, a foreign land in a foreign time.

Behind Marc, the worry on Charlie's face has returned tenfold. He's holding Kay's hair back for her. She's no longer vomiting, but she's looking in my direction, over my head as well.

I turn around, curious to see what everyone is fascinated by.

I stop breathing when I see it: the sign. *Welcome to Fabulous Las Vegas, Nevada!*

CHAPTER 3 - GRACE

"There," Kay says and stops in her tracks to point at a spot far in the distance: the cemetery and funeral home. This snuffs out all discussion and we share a sigh of relief. At least we know where we are in Vegas, and we're not stranded in an endless desert. As for *when* we are, that's another story. We've been walking for a couple of hours and it's cool out, which tells us it can't possibly be August like Kay's and my last stint here. Even though the sun has risen, there's a cold, brisk wind and when a cloud hides the sun, even for a brief moment, it's cold. And then there's the biggest and most puzzling question, one we've been discussing on and off the entire walk. *Why?*

Why are we in Vegas and not Germany? How could Adalia give us that speech about Dr. Messie paying for his crimes and then, moments later, abandon us? She is the one who set everything in motion for this life-travel trip. And not only that, but she was the one who intervened on my last trip to Vegas, warning me that cloning souls in the past resulted in future soul losses. She was an old woman by then, and when I discovered that she was Leo's grandmother, it became clear she'd been trying to stop Dr. Messie in the past for a long time. It was confirmed when we learned that she'd fled Nazi Germany during the Second World War and married Leo's American grandfather. That's how we knew she'd gone to Germany, and when. It's why we asked her to take us there. Adalia is the key to this whole mission. Now it just feels like we've been left to fend for ourselves without the mastermind.

So did Adalia send us here by accident? *Of course not,* according to Marc; *there must be a purpose.* The whole walk he defended Adalia like he'd known her all his life, not only recently met her.

Charlie usually plays the reasonable one, but even he couldn't find a logical argument. "You're right, Marc. She screwed us—*on purpose.*"

I didn't want to say anything because I felt like I'd have to pick a side: team Marc or team Charlie. Besides, I didn't know what to think, especially given my hesitation about going to Germany in the first place. I only knew that I felt betrayed by Adalia. And I didn't know what to make of Kay's bizarre behaviour. With Adalia's help, Kay had recently taken Peter, her little brother, off life support, so it could've been her way of turning a blind eye to the possibility of Adalia screwing us over. But still, she was acting like Vegas was nothing more than a pit stop, blissfully saying things like, "As soon as we get to Germany, I'm trying schnitzel. Have you ever tried schnitzel?"

We approach the cemetery where Leo and I first saw each other and I bite my lip, suppressing a wave of guilt. When I catch myself recoiling from Marc, I inch closer, with purpose. I remind myself I can't win his trust and forgiveness if I revert to my bad habit of pushing people away.

"Well, with no funeral service to crash, I guess we'll starve to death. Ha! Good thing we're already at a graveyard," I say, covering with a corny joke no one laughs at. I avert my eyes from Kay, who is watching me with pity, and I don't need to guess what that knowing look on Charlie's face means. He has a way of reading me and I'm sure he's scrambling for the right thing to say to bail me out of my discomfort, like always. Even Marc, whose jaw tightens, senses I'm overcompensating, and he barely knows me.

"Kay, is this where you and Gracie came to find a taxi last time?" Charlie asks, saving me.

"Yes. The phone's that-a-way. I'll show you how it works in a sec. First things first—there's a bathroom inside that funeral home and I need to rinse my mouth." As she leads the way, I hear her clicking her tongue off the roof of her mouth and catch a glimpse of her sour face. "Barf breath. Right, Marc?" She grabs his arm and pulls him along.

During our long trek, Kay stopped a few more times to up-chuck. Charlie held her hair each time and rubbed her back while I uselessly plugged my index fingers in my ears and squished my eyes shut to drown out the sight and sound of my best friend.

Marc has also been sick, and that is what troubled me most. He's complained of blurry vision and stopped several times just to sit on the ground, his arms stretched out as if to stop the world from moving beneath his feet. He insisted it was just his head, not a big deal, and has nothing to do with that drink he didn't finish. A possible bleeding brain is a big deal in my book, but I hope he's right about the drink having no effect. He's here and we all took a beating in that storm. I rub at my own throbbing head, convinced the daylight will be the final push needed to induce a stroke.

When we enter the funeral home, it strikes me how different everything is. The wood panelling on the bottom half of the wall is now a deeper tone. On the top half, the wallpaper has changed from a dull-coloured flower pattern to a simple, ivory-embossed one. Even the furniture: the high-back, dusty-rose armchairs have been swapped out for classic midnight-blue ones, their curly wooden arms stained almost black to stand out from the wood panelling behind them.

I back out like I've entered the wrong place and exchange a glance with Kay.

"Maybe they've renovated?" She words it like a question and shrugs.

Although the same thought occurred to me, the decor doesn't strike me as crisp and new. The chairs are already worn in, with butt outlines denting and fading the fabric, and the wallpaper is peeling in a corner or two.

We're approached by a petite, mousy woman, mid-twenties, wearing a black pantsuit. She wears no makeup and her dull, dirty-blond hair hangs pin straight to her shoulders. Her name tag reads *Amy*. What a forgettable name for such a forgettable face.

"We're not open yet. May I help you?" Her voice is soft, like someone offering condolences at a … a funeral home. I stifle a laugh at my dumb joke.

I don't know why I expected the place to be unattended. Al-though there's no service ongoing, they wouldn't leave a building unlocked and unwatched. As usual, I have nothing to say when caught off guard and always find myself trying to look innocent.

"Hi, Amy. We're looking to visit a beloved relative," Kay jumps in with a regretful frown, one hand over her heart respectfully. The rest of us stand mute.

"We'd like to freshen up first, of course. May we use your facilities?" Kay asks with a bowed head. When Amy doesn't respond or point us in the right direction, or even move out of the way to let us through, Kay adds: "We've travelled a long way to pay our respects and encountered bad weather."

Kay's explanation of how we look—*weather?*—is laughable. I feel like a human torpedo that crash-landed in a typhoon. This is Vegas, so anything goes, but I'd pay to hear Amy's thoughts. Our clothes (styled for 1930s Germany) are filthy from getting caught in the storm and dumped in the desert. Kay and I have matted hair. Bloodshot-eyed Marc has a mangled arm with a red ribbon tied around it in a neat bow. Charlie's the best kept out of our group, and he's wearing a sweater that he used as a pillow for Marc. It's a dark sweater but there is no mistaking what it's stained with: blood.

"Um, ya, sure. Right over there," Amy says, throwing a thumb over her shoulder without taking her eyes off us. "What's the name?" she asks, remaining professional by not reacting to our stench as we awkwardly squeeze around her toward the restroom.

I take a discreet whiff of us; now that we're indoors, our scent is pungent. We haven't completely dried out and we smell like a clan of cats coming in from the rain.

"I'm Grace. This is my bro—"

Kay jumps in. "You mean our relative, right?"

Amy nods, holding her breath.

"David Williams," Kay says in a sad voice.

"Allow me to look up where he rests, while you freshen up," Amy offers, then asks us to sign the guestbook before she finally moves out of the way and leaves us.

When we've made it out of earshot, Kay narrows her eyes at me. "Why would you give her our names?"

"I want to be more honest," I reply innocently, though now that she's making a big deal out of it, I realize I need to learn how to better pick my moments of honesty.

She tightens her lips, shoving the restroom door open with a hip. "Incognito—that's what you need to be."

Fifteen minutes later, and with cleaner faces, Amy intercepts us as we leave the building. "Third laneway and make a right to the Williams' family burial plot."

She reminds us once again to sign the guestbook. We lie and tell her we will.

Kay heads to the pay phone with Charlie to call a taxi and I make my way to the gravesite where I know Leo's father, David Williams, was laid to rest. Amy said it was the third laneway, but I don't need directions. I remember exactly which tree Leo was standing under the day I first saw him. Guilty nostalgia forms a ball in my gut as I approach it.

"Where are you going?" I didn't realize Marc was following me and his voice cuts in at the exact moment I see the plot beside David Williams. The memory of Leo's death pulls me down hard on my knees, and my heart hurts when I touch the ground above the spot where he lies. Leo. The man I loved. The man I killed.

I glance over my shoulder at Marc. He stares at the gravestone, unmistakably shocked, jaw clenched and lips drawn in a tight, straight line. To leave his body in the future to become Marc, he meditated for months and induced a continual code 33; he suffered through flashbacks of his past lives and deaths, reliving Leo's death over and over. Marc once described it to me as a recurring nightmare. I imagine he must feel like he's standing at his own grave.

Marc shifts his gaze to me and I sense anger burning beneath his cold scowl. It frightens me. The way he looks at me, it's like he sees me for the first time, for what I really am. A killer.

I should say something, but all the words have lodged in my throat in the form of a bitter ball of guilt, and all I can manage is a weak "sorry" that even I can barely hear.

He responds with an abrupt U-turn and leaves.

"I'm sorry." I reflexively call out another apology. I've done this a few hundred times since our dinner at the historic CN

Tower, when we both confessed. I confessed I had killed Leo, and Marc told me Dr. Messie had ordered him to come back to kill me.

Like always, he ignores me. He walks quicker, hands in pockets, shoulders hunched to his earlobes.

Defeated, I turn my attention back to the gravestone and take a deep, shaky breath. "Hey, Leo," I say to his face, chiselled into the stone.

Not only is the image not to scale, but the serious business-like face doesn't reflect the laid-back, flirty spirit I remember. Sometimes he was even sweet. "If your crazy logic is real, we'll see each other in all our future lives. You and I, we're soulmates," he said right before I killed him. I will carry those words with me until my dying day. I miss Leo. And even though his soul has morphed and moved on and on to become this Marc, it isn't the same. Yes, he's still my soulmate, but something is missing, and I know Marc feels it too.

I retrieve a small item from my pocket—a wine cork from my and Leo's picnic at the Grand Canyon on the night I pushed him to his death. I twist it around between my fingers. It's the new thing I carry around to torture myself, adding to my old habit of wearing Dad's copper watch, which I haven't parted with since the night of his suicide—another death I sometimes blame myself for. Although the stained cork has faded in colour and has long lost its scent, I'll never forget the smell of the wine on Leo's breath when his lips touched mine. All I have to do is close my eyes and I can still feel him kissing me. I can feel his fingers weaving into my hair at the nape of my neck, pulling me in close enough to sense his breath in sync with mine. That kiss was what sealed the deal and removed any doubts about who he was—leading me to kill him, then run for the shuttle two days ahead of schedule.

My eyes snap open at that last thought. It hits me that we have no way home. The shuttles ended only a couple of days after I killed Leo. While Kay went on about schnitzel, and I avoided Charlie and Marc's argument about Adalia sending us to Vegas instead of Germany, no one mentioned a solution. It went without saying that we'd hop a shuttle out of here ASAP. Metagenesis can't be stopped from here or now.

"How the hell are we getting out of here?" I ask Leo.

His stone lips don't move; his eyes reveal nothing.

"Uh, Grace?" It's Kay. I spot her down the row a couple of plots away, staring at an unfortunate someone's gravestone. I was so lost in my world of Leo that I didn't hear her approach. "Didn't we leave here in the year 2000?"

I glance at Leo's gravestone, with the date of his death clearly marked as August 22nd, 2000, only a few days after his birthday. I look back at her. "Ya?" I answer-ask, rubbing my clammy palms on my thighs. Then something in my gut pulls my attention back to the engraving on the stone. It reads: *David "Leo" Abruzzo*. His name sends a cold sensation slicing the inside of my belly from the bottom up. Why? Is it disappointment that I didn't know his real name, just like I still don't know new Marc's? I knew Leo only by his nickname, his zodiac sign. I later learned his given name, but he failed to mention his surname to me. That must be what's putting me off, yet—

"Grace, are you listening to me?"

I rise off my knees and turn to her. "Ya, I am. What'd you ask me?"

"When did we leave? What year?"

"End of August, 2000. Why?"

"Given this fresh pile of dirt, this beau was recently buried, and it says he died February 28th, 2006. The shuttles are done. How are we getting out of here?"

Kay walks over to me and we stare at each other. She's my mirror image, eyebrows scrunched, pupils giant with trepidation. She's preoccupied with the date, but not me. Yes, the fact that we're here six years after the last shuttle is shocking—I am thoroughly shocked—but it isn't the source of why I suddenly feel sick. What is it about Leo's name that's spreading fear in my veins like a virus? I search every dark corner of my mind for an explanation and come up empty.

Charlie approaches us then and nods at Kay. My face flushes when he gives me a weak smile that tells me he saw me on my knees, begging for Marc's forgiveness. Then he looks at Leo's gravestone and his shoulders sag. "Leo died in August? It's too cold. No way is it August now."

"It's not even the year 2000, Charlie," Kay moans. "The shuttles are over. We're stuck here."

He rakes a hand over his short coils and utters a quiet curse.

Staring at the stones in front of us, we share a moment of silence and let the gravity of our situation settle in. I glance from one grave to the other. I see Leo's and his dad's, both Davids. They don't share the same surname: I recall Leo telling me his parents never married. He didn't get along with his dad and I bet he'd be upset his gravestone didn't just say "Leo."

"We have to find the old woman, Adalia. She can help us," Kay says.

I see Kay's logic, but... "Adalia was really old when she approached me here in Vegas. She could be dead."

"She better not be dead!" Kay yells at me like I have control over the old lady's state of being. "She has to get us to Germany!"

"Or back to Toronto," Charlie adds. I like his idea better. Then he mutters that we don't even have the vial, making Kay's idea pointless.

I shift from foot to foot, feeling like I should be the one to suggest something, but what? If we go to Germany—which I don't want to do—we have no vial. If we return to Toronto, we have to come up with a new plan. And if Adalia is dead, we're not going anywhere.

Charlie chimes in with his big-brother voice. "Girls, if she were dead, wouldn't she be here, buried with her family? David was her son. Leo was her grandson. And I assume that guy there," he points to another tombstone, weathered and much older than the others, "her late husband?"

Kay gasps, her hand flies to her mouth. "Brilliant observation!"

Charlie and I share a smile at how easy it is to please Kay. He's right about Adalia, though, and it gives me a flutter of hope—albeit a small, wee, tiny flutter. Given that she's the one who sent us here, she might not want to help.

"I hate that she did her 'trust me' speech before screwing us," Kay says, then mimics a young Adalia with a dramatic head bob. "*Trust me.* What the heck does that even mean?" She throws up her hands.

"If there's a way out of here, the old lady is it, whether we trust her or not," Charlie states as a matter of fact.

"Wait," I say, a long-shot idea forming. "Adalia may not be the *only* way."

Charlie and Kay tilt their heads in unison.

"Jordan was here, too."

Kay's lips curl into a smile. "Find adult Jordan?"

"Wouldn't he have gone back home?" Charlie asks.

"He couldn't. He got caught snooping and was chased out, re-member?"

Many years after being cured, Jordan not only learned the truth about the cause of Metagenesis, but he learned that Dr. Messie had known it all along: time-travelling was supposed to be the next big thing in tourism; instead, it caused future soul losses, ceasing the cycle of reincarnations. That was why adult Jordan came to Vegas and asked me to let him die as a nine-year-old, telling me that if he hadn't been cured, the human experiments—which had been de-nied by the Ethics Review Board—would've stopped. Metagenesis would've been over.

"Then it's settled. We find Jordan," Charlie states with an en-couraging nod.

Kay claps her hands together. "Great!"

I half smile at the two of them. I'm not super enthusiastic, even if it is my idea. It's been six years. Adalia and Jordan could be anywhere in the world, which means we may never find them. I'm relieved (though I'll never admit it) that we didn't end up in Germany, but I'm horrified at the thought of being stuck here in Vegas. If we're stuck, Metagenesis will continue to spread until it's game over for humanity. And there's something else I can't put my finger on... about Leo...

Kay cuts in. "Grace, are you with us? You have the stare of a blind cavefish."

"David Abruzzo... Does that name mean anything to you?"

Charlie and Kay make sad eyes at me and shake their heads.

"Hear me out. What if he was important and I killed him?"

"Stop torturing yourself," Kay says.

"I'm not, it's just, I don't know." I shrug, searching Leo's stone face for an answer. "His name... it's... familiar."

She squeezes my shoulder and Charlie gives me a pep talk. "Gracie, millions of things must run through your mind about what you did. You must constantly play out how things could've been different, all the 'what-if's. I can't begin to imagine what you're going through. But Metagenesis is Dr. Messie's mistake, not yours."

Kay takes the torch like the two of them are a tag team who've practised this routine in case of a Grace emergency. I feel like I'm being handled. "We have a plan to make things right and we mustn't veer off it now. Dr. Messie must be stop-stopped."

A smile inches up my cheeks at Kay's "stop-stopped" expression. Her habit of blocking negative energy keeps her from using the word "kill." Neither mentions that the plan is null and void, thanks to Adalia. And even though their explanation does nothing to tame the inner voice screaming for me to think harder, what they say makes sense. I know my mind looks for Leo all the time and grasps at ways to torment me with his memory. The wine cork in my pocket doesn't help. But following my instincts has always gotten me into trouble.

Kay offers another shoulder squeeze. "All we have to do is find Jordan or Adalia. Piece of pie!"

"You mean cake." Charlie smirks.

She bats a hand. "Everyone knows pie is easier. And once we hunt Dr. Messie and stop-stop him, Metagenesis will be over. Simple. As. Pie."

"Sure, pie. Whatever you say," I reply.

"That-a-girl." No-negative-Kay ignores my sarcasm and grins like a fifth-grader who just aced a complex word in a spelling bee.

"What if we can't get back? What if we can't find adult Jordan or old-woman Adalia? It's been six years." I look to Charlie first. I want him to reassure me using reason, not optimism like Kay. But his expression tells me I took the words right out of his mouth.

"Quit singing the blues. Of course we'll find them!" Kay's tone is optimistic as per normal, but she's not stupid. Her eyes say what Charlie and I think: *without Jordan and Adalia, we're all dead.*

CHAPTER 4 - MARC

An hour and a taxi ride later, I find myself sitting on a plush bed in a high-end hotel room, scrubbing water out of my hair from a shower fit for a king. I bite my tongue as I listen to Grace and Kay argue in the bathroom about the best way to find Jordan. They speak freely, like I'm not in the room, or like the running water and hum of the bathroom fan distort their disagreement. Kay is insisting on going to some diner to ask for help from a waitress they befriended the last time they were here.

"And exactly how is Camilla supposed to help us, Kay? She knows how to hide *from* people, not find them."

Camilla, from what I gather, is the waitress. When Grace had recounted her Vegas journey to me, she mentioned she'd made friends with a woman on the run from her past, abusive relationship. Grace doesn't instantly like people, but it was clear she had felt a connection to the friendly waitress. However, Grace has zero interest in talking to Camilla and goes as far as accusing Kay of wanting to find her just to catch up and gab. It seems to me like a stupid accusation until I hear Kay's response.

"Aren't you at least curious to see how her wedding went?"

"Seriously?" Then Grace follows up with a suggestion of her own, to search for Jordan Dartmouth the same way they searched for the "subject."

Kay reminds Grace how long the phone-book process took, and that Jordan might have left Vegas long ago. "And if he hasn't left, he's probably incognito!"

The way they refer to my past life, Leo, as a "subject" in a phone book, makes me sick. With each passing minute, it becomes more and more apparent that I don't belong. I didn't belong in Toronto. I don't belong in Vegas. I don't belong in this body, and I will never belong to this family.

Charlie returns from the vending machine and immediately tries to distract me with small talk when he realizes I'm eavesdropping. He's a good brother-in-law, but his loyalty is to his little sister, Grace—or rather *Gracie*—whom he notoriously defends.

"Marc, check it out." He tosses something shiny at me.

I catch it by reflex. It brings an instant smile to my lips and I chuckle despite my mood. It's a can of fucking Pepsi.

Charlie makes a sour face. "It smells like ass in here. Wanna go torch the pile of wet clothes? Or at least get outta here for a few minutes to let the ladies finish up?" He tips his chin toward the open door. His tone tells me it's a command and not a suggestion.

Happy to stop the movie reel rolling in my head of Grace on Leo's tombstone—*my* tombstone—I oblige. What she did to him is more than a flashback for me: It's a living nightmare. And each time she apologizes, I relive the apology she screamed to him/me while I clung for life at the edge of that canyon after *she pushed me into it.* It's like I'm in an arranged marriage with a lunatic. And right now, I'm this close to shouting at her to shut the fuck up. I can never seem to decide how I feel about her: love, anger, desire, regret. But at this moment, her shrill voice echoing from the bathroom has the same effect on me as a fork scraping a dinner plate. She's making my skin crawl.

"Where to?" I ask, leaving the can of soda unopened on the dresser and following Charlie out of the room. Getting to know him isn't a bad idea.

I don't think Charlie has a plan for where to go. He simply wants his sister out of my earshot. In the lobby, he eagerly accepts when I suggest we grab a seat at one of those bars at the casino-hotel we've checked into. It's hardly noon, but we take seats at the marble counter and order two strong drinks, then wait in awkward silence for the bartender to return.

I take in the scene around me. Roman palatial, just as the name Caesars Palace suggests. We really went all out, according to the ladies. I have to wonder if Adalia screwed us, helped us, or suspected something. The way she wished us success, but then looked at me the way she did… It was like she was asking me specifically to trust her, or she was telling me that she didn't trust me. Then she made me responsible for the money and again I tried to read between the lines: was she testing me?

According to Grace and Kay, it was a shit-ton amount of money. I know nothing about spending it, so they've taken over and insisted we weren't going to scrimp. I hated the shopping spree, but I admit I like my new outfit. Grace picked something out for me but I refused to entertain letting her dress me. Instead, I chose black fitted jeans, a black button-down shirt, and a thin black leather jacket. She made a face at my colourless choices and I took pleasure in telling her I was in mourning. That shut her up.

The bartender slides two short drinks in front of us on little coasters shaped like the coliseum. "That'll be eighteen dollars, please. Do you want to start a tab?"

"What's a tab?" Charlie asks.

The bartender hesitates. "Pay later?" he says, his pierced eyebrow rising in unison with his voice.

Charlie pulls money out from a fat wad of bills wrapped in his shiny copper money clip that matches his pinky ring, both of which he bought here. "No tab," he replies.

It always trips me up when Grace, Charlie, or Kay ask stupid questions about the customs of this era. It's like the 2080s generation collectively decided to ignore the recent past and start fresh. I'm no expert myself, but I know what a tab is and I'm from another hundred-plus years *post* Grace/Charlie/Kay. And they're so oblivious. I was too scared shitless on the plane to notice the US currency Adalia had taped to my chest, but as soon as I peeled off my shirt… how could these numbnuts not have noticed? Ha! The thought of money makes me laugh, remembering how the last time Grace and Kay came here, they had a piggy bank. *A piggy bank!* I glance at Charlie, innocent and naive. In fact, it's naive of all of them to think stopping one man will stop Metagenesis. Idiots.

"How do you like our odds of finding the kid and the old lady?" I ask, trying to get some conversation going.

"I don't," Charlie responds, and we both fall silent again. I bet I know what's running through his mind: if the shuttles have ended, what can Jordan or Adalia do about it? No one has asked these things aloud and I'm not going to be the first. I'm just along for the ride—you know what they say, go along to get along. But if we find Adalia or Jordan, I guarantee they're going to be as pissed as I am when they realize Grace ignored their warnings.

"What's up with the copper ring?" I try again and I'm glad I do, as it breaks the ice.

Charlie smiles as he tells me about his good-luck charm, a piece of metal he used to wear around his neck as a kid. A gift from an old family friend he never met.

"I had it made into a ring. Not sure why," he says, fidgeting with the thin band.

"I thought you bought that ring here to match your money clip, you stylish motherfucker," I joke and back-slap his arm.

Charlie enjoyed the shopping spree more than any of us. He tried on every outfit in every colour before settling on a few quality pieces. The storekeeper said he had an impeccable fashion sense and nodded in approval at all of his choices.

"You got it all wrong. I bought the money clip to match the ring. I couldn't say no when they offered to buff it." We both laugh. "That reminds me—I need to buy some nail polish."

"Nail polish?"

"The clear stuff, to keep it from going green," he says, thinking he's defending himself, but it only makes me laugh harder.

"Adalia said you weren't allowed to bring anything, you sly fox."

"Gracie did. She smuggled that watch of hers back and forth."

I nod. "True, true."

He doesn't mention that she also snuck in that wine cork they think I don't know about. I'm itching to find out, without having to ask, which man she shared the wine with: Leo or *her* Marc? She never talks about either of them unless I ask, which I never do. Questioning goes both ways and I don't want to answer any of hers in return. But still… I clench my jaw, push the thought aside.

"Do you have any questions? You know, stuff you don't want to ask Grace?" Charlie asks, his eyes focused on his drink. What is he, a mind reader? "You and I were pretty close before you two split up. After, it was just weird, you know? I knew she was pushing you away and causing all the problems but... she's my sister, so..." He trails off.

I blow out a breath, puffing my cheeks. "I don't know what to ask," I admit, instead of bringing up the wine cork. That would reveal more about me than about her. "Like you said, '*she's your sister, so...*' What am I allowed to ask? What are you going to tell me that she hasn't already?"

Charlie looks at me with a raised eyebrow.

I plow ahead before he can answer. "Everyone wants to protect Grace, shield her from her mistakes, ease *her* pain. But you all seem to have forgotten that I'm the one in the dark about everything." I slap an open palm against my chest with each point I make. "I'm an outsider. I don't belong in your little family." Slap, slap. "Grace isn't even my wife, by the way. Let me tell ya, if there was an award for tolerance, I'd take first prize for not walking away from that woman. It'd be easier to leave her than to stumble around trying to learn how to be Marc. And why should I? I don't owe Grace my time, or an explanation, and definitely not my forgiveness. How can she expect..." I pause, catching my breath. My heart is pumping rage. "How can any of you expect me to forget what she did, what I sacrificed to be here, and the life I left behind?"

"No one's asking you to forget," Charlie says, full of genuine sympathy.

"How else am I supposed to assume the role of Marc?" I make an effort to lower my voice and cool down despite my boiling blood, but stopping my rant is out of the question. "Grace got us all into this situation, and now I should suck it up like you and Kay have, right? You two stick by her no matter what. So whatever I ask you, I'm sure you'll answer strategically to help your little sister, not to ease my mind. You made it clear—in your own words—even when she's the one who causes the problems—" I stop mid-sentence and let out a sigh. There's nothing more to say and I'm taking it out on the wrong person. I turn to my empty drink and raise my hand to get the bartender's attention for another.

Charlie tells me, "Make it two more."

I hold up two fingers; the bartender nods.

Charlie studies me as he considers my response. "Are you really thinking about walking away from Grace?"

I laugh. Holy shit, he's relentless. "You're a good brother, Charlie. I can't fault you there," I say, calmer.

"Are you?" he insists.

A shrug is the best answer I can give. Sometimes I want to leave. Sometimes I want to stay. Most times I wish I could go home, to Rachel, though I'm quite sure she wouldn't have me back after what I did to her.

"OK. You're right," he admits with a meek smile. "I was planning on telling you stories about Grace's childhood disguised as my own, fill you in on what my sister was like before... before everything. Things the original Marc would've known that made him care about her."

"And get me drunk like a cheap date so I fall for your bullshit?" I ask with a crooked smile, glad one of us is being truthful.

"You're not a cheap date," he says and takes another twenty out of his pretty money clip, then leaves it on the bar in exchange for our drinks. We both chuckle. "Let me make a peace offering," he says. "I'll tell you something about my sister that she absolutely wouldn't want you to know."

I straighten in my seat. "What do you want in return?"

"Gold stars, because what I'm about to tell you, even the original Marc didn't know."

"I'm listening."

"I'm sure you've heard about how our dad died." Charlie pauses, watching my face for a reaction.

Their dad's suicide a few years earlier was what changed Grace, caused her to push everyone away. It doesn't take a genius to figure that out. But no one knows for sure why their father took his own life. He didn't leave a note. I've always wondered, but have never had the balls to ask, what pushed him to it? I had a hunch, and in the days I got to know Grace in Toronto, I asked about their mother. "Mimi left when Charlie and I were little," she'd said. "It broke my dad." I didn't comment on the way she referred to her mother by first name, but it said a lot. And when I asked why

Mimi had left, Grace shrugged and her lips tightened into a thin line. It was her way of saying I wasn't to ask anything more. I wonder if Charlie will share the family secret with me now.

"Did she tell you about her one-minute mistake?" he asks.

I scrunch my brows. "Her what?"

"She always said that if she'd arrived a minute later, she would've been spared from watching Dad die, or a minute earlier and she could've saved him." Charlie turns his attention to his drink, wipes the condensation off the glass, the memory of their loss making him fidgety.

I nod slowly as I remember Grace recounting how she'd heard her dad's neck snap and the significance of the watch she wears. "Ya, she told me."

Charlie keeps his eyes on his drink and we reminisce. He thinks of his dad while I kick myself about my own one-minute mistake: the day I asked Rachel, "Is there someone else?" The silent minute that followed seemed never-ending, but it was no more than sixty seconds, I'm sure. I was about to wave a hand to dismiss my question before she could say something that would split my life into a distinguishable before and after, but then she replied, "Not how you think." Rachel had visibly swallowed, staring at me without blinking. The knot in my chest tightened and I was unable to either breathe or speak. She took this to mean that I wanted to hear more, but I didn't. I wanted her to laugh it off and assure me, *of course not, you're my one and only!* But what Rachel said was: "He's gone."

I wish I had never asked. I should've ignored the moments when a memory would cross Rachel's face, and her gaze would shift, telling me she was slipping into the past. Why had I let those sixty seconds pass? I'd had a whole minute to dismiss the question and stop the train wreck that came next. And what a horror show that was.

Charlie clears his throat, pulling me away from Rachel, at last deciding to let me in on the long-kept sibling secret. "Did my sister tell you why she was late?"

"Late?" I ask, my curiosity piqued. I hope I don't regret what comes next, this time. Secrets have a way of getting me into trouble.

"I didn't think so."
He blows out a nervous breath.

CHAPTER 5 - GRACE

Our diner has changed quite a bit and it amazes me that Kay doesn't remember what it was like before. When I commented on the employees' new, tight, faux-leather, waist-high pants and vibrant, oversized tops, Kay said they all looked the same to her. All I could do was shake my head at her in awe. The diner is no longer fifties American flair; it's now retro American. They've swapped out the Thunderbirds, Buicks, and old Chevys for Trans Ams, Camaros, and Monte Carlos. At least when we taste their burgers, we both agree it's like nothing has changed at all.

"So?" Charlie asks Marc. My brother's waiting for a reaction before trying his own burger because he's already decided he doesn't like the salty fries, forcing me to suppress an eye-roll when he warned me against eating them. "Not worth the risk of high blood pressure," he said. My always-cautious brother has never risked a thing in his whole life.

Kay doesn't care what anyone thinks and is already half done with her meal, but I care—perhaps too much. From the edge of my seat, I watch Marc, hoping he's satisfied with his burger, desperate to turn his mood around. He's been off all day, though I admit I don't know the real him, so it's hard to say what "on" would be like. All I can say is that it feels as if we're in a wordless fight that started at the cemetery. It's still strange, him eating meat. My Marc was a vegetarian, so when new Marc ordered a side of bacon, I must've flinched because he shot me a look, then doubled the order. It's hard to reconcile that this man in my husband's body isn't the one I married, but if I don't, what will happen to us?

Marc gives us a slow nod. "Yup," he says with a full mouth and an exaggerated thumbs-up, still drunk from bonding with my brother at the bar. "I approve."

I smile and lean back in my Trans Am bucket seat and return to picking at my meal. I'm happy Marc likes the food, but also happy to see the start of a real friendship between him and my brother.

My Marc and Charlie were not just family—they were friends. Usually, my brother takes my side on anything without question, but when I announced to him that I had split from Marc, it was Charlie who begged me to reconsider. For weeks, I would show up at his place for our weekly Sunday brunch and he'd be mopey when I let myself in with only Jordan in tow. It was like he was hoping I'd changed my mind and Marc would suddenly be with us. The two of them had a lot of common hobbies: trivia nights at the bar, they played on a men's soccer team together, and they used to have a weird who-can-grow-bigger-watermelons competition. Marc usually won. After I kicked Marc out, Charlie stopped doing all his favourite things, like he was the one who'd been through a separation. I remember saying to him, "I didn't ask you to stop being friends with him. If you want to be his friend, be my guest." I didn't mean it, though, and Charlie knew it.

As for the possibility of a friendship, new Marc had turned his nose up when I asked him if he liked soccer, and I have no idea if he's any good at trivia. But hope blossomed when I saw the way he eyed what used to be a vegetable garden outside my trailer, with curiosity. And now, bonding with my brother about burgers... I never thought I'd see that.

Charlie nods to the customers seated on tall, leopard-print stools around the high counter, watching the TV, then comments, "Those people are just glued to that thing as if under a spell."

"Ya, but did you read the ticker at the bottom?" Kay asks. "That poor couple was just making out. They only turned the heat on to keep warm, not realizing a running engine in a closed space could kill them." She holds up a finger like an idea just came to her. "Or wait a sec—" She sits up tall. "Do you think they did it on purpose? It's like Romeo and Juliet, except their poison was carbon monoxide, dying in the garage wrapped in each other's embrace." Kay has a dreamy look on her face. "It's a romantic tragedy."

We all laugh at her and she looks at us, clueless. "What?"

"You're glued to the TV, same as they are," Charlie points out with a giant grin.

Kay bats a hand to dismiss my brother's comment before she jams more food into her mouth.

Our waiter, Josh, approaches the table. "How're the first few bites? Everything a'ight?" he asks, dryly.

The food is good, but the service has gone downhill. This kid's got nothing on happy, hardworking Camilla.

Camilla was chatty, lovable, and perfectly flawed. I often think about her. Though we didn't come to the diner just to find out—like I jokingly accused Kay of wanting to do—I do wonder if she ever managed to reach her weight-loss goal to squeeze into her little wedding gown. Kay and I would laugh when we'd spot her sneaking fries off customers' plates before serving them, and then she'd complain to us that she hadn't lost a pound in weeks. Did she marry that guy, Eddie? Did he keep her safe and make her happy?

When we first came into the diner, we asked about Camilla. Josh said no one by that name worked here. Since he looked younger than my socks, we insisted he ask his co-workers if they'd heard of her.

"Everything is a-m-a-z-i-n-g," Kay says with her mouth full, and then crams in yet another fry.

Waiter Josh smiles at her in such a way that it wouldn't surprise me if he jotted his number down on her bill. Then he addresses us. "Well, I asked around back about a Camilla, like you said. Manny's been here the longest and he ain't heard of any Camilla."

Kay and I exchange a look. She's mid-chew and about to say what's on my mind, but her mouth is too full.

"Manny?" I ask with a smile. "Would you please tell him Kay and Grace say hello?"

Josh nods yes but doesn't leave, watching Kay or, more accurately, watching Kay's chest.

She speaks, not caring that her mouth is full. "Now? Can you go *now* and tell Manny we say hello? Bye, Josh!" She shoos him away with a flick of her wrist.

"That's weird. Why would Manny say he doesn't know Camilla?" I say.

"Who's Manny?" Charlie asks just as the quiet cook approaches our table.

I remember him as a silent, serious man, and I also remember that Camilla liked him, so I greet him with a warm smile. "Hi, Manny."

Kay squeals, bounces off her seat with open arms and greets him like he's her long-lost twin. Manny doesn't smile but returns her big hug with the same affection. He has a kind face, and the years haven't done much to age him, other than a few lines around his dark, beady eyes.

"Choo look the same, like last time," he comments in a heavy Spanish accent. His voice is soft and low. "Camilla run away. She hide from a bad man. We don't say her name, in case."

"Eddie?" I ask, lowering my voice and glancing around the restaurant.

Manny makes a "tut-tut" sound with his tongue and shakes an index finger, indicating the bad man is not Eddie, thank goodness. "No, she and Eddie they hide together, with keeds."

"They have children?" I ask, thinking about how happy that must've made our Camilla, and it angers me that someone is threatening that happiness. When she thought I was on the run, she empathized like she'd been through something similar, telling me that people came to Vegas to stay hidden. Whoever she was hiding from must've found her.

"Two keeds. Baby has your name," Manny says, nodding at me.

"Bless her kind heart," Kay says with a hand over her own heart. "She must've really liked you, Grace."

I swear her eyes are pooling with tears of joy, and I chuckle. My best friend is a people lover, through and through. It's by far her best quality.

"Manny, we're not actually looking for Camilla," I tell him, lowering my voice when I say her name. "We're looking for someone who used to hang out here, a young man who was following us around. It's a long shot, but we thought she might've remembered him since she used to work all the time."

"The keed," Manny says. And I'm wondering if he's still talking about Camilla and Eddie's kids, or if he's actually listening to me. "The keed," Manny repeats, pointing to the corner. We all turn our heads to look at the spot he's pointing to, like Jordan is sitting there now, in that Mustang seat, right over there. "Young man, he used to seet there, pretend to read the journal newspaper. Watch you."

Wow, Manny was observant.

"You know who we're talking about?" I ask, amazed at his memory.

"I never forget. It's not every day choo meet a man who keels."

Did he just say "kills"?

"He murder someone, a man. Four, five years ago. He should be in a jail. He get away with it. He no pay for his crime, everyone know he did it, like OJ. Big trial. Big story. Why's you looking for the Swiss boy?"

"Murder? Jail? *Swiss*?" Kay asks, then side-eyes her orange juice and mutters, "OJ?"

My appetite instantly disappears, the emptiness in my tummy replaced with another bout of guilt. I never thought my son would be in trouble with the law. But even if I had thought that, not in a million years would I have imagined it would've been for murder. What's worse? He's guilty.

Jordan shot and killed Dr. Messie's hitman, Mister, in those caves. But he did it so Mister wouldn't carry out the hit on Leo. Once injected with the syringe, the subject had to die soon after. Cloning a soul only worked with the completion of a life cycle. Jordan was trying to stop Metagenesis by saving Leo's life. But it was all for nothing. With Mister dead, I carried out the hit on Leo myself, pushing him into the canyon. Jordan isn't the only one who got away with murder, but I'm the one who should've been on trial.

No! Dr. Messie is the one who should pay! I hear Charlie's voice in my head, reassuring me. When I came clean to my brother, he made it his daily task to assure me I wasn't the horrible human I felt I was. *"Dr. Messie is the cause of all of this."* Charlie would recite

41

variations of this to me over and over. *"His family proved the theory of reincarnation. His family discovered life-travelling was possible.* He *is the one who created the new plague, Metagenesis. Not you, Gracie."*

I'd argue that I had played a part in the current state of mankind, to which he'd say, *"But Dr. Messie was the one who tipped the first domino."*

I love my brother. Now, he reaches across and covers my trembling hands with one of his, stopping my watch from clinking on the table.

"Dartmouth, it sound Swiss, German or something," Manny replies to Kay.

It's an English name, when there was such a country before the borders went away, but sudden nausea prevents me from opening my mouth to correct Manny. I can't even look at him anymore. My vision is wobbly and I focus on the small speckles of the table's design: they look like what white noise would sound like. The odour of meaty meat mixed with greasy fries is making my stomach churn. Marc is still eating his burger smothered in bacon through all of this, buzzed from booze, and not at all concerned about our son. The fact that my vegetarian husband is eating meat is just another reminder that he isn't *my* Marc, which means Jordan isn't *his* son, so why would he care?

"Manny, how do we find him? Does he still come here?" Kay asks.

"Not in a long time. Maybe choo look on the Internet. There is a Internet café two doors that way." He points.

They talk a little longer, but I don't contribute to the conversation. I can't make out what they're saying, anyhow; they may as well be speaking in a foreign language.

Charlie and Kay rise from their seats, packed boxes in hands. They say something to me and I start to mechanically rise with them.

Kay touches my shoulder. "No, no, you stay here with Marc." She looks to my brother as if tagging him in to back her up.

Charlie takes the reins. "We'll research at the café. Try and finish your food."

Marc and I are alone again. I can feel him looking at me and I lift my gaze from the speckled table to meet his eyes. I pout at how uninterested he seems, sucking back his Pepsi with a detached, cold stare. We should talk, and there's no shortage of topics we could and should cover, but I'm too stunned to try.

After a long silence, I ask, "Which way did Manny say the Internet place was?"

"Why?" His tone is bland, his stare blank. Emotionally, we're worlds apart.

"Which way?"

Marc throws a thumb over his shoulder. I get up and leave without saying a word and he doesn't stop me. I pause at the door to glance back at him, curious if he'll look at me, but he doesn't. He beckons the waiter and asks for a refill. Their physical body is the only thing both Marcs have in common.

I push through the door and make my way to the Internet café. Once inside, I survey the small space. Sitting behind the cash register and staring at a boxy screen is a scrawny, beer-bellied employee who looks like he hasn't showered or shaved in days. The place is packed but quiet, save for the click-clacking of keyboards. People are sitting at almost every table in front of boxy little TV screens, some with giant headphones on. No one is interacting except for my best friend and my brother.

I spy on them for a moment. Charlie is a bit smitten with her—leaning in too close, his hand on the back of her chair—which is cute but… Kay isn't the keeping kind. She and I have been friends since we were twelve and the two of them have never liked each other. Charlie has a quiet, agreeable demeanour and always thought my best friend was annoying and too cheery. Kay is outgoing and rebellious and always thought my brother was dull and too serious. Watching their kinship these last few days makes me worry—for my brother, not for Kay. She's a heartbreaker, never lasting in any relationship and usually dating guys old enough to be her dad and rich enough to run a kingdom. She loves people but bores quickly.

They both rise from their seats like they're done.

"No, wait!" I shout. All at once, the patrons in the café and the bored employee turn their heads toward me like synchronized robots, then back to their screens.

Charlie and Kay offer me identical pity-smiles as I approach.

"So? Is their Internet as good as our Instant-net? Did you find Jordan?" I ask, keeping my voice down, but not enough, according to the look I just got from a patron two spots over.

Kay takes the lead. "Actually, yes. We were just coming to get you. Figured you'd want to be the one to talk to him. It looks like you can chat right here on the computer. Matt helped us. I'll show you."

"Matt?" I question, but they ignore me. Kay looks at Charlie, raises a brow.

"Uh, where's Marc? Outside?" he asks, glancing over my shoulder. I tell him Marc is still at the restaurant. Charlie opts to keep him company, returning Kay's look with a stern nod before leaving us, as if to tell her, *Tag! You're it, Kay!*

The employee clears his throat, eyeing us.

"Sorry, Matt! We'll keep it down." Kay flashes him a flirty smile full of teeth.

He nods back, satisfied and flattered.

"Sorry, Matt," I mimic under my breath, batting my lashes at Kay.

She shushes me but also giggles, calling me a hill myna.

"A hill what?" I ask and she shushes me again, poking me with an elbow.

"Like a parrot, but one who screeches," she whispers, then makes a screech-like face with bulging cross-eyes, and I almost lose it. For two short seconds, I'm reminded that we're best friends. I want to go back to that simpler life, the one where we used to get kicked out of classes, museums, and even loud bars, on account of our bad behaviour.

We sit and Kay pulls the keyboard and mouse to her. "Before we get to Jordan, let me show you what else Matt helped us find," she says with a sideways smile. "Something funny and someone useful." She types "Adalia Messie" in a box titled "search," and a little hourglass spins around on the screen. "It's a turtle compared to our Instant-net, but it's better than those phone books," she mutters, breaking up the eternity the search seems to take.

"So it *is* like our Instant-net? You can find info on, um, any-one?" I try to sound nonchalant and not like a woman eager to type her murdered lover's name, Leo—whom she murdered—into the search box, to scratch an itch.

"Grace." Kay enunciates my name like a warning. When a list finally appears, she clicks on an article about a funeral home. "Adalia's late husband's family owned that place. Isn't that hilarious?"

I don't smile. I don't think it's funny.

Kay clears her throat. "Sorry. Too soon. Bad taste." She clicks an X, closing the page, then opens another article featuring volunteers at a nursing home. There's a picture showing a group of elderly people—all women except for a man in a wheelchair and a beefy nurse beside them. Below the image are their names, but I don't need to read them. I recognize the old woman in the centre as the same one who begged me to stop my search the last time we were here: it's Adalia.

"Now with *two* people who can help us, we're *two* steps closer to Messie," Kay states with a proud smile.

Relief warms my chest that Adalia is alive, but it's short lived. "I don't think that's how it works. And besides, did you read the headline?" I point to the article's title: *Dementia: Causes, Symptoms, Treatment.* If there is a way to Germany or back to Toronto, old-woman Adalia is not it.

"Nuh-uh, don't you start, Grace." Kay turns a cheek and holds a hand up to my face to block my negative talk. Then, energetic as ever, she wastes no time divulging her plan. "Charlie and I have talked about it and decided it's best to divide and conquer, like last time. You can talk to Jordan because he's your son and all. Marc can just, I don't know, do whatever. And your bro and I'll visit the old woman because, um, she might be mad at you. Anywho, meet back at the diner afterward for a milkshake break, say around three o'clock?"

I sigh. Why does she get dibs on my brother?

"Great!" she exclaims like my silence must mean I agree. Beer-belly employee, Matt, clears his throat again, but this time Kay's too excited to care. "Let me get you to that chat screen, then I'll leave you to it."

Without giving me a freckle of prep time to face my son, she turns her attention back to the computer and types "Jordan

Dartmouth" into the search box. "Should I send Marc in?" she asks.

"Uh, not yet," I tell her.

She side-glares at me but doesn't dig.

My eyes flood when a whole list of Jordan-related things appear. There are pictures of Jordan in handcuffs, being led out of a bar; a mug shot; him in a courtroom. There are also news articles about his crime, the trial, and the outrage when he was found not guilty by a jury of his peers.

Kay pats my shoulder, not a comforting pat, but more like she's in a rush to get back to Charlie. She hastily chooses an article from an entertainment magazine. It's an article showing Jordan entering his place of work, an office building, holding up his jacket to shield his face from cameras. An entertainment magazine? I give her a puzzled look and she answers every possible question she thinks I might have, to speed things along.

"Lucky for us, seems he was kind of popular because of that trial. You know how people flock to gossip like flies on poop." She's no longer whispering. "We couldn't find a personal phone number or address for him, but if this info is correct, he works at this mining company here." She clicks on the company's name, Valle Tinto, then clicks a few more times and arrives at an employee contact page. "See?" She points to a button labelled "chat," which looks like an old-fashioned phone.

"Do you want me to stay?" she asks, but she's already rising from her seat.

"No, of course not. I'll—"

"Bye!" she calls over her shoulder, at the door before I even finish telling her that I'll be fine. I'm glad we're not wasting any time, and I don't want anyone to worry about me, but a little compassion might've been nice.

I suck in a breath and click the video chat button. A green light blinks to life on a bulky camera perched on top of the computer. The screen says, *Video connecting to Jordan Dartmouth... standby...*

I release my breath only when moments later, the message changes to say *Unavailable*. My pulse slows. What now? I check my watch. I've got hours to kill—it's only noon. Well, I might as well scratch an itch. "David Abruzzo," I type into the search box.

The hourglass spins, fills, and refills, repeat. The longer this takes, the louder the sensible voice in my head tells me I'm being stupid. Charlie and Kay are right: I'm torturing myself, and this feeling about Leo that I can't shake is guilt, not familiarity.

I point the cursor to the X button to close the screen. I hover over it, almost click it, and I half rise from my seat to walk away, my butt levitating off the chair. But then the search produces a list: an obituary, some news articles. I relent. I begin my torment session with the obituary, reading over it slowly.

That other voice in my head starts up again, the bitchy one that keeps telling me I'm missing something vital, and it works me up into a ball of anxiety. *Stop obsessing, Grace. Leave! Go for a walk!* But then I reach the customary list of those who have survived and predeceased Leo, and I almost vomit my burger.

CHAPTER 6 - MARC

I watch Grace and Kay through the café window. Charlie suggests we go back to the restaurant to wait, rubbing his arms as if we're in the goddamn Arctic. I decline, curious as to what Grace is up to. Anxious to get my attention off his sister, Charlie ups the stakes, telling me it's imperative we speak to Manny—something about transportation. I shake my head again as Kay comes outside and joins us, her giant smile disappearing when she sees me. I don't think she likes me. She's nice to me only around Grace.

"Hey, Marc. Did Charlie fill you in?"

"Ya, sure. Adalia or whatever," I reply, still watching Grace, her shoulders rising and falling with a deep breath before she squares them with the screen in front of her. I move to go inside and join her, but Kay places a hand on my arm.

I raise a questioning eyebrow at her.

"Give her a few minutes, would you?" Except she's not asking.

"Why?" I play dumb. I have a few guesses: Leo, Leo, and Leo.

Instead of answering me, she tries to distract me. "Let's head back to the diner. You might need transportation too, in case you two decide to go see Jordan in person. He's in another state."

If stabbing myself in the eye were number two on my top-three-things-I-never-want-to-do list, going with Grace to visit her delinquent kid would rank as number one. I hardly knew him as a kid; there wasn't much time between my arrival in Toronto and our departure to ~~Germany~~ Vegas, but he was always a weird kind of quiet around me. It made me think he could see right through me, like he sensed I wasn't his dad in the same way a sniffing dog detects drugs no matter how well you disguise them. So I avoided him.

"Is that what you want to see Manny about? Transport?" I direct my question to Charlie, who nods.

He rubs his hands together, eager to go back to the diner. "Shall we go, then?"

"You two go ahead. I'm gonna keep my *wife* company." I take a swift step around Charlie and Kay before they have time to even exchange a look with one another. I'm sure they'll talk smack about me when I'm out of earshot, analyze the tone I used when referring to my wife, discuss my remarks about wanting to leave Grace, if they haven't already. I get the feeling I'm a hot topic between the two of them and I don't give a hot shit.

Once inside, I watch silently over Grace's shoulder as she flips through images and headlines on the screen. She pauses on a portrait of a man with a big, confident smile, so entranced by it she doesn't sense my presence. I grab a seat next to her, making her jump when I plunk down on the creaky chair and it swivels on its little wheels.

"Hey," I say. I couldn't fake a grin if I tried.

In a panic, she taps a bunch of buttons and the screen changes. "Uh, hi." Her gaze shifts between the computer and me, once, twice, three times.

I don't budge each time she meets my eyes. I was caught off guard at the cemetery when I approached her at Leo's grave—*my* grave—but not this time. I know who that smiling man was on her screen.

"Are you done yet?" I stare coldly at her. I like her even less now that I know about her one-minute mistake. Not because I blame her for her dad's death, or that it's one more thing she has in common with Rachel, but because it's one more thing she kept from her Marc. I'm pissed off on his behalf, and I know that makes no sense at all.

Grace swallows. "Yes. Sorry." Then she begins babbling a list of suggestions and excuses, peppered with apologies; killing time before trying to call Jordan again, so sorry, didn't mean to upset me, didn't see me standing there, sorry, we should grab a coffee or go to a casino or go for a walk or back to the diner, or sorry blab sorry blab blab, before finishing off with: "We can try Jordan again later?"

The cashier clears his throat and jabs a thumb over his shoulder to a sign: *quiet time in effect daily until 6 p.m.*

She even apologizes to him. Then, lowering her voice, she asks me again, "Can we go now? Please?"

Neither of us makes a move and so I nod toward the door, indicating for her to lead the way. We both rise, but when she starts to leave, I don't follow. Instead, I take her seat and turn to the screen to retrieve what she was looking at. I feel her turn back to me.

"You can go now." I dismiss her without looking at her.

She doesn't move for a few moments. I can see her in the screen's reflection, standing there, wringing her hands together. Their mannerisms resemble each other, my wives, which makes it more difficult to hate Grace and equally difficult to stay with her. When sensing there's no right thing to say to me, which there isn't, she leaves me and heads to the cashier.

I don't know what I was expecting, but aside from the eyes, Leo looks nothing like who I am now—Marc—or like who I used to be. I scroll through the images, scanning the headlines, then stop at a picture of the Grand Canyon. My heart races. This is the image from all of my nightmares. Rachel, Grace, reaching for me as I let go of the ledge and fall to my death.

Grace returns moments later and takes a seat at the only available computer, a row ahead of me, two spots to the right. She wouldn't dare search up Leo again while I'm sitting right here, would she? My anger simmers down when I realize she's trying her kid, Jordan, again. This time he answers the video call, filling the screen waist up.

Seeing the kid as an adult seems crazy when just days ago, we left him in Toronto and he was nine. Even from this distance, I can see the burn scar on Jordan's cheek that Grace told me about, from when he tried to save her life and failed. In two years, when Jordan is eleven, Grace is supposed to set fire to the Recycled Souls Laboratories in Toronto, where she is supposed to die. I sit up tall for a better view, my curiosity torn between Leo on my screen and adult Jordan on hers. I look nothing like Leo, but Jordan? I'd say the kid and I are about the same age, and with his scruffy, unshaven face and bushy brows, we could pass as brothers. It's uncanny.

"Hi," she says, her voice small and careful.

He doesn't return her greeting and I almost feel sorry for her, the way his face changes in under three seconds from boredom to something between shock and anger. He's staring at her with the same amazement one would have on seeing Satan in a tutu.

"Hi," she repeats. He still says nothing. She fakes a cough. "Dad's here, too. I can get him if you want?"

Shit! Please say no, please say no.

"Is he?" Jordan replies. "Are you sure? Is *my* dad here? How's Leo?" he accuses, backing away from his computer. "It's best you don't answer that, *Grace*—this isn't a private connection. Where are you—at an Internet café, for fuck's sake?" Shaking his head, he stands up and then disconnects.

My jaw hangs open. What a twat he is. And I don't give Grace the credit she deserves when without hesitation, she calls him right back.

"*What?*" Jordan's voice comes through even before the pixels merge into an image.

"Please don't hang up," she says, too loudly for the liking of the cashier, who clears his throat again. Grace lowers her voice, making me strain to hear. "We need your help to get back home. Please."

His face contorts into a mix of shock and disgust. "*Home?* There is no way *home!* The shuttles ended two days after you left! Why are you even back here? And why aren't you dead?"

Grace bends at the waist as if slugged in the gut, his last question knocking the wind out of her. But her posture recovers in an instant and she plows on.

My chest stirs with a bit of both pride and sadness at how similar she is to Rachel. Persistent. A little nutty. Tough as nails. They say only the eyes carry over from life to life. I beg to differ.

"There has to be something we can do. You must know something that can help us. Adalia was supposed to take us to Germany, to put an end to Metagenesis, but she backed out and sent us here." She pauses. Jordan isn't reacting, but he's also not hanging up. Grace adds, "Adalia is Dr. Mes—"

"I know who Adalia was—she was the Doc's little sister. What do you mean 'supposed to' and why was she helping you?"

Grace hesitates, glancing around the room, choosing her words. Most people are too engaged in their own Internet sessions to pay her any mind, but some—myself included—are hanging on to Grace and Jordan's every word. Even the cashier has stopped clearing his throat at her. "We asked her to help us, umm... *stop-stop* Dr. Messie and then ..." She pauses as if something has just dawned on her. "Jordan, why did you say 'was'?"

"What are you talking about?" he asks. His tone may be rude, but the topic of Adalia has gotten his attention.

"You said 'Adalia *was* Dr. Messie's little sister.' You 'know who she *was*.' Past tense?"

I catch myself nodding my approval at her observation. *Good ear, Grace.*

He stares at her before answering, as if deciding what to say, how much to trust her. Who can blame him? "You first," he says after a long pause. "Why'd you ask Adalia to help you? In fact, how do you even know her name?"

Interesting. I bet he and Adalia never met here in Vegas, and he never connected the dots between Adalia and my past life, Leo.

Grace replies, "Before you approached me that day on the bench at the Canadiana Hotel, Adalia tried the same. She asked me to stop looking for the subject. Told me what would happen to your dad if I didn't stop."

My stomach clenches. There's that word again: "subject." And the way she skirts around what she did makes me want to choke her. What would *happen* to his dad? That vial was what happened. She stabbed Leo with it, which made Marc lose his damn soul, and then, voila!—here I am, replacement Marc!

"Your turn," she says in an even tone.

Looks like he'll have to feed her some info if he wants more. As pissed as I am, I can't deny that she's playing her hand well.

"Adalia went missing without a trace a few weeks before I was chased out. I didn't know she was here. Your turn," he says, and then waits for her to divulge more.

They play this game a few more times. But they're talking only about Adalia and I don't see how that's going to help our get-out-of-Vegas-2006 plan. I keep an ear open but train my eyes back on Leo, on my screen.

While I listen to Grace explain why they reached out to Adalia, assuming she must have gone to Germany as a young woman to stop-stop Dr. Messie herself and failed, I scroll through images of Leo and my blood boils in my eardrums. I know Grace is sorry for what she did. I know she's trying to make amends, but for some reason, the sorrier she becomes, the higher my wall of anger builds.

By the time Grace tells Jordan that Adalia was Leo's grandmother, I'm pissed off all over again, and so I don't care that the kid lets out a wicked laugh at her expense.

"I can't believe I overlooked such a fun detail," Jordan says, like an asshole.

I shouldn't be scrolling through pictures of how Grace victimized Leo—*me*—if a fresh start is what I'm after. Rachel was my main reason to travel back; starting my life over was the other. As for killing Dr. Messie—well, that was just a lucky bonus. Leo is a ghost to me and for this reason alone I shouldn't give a shit about what Grace did to him. Instead, I should tell her I know about what she did on the day her dad died, and tell her the truth—at least about Rachel—and snatch up my one chance at a life redo. Those are the things I should act on but can't seem to bring myself to. I sigh and tune back into the conversation in front of me.

During one of Jordan's turns, he tells Grace that Adalia was presumed dead. But before her disappearance, she gave him access to something he never should've been privy to: a letter, which led him here six years ago to find Grace. "She told me I deserved the truth. I thought that was why she'd gone missing, that she had been… stop-stopped. I didn't know she left for Germany." After a long pause, Jordan says, "I'll think about it."

"Think about what?" Grace asks.

"Helping you and Marc."

"Dad," she says firmly.

He rolls his eyes.

"So you do know a way back? A shuttle? It's not too late?"

He shrugs a maybe.

"Then what's there to think about? Do you realize what's at stake? If we don't get back to Toronto, Dr. Messie can't be stop-stopped. And then Metagenesis—"

"How gullible are you? You think Dr. Messie was a one-man show?" he scoffs. "Stop-stopping him is the least of my concerns," he says callously and laughs like the idea of finding the doctor is child's play.

I don't know what to make of his comment, but it makes me perk taller in my seat.

"What's so funny?" Grace's voice rises; so does the cashier's gaze, but he doesn't hush her. Nosy prick.

Jordan shakes his head at her like she's a dumb kid. "You have no idea what you've done, do you?"

"Why don't you tell me?" she spits back at him.

"You're at a goddamn Internet café," he shouts at her, enunciating the words *Internet* and *café* as if each syllable is a complete sentence. "OK, look," he says, calmer, raising a palm to the camera. "Morgan Bell is my lawyer—look her up. I'll let her know my brother and sister will be calling. Got it? Brother. Sister. Go to her office and call me back from there. You'll have privacy and a secure connection."

"Can't we just meet in person?"

"No. I'm away for work."

"We can come to you."

"*No!*" he shouts, panic in his eyes. Then he rakes a hand over his head and puts on a deliberately calm face and matching patient voice. "If you need a place to stay, you can go to my condo. I'll let the doorman know. He has my keys." He jabbers off a Vegas address, asking her to repeat it back to him. Then he brings his face close to the camera and lowers his voice just loud enough for me to hear. "And stay out of sight. It's not safe here for either of you. *Capiche?*"

"What? Why? Tell me."

My question exactly.

"I can't! In-ter-net ca-fé." Then he disconnects.

Grace's whole body moves with each breath she takes, like she's trying not to cry. Part of me wants to comfort her; part of me thinks she deserves it. Then she glances over her shoulder at me and I quickly focus my attention back on my terminal. I pretend I didn't see or hear what happened, even though you'd have to be deaf, dumb, and blind not to have followed along. Besides, she caught me looking away. She probably thinks I'm sparing her embarrassment. I'm not. I just don't want to engage. What would I say?

To make it more believable that I was using the computer all along, I exaggerate the task of shutting down the Leo screens, testing the durability of the mouse with each hard click. As I hit the Xs one by one, another heading with the Grand Canyon flashes by, tempting me once again to tumble down the Leo rabbit hole. That's when I spot someone I recognize and do a double-take.

I glance up at Grace; she's watching me. I plant an awkward smile on my face—the wrong thing to do when your wife is about to snap. She gets up and leaves, sobbing on her way out. I should follow her. A better man would. Instead, I look back at the screen, wondering whether she saw what I'm seeing. I squint, trying to convince myself one way or the other, but then I laugh. Nah—can't be. His face is mostly hidden; that could be anyone's fat body. No way is that Dr. Messie standing there. That would mean he's here, in Las Vegas, right now. I click *end session*, deciding to go tend to my wife.

CHAPTER 7 - MARC

Talking to Jordan will get us about as far as Morgan Bell's office is: an hour from the middle of nowhere. But I want to hear what he has to say before anyone else does, feel him out, see what he's up to, which was why I came alone. I left Grace abruptly and deliberately rudely. "See you at three p.m. for milkshakes," I said out of the blue. And when she called after me, asking me where I was going, I ignored her. If I'd been nice, she'd have come after me.

As for Jordan, he could've told Grace what we needed to know over the video. So why didn't he? At the mention of Adalia, his attitude mysteriously changed from not wanting to help, to thinking about it. And then he laughed at the absurdity that Dr. Messie was a one-man show... The kid's luring us to meet his lawyer with the offer of help. Why?

Morgan Bell's office is sandwiched between unoccupied units with yellowing *For Lease* signs propped up in their windows. I enter a small waiting room. There is neither seat nor wall space available because it's bursting at the seams with sketchy-looking people. There's a biker in leather holding a chihuahua, seated next to a man in ratty clothes whose face is bloated from years of drinking. Across from them, a woman leans on the wall; she's wearing too much makeup for this time of day—smudged—like she's been up entertaining since yesterday and I'm not sure she's a "she." Her skirt is too short and her top is too tight, revealing manly pecs. *This* is the lawyer who got Jordan a murder acquittal?

A phone rings in the distance and goes unanswered. I don't see a receptionist, though by a man's yelling from beyond one of two closed doors, I assume there should be one.

"Lucia! Lucia? How many times do I have to tell you it's your job to answer the phone?" The yeller barges out from one of the offices. He sees me standing in the middle of the waiting room, adjusts his jacket—which looks two sizes too big—and places a toothy grin on his grumpy, fake-tanned face. He has perfect teeth, too shiny, too white, and all equal in size.

"Have you been helped? Lucia must've stepped out for coffee."

"I'd like to see Morgan Bell. I don't have an appointment, but she's expecting me. I'm Jordan Dartmouth's brother."

"Morgan!" the man yells, his smile gone. "It's for you!" He bangs on the office door adjacent to his.

A stunning woman, Morgan, greets and invites me into a cramped office. "Please excuse my officemate, Dan. It's been a long day." A midnight-blue skirt suit hugs her hourglass figure and she wears shiny red shoes, showing off her perfectly shaped calves. Those shoes trigger an unwelcome memory.

She leads me to a polished white-leather loveseat in front of a large TV. A desk littered with garbage and files sits facing a small window. "I was in the middle of organizing—please excuse the mess. Jordan mentioned you'd be calling first."

"I was in the neighbourhood," I lie. My pulse is going wild, but not because of my lie.

"Give me a minute to borrow a webcam from Dan's office. Can I get you something to drink? Coffee, tea…?"

I ask her for a Pepsi, and she dashes out.

I survey the office in her absence. A lawyer who dresses like a million bucks yet works out of a scuzzy office is odd, but it's also a turn-on. What is it about her? There's a framed photo on her desk, facing the other direction so when she's seated at her computer, it's in her sightline. The picture is for her benefit, not her clients'. I'm dying to walk over and snatch it up for a look-see, but she returns before I give in to temptation.

Morgan hands me a can of soda, not Pepsi, and asks me if it's OK, not waiting for a response as she goes to the TV. I open the can and take a sip, and decide I don't like it. Then I watch her as she plugs in the ball-shaped camera, setting it on top of the TV, and fidgets with it until a red light comes on. When she's done, she smoothes her hair with one hand and then glances at me, noticing me noticing her. "You're not a no-name-brand kind of guy, huh?"

"It's fine," I tell her, and force another sip of the watered-down brown soda.

"Well, everything is set up. I already spoke to Jordan. He'll just be a minute. I'll give you privacy as soon as he answers," she says, taking a seat beside me and crossing her long, slender legs.

"Thanks." I do everything I can not to adjust my collar.

For an awkward minute, we sit so quietly that the waiting-room noise can be heard crisp and clear; a chair scrapes against the floor, the elusive Lucia answers a phone, water runs from a nearby faucet.

"Jordan mentioned his sister would be here as well. Grace?"

"She wasn't feeling well." It's not a complete lie. The kid had her shaken up pretty good. It's one of the excuses I gave myself to come here without her.

"Send her my regards," Morgan says.

We fall back into silence until the TV flickers to life. She greets Jordan, then leaves us, giving me a shy smile and apologizing for the terrible soda on her way out.

On the screen, Jordan sits at a table in a boxy grey room no bigger than our hotel's bathroom. He's amused to see me, in a sadistic sort of way. First, with a sarcastic eye-roll, he asks me how he should address me. "Leo, Marc, Dad...?"

I know the kid doesn't owe me the benefit of the doubt—as adults, we're strangers—but what'd I do to piss him off? And yet, in return, I can't help it—I give him the finger. Truth is, the feeling of dislike is mutual. I don't know what his reasons are, but I'm well aware mine are petty and illogical: not only is he the reason Grace chose to kill Leo, but I worry he'll sabotage my fresh start if I decide to stay with her.

"So, Marc—can I call you Marc?—how is it, pretending to be someone you're not? Even if I didn't know that vial didn't work, because Dr. Messie never perfected it, I'd know you're not my dad. You have his body, but you're nothing like him. You're a resentful little black sheep, aren't you? Suddenly thrown into a life you don't belong in, with the woman who made that happen."

He's good, I admit, at knowing exactly which nerve to hit. And it seems my impression of him as a kid, comparing him to an imposter-sniffing dog, was dead on.

"Speaking of, where's my mom? Why isn't she there?"

"She doesn't need to be here. Now tell me how to get out of this decade."

"Whoa, whoa, whoa," he says, putting up a hand to slow me down. "We haven't seen each other since... well, we've never seen each other—and you're expecting me to give you the world without even a smile in return? This is not a one-way street. You can't just take, take, take, Marc. Where are your manners?"

If he were here physically, my hands would be squeezing his neck. "So you want something from us? I'm not surprised. But if you're looking to get some pent-up childhood anger out of your system, I'm not your dad and could give two blue fucks, so you'd be wasting your time," I say, clenching my teeth. Then I get up and walk over to the camera. I want to make sure he can read the I-don't-give-a-shit-look on my face. "What do you want, *kid*?"

Jordan crosses his arms over his chest. "This is about what *you* want," he says, dropping the attitude a notch. "What do you know about my mom's parents?"

Not much would be my honest answer. Her mother abandoned them and, in my opinion, her father hung himself because of it. Between those two traumas, there isn't much else to know. Though Grace loved her father deeply, by all accounts he was an absentee who spent most of his time gambling, and who left Charlie to look after his little sister, something that continues even now.

"What are you fishing for?" I ask.

"Do you want to go home or not?"

"Home?" I scoff. What a joke. I'm just at home here in our Vegas hotel as I was days earlier in Grace's Toronto container home.

"I can get you home, little black sheep. Your real home—whenever and wherever that is," he says, as if reading my mind. Then he looks me up and down and adds: "As Marc, of course."

I chew my lip. Home to Rachel? My heart clenches when I think about that conversation we had the first time she walked out of my life. I wanted to die when she admitted that she still loved her first husband. As if that wasn't enough, I followed up by asking her: "Do you love me the way you loved him?" I felt instantly pathetic when Rachel looked at me, pitying me with her eyes. "That's not fair," she replied. "So that's a no," I snapped back. Even now, it hurts. And yet, I'd give anything to see her again, even though she wouldn't recognize me in this new body.

Jordan smiles, knowing he's piqued my interest. "Has my mom ever mentioned meeting a Camilla and Eddie when she was in Vegas?"

I nod, uneasy about cooperating but too curious not to. Jordan rolls out a strange line of questioning, wanting to know all about Grace and Kay's friend, Camilla, and Camilla's fiancé, Eddie. I don't know why any of it is relevant, but my mind is too busy processing the idea of seeing Rachel that I give one-word answers even though I don't want to.

"Where are they now?" Jordan asks.

"Hiding."

"Where did Eddie work?"

"Gym."

"Doing what?"

"Security."

"Security? How fitting." He chuckles to himself. "Where?"

I stop answering his questions, my common sense kicking in.

"Where?" he repeats.

Drawing my lips into a straight line, I consider what Manny said about Camilla running away and hiding from a bad man. That leads me to consider what I know about Jordan: nothing. Is he the bad man? And I wonder... There is a huge black hole between Grace's death when Jordan was eleven and the man he is today. The kid was Dr. Messie's protégé, spending more time with the doctor than with his own family.

A nagging feeling creeps up on me when I think about Jordan with Dr. Messie. I shove my selfishness aside on a whim to ask: "Do you know where Dr. Messie is?"

Jordan seems surprised at my question, but not confused by it. He swallows and shuffles in his seat. I hear it scrape against the floor.

"No," he answers, but what's peculiar to me is that he doesn't ask me why I would pose such a question. And that to me is very telling.

"I don't know anything else about Camilla and Eddie." It's the truth—and even if I knew more, I wouldn't say—but I make it sound like I'm holding back to piss the kid off.

He jumps out of his seat and whips around to the front of the table, shoving it out of the way to get to the other side faster, then looms right close to the camera. His angry face is huge on the screen, taking up all thirty-two inches of the TV. "You and Grace need to watch your backs," he utters, gritting his teeth so hard I'm amazed they don't crack.

I'm scrambling to make sense of what little information I have, which is no information at all—just a grainy picture on the Internet that resembled Dr. Messie. But I know I've hit this kid's bull's-eye, so I take another shot. "You feel indebted to Dr. Messie, don't you? You're not going to help us. You're protecting him."

"Dr. *Messie?*" Jordan laughs like I just told him the Easter bunny eats kittens for dinner. "You have no idea who your enemy is."

Jordan's threat lingers between us and we stare at each other, neither of us backing away from the camera. Then his hand covers the lens and the connection comes to an abrupt end, leaving me staring at a blank screen. I bet his camera is in pieces now. I may be confused about a lot of what just happened, but I'm not confused about who my enemy is: Dr. Messie *and* Jordan.

CHAPTER 8 - GRACE

Marc sits across from me with a bouncy knee. We both ignore the menus in front of us. "They're late," he says, then slurps the last of his water, shaking an ice cube from his glass into his mouth.

"I'm sure Charlie and Kay will be here any minute," I assure him.

He checks the TV for the time, and murmurs around an ice cube, "It's awready been ten."

"Kay said *around* three, not *at* three. Relax."

He shuts up, but he doesn't relax. New Marc's temperament is the exact opposite of my Marc's. His moods change directions as often as the Toronto weather did in the weeks leading to our departure. And no matter how hard I try to ease his anxiousness ahead of my own, he never rewards my efforts.

But I admit, when he followed me out of the Internet café and pulled me into his arms, it shocked me stiff. Without saying a word, he rubbed my back until I melted into his embrace, letting me sob like a child. Then I backed away from him, searching his face for the connection that had been missing between us. He said nothing, but he dried my tears with his sleeve stretched over his thumb and offered me a true smile and a gentle kiss on the top of my head. His gesture brought on more tears.

"I'm sorry for everything," I mumbled another apology through hiccups and sobs.

"I know," he gave the same reply he always does when he bothers to reply at all. What he didn't say, and I fear he'll never say, is *I forgive you.* Then he took my elbow, suggesting a walk to calm down, and his grip was anything but kind. Gentle Marc had slipped away as had my desire to mention the obituary. Admitting that he might be right about Adalia was one thing, but telling him how Leo played me for a fool would take a special amount of courage.

An uncomfortable silence hung between us as we walked, lasting a few blocks. Then, out of the blue, he turned to me and said, "See you at three p.m. for milkshakes," and he left. It was so weird. I called after him, asking him where he was going, and he ignored me. Yesterday's Grace would've stampeded after him, insisting on an answer. The less-confident Grace of today welcomed the chance to spend the rest of the afternoon (and a good chunk of cash) playing blackjack.

Now, Marc's silence lasts precisely five minutes. He spits a cube back into his glass and complains, "It's now three-fifteen."

"Maybe we should've just gone to the lawyer's without them," I say.

"Lawyer?" he huffs. "I'm not going to see no lawyer. Why didn't Jordan just tell us whatever he had to say over the video chat? 'The shuttle will be at xyz at such and such a time.' What more is there to say? The kid is up to something and we should avoid him, not play nice with his lawyer."

"I agree," I say quietly. What he says makes perfect sense. But Marc continues as if he didn't hear me and I still need convincing.

"We don't need the kid or his condo. We have Adalia and a hotel room. We should've gone to the nursing home with Charlie and Kay, find a way out of this mess together. I'll bet that's what's delaying them."

"I agree," I repeat louder, gearing up to tell him about the obituary. Well, the part about Adalia.

"You do?" he asks, relieved I'm not arguing.

"I do. But I have to ask, why the blind trust in Adalia?"

He observes me for a moment before answering. "She was Leo's grandmother, for shit's sake." What he says is rude, but he says it cautiously, like he's trying to read between the lines.

"Until I saw the obituary, I thought she had chickened out," I offer.

"Obituary?"

"I'll get to that. But first, be honest with me. You're pretty insistent that she had a reason for sending us here, and I want to know *your* reason for believing that. Because young Adalia in 2080 Toronto didn't know who her grandson would one day be. We never told her, and Dr. Messie kept her in the dark. She didn't even know the subject's name."

"You mean Leo. She didn't know *Leo*'s name," he spits back at me.

I bite my lip. Why can I never say the right thing?

His jaw stiffens and I sense he's about to shut me out again, but he surprises me and starts talking. "Ask yourself this: if she changed her mind, then why go the extra mile and send us to Vegas in 2006?" Then he reaches into his pocket and pulls out a dollar bill. "American currency. Not German. And..." He holds it up close to my face, pointing a finger at the year. "It's from the late nineties."

My mouth hangs open. None of us could make sense of why she sent us here, and aside from Marc, we simply wrote it off as being screwed over. We never looked at the date on the money, much less considered its currency, as he had. I scrunch my forehead, wondering why he hasn't shared this before.

Marc stuffs the dollar bill away and his face softens. "Look, maybe Adalia screwed us, maybe not. I have no idea. But she was Leo's grandmother and that should count for something. Now, what about the obituary?"

Shame travels up my neck and I feel my face flush. Thinking about what I read makes me feel like a fool all over again. But as a general rule, I don't reveal Leo-related things to Marc. So I decide to leave out who survived Leo (his wife) and instead tell him who didn't. "The list of people that predeceased Leo included an Uncle Claudio."

I don't know what I was expecting, but a blank stare from Marc wasn't it. Had he also seen the obituary at the café when he sat down at the computer? I clear my throat and try again. "Claudio, as in Dr. Mess—"

"Ya, ya. I know his first name." He stares at me for a moment, his expression still blank. "You're suggesting Dr. Messie is here," he states, his voice neutral.

"I'm suggesting he *was* here. Predeceased."

"Got it. So he's dead. Why mention him in an obit? I don't get it."

"Me neither."

"Well, he was her brother, after all." He shrugs and goes back to chomping on ice, his gaze drifting to the TV as if this new information has no importance. Not only do I feel ignored, but his reaction makes me question myself. Am I overanalyzing? I open the menu in front of me, pretend to read it as I bounce ideas in my head. Was Dr. Messie here, and now he's dead? Or maybe Adalia mentioned him in the obituary to send a message or a warning? But for whom, and about what? Or is all of this irrelevant, and she just mentioned him because, as Marc said, he was her brother, after all?

From the corner of my eye, I spot our waitress making her way back to our table. It'll be the second time she's come around in the twenty minutes we've been waiting for Charlie and Kay. I flip through the menu to the beverages, feeling like I should at least order something. The waitress arrives at our table, refills our waters, and asks if we're ready to place an order.

"Nope," Marc replies without taking his eyes off the TV.

"I'll take a coffee, please—black," I say with a smile to balance Marc's rudeness.

"Yes, ma'am," the waitress awkwardly replies, then strolls away.

"What's wrong with you?" I scold Marc. "Do you want her to spit in our food?"

He shrugs, still watching the TV.

I turn to see what's got his undivided attention. "What the?" I say, almost laughing at the absurdity of the ticker story: female inmates on a hunger strike demanding healthier food options. Where and when I'm from, criminals are euthanized for petty crimes.

"Buffets of quinoa and salmon should be the standard," Marc says. "Or bacon. At least bacon." I turn back to face him, shocked that he's making a joke. "You should've seen the story just before." He nods at the TV, but keeps his eyes on me, wearing a rare smile. "A group of palliative care patients disappeared, apparently leaving a note like a bunch of teenage runaways. Can you picture it? A group of almost-dead people on a rendezvous before kicking the bucket? Where would they go? Skydiving?" He chuckles at his own joke and then watches me for a moment, like he's measuring my mood. "Grace, I need to tell you something."

My heart starts hammering, but I keep my face as still as possible, making sure I appear calm and receptive. I don't want to risk spooking him away by saying the wrong thing, so I keep quiet. I don't even breathe. Marc never looks at me like that, and he never ever volunteers information. His Adam's apple bobs and an eternity passes between us before he finally speaks.

"About our plan," he says. But something about the way he says it makes me think it wasn't what he was going to say. He's changed his mind.

I release my breath and try not to let my disappointment show. "What about it?"

He stares at me and the table starts shaking from his knee jiggling again. He looks like he's struggling to come up with something to say; an opinion, a suggestion, anything. Lucky for him, my brother and my best friend arrive at that exact second.

"Hey," Charlie says, sliding in next to Marc while Kay takes the spot beside me in the Trans Am bucket seat.

Judging by Charlie's frown, and the way Kay smiles and waves at Manny—polite, but not in her usual upbeat manner—they don't have good news. When they read our faces and body language, they assume the same.

My brother slaps a hand on the table. "Shit!" He slumps in his seat.

Kay shoots him a look—she doesn't like cursing—and then she gets right to it. "Long story short," she says without an ounce of enthusiasm, "talking to Adalia was like drawing blood from a vampire." She explains that Adalia was beyond senile, muttering nothings, eyes unfocused.

"Anything of value?" I ask, eager for any morsel of info that might shed light on the obituary.

"She knew who Leo was," Kay says, tilting her head with a gentle smile.

Marc violently rattles the ice in his glass. "Anything else?"

Kay shakes her head. If she notices the tension between Marc and me, she doesn't let on. Charlie, on the other hand, keeps giving me that worried, big-brother look he used to give me when he knew I was in trouble. As a child, I loved the way he always fixed my mistakes when I couldn't. But the older I get, the bigger my mistakes get, and Charlie can't fix them anymore. When he looks at me, I wonder if it's my pain he feels or his own, for failing me.

"Kay, what did Adalia say, exactly?" Marc asks.

"Her eyes just glossed over and she kept mumbling completely paranoid nonsense about ice ages, like she was from another planet. Honestly, she didn't even recognize us. When we asked about her brother, she said she didn't have one. Can you imagine forgetting your sibling? We questioned her over and over, hoping to conjure up memories. We asked about Dr. Messie, using his first name, his last name. We even asked if she'd ever heard of Hitler, or Elvis, or the Queen of England. It was brutal. Then, for a split second, she seemed to snap out of her trance. 'My brother is a doctor,' she said, all proud, then went on to say that he was at the gates of heaven, where—get this—they don't allow dogs."

Charlie cuts in, calling Adalia "bat-shit crazy."

"Use your words," Kay scolds him. "It's dementia."

He smirks. I'm catching on that he swears on purpose because he knows it'll get a reaction out of her.

Kay picks up again. "Can you imagine a saint at the pearly gates of heaven with a big ol' book of names? 'Welcome, Dr. Messie! Back of the line, Fido!' Let's be real. I don't think Dr. Messie's ever even made Santa's nice list."

"Dogs?" Marc asks.

Kay makes a face and twists her palms up as if to say, "Who knows?"

"Nothing else? What did she actually say?" Marc persists.

"Holy cats, Marc! You're being awful pushy. No, nothing else, nada, zilch, nein. Is that clear enough?" Kay snaps.

He puts his hands up in surrender. "OK. Chill. It's just that Jordan was a bust, so we had our hopes set on Adalia."

"He wasn't a complete bust." I jump in and correct Marc. "He said he'd think about helping us. Told us to go to his lawyer's, to call him from a private connection. Even invited us to stay at his condo in Vegas."

"Oh my gosh, this is great news!" Kay exclaims, practically yelling. "The way you two looked when we first got here, like two sad goats on their way to the slaughterhouse, we thought there was no hope at all!" She leaps off her seat. "Hey, Manny!" she shouts across the diner, bursting with excitement. "Make it to-go!"

"Make what to go?" I ask.

"I called ahead to place our orders. We were famished," Kay replies, rubbing her belly, suddenly alert and eager. "I got the double chocolate mint mocha shake. I can't wait!"

Charlie laughs, keeping his eyes on Kay.

She bounces over to the counter to collect their orders. I hear a "Woo-hoo!" as she pumps a fist in the air.

"Don't get excited. I already spoke to the kid. He isn't going to help us," Marc tells Charlie and me.

"You did?" Charlie asks, taking the words right out of my mouth. Only Charlie doesn't seem as stupidly blindsided as I am.

Marc avoids my glare as he tells Charlie he went to see the lawyer already, using her first name, Morgan, as if they're friends. "Grace was too upset over Jordan. I was trying to spare her."

Spare me?

"And?" Charlie asks, raising an eyebrow with a nod, as if approving of Marc's protectiveness of me.

"And nothing, nada, zilch," he says with a sheepish grin. "Same as Adalia, only a different kind of crazy. I think he's just out to hurt you, Grace," he says, finally meeting my eyes. "That's what I wanted to talk to you about. And I already knew about Dr. Messie."

"What about Dr. Messie?" Charlie asks.

"I'll let Grace tell you about the obituary." Marc keeps his eyes on me when he responds. I guess he has seen the obituary after all. Now he knows that Leo was married, and his wife's name was also Rachel. But Marc has been punishing me since the cemetery, and so I don't believe his bullshit about sparing me from Jordan. What's he up to?

CHAPTER 9 - GRACE

Charlie and Kay are too distracted googly-eyeing each other to notice my mood. The only person who does is the concierge at Jordan's condo, who introduces himself as Oscar, cross-references our names with a list, and then offers me a pity-filled smile.

"I seen you two shiverin' outside. If I'd known you were Mr. Jordan's family, I'd-a let y'all in," Oscar says, his tone apologetic. He's referring to Marc and me. We split into two taxis, not wanting to crowd four of us in one. Kay got dibs on my brother, and Marc and I shared the other, which arrived a few minutes before theirs. We stood outside, ignoring each other while we waited for them.

Charlie asks, "Does Jordan usually come home on the weekend?"

We're hopeful that he will. Today's Thursday.

But Oscar tells us he rarely comes home at all. When he sees how deflated we are, he adds, "But maybe now that he has out-of-town family visiting…" Then he nods to the takeout bags cradled in Kay and Charlie's arms. "Whatcha got there?"

This question is all that's needed for my chatty best friend to become close personal friends with Oscar. She leads him in a conversation that starts with burgers and milkshakes and ends with him telling us all about his lovely wife (Linda), her food allergy (shellfish), and where they spent their last Christmas vacation (a hospital in Puerto Vallarta on account of paella that falsely claimed to be seafood free).

On the slow elevator ride up, Marc worsens my mood. He expresses his distrust of Jordan: "Grace's son" this and "Grace's son" that. I hate how he's been referring to Jordan as solely mine lately. I also think he knows it, and that's why he does it. Charlie and Kay don't jump on the bash-my-son bandwagon, but Marc won't let up. "Grace's son isn't going to help us. Why would we leave a perfectly good hotel room to come here? We should try Adalia again—now, together."

Though we've all agreed that he was right about Adalia sending us here on purpose, given the currency and the obituary, we've also agreed that she probably didn't plan to greet us with dementia.

"Marc, she's not well," Charlie repeats the same line from before we left the diner. "And we *will* give her another try. People with dementia have good days and bad, so you never know. But we also need to try Jordan, too. He lives here. Either he comes home so we can talk, or we find something in his home that points us in the right direction. Tomorrow, we'll split up again, revisit Adalia, revisit Jordan."

"In person," Kay adds. "None of this video shenanigans where he can hang up on us when he's through. So immature." She shakes her head, then exchanges a glance with Charlie, and then they both glance at me. "Grace? You OK?" she asks.

I fake a smile and tell a white lie because I'm tired of being pitied. "Maybe a little hungry." Food is the last thing on my mind. What is top of mind: stopping Dr. Messie and Metagenesis. And so are Jordan, Adalia, Leo, Marc… people I once trusted.

When we reach the penthouse floor, there is no door to unlock or open, even though the keychain holds two keys, the first of which worked in the elevator, and we spill right into a foyer. Jordan's condo resembles more of a palace than a penthouse. We stand still and speechless, admiring the cathedral-like ceilings adorned with colourful murals. A huge stained-glass window takes up the majority of the back wall and sunlight spills through it, filling the space with a soft, colourful glow. Aside from a loveseat and an armchair, the only other item in the whole place is a giant, ornate clock standing tall and regal against a wall. I can hear its cogs and wheels moving slowly, the pendulum rocking back and forth. Other than the mural, there is no art on display, just a bunch of pockmarks on the walls like things were once pinned all over them.

Charlie, Kay, and Marc fix themselves plates in the kitchen. Even if I were hungry, I'd prefer to eat mud than be near Marc right now, so I wander into the living room.

"That kid is an asshole," Marc says, speaking quietly enough to make it obvious he's not talking to me, but like he still wants me to hear.

When and why did he pick up the habit of calling him "kid"? I hate it. I throw a dirty look at him and then blink back tears when I catch Charlie giving him a knowing nod.

Kay leans toward Marc, as if closing the distance will stop me hearing her. "He's more of a louse," she says, keeping true to her clean vocabulary.

I reluctantly agree, but it still hurts to hear them say it. It's been a long day, and in any case, I prefer to focus on how Jordan can help us, rather than his attitude. I have so many questions.

I run my hands over the teeny holes on the living room walls, curious, and then roam around the condo. I try in vain not to eavesdrop while I snoop around my son's home, hoping to catch a glimpse of who he really is and who his friends are—specifically, a hint about how he can get us home.

"I'm surprised how different he is," Kay says as I cross paths with them. They're coming into the living room with their plates and I'm taking their place in the kitchen.

"He used to be so mild-mannered," I hear Kay say.

I pull open kitchen cupboards and drawers; they're empty.

"He killed someone," Charlie says. "Regardless of why he did it, it must've affected him."

I whip closets open in the front hall and slam them shut; they're empty.

"I agree. Committing that kind of sin must really change a person." That was Kay.

I stomp off to the next room.

"Like Grace." Marc doesn't bother whispering—he wants me to hear. After a long silence, he clarifies his remark for everyone, "Grace is a cold-blooded killer, too."

I smack my head off the corner of a cupboard door in the bathroom, cuss and wince in pain from both the fresh cut on my scalp and Marc's words. Blood drips on the white marble tile. I grab a wad of toilet paper, the holder crash-bangs on the floor and the roll falls off and unravels all over the place. "Shit," I mutter. I make a tissue ball to stop the bleeding before plodding my way to one of the three bedrooms.

"What a crass thing to say, Marc, especially given her reasons. And you know she's sorry, so back off her," whispers Charlie.

Do they not realize I can still hear them? Whispers echo in a living room shaped like a concert hall. I check all the bedroom closets, the built-in drawers, the baroque chest at the end of one of the beds. Empty, empty, empty!

"You can't apologize for killing a person and expect to carry on like everything is OK," Marc continues, louder than before. "Leo was a person, not a houseplant."

"Carry on? You don't know her at all, if that's what you think she's doing. She's trying to make up for her mistakes, Marc. When are you going to stop punishing her?" Charlie whisper-yells.

That's the million-dollar question.

"Does it ever get tiring, wrapping yourself around her finger?" Marc asks.

"Stop! This negative chitchat serves no purpose. You're just weaving your friendship into a hell-bound handbasket," Kay says.

"What the fuck does that mean, Kay? Why don't you just say what you mean?" I can't believe Marc swore at her, and I half expect Charlie to take a swing at him.

"Charlie!" Kay's tone tells me I was right. "Please, don't engage. It'll only give him what he wants," she sneers, then calls out, "Grace, honey?" She's probably checking to see if I'm paying attention, which I am but would never admit. "You all right in there? What's all that banging around?" If she's so concerned, you'd think she'd rise off her butt to come check on me. She's supposed to be my best friend. She should be defending me alongside Charlie instead of refereeing between him and Marc.

I emerge from Jordan's empty bedroom, come into his empty living room where—with plates of takeout from the diner on their laps—my husband, my brother, and my best friend discuss my crime, guilt, and sentence as if I'm not even there.

"Does anyone care about getting home, or going to Germany, or finding Dr. Messie? How about Me-ta-gen-es-is? See this?" I jingle the stupid keys in their smug faces. "Isn't anyone curious to know what this extra key is for? There is nothing in this entire place it could unlock. I checked. There are no locks on any of the doors or cupboards, it's not the right size for a vehicle, it's not for his elevator, and there is no front door."

They're looking at me with "so what?" faces, like I'm making a big deal out of something minute and irrelevant. Maybe I am, but those pinholes in the walls are screaming out to me. And isn't this why we came here instead of returning to our hotel?

"There is nothing in this whole condo that says my son lives in this place, but he's been here for six long years. What's he been doing? Why's he still here—in Las Vegas? He gets away with murder and decides to live in a city where he's hated? He knows a way out of here, and is reluctant to share it with us?"

Charlie and Kay's expressions change with each question I blurt out. They glance at each other, then back to me. I can't tell if they're on board with me or if they're worried I'm losing my mind. What's worse is the satisfied smile that spreads across Marc's face like he's happy about it.

I wave out a hand. "What was on these *walls*?"

"You think there's more going on?" Charlie asks.

"Of course." I throw my arms in the air. What a stupid question. "He's *my* son." I scowl at Marc when I take ownership of Jordan.

Again, Charlie and Kay look at each other, talking in code with eye movements.

I spin around and stomp away to the elevator.

"Where are you going?" Kay asks, the springs on the couch creaking as she finally rises.

"To find out what this key unlocks," I call over my shoulder. I don't wait for a response from anyone as I enter the elevator and press the button to take me back to the street.

Kay runs toward the elevator but arrives in time to smack her palm on the door as it closes. "Grace, wait," her muffled voice comes through as I descend.

I have no intention of waiting. Now that I'm gone, they can properly speak about me behind my back. As for me, I've got more important things on my mind, such as finding a way home to stop a mad scientist. I don't want to sit around waiting for Adalia to have a good day, or for Jordan to get over himself. If either of them knows a way home, I'm going to look for it until I find it.

"What can I do you for, Grace?" Oscar asks.

He seems like a thoughtful man, though I'm basing my opinion on his ability to remember my name and his bushy grey brows, which are in a perma inward slope. It could also be his blue uniform, stirring up memories of my dad. My dad was wearing his security guard uniform the day I found him dangling from that rope, one minute too late.

I ask Oscar if there's a locker room in the building. He kindly points me in the direction of the condo's lockers, but tells me Jordan doesn't have one assigned to him.

"What is it you lookin' for, sweetheart?" he asks.

"A way home." I almost tear up saying it, and when his brows slope even more at my response, I have to change the subject before I turn to putty. "Any idea what this key would be for?"

Oscar takes the key, turns it around in his hand. "Looks like a storage locker."

"But you said—"

"One of them big storage facilities folks rent out, though I couldn't tell you which one." He hands the key back to me.

I thank him and leave, declining his offer to call me a taxi. I don't want to wait in the lobby—it'd give Kay time to catch up to me.

Time to chase down a storage facility. Whatever you're hiding, Jordan, I will find it.

CHAPTER 10 - GRACE

I didn't go to Jordan's storage facility. I wouldn't even have known where to begin the search for it without asking him when all I have is a key. And there was no way I was going back to the condo. I thought about going to our hotel room, since we hadn't checked out in case Jordan's condo was a dump. That's where I asked the taxi to take me. But when I arrived, I got sidetracked by the neon signs calling me to gamble on their gaming floors. The idea of losing myself in a round of poker almost won me over. I walked right up to the entrance and stood there long enough to make the security guard question and offer me help. The guard was an old lady, super old, and it made me think of Adalia.

So here I am.

Adalia stares out the window, but not at the stunning vista rolled out in front of her. Her eyes are vacant like she's in a far-off land in her head. The floor-to-ceiling windows offer scenery only big spenders could afford in the fanciest resorts. It seems a waste for the Red Rock Nursing Home to be front and centre to this view. The beautiful backdrop of a nightly orange-pink sky is lost on most patients in this care facility. Tonight, the redder-than-Mars sun hangs low, inching its way behind the rust-coloured formations in the distance. A film director couldn't have staged it better. It's breathtaking. And it has no effect on the old woman. I frown. This is going to be a waste of time.

"Here you go, ma'am." The young attendant returns with an ornate, high-back chair for me and places it next to my Grandma

Addy—or so he thinks. The obituary mentioned that Leo would be missed by Grandma Addy, so I went with it.

I thank the attendant and take a seat. The chair may be gorgeous, but it's so hard I wouldn't be surprised if its maker had chiselled it right out of the red rock landscape. They certainly don't want people to overstay.

"Visiting hours will be over in fifteen minutes," he reminds me again with a stern look and then leaves us. At first, he tried to get me to come back the next morning, telling me she'd already had a busy day with far too many visitors. But I was adamant that I needed to see my grandma now, and I promised to leave at seven—sharp.

"Adalia, it's me, Grace." I pause for a reaction. I almost expect her to snap out of her dementia long enough to strangle me for what I did: ignoring her warning, killing her grandson. She doesn't budge. "We met a long time ago in Toronto, 2080, when you were young, then again six years ago, here, in Vegas. You asked me to trust you. That's why I'm here. Can you help us get home so we can stop Dr. Messie?"

Still nothing. She doesn't even blink.

I sigh, survey the room: lavish furniture, expensive drapery, intricate artwork. There are tons of framed photos and trinkets on her nightstand and I go to them, start skimming them. Most of the photos are of Adalia with her family at different stages of their lives. I especially love the one of her wedding. She was a beautiful bride. I'm a little jealous that she was able to leave the Metagenesis mess behind to start over, even if her motive was to kill her own brother. She lived a full life in another era, as if that was where she belonged all along; she had a long marriage, a son, a grandson... I bite back guilt when I recognize one of the photos: Adalia with her arm around a smiling Leo. I remember this photo from Leo's bookshelf the morning after spending the night at his place. I pick it up.

"Put that down."

I turn back to her. "Adalia?"

She's still staring blankly out the window, into la-la land. If I believed in ghosts, I'd swear one just spoke to me. Taking the photo with me, I sit back down and shuffle the chair closer to her.

It must weigh a hundred pounds, making me wonder if the attendant moonlights as The Incredible Hulk.

"Do you know who this is?" I ask, and place the photo in her lap. Kay said Adalia remembered Leo, so it's a good spot to poke at if there is one.

She bows her head; her lips curl up for a split second, but the smile is gone as quick as it appeared. I saw recognition in her eyes, though. I'm sure I did.

She turns her stare back outside and we sit in silence for a time before I give it another go.

"I saw Leo's obituary and what it said about his Uncle Claudio."

She looks at me then. Her old eyes have a bluish hue to them. They're dull and seem to have shrunk with age. At the mention of Leo's name, they twitch, but I still don't get a vocal response. Instead, she gets up out of her chair.

I half rise out of mine to snatch the picture before it slips off her lap. "Should I call someone? Do you need something?"

She ignores me and paces around the room, muttering under her breath. She opens a closet at the far end of the room and shuffles a pile of pretty memento boxes around, peering into them one by one.

I'm unsure what to do and head over to the door to get the attendant, but see the clock on the wall and decide against it. Visiting hours have ended and he'll kick me out.

"Adalia, why don't you come back and take a seat?"

"The world, the world is ending… ice and fire…" She rattles on like I hoped she would, only she sounds as crazy as Charlie and Kay said. I should leave. Coming back to visit on the same day was a stupid idea.

She's rummaging through personal belongings in the dresser. I approach her and try to get a rise out of her for the last time. I bring the picture with me and park it in her sightline. What's the worst that can happen? If she's crazy, she won't know the difference. No harm, no foul. I go at her with the unabridged, cold truth.

"My name is Grace. The man in this picture is your grandson, Leo," I say it with the enthusiasm of a sloth, to keep from falling to pieces. "I killed him to save my son, Jordan. Dr. Messie, your brother, who created Metagenesis, made me do it. I need you to help me stop him. It's why you sent us here, isn't it? Except we were all supposed to go to Germany—together. Do you remember?"

She takes the picture and places it in the top drawer with no emotion, then moves down to the next one. "I don't have a brother," she says.

I sigh. I think it's time to leave.

But then she adds, although barely audible, "He's dead to me."

My mouth hangs open. She said those exact words to us on the flight. "What did you just say?"

She doesn't repeat herself, but she does stop sifting through her stuff, apparently finding whatever she was looking for. A small smile spreads on her face, one of relief, and then she turns to me, the film over her eyes not as thick as it seemed moments earlier. She grabs my hand. Hers are ice cold, her fingers knobby.

I look down to see what she is shoving into my palm. It feels like—I give my head a shake and look again. It's still there in my hand; I didn't imagine it. A little pink vial. My breath catches.

I meet Adalia's eyes again. She's still holding my hands, squeezing.

"Is this…?"

She nods once.

I raise an eyebrow. "Why was Dr. Messie mentioned in the obituary? Was he here?"

She frowns but also squeezes my hands hard. I'm close. My heart rate picks up to triple time. I lick my lips. "Adalia, is he still here, now?"

She nods again.

"Do you know where?"

She releases my hand, tucks her hair behind her ear. And nods. Vigorously.

CHAPTER 11 - GRACE

The good news is that I have the pink vial. The bad news is that Adalia still has dementia. She doesn't know where her brother was or is or will be. Right after she gave me the vial, squeezing it into my hand, she began rambling about her brother in heaven standing at the gate with no dogs, same as she did with Charlie and Kay. Then she chose a trinket sitting among her photo collection and shoved it at me. "Be kind!" she shouted when I tried to give it back. I glanced at it. It was a flat stone with a carving on one side of two children holding hands. "Be kind!" she repeated and that was when she really ramped things up, screaming nonsense about fire and floods and "No dogs no dogs!" When I tried to put the stone back in its place, she went ape-shit. *"Kind!"* she screeched, her eyes wild. The attendant dashed in to save the day, asking me to leave with a glower.

I felt terrible guilt, blaming myself for setting off her episode, or worse: what if losing Leo was what made Adalia sick with dementia in the first place? I watched from the doorway as the attendant soothed her and walked her back to her spot in front of the window. She sat, tucked her hair behind her ear, and quietly drifted back into her daydream. I didn't dare re-enter the room to put her stone carving back, just in case it set her off again. I slipped it into my jacket pocket with the intention of returning it another day.

By 10 p.m., I'd dropped an unspeakable amount of cash on a bunch of bad hands at Mandalay Bay's casino. You'd think that would've been enough to send me back to my waiting family at the condo—that, and the fact that I'm desperate for sleep. Instead, I'm on the pedestrian bridge of the New York New York hotel, watching a roller coaster zip through the skyline. There is no comfort to be found at a blackjack table and even though I know this, I'm foolishly contemplating playing a hand or two in their casino. But I chose this spot because it reminds me of my dad—or more accurately, it makes me think of Mimi, my mother, whom I don't remember.

I spend a long time on the bridge, my mind running wild. This is why I'd rather be at a blackjack table, to stop the first thought from looping around to the next. I shake my wrist out of habit, feeling Dad's copper watch. Charlie and I scattered Dad's ashes at the real Statue of Liberty. That was also where he proposed to Mimi. Sadly, that's all we really know about her. Even Charlie, who was five when Mimi left (I was only three), has little memory of her. He remembered stupid things a kid would: her favourite colour was yellow, she liked French fries, she was nice. I've always believed he misremembered her character. If she was nice, why'd she leave us? Dad blamed himself, making the topic of Mimi taboo. Until now, I never understood how you could blame yourself for being left behind. I'm slowly coming to terms with losing Marc, and the person to blame for that is me.

I'm a lot like my dad. If I'm not careful, I'll be trapped in the same dark hole he never climbed out of after he lost his precious Mimi. Not wanting to fall prey to another blackjack table, something else my dad would've done, gives me the motivation to grab a taxi and head back to the condo. Avoiding Marc won't delay the inevitable. Besides, I have news to share with everyone. I have the vial. And a little stone carving of two children… I shake my head.

I had assumed everyone would be waiting up to scold me for my disappearing act and I planned to use the vial as my peace offering. But when the elevator door opens to Jordan's condo, it's almost dark, as if empty. There's a silhouette sitting in the wing-chair facing me, legs spread comfortably, arms on the armrests with a drink in hand. Some light seeps in from another room, but the man is sitting in the shadows, as if on purpose. From the foyer where I stand, I see only his outline.

"You're back," he says matter of factly. It takes me a second to place him: Marc. He sounds different. Ice rattles as he raises his glass to sip. "Did you find out what the key is for?"

"A storage room." Why is he sitting like that? The armchair looks like it's been deliberately moved to face the elevator door, like he positioned it just so, to confront someone: he's been waiting for me.

"A storage room? What's in it?"

"Haven't gone yet." I cross the threshold cautiously, tuck the keys into my jacket pocket, tug at my skirt—stall. I want to tell everyone about the vial but... I survey the room. It seems like we're alone.

"They've gone out. Check out of our hotel and then some all-night grocery place," Marc answers my unasked question. "You had the only keys so one of us had to stay behind. I volunteered." He takes another sip, holds his glass out in front of him. "Want some?" His voice is low in both volume and octave. He is too calm, and it makes me nervous. "I won't bite," he says nonchalantly and shakes his glass, clinking the ice cubes around.

I reach for the light switch on the wall.

"Leave it off," he commands in an almost whisper.

I swallow hard and my chest heats up. I take my jacket off and hang it on the hook to my left, then unglue my feet from the floor to approach him. When I reach for the drink he's offering, he pulls his arm back before I can grasp it and his other hand simultaneously snatches my wrist and pulls me onto his lap in one smooth motion. My breath catches in my windpipe. I sit completely still, stunned.

Marc takes another swig before setting the glass on the floor beside him. "Come here," he whispers as he adjusts my position on his lap, his hands using my hips as handles. The smell of alcohol drips off his words. I'm surprised to feel his erection against my thigh and his hand pushing its way up beneath my skirt.

I spring off his lap, taken aback. My blood thumps in my eardrums and even the tips of my ears throb. He laughs, drunk, and rises from his seat. I back away from him as he lazily walks toward me like I'm his prey who knows she's been caught by her predator. But unlike an animal about to be a victim of an attack, I want to be devoured by him. It's just that guilt, lust, and longing are all the wrong reasons. He doesn't sound like my Marc. Well, his voice does—just not his tone or choice of words. When he walks through a streak of light, I can see enough to detect drunken desire on his face, his eyes undressing me.

"Will you tell me your name?" I ask under my breath, certain that if I hear his name, it'll send me running away from him instead of toward him.

"Please," I plead as my back hits the wall.

He doesn't stop his approach and when he reaches me, he covers me with his body, roughly grinding himself against me. My hands sprawl over his pecs to keep him from coming closer.

He doesn't ease off.

He ignores my resistance, cranes his neck, and breathes in my ear. "I want you." He lets his teeth catch my lobe before kissing the spot just under it. I melt. This is the first time he's shown any desire for me—good or bad—since he looked at me with disgust at Leo's gravesite, the moment he began to openly hate me.

"Do you want me?" he asks and then brings his face to mine, nose to nose. He searches my eyes for an answer. My hands tremble on his warm chest, his heart beating fast under my palms. He's not Marc, not really, but he feels like him. His breathing is heavy; so is mine. I don't respond but I also don't stop him from hiking my skirt up and slipping his hand beneath my leggings, over my panties, and stroking. I move my hips in anticipation. A tremor runs up my back and I dig my nails into his chest. He presses all his weight against me, then forces one of my arms off his chest and pins it against the wall.

"Can I have you?" he asks, looking me dead in my eyes and caressing me heavily.

He bites his lower lip as he waits for me to grant permission. I almost deny it. I almost push him away with my free hand—almost. Instead, I unhook my claws from his chest and let my free arm fall limp to my side, giving him the green light to have his way with me.

But Mark misinterprets my surrender for denial, and comes to a full stop. He releases my wrist and his fingers travel down my sides, leaving behind a trail of goosebumps, his eyes still on mine.

Then he takes a small step back. I panic, confused by a sudden feeling that I need this to happen, that it will magically solve everything between us. I'm close to tears because I do want him and I am desperate for him to want me too, even if it's the alcohol talking. I've felt so alienated since he's withheld his love that I'll take him any way I can.

I grab at his belt and pull him back to me, catching us both by surprise, and the doubt in his eyes disintegrates.

He slides down to his knees, fusses to pull my leggings down, off my buttocks, halfway down my thighs. He doesn't take them right off and before I can help him undress me, he ducks his head under my skirt, lifts the edge of my panties, and his tongue flickers my sweet spot. Fingers penetrate me and nearly send me over the edge, but not quite. He stops just before and makes his way back up.

He kisses me hard, squeezing my breast with one hand while messing with his belt buckle with the other. I hear the clasp come undone and he stops kissing me, flips me around, slamming me against the cool wall, then twists one arm behind my back. I'm sure he's bruising me and I don't know why I like it. His roughness is foreign; *he is not my Marc*, I remind myself. I should want him to stop.

"Tell me your name," I insist through my panting, a fleeting moment of clarity hitting me. If he admits that he isn't my husband and doesn't love me, maybe I'll snap out of this trance.

"Are you sure you want me?" he breathes into my hair as he presses up on me. "Yes or no?" His buckle clangs when it hits the ground with his jeans and he rubs up against me, bare. But he waits for an answer.

I nod yes.

He uses his legs to spread mine, widening my stance with his feet and pushing against me, stretching my panties to one side. I bring my hands up to a push-up stance on the wall in an attempt to raise my face off the surface.

"Say it!" he commands.

I whisper a *yes* barely heard over the sound of my pounding heart.

"Louder!" he shouts in my ear as he pulls out my hips and enters me with force. I start to cry, mourning the loss of my Marc, though not loud enough for him to notice. But even if he did, I doubt he'd care, so long as I don't change my mind about sex.

"Say it!" he shouts again as he grips my hips and pumps, my cheek scrubbing the wall. I'm clenching my fists and my nails dig into my palms with each thrust.

"What's your name?" I shout through gritted teeth, tears streaming down my cheeks as he humps me harder and harder, faster.

"Say it!" He grabs the side of my head and a fistful of hair, his elbow jabbing into my back.

"Yes!" I shout back, desperate for this to be over yet yearning for him to keep at me and to take what he wants, to push harder, deeper, faster. "Yes! Yes!" I shout repeatedly each time he demands me to, over and over until his words evolve and morph into growls and grunts.

And then he finishes.

But not me, I don't finish.

My mood is ruined by the reminder that I'm being fucked by a total stranger and feeling dirty about wanting more. I don't think he cares that I don't finish, that he leaves me unsatisfied. He slips out of me, yanks my leggings up halfway, not bothering to fix my underwear or wipe away the warm, wet mess. I turn around and lean against the wall, spent, and watch as he slides his legs back into his pants and then saunters away as if nothing happened. He flops down onto the chair, picks up his half-finished drink from the floor beside him and chugs. His breath in his cup is loud and I can hear each swallow of drink, which he finishes in four big gulps.

"My name is Cyrus," he says coldly, watching me.

I openly cry, realizing once and for all that my Marc is gone and what just happened tonight was the absolute end. So I sob as I lean against the wall. And what does he do? He reaches to the other side of the couch for a bottle, refills his drink, and holds it out to me again, like a carrot to a donkey, an ass.

I've never felt so alone.

CHAPTER 12 - GRACE

The sun has barely risen so I'm shocked to see that Kay has, too. She's sitting at the raised counter, staring off into space. I contemplate going back to bed to bury my head underneath the blankets. I was hoping to be alone. But then I notice how quiet she is. I know she's never been a morning person, but she hasn't even greeted me or acknowledged my presence.

"Morning," I say as I make my way to join her.

She jumps and knocks over her coffee. "Darn it!" She scrambles for paper towels.

I beat her to it and wipe up the mess.

"Didn't mean to startle you. You OK?" I ask.

"Thinking…" Then her eyes mist. "About Peter."

I never know what to say to people in need of comfort. Instead of saying the wrong thing, I give her a side-hug, refill her coffee and pour myself one too, then slide into the seat beside her. Though I have no intention of unloading what happened with Marc last night, I do want to bring up my visit with Adalia, just not in the middle of her grieving Peter. That wouldn't be—

"So what'd you find out about the key?" she asks, suddenly alert and eager.

"Uh…"

Then she sighs. "All right, let's get Peter out of the way. I was *thinking* about him, not grieving for him. I did that long before Adalia helped me take him off life support. I grieved when he first lost his soul, again when my parents sold him to Dr. Messie in the name of science for a quick paycheck, and every time I visited him in that clinic afterward."

"I'm sorry you lost your brother, Kay." It's not the first time I've expressed my condolences to her, but I don't know what else to say.

"Me too," she says. "But even though I'm sad he's gone, I'm not as sad as when he was hooked up to those machines and there was nothing I could do about it. My brother died long before his heart stopped beating. Doesn't mean I don't sometimes think about him. It's perfectly normal. I'm fine. Really."

"You're like a self-charging battery," I say, marvelling at the way she counsels herself. She's such a low-maintenance friend.

"I don't get it," she replies. Then, like a flipped switch, she waves me off and changes the subject back to her question about the key.

I tell her it's for a storage locker and she doesn't seem impressed. But when I tell her about my visit with Adalia, she leaps off her seat, yelling, "*OH MY GOSH OH MY GOSH OH MY GOSH!*" until Charlie comes out of the room.

"What the fuck, Kay?" he says, rubbing the sleep out of his eyes.

She's so excited that she doesn't flinch when my brother swears. It takes him offering to cook us breakfast to get her to sit back down and calmly tell him what she's all worked up about.

I stare into my mug of coffee-gone-cold and tune out the chatter around me while Charlie makes us breakfast. I don't share Kay's enthusiasm as she excitedly talks about me getting the vial, comparing me to some clever animal I've never heard of. She talks right over me when I remind her of the bad news: we need to find Dr. Messie to stab him with it. I don't bother inserting myself into the conversation again.

When Marc—or Cyrus or whatever his name is—enters the room, he acts as if nothing happened between us last night. He skillfully looks through me without calling awareness to his talent of making me feel invisible.

"Good morning, *Marc*," I say, enunciating his name purposely.

This catches his attention and he locks eyes with me for a split second.

"Good morning to you," he replies with a smile on his face but not in his eyes, then brushes my cheek with his lips to almost kiss me.

He pays me just enough attention that Charlie and Kay would think everything is fine between us, but not enough to satisfy the jagged hole he's dug in my heart. I can still smell lingering alcohol emanating from his pores: it sends a shudder through my ribcage. I shrug last night away and tug my sleeve over a bruise forming on my wrist, from his grip.

He doesn't sit next to me. Instead, he takes the seat at the end of Jordan's long breakfast bar. He might as well be in Siberia.

"Grace, you want some sugar or milk for that coffee?" Kay asks.

"You're staring into the mug like it's gonna tell you your fortune or something." Charlie says as he swaps my coffee cup for a fresh hot one, steam rising from it.

I glance up at them and try to smile but can't manage to even fake one for their sake. Marc's presence has rattled me. "I'm just thinking," I say absently.

The room grows quiet, like I'm supposed to share what I'm thinking. I don't. I stare back into my mug and ignore the uncomfortable silence that follows.

Kay pushes a sugar bowl and milk carton toward me. I ignore them and instead wrap my hands around the cup, absorbing the warmth, careful to keep my bruised wrist covered. I take my coffee black, anyhow, a fact everyone seems to have forgotten about me.

Charlie places a plate in front of me, eggs, scrambled, arranged in a smiley face like he used to do when we were kids and he knew I was upset. I haven't eaten since lunch yesterday and should be in the early stages of starvation, but the aroma of eggs turns my stomach.

Eventually, the chatter starts up again, though Marc remains out of it. Imagined or real, it feels like he can read my thoughts as clear as if they were in a cartoon dialogue bubble over my head. My mind is swimming with scraps of a bad dream. Can he sense it? Not the usual Dad-suicide dream. Instead, Leo haunted me all night, leaving me nearly sleepless. We walked along the canyon and he rambled about his job and no matter what I did, I couldn't change the outcome. I killed him over and over and each time he yelled that he wasn't a houseplant. I'd wake, fall back asleep, and repeat the nightmare.

"Don't you agree, Grace?" Charlie asks.

I have no idea what we're talking about now, and from the corner of my eye I can see the smirk on Marc's face, like he really was in my head. I hate that I feel exposed—to him, no less.

My heart pumps harder and my face burns up, telltale signs that I'm heading toward an epic meltdown, and I decide to escape before the dissolve. I get up and leave, grabbing my jacket off the hook on my way to the elevator.

As the door begins to close, Kay jumps in with me at the last second. "Not this time you don't," she scolds as the elevator descends. I don't have to look at her to know that she's scowling at me. "Where are you going?"

"I want to find the storage unit," I tell her.

"What for?" she asks in a snarky tone. Why is she suddenly mad at me? "We have the vial, and Adalia said Dr. Messie was here. We need to find Dr. Messie. Who cares about Jordan's locker?"

"At some point, we have to get home. Whatever is in there could help us."

"You're being sneaky," she accuses, still boring her eyes into me. "What happened to your face, by the way?"

"Huh?" My fingers go to my cheek and I blush when I touch the spot that was scrubbing against the wall while Marc was—

"Something happen between you and Marc last night? You two have been oil and vinegar."

I drop my hand, ram the button urgently, and concentrate on the little dial flashing down. It's going so slow I wonder if it's powered by gerbils. "I don't want to talk about it," I reply, knowing that if I do, I'll crumble.

When the elevator reaches the ground floor, she comes off with me. I question her with a look. She's wearing jogging pants and the short-sleeved shirt she wore as pyjamas. Her hair is a mess—morning hair.

"I'm coming with you, Grace."

"I don't want the company," I tell her bluntly.

She gasps as if I've just slapped her.

I huff and walk off. Truth is, I don't know where this damn storage room is, and my plan was to brainstorm. Alone. At a casino.

I deliberately don't grab a cab right away. Kay's got to be freezing with no jacket and I'm hoping she'll give in and turn back. I walk a bus-length ahead of her and take pleasure when the wind blows in my face and stings the fresh wall-burn. I smile as I picture how cold she must be, but when I turn around to give her stink-eye, I catch her hailing a cab. With her back turned to me, she doesn't see my surprise that she's already given up. I'm half-relieved, half-disappointed. I keep walking.

I shove my hands in my pockets for warmth and my fingers brush against something smooth. It takes me a moment to place what it is: my souvenir from Adalia. I pull out the stone carving and look it over as I walk. It's nothing special, a flat stone about the size of my palm with a carving on the side of two kids holding hands. Turning it over, I read the inscription on the bottom and suddenly realize why she gave it to me.

If more humans were like you, the world would be a better place. It's too late for me, but not for you. Stay good, little sis.

It isn't signed, but Adalia has only one brother. "Be kind," I say quietly as I consider her words. It's impossible to know when Dr. Messie gave this to her, or under what circumstances. But she kept it... and then gave it to me along with the vial, knowing that I plan to kill him. It's clear she wants me to go through with it, but I'd say she's asking me not to be cruel about it. *Kill him kindly?* I chuckle at the paradox. I don't believe Dr. Messie deserves kindness, but apparently she does. What is she, a saint? But it's probably something as simple as sibling loyalty: he is her brother.

I tuck the stone back into my pocket, still determined to return it to Adalia, and I round a corner to grab a cab. Kay hasn't passed me in hers, so they must've pulled a U-turn. I turn and stick out my arm to hail a cab and am caught off guard to see one right there, keeping up with me at a crawl. When it pulls up beside me, my jaw drops. Kay's in the backseat, warm, wearing a glowing smile.

I stop in my tracks, fold my arms over my chest, and put on my pissed-off face.

She rolls down her window. "Getting rid of me is like trying to sweep sand off the beach. Want a ride? It's much warmer in here."

I turn around and ignore her, walk at a brisk pace. The cab crawls beside me, not as discreetly as before, and cars behind it start to honk at the driver for holding up traffic. Someone yells, "Move it, jackass!" out of their window before weaving around the taxi, cutting off another vehicle, who then honks and yells at that guy.

"I know you're upset about whatever is going on between you and Marc. But why are you taking it out on me?" Kay shouts.

I walk faster, tears welling in my eyes.

"Oh for crying out loud, get in the car, and I won't ask about him again. Satisfied?"

She has said the magic words to stop me in my tracks. I squeeze my eyes to halt the tears, *I will not cry*, and then climb into the taxi next to my best friend.

Kay puts on a genuine smile. "Atta girl," she says. She pats my knee and plants a huge kiss on my cheek, then moves closer to me. We're practically snuggling. It's a bit overdone, but I chalk it up to her victory celebration at my easy surrender.

"Where to?" the driver asks. He has a raspy voice like he's been smoking for a hundred years and his car smells like a pine forest on fire. There's a little tree hanging from his rear-view mirror and a non-smoking sign on the windshield. I bet he thinks the pine masks the smell of his smoking habit in his non-smoking cab.

"Ladies?" The driver makes eyes at us in the rear-view, waiting for direction.

I wanted to go to the casino, blow off some steam. But that's not something I do with Kay. Now I don't know where I want the driver to take us.

"Show Randy the key, Grace."

I look at her. "Huh?"

"The key to the storage unit. Does it have a logo? Maybe he knows it."

I pull out the keys.

"Randy, hon, do you know where that is?" she asks, then nudges me to show him.

I reach across the middle console so Kay's newest friend, Randy the driver, can see the logo on the key—a brilliant idea I wish I had thought of after leaving Adalia. It would've saved me a lot of money, and heartache.

"Yes, ma'am." The driver winks at Kay. "I know exactly where that is."

CHAPTER 13 - MARC

By taking a long shower, I successfully avoid eating breakfast with Charlie. When I come out, the kitchen is clean and he's got his shoes and jacket on. Was he waiting for me or hoping to be gone before I finished my shower? In any case, I decline the offer to go with him to see Adalia again.

"What's the point?" I ask.

He tells me he hopes she's having a better day so we can ask about Dr. Messie again, now that we have the vial. "Besides, it's better than waiting around for my sister and Kay to come back from wherever they went."

When I don't budge, he says, "Suit yourself. If you go out, the concierge has extra keys. I asked. No need to repeat last night."

I know he's referring to Grace taking what we thought was the only set of keys, but my face heats when I think of how I behaved last night. I was a real dick.

Charlie places a cell phone on the counter, calling it a throw-away, and tells me they bought two at the supermarket last night, and he's taking one with him now. He warns me to keep it charged. "It's not heat-powered," he says as he writes the number for his phone on a pad of paper and slides it in front of me. "Call me when they're back." He doesn't leave, though, probably smelling my shame. He lingers and then asks, "What's going on with you?"

"Don't know what you mean," I respond, picking up the pen and doodling on the pad of paper. I'm in no mood for a heart-to-heart. Just because we bonded over a few drinks the other day doesn't mean we're best friends.

"Cut the bullshit, Marc," he unleashes his frustration. "You've been a real prick since we got here. And ya, I get that you're trying to adjust and you're pissed off, but something else is up. Tell me, why'd you *really* sneak off to see Jordan the way you did? No one is buying your story about protecting my sister's feelings, least of all me."

I like him better when he's being straight with me, and I almost smile. I express my amusement by drawing a happy-face stick man. "I wanted to know if the kid was serious about helping us, and now that I know he's not, I'm pissed. That's it."

"Bull. Shit."

"What do you want me to say?" I snap, slapping down the pen. I wasn't expecting him to buy that line either, but it *is* mostly fact.

"The truth." He folds his arms across his chest.

I hold eye contact with him. For some reason, I hate lying to Charlie, which is why I decide to tell him the truth he's expecting to hear. "I wanted to know if he could help me get back... to *my* home." I didn't realize how badly I wanted this until I choke on the last three words as I speak them. A shiver runs through me when I think about leaving Grace. If I'm being honest, I've already left her. Last night, I flipped her around because I couldn't even look her in the face when we were... while I was... because I wished she were Rachel and I were Cyrus.

Charlie unfolds his arms and lets out a deep sigh. I'm not sure if it's pity for me or for his sister, but whichever it is, it's written all over his face. "And?"

"And nothing." I keep my eyes on his, hoping he'll see honesty there and stop asking questions.

He leans across the raised counter and watches me for a moment. "I'm sorry for everything you've been through. And you're right. You don't owe my sister anything. I won't hold it against you if you leave."

It's funny. When Grace apologizes, it infuriates me. When Charlie does it, it makes me feel seen. "Is this the part where you try to convince me to stay?"

"Nope. If what Grace did isn't something you can move past, staying won't be good for either of you."

Charlie's not a bad guy. Under another set of circumstances, we could even be friends. I pick up the pen and start cathartically doodling again. It distracts me from the kindness he's showing me, that I don't deserve.

"You know what, Charlie? Sometimes I think I could stay here in Vegas, start fresh. We're in the land of entertainment. Casinos, live theatre, plays, musicals, what's not to like? I used to love theatre." I hesitate. Not sure why I shared that bit. Next thing you know, I'll be gushing about the all-access theatre pass I bought so I could run into the pretty girl from the museum who loved Greek tragedies. I'd sit a few rows back, working up the nerve to ask her out, promising myself I'd do it at the end of the play. Yes, I loved theatre, but I hated Greek tragedies, so I'd fall asleep every time and miss my opportunity. When I'd wake, the play would be over and she'd be gone. Until one day, the pretty girl shook me awake. "I believe you've tortured yourself long enough. I'm Rachel. Want to take me to dinner? I hope you like sushi." I lied and told her I loved it. It was a lie I kept up for the duration of our relationship, especially once I learned that her late husband had hated it. I wanted to be different.

I scribble hard on the notepad, the pen ripping through layers, symbolically scratching Rachel from my mind. "Do you ever think about staying, Charlie?"

"How so?"

"Just… staying. It's 2006. There's no Metagenesis here. Dr. Messie doesn't have to be your problem."

"We have a job to do. Staying here would be selfish."

"And yet you wouldn't hold it against me if I did?" I scoff.

"Killing Leo was selfish. And I didn't hold that against Grace."

My hand freezes stiff on the pen and I look up at Charlie. He flexes his jaw while I pick mine up off the counter. I'd bet years off my life this is the first time in the history of Charlie that he's ever expressed discord with his precious baby sister, Gracie. It's no small feat and I'm stunned into appreciative silence.

Charlie straightens and zips up his jacket to leave. "When they get back, have Kay call me and I'll get her out of your hair so you and Grace can talk. I hope to see you later, but if I don't, that's fine too. Take care, Marc." Then he leaves.

For twenty minutes I watch the clock, because there's nothing else to do in Jordan's place, and then I decide to run out to the corner store to grab another bottle of whisky. If I'm going to be alone with Grace, I may need a little help, though that didn't go too well last night.

I sit on a bench in a parkette across from the condo, obsessing over what I might say or where to begin, or even if I'll bother. Starting with Rachel would be the most logical. When I think about that, I think about how Rachel and Grace are similar... but at least Rachel talked about her first husband, Darius. Grace never brings up Leo or *her* Marc. But I know better than to ask, having learned the lesson from Rachel.

Though Rachel spoke of Darius here and there, she had nothing left of his—not one souvenir. This fact messed with my head; sometimes I'd worry he wasn't really dead, and other times I'd hope she'd made him up and he'd never really existed. Both scenarios were completely irrational and I knew it. Even still, I couldn't help my petty behaviour, trying to catch her in a lie.

"Who is he?" I asked her once. Wish I hadn't. Dead or made up, it's not like I really wanted to know.

She turned to face me, crossed her arms over her chest, and corrected me. "Who *was* he. He died."

But he was very much alive in her head. He was in all our silent moments, the ones I tried to fill but couldn't because one-sided conversations were exhausting. And each time I'd stop talking, he'd be there, between us. He was the unmentioned ghost in the room, my competition. I was never going to win. One time she told me that if she'd known her previous relationship would have caused so much drama, she never would have told me. This infuriated me.

"So you would've lied to me?" I snapped at her, to which she exhaustedly replied, "You're twisting my words, Cyrus. Stop." When I'm being honest with myself, which happens after I've behaved like an asshole, I can admit I'm jealous of how much Grace loved *her* Marc, just like I was of Rachel's dead husband. My jealousy was what drove her away—well, mostly.

A quarter of the way through my whisky, a taxi pulls up in front of the condo. I hold my breath, expecting Grace and Kay, but it's a false alarm. Then another vehicle pulls in behind it, a dark sedan, and from its passenger side, Jordan climbs out. I rise off the bench and wave, catching his attention. What's this kid up to? I'm not happy to see him again, but better him than Grace. No amount of whisky can prepare me for a chat with her. Besides, before any conversation takes place between us, I need to decide what I want. If I want to stay with her, I'll have to keep living a lie. If I tell her the whole truth, she'll want to kill me all over again.

CHAPTER 14 - GRACE

We drive a long way. I didn't think it was possible to outtalk Kay, but Randy does it. When a news report comes on about the missing palliative care patients, he talks right over it, excitedly giving his spin on the situation. Randy's second cousin, Angie somebody, works for the medical examiner and says bodies are turning up dead from copper poisoning. But someone else from Randy's family tree is a priest (or was a priest, I can't keep up), and he says they're ritual killings. This inevitably leads to Randy's opinion on the state of the world these days, young people, immigration, and his political views. Kay nods politely, adding her two cents here and there. It's funny to see her in the position of listener. As Randy rambles about his twelve-year-old cat with liver problems, Lexi, he turns in to a plaza and I give Kay a look of relief. She's not as discreet, placing two fingers to her temple and pulling the imaginary gun's trigger, then going cross-eyed. I stifle a laugh.

"You two sweethearts take care. Work things out. Life's too short. Besides, alligators are dangerous, even baby ones," Randy says as we shut the door behind us.

I give Kay a questioning look as we make our way toward Laughlin's Only Storage, a giant building with bright-orange garage doors.

"I told him my girlfriend was leaving me and I had to stop her from running into the arms of her horrible ex-lover," she says. That explains the wet kiss she left on my cheek. But...

"Does he think my ex-lover is a baby alligator?" I ask, raising an eyebrow, dying to hear this explanation.

"He thinks your ex-lover has a baby alligator who roams freely in the home," she says, dissolving into laughter. "And I told him that although you got along with Abigail, I feared she'd eat you alive if you showed up unannounced at breakfast time."

"Is Abigail the alligator or the ex-lover?" I ask, barely able to get it out without laughing. "And why such an elaborate lie?"

"I got a little carried away trying to convince Randy to help me stalk you with his taxicab. How else was I supposed to explain that my situation was so urgent, I couldn't spare two seconds to get out of my pyjamas and slippers? The story just kind of got away from me, know what I mean?"

"Slippers?" I look down at Kay's feet for the first time and then completely lose my composure, bending over, hands holding myself up on my knees, howling. She's wearing giant, pink bunny slippers. I don't know how I hadn't noticed in the elevator.

"C'mon, sexy lover-girl!" she cackles and smacks my ass, which just makes me laugh harder.

I grab at my belly, my sides splitting. "And pyjamas. Are you even wearing a bra?"

"Is it that obvious?" She cups her hands over her breasts.

"Very. Here, take this." I shake my jacket off and offer it to her, just like the old days.

"Thought you'd never offer." She winks at me.

When we were kids, Charlie used to ensure I left the house over-prepared, unlike Kay, so I always had an extra layer for her. I used to think she did it on purpose, hoping her parents would notice her. Her miniskirts got shorter and shorter and she'd bare-leg it in the middle of a snowstorm. Of course it never worked—her parents noticing her, that is.

Still chuckling and making jokes about Kay's bunny slippers, which we've nicknamed *Abigail* and are now filthy from walking the streets, we search the storage area for the orange unit matching the number on Jordan's key.

"Why wouldn't Jordan store his stuff in his empty condo?" I ponder out loud when we find the right unit.

"Isn't this exciting? I wonder what we'll find. I bet he's an art collector," Kay exclaims. "Or an art *thief!* Like a mastermind from the underground art world."

"Really, Kay?" I smile at her.

"Totally kidding," she says. But I can tell she's only partly kidding by her eyes, wide like a kid on a real-life treasure hunt. It's funny how she went from thinking this was a total waste of time to this.

I unlock Jordan's locker and lift open the heavy metal door. A sensor turns on overhead fluorescent lighting, bringing the room to life, and our good mood comes to an abrupt halt.

In awe, we wander to the centre of the room where a single wooden chair sits, facing a wall. Like in any normal storage unit, Jordan's storing contents of his home. In one corner, furniture wrapped in wasteful cellophane has been organized like 3D puzzle pieces to fit perfectly on a wooden skid. A pile of boxes lines the wall to our left, with large labels indicating the rooms they belong to. Is he planning on moving? But what really captures our attention are the newspaper articles displayed like artwork on the wall facing the wooden chair. This explains what must've been decorating Jordan's pockmarked but otherwise bare condo walls.

"Oh my gosh!" Kay expresses my thoughts. I'm speechless. "What is this stuff?" She moves around the room from wall to wall, examining the pinned-up newspaper clippings, the whiteboards with shorthand scribble, photos of people and places.

I know exactly what this is. I saw some of these newspaper clippings at the Internet café. What I don't know is why? Why is Jordan obsessed with Leo?

CHAPTER 15 - MARC

Jordan crosses the street and my prayers go unanswered. He doesn't get hit by a car. He's got a big smile on his face, weirdly happy to see me. "You're just the man I want to talk to. Let's take a walk," he says.

"A walk?" I raise an eyebrow.

"Hey, I know we didn't get off on the right foot. But I do want to help you."

If I weren't curious about what he's up to (and about getting home—if that's what I want), I'd tell him to fuck off. I don't like being told what to do.

He doesn't say where we're going and we walk in silence for a while. It's warmer out than the other day and the sidewalks are busy with clusters of tourists. Each time one approaches from the opposite direction, we're the ones who walk in single file to let them by, Jordan letting me go ahead.

Every once in a while, he pulls out a phone and click-clacks on a tiny keyboard. "Sorry. Work," he says.

"So, kid. Show me yours and I'll show you mine?" I joke to get things going.

He smirks but doesn't bite. Instead, he makes small talk. Asks me if we need anything at the condo, tells me Oscar says we're nice people. "I didn't realize Kay and Charlie were here, too. Hey, does my family know you're thinking about leaving them?" He phrases the question like he's genuinely curious.

I hold my breath, feeling exposed.

"Do they?" he insists.

"Maybe. Can we just get on with this?" I ask, getting annoyed. Whatever he has to say could've been said on the bench at the parkette. "Look, kid. I can go first but I have no idea what you want from me," I offer with my palms out, showing him they're empty. "Is this about your storage unit?"

"My storage unit?" he asks, and I immediately regret my question. By the shock in his tone, I don't think he meant for us to have that key.

"There was an extra key on the keychain." I shrug like it's no big deal.

He takes a minute to contemplate and then gives his head a little shake like he's mentally tucking my comment away in his back pocket for later. Then he asks, "What did you do for a living?"

It's a strange question, but I don't see the harm. "You don't know what your dad did for a living? Agriculture or something like that. A regular dude with a green thumb." I put up both my thumbs and offer a giant toothy smile.

Jordan shakes his head. "I don't mean the original Marc—I mean *you*. What did *you* do for a living?"

I don't answer for a long time and now when groups of tourists approach, Jordan doesn't move for them; they have to move for us. He watches me expectantly.

I loathe answering questions about my own life. It's like being reminded of a dull toothache: pure agony. Each time the topic comes up, I hunger for my old life—not a craving, but a feeling of emptiness that I'll never be able to fill. And I don't want to satisfy these people's curiosities. I like being a mystery to them. My life is the one thing that I can hold on to and no one can take from me, if I just don't tell them. It's the only thing I have left of me that belongs only to me.

"Why do you need to know?" I ask, trying to keep the mood light with an upbeat tone, but he sees through it and shakes his head at me. He is both annoyed and amused.

"You get weird-ass uncomfortable talking about yourself. How am I supposed to trust you?"

My eyes go back to my feet. We're at a crosswalk now and the light is green, but neither of us starts to cross. I move to the side, lean on a nearby phone booth covered in flyers. I take a closer look and laugh out loud when I realize they're of naked women. There's one with the red shoes. She reminds me of Jordan's hot lawyer, Morgan; makes me feel that tug in my gut. Jordan laughs, too, at my reaction. The naked ladies have broken a spell.

"Everything is foreign here," I say, avoiding his gaze.

"You barely got used to Toronto—Vegas must be a shock," he offers and then waits patiently for me to get back to his question. He doesn't take his eyes off me.

"OK, kid. I get that you're asking me random questions to de-cide if I'm trustworthy. What if I told you something about your mom instead?" He opens his mouth to argue but I hold up a hand to stop him, then I babble out the one-minute mistake. "Did you know she had an abortion? The day her dad died. Apparently, abortions only take a minute. Then she stopped in on her dad for tea—a fucking tea—like she'd been out running errands. But she was a minute too late and arrived to find her dad at the end of a swinging rope, his feet still kicking at air. Your mom made it sound like she and Marc were perfect until her dad died, and I'd bet Marc thought so, but she lied. He wanted more children; she didn't. Her dad's suicide was just the breaking point. In any case, she only ever told Charlie." I feel my blood pressure rise with an-ger, as if it were me Grace hid her pregnancy and abortion from. "Charlie told me, and now I've told you."

Jordan's eyebrows are fixed halfway up his forehead. "Wow! I don't know what to say."

I smile, satisfied to have shocked him speechless, hoping my tactic of avoiding the subject of myself has worked. I lift off the phone booth. "Walk and talk?"

He follows obediently and we walk quietly for a bit, then he takes the lead, bringing us through an empty green space toward a warehouse—probably an abandoned one, judging by the vacant lot.

"I don't know where to begin," he says.

"At the beginning?"

He inhales deeply and kicks off his story by asking me if I know what the Halation is. I answer that of course I do.

"The protective barrier encompassing the earth like sunglasses?"

"I said, yes, kid. I know what the Halation is."

"Great." And without missing a beat, as if he'll lose his nerve if he does, he unveils his motive for never leaving Vegas. "When Leo died, I wanted to know who he was. At first, it was curiosity about my dad's past life—your past life, I guess—and to fill my time." His eyes shift to his feet and stay there when he admits wanting to know more about his dad. He walks quicker so he's just ahead of me. "Besides, Leo's family was wealthy, so his death was all over the news. It was hard to miss," he adds with a shrug. "What got me was how the journalists focused on his company. Some called him a dreamer, but others suggested he was doing something groundbreaking for the environment. It got me wondering: what if those killed in the past were important to history?" He stops walking and turns to face me. "I wanted to know how Leo's absence would affect the future. That's when I looked into his company and his research and it didn't take long to put the pieces together." He pauses and watches me.

"Why are you drawing this out?" I'm holding my breath, wanting to shake the rest of the words out of him and at the same time shove them back into his mouth. Panic is rising inside of me because I already know the answer without having to hear it. His question about the Halation, coupled with his quick explanation about Leo's company, is enough. It's like he's dropped a bomb that hasn't yet landed—I see it coming, and there's nothing that can be done to stop it.

"Leo was accredited with discovering how to slow down the progression of Planet Earth's collapse, though history knew him as Leonardo Abruzzo. He started the company from the ground up and funded all the research. Leo invented the Halation."

There it is—the exploding bomb. "Kid, are you fucking with me?"

"Wish I was. Killing Dr. Messie might fix the Metagenesis problem—emphasis on *might*—but when my mom killed Leo, she created a much bigger problem. Without Leo's intervention in the year 2034, the southern hemisphere will continue warming up until it's an uninhabitable inferno and the northern hemisphere will turn to ice. He left a ton of research behind, but none of it relates to the Halation, at least not directly, like he was nowhere near the discovery when my mom killed him."

"The Halation wasn't a *permanent* solution," I point out, even though I know it's a dumb rebuttal. It may not have halted the inevitable end, but it was slowing the process down by hundreds of years.

"Close enough, don't you think?" Jordan says, tilting his head at my idiotic comment. And then the kid closes with: "Now that Leo's dead, the world is going to end sooner—kaboom!" He uses an amused tone, as if explaining the punch line to a cheesy joke, but I can tell he's nervous.

"OK, but I came from another time, a hundred years ahead, and everything was fine," I say, desperate to invalidate his reasoning by pointing out a flaw, because if he's right, then we're all doomed even if Metagenesis is stopped.

"You left at the exact moment my mom killed Leo. Your future still had the Halation in its history. Let me ask you this..." He holds up a finger, confident that the next thing he says will drive the point home. "How was the weather when you left Toronto to come here?"

"The weather was off," I admit in a hoarse whisper. The weather was causing flight delays and cancellations; soundless storms, red lightning, tornados, heat waves, followed by snow and baseball-sized hail. I don't have to elaborate for Jordan; he can read it all over my face.

When I don't say anything more, he tips his head to force me to look at him. "If it clarifies anything for you at all, Marc, everything was fine throughout my entire childhood with the climate, and we had the Halation to thank."

"Holy shit," I say, anxiety rising from my gut. I remind myself to breathe and I also remember the bottle of whisky in my hand. I twist off the cap and take a few burning swigs.

"If you ask my mom, she'll know what the Halation is because she was here when Leo died—she killed him. But Kay wasn't here. Kay left Vegas when she got into that big fight with my mom. So if you ask her, or if you ask Charlie, they won't know what the Halation is because they were in the future when Leo was removed. Kay and Charlie will remember the weather as always being chaotic, and the name Leonardo Abruzzo will mean nothing to them."

I think back to the boarding lounge on the day we left Toronto. A handful of passengers had expressed outrage at taking off in the weather and demanded refunds. However, most complained about another lengthy delay and wanted to travel regardless. I remember thinking Charlie and Kay were rebels joining the group who wanted to fly. "It's just a little rain," Kay had said while Grace and I stared out the window at hail the size of my fist, pummelling down on the runway.

Jordan waves a hand in front of my face, bringing me back to the present. "Earth to Marc? Are you there?"

"Holy shit," I repeat. Meaningful words elude me.

"Hence the reason I want to know what you did for a living. It has nothing to do with me trusting you. Before you go home, I want your help—need your help, to give me info on the Halation. If you can't, Earth is going to die."

"How in the blue hell can I help with *that*?" I ask, shaking my head, dumbfounded.

"I'm an aerospace engineer and my lab partner's specialties also lie elsewhere. We're having a hell of a time getting things going."

I stare at him, my mouth agape.

"I'm a rocket scientist," he clarifies, misreading my expression—I know what an aerospace engineer is.

"And you want me to do what?" I ask. "You said you could get us home, which means there is still a way to life-travel. Why not travel back and stop Grace from killing Leo?"

Jordan purses his lips, annoyed. "Don't you think we already thought of that? Something shifted the day Leo died, like history restarted from that point on and can no longer be interrupted. After he died, it became impossible to travel back before the date of his death. I bet you all arrived at the wrong time, didn't you?"

I curse under my breath. He's bang on. Adalia sent us with currency from the late 1990s. What if she was trying to send us back to undo Grace's mistake? I make a mental note to visit Adalia myself—alone. Sparking her memories in the presence of others may not bode well for me.

"What I'm hoping is, somehow you remember things about your past self, Leo, or that you worked or studied in a field that could be helpful. My dad specialized in agriculture research. Leo was an environmental engineer. Do you also have a green thumb?" His lips lift into a hopeful smile and he holds up his thumbs, mimicking me earlier.

I begrudgingly divulge another snippet of myself. "I'm an urban designer."

The kid's smile disappears.

"I make cities," I say, but I know his sudden mood swing isn't because he doesn't understand what an urban designer is. "I specialize in sustainability, and that's pretty much the extent of my green thumb." I'm oversimplifying, but I'm basically saying that I'm useless to his cause. I toss in a stupid joke that I sometimes grow my own pot, hoping to get a laugh, but he grimaces. Then I add, "Sorry, kid. Looks like we're all fucked."

"I was afraid you'd say that." His eyes move behind me, and he nods. "Go ahead, take him."

Before I can figure out that he isn't talking to me, I'm blinded by a cloth bag thrown over my head. Hands grab me, and something is shoved under the bag inside my mouth, muffling my shock.

CHAPTER 16 - GRACE

"**W**hat the hell is up with Jordan's Leo obsession?" I vocalize my thought, clearing the frog in my throat.

Kay spins around and gives me a screwface. "Leo?"

"The newspapers—they're about Leo."

She squints at one of the walls and moves right up to one of them. "What do you have, micro-superhuman eyesight? How can you possibly see what's on these? Even a buzzard would go cross-eyed."

"That one, there." I point at the article that initially stood out to me, and I shyly confess. "I've seen it before. On the Internet. I searched Leo's name at the café."

Her chest rises and falls with a melodramatic sigh. "I figured as much."

I put my hands up in surrender. "I know, I know. I'm a sucker for punishment. You don't have to tell me."

She walks over to the article I'm referring to, the one with the front page of the paper picturing the Grand Canyon with the headline "*MAN FALLS TO HIS DEATH.*" The subheading named Leo as the CEO of a groundbreaking environmental company. I approach as well and examine a few of the others on the same wall.

"*COMPANY PLUNGES WITH THE FALL OF A GREAT LEADER*"

"*CONSPIRACY RUMOURS SCARE INVESTORS AWAY*"

"ENVIRONMENT CURE GOES BELLY-UP—CHAPTER 11"

"This is weird," Kay says.

"Very. Seems Jordan was obsessed with Leo's life and death, but mostly with his company. Environment cure?"

"No, no, I mean *this. This* is weird." She points to the same article, the original one about Leo's death.

Nerves stir in my belly. In my nightmares, I relive the moment in the picture all the time.

"Isn't this Leo's car? It's a sweet ride but…"

I glance at the car. "What about it?"

"I thought you said you drove Leo's car to catch the shuttle in the desert? What's it doing in this picture? How'd it get back to the canyon?"

I squint and home in on her index finger, pointing at Leo's car. *It can't be.*

"I guess I drove a different car, maybe?" I tell her, even though I know I didn't.

"Uh, Grace?" Kay's eyes are wide as teacups, unblinking.

I assume she's looking at the obituary, which lists Leo's wife, Rachel, but Kay hasn't moved from the picture of the car at the canyon. Her face is pressed almost right up to the paper.

"Grace? *Graaaace*!" she's shouting.

The louder my name gets, the faster my heart drums.

"What? What is it?"

She can't seem to say it, just keeps shouting my name and jabbing her finger on the picture like a woodpecker. I try to look but her damn finger is in the way.

"What the hell is it, Kay?" I snatch her hand away so I can see, and when I do, my heart stands still.

It's Dr. Messie. Was it him who drove Leo's car back to the village?

"Kay, as shocking as this picture is, we already knew he was here."

Kay looks back at the picture, her expression pensive like she's trying to solve a riddle. Then she shakes her head as if she's giving up and backs away, starts pacing the room behind me, leaving me to stare at the wall alone. The man in the picture appears older than the Dr. Messie from our time, and truthfully, he could pass as any other fat old man. But it's his white outfit that gives him away—that belt, those shoes. It didn't take us long to identify him, which means Jordan must've as well.

"Jordan knew we were looking for Dr. Messie and yet he kept these details from us. Why?" I wonder aloud.

"Because he's probably working with Dr. Messie," Kay replies.

I whip around and glare at her. She's standing still now, wearing a long face, holding a black backpack.

"Jordan would never collaborate with that monster! He was trying to stop Dr. Messie. That's why he came to Vegas, remember? What would make you say something like that?"

"This," she replies and holds up the bag for me to see. It has a logo on it from Recycled Souls. The logo is an ouroboros, a snake eating its own tail, symbolizing reincarnation, immortality, eternity. Dr. Messie's laboratories and clinic bear this same logo.

I chuckle, appalled that my best friend would even suggest what she just has, and relieved that she's wrong. "Kay, we all have a backpack from Recycled Souls. They're a dime a dozen. Adalia even gave us one the first time we came here, remember? So if that's what you're basing your opinion on…"

"I'm basing my opinion on what's inside." She reaches into the bag and pulls something out, then hands it to me.

I take it. It's a note written on Jordan's company letterhead, Valle Tinto.

I saw you in the paper, so I know you're here. I'm easy to find yet you haven't tried to kill me for betraying you. I'm hoping that means you need me, because I need you, too. I want to call a truce. Can we meet? If you prefer a public location, there's a bench in front of the fountain at the Canadiana Hotel. I'll be there every Saturday at noon until you show. – JD

"Flip it over," Kay says.

I agree to a truce. But I'd like to speak over the phone first. 702-716-2292 – CM

"Claudio Messie," Kay says, like I don't know who the fuck CM is.

CHAPTER 17 - MARC

Blindfolded and gagged, I don't understand the need for the burlap sack loosely thrown over my head: I can't see through a blindfold. Jordan puts me in a car and tells someone he'll meet us there.

"Sorry, Marc," he says with no emotion, and then buckles me in as if concerned for my safety in the event of an accident.

Thirty minutes later, I'm doing everything I can not to retch. It's not the whisky I guzzled earlier that's making me nauseated, though I'm sure it's not helping. It's the gag. Held in by the same duct tape binding my hands behind my back, it tastes like an old dishrag. I cough hard, draw in air from my nose and cough it out rather than sucking the odour into my lungs. The task is futile, bringing me dangerously close to hyperventilating. *Stop it! Breathe slow! It's just a cloth—Focus!* I force my body to go slack, loosen my shoulders, and slouch. I need to relax.

My eyes water under the mask as I try to concentrate on the one thing that's not tied back, gagged, or blinded: my ears. No one has stuffed cotton in them and they work perfectly fine. Every so often, the people in the front talk to each other, and if I could quiet down enough, I might be able to hear something valuable.

The chatter starts up again and I strain to listen, sitting perfectly still, trying to mute the sound of my breathing and heartbeat. Then a hand reaches underneath the sac, startling me. I didn't realize there was someone beside me. Duct tape is ripped off my mouth in one movement and I urgently push with my tongue, trying to rid the cloth from my mouth, then a hand yanks it out for me. Relieved to be free of the dirty rag, I break out in a coughing fit. My lips swell, pulse, and burn where the tape was and my face feels like it's just gotten a wax job.

"See? He didn't pass out," says a woman to my right. She sounds tough but petite. "He's fine," she informs someone, as a matter of fact. "Marc, if you make a peep, that sock is going right back in your trap," she says and the thought of someone's filthy sock in my mouth has me raking my tongue over my teeth and spitting into the sac.

I'm not going to make a peep, anyway. I'm far too interested in what they have to say—what Jordan wants or plans to do with me. I'm all ears. But now everyone is quiet and it's just the radio keeping me company. It plays a catchy tune about "hips don't lie." The radio woman's voice is both yodel-like annoying and oddly pleasing.

On the plus side of being kidnapped and thrown into the backseat for a bumpy ride, the hand that ripped the tape off my lips managed to loosen the blindfold. It slips off with each bounce of the vehicle and we've been bucking wildly for a good fifteen minutes like we're off road. Where the hell is this kid taking me, and why?

Our butts bob and smack off the seats in silent darkness for at least an hour, and as a result, the blindfold falls right off my face, rests on the bridge of my nose, acting as an odour filter. But I can still smell the sock, the bag, and now that new car scent, all of which is making me uncomfortably hot. I'm having difficulty breathing and need fresh air badly. I'm about to speak up—or beg—when the vehicle slows and makes a sharp left turn and then finally comes to a stop. The driver kills the engine.

The driver's door opens, he gets out and the car door slams shut. The woman beside me doesn't move. Although the passengers have been silent, the terrain was anything but. And now that the car is parked with the motor and music off, I can hear the woman's presence beside me, her breathing in high definition.

"Where are we?" I ask.

The woman sighs but doesn't reply.

"Let me speak to Jordan."

She shuffles away from me and opens her door like she's leaving, too.

"Please, wait!" I shrink at my pleading, disgusted with myself. "Let me out of the car for half a minute. I just need some air. How's a guy supposed to breathe underneath this bag? And I gotta take a piss!"

She closes her door and then reaches across my lap. I flinch—and hate myself for it—when she brushes against me. I hear the window lowering beside my head and realize she's cranking it open and thankfully not shoving the sock back into my mouth. A cold breeze seeps through the bag and I suck it in with great relief.

She also rolls down her window, creating a cross breeze before she opens her car door again. "There. Now hush," she utters before telling me someone will let me out to pee soon, like I'm a pet poodle, and then leaves.

Good. Get out, bitch. Now that I'm alone, I can think. And listen. My captors can't be more than a hundred feet away, the open windows giving me both fresh air and a backstage pass to a performance I haven't paid for. It's like I'm sneakily hiding behind the curtains. I may not be able to see the actors, but I can hear them. And if I close my eyes, I can imagine them acting out the scene that their dialogues paint in my mind.

"This was a bad idea." Male voice; my driver. I picture him to be tall and dumb.

"Shut up and hurry up," female voice, not the one who was sitting with me. There's something familiar about her voice. "You! Pick up another shovel and help with the digging." Did she say "digging"?

"This should've been done by now," says petite tough woman, the one who was sitting beside me.

As if on cue, I hear the distinct sound of a shovel hitting earth and then earth hitting more earth, like it's being heaved over a shoulder into a pile. For what? I gulp.

"This better be the last man we have to bury," she says.

They're going to bury me?

CHAPTER 18 - GRACE

Other than the storage facility, the plaza is home to a Department of Motor Vehicles, a 7-Eleven, and an employment centre. Kay and I are in front of the 7-Eleven, where we told the taxi dispatch we'd wait. We've been silent since we left Jordan's locker, after taking our time sifting through it. We didn't find anything else linking him to Dr. Messie, which led me to suggest Jordan may have been luring Dr. Messie to finish him off, and not inviting him to collaborate.

"Maybe that's why Jordan doesn't care if we find Dr. Messie or not. Because he knows he's already dead," I surmised.

Kay agreed that it was a plausible explanation, but she did it carefully, like she wasn't convinced. I don't know if I believe my theory, either. But at least we've dropped the subject.

Now, Kay seems to be trying to tell me something with just her eyes, staring at me as if I might combust.

"What?" I finally ask her.

"Nothing."

A minute goes by and she's still staring. "Do I have something on my face?"

Her worried expression morphs into the smirk of a master trickster. "Let the record show that I kept my promise about not bringing up Marc. Technically, you did."

"Huh?"

"To answer your question: yes, Grace. You have something on your face. It's red and scuffed. And since I'm still keeping my promise, I'll just mention that I saw your wrist when you reached across in the taxi to show Randy the key. So, did the person I'm not supposed to talk about, Marc, do that to you? I mean, since you brought it up and all."

I bristle and fold my arms over my chest. "It's not what you think," I say, then lean against a newspaper stand. "He hurt me, but not physically. Can we please leave it at that?"

Kay also folds her arms across her chest. "Nope. Spill it, Grace."

In my head, I pray for the taxi to show up to rescue me while I tell Kay as little as possible about the angry sex session I wholly regret. I mumble, "Yes, it was consensual," and I blush when I explain that the scratches on my face are from the wall. Then I jump to the end, where Marc told me his name was Cyrus. I use a casual tone, not wanting to let on how badly I'd like a redo of last night so I could knee him in the groin when he asked if he could have me. "That's it. That's all I want to say about it."

"Did you two have a conversation at all? Or did you just beat cheeks?"

"*Beat cheeks*, Kay?"

"Sorry, too blunt. Did you talk? You two need to talk."

When I repeat that I don't want to get into it, Kay examines me like a therapist would a patient, and then, seemingly satisfied, she suggests grabbing lunch, rubbing her tummy for effect. "I'm starving," she says, dragging out the 'r' in starving.

I'm beyond grateful she's letting the topic of Marc go and I give her a "thank-you" smile.

I'm also hungry. I'm going on twenty-four hours without food, but I suggest returning to the condo to share what we've discovered with Charlie and Marc. "Jordan's weird Leo obsession and his note to Dr. Messie...?" I add when she makes a pouty face.

"I'll order the quickest item on the menu. Promise. And I always keep my promises." She winks.

"You want to eat at a restaurant?" I eye her slippers.

"I'm a trendsetter, Grace." She smiles and does a little walk and twirl, thrusting her hips left and right on an imaginary catwalk.

"They do look hot on you. No wonder Randy liked you."

"Jealous?" She bats her eyelashes and we both laugh.

I tell her I bet he wanted to beat her cheeks. I enjoy the shock on her face and the laughter that follows.

"Ew! I bet he's one of those weirdos who talks about his cat while he's doing you," she says. "Lexi loves belly rubs… grunt grunt," she adds in a gruff man-voice and gyrates below the waist.

Getting in the taxi to the condo, we stop the dirty best-friend talk. Kay strikes up a conversation with the driver, making another new friend. She asks him for restaurant recommendations, asking him to describe the main dish of each one, slowly. She grips her belly each time he does, which encourages more elaborate descriptions. She oohs and aahs and asks specific questions about the sauces, her mouth in an O shape. I'm becoming uncomfortable, like I'm in a car with a couple groping each other. When we arrive at the condo, not to my surprise, the driver offers to wait for us so he can drop us off at his favourite restaurant. Even though Kay tells him we might be a while, she wants to shower, he's happy to wait.

"Anything for you, Kay."

"You're too kind," she replies with a hand on her heart.

I chuckle. How does she make everyone like her so quickly?

Once inside, I find a note addressed to me, posted on the fridge, at the same time Kay spots the throwaway cell phone she'd told me about, with a notepad sitting next to it.

"This must be Charlie's number," she says excitedly and calls him right away.

I stare emotionless at my note while listening to her one-sided conversation.

"Charlie, you'll never believe what we found at the storage—" She stops abruptly and then her excitement level hits a new high. "Wait, what?… You did?… How?… Oh my gosh!… That's fantastic! We're on our way!"

CHAPTER 19 - MARC

I'm queasy from the car ride and the taste of dishrag in my mouth, but the thought of being buried off road is motivation enough to figure my way the fuck out of here. I tuck my head between my thighs and clamp my knees on the burlap bag. Blood rushes to my head and I shake off the nerves. I strategically pull away from the bag bit by bit, rising slowly so as not to mess it up. When I'm sitting up again, I chance a look out the window. It seems like we're in a giant cave. I count five figures illuminated by car headlights: our car's and another's parked to my right. I can't tell if any of them are Jordan, but two people are inside a hole, digging. And yes, the hole is big enough for a body. No one is paying attention to me, but even if they were, they wouldn't be able to see me because I'm not the one lit up by the spotlight. It's a golden opportunity.

I shimmy to the other side of the car—there's more room behind the passenger seat—and stretch out, trying to weave my arms under my butt so I can get them in front of me. But it's still too cramped back here and I'm far too big. Sitting up, I survey the inside of the car for anything I can use. There's nothing in the backseat. I peek through the middle console to check the front seats, but then freeze when footsteps approach. *Shit!*

"This isn't what I signed up for," a man says.

I panic and duck back into my spot, looking for the stupid bag—not that I could get it back over my head if I found it. Then a car door opens, but it's not this car, it's the one beside me. I sit perfectly still, not making a sound or moving an inch, silently begging for them to leave.

"Me neither, but you have got to get a grip. It's too late to grow a conscience," petite tough woman quietly scolds him like she doesn't want their group to overhear this side talk.

"We could turn ourselves in. Make a deal, witness protection, or whatever. Like in the movies. We could go to Hawaii," he tells her.

"They're not going to send us away on an all-expense-paid permanent vacation. People are dead, Saeed."

"I know, I know."

There's a long pause in the conversation and I worry they've noticed me, but then Saeed asks in a low voice, "What about Grace?"

Hearing my wife's name sends a chill up my spine. If they hurt her… I blink and give my head a little shake, shocked at my instinctual reaction to protect her, given how mixed up I feel about her.

"What about Grace?" petite tough woman asks.

"Isn't she gonna wonder where Marc is? What if they come looking? Maybe we should, you know, take care of her?"

"*Take care* of Jordan's mother? Do you have a death wish? Listen, Marc and Grace are on the outs, anyway. He was gonna leave her, and now it'll look like he finally did."

"How many more bodies are we gonna have to bury?" he asks.

"Marc is the last experiment." A long silence follows and I hold my breath, hoping they're not coming to check on me or let me out to pee.

"Gimme the gun," she says.

Holy shit, holy shit.

A gun cocks and re-cocks before she speaks again. "Let's get back before Jordan loses his temper on Tweedle-Dee and Tweedle-Dum. You know how he is."

Footsteps lead away from the vehicle and when I'm confident they're far enough, I throw myself to the other side of the car.

With my hands behind my back, I lean up against the car door, fumble around until I find the handle and pull. It clicks open and I cringe when the interior lights flick on. I've got to move fast. I let the gap widen and slink out of the car, closing the door softly to kill the light. Once outside, I lie on my back and writhe around in the dirt to get my hands under my ass, under my legs, and out in front of me. I've never been flexible, but it seems the real Marc was, thank God. I use my teeth like little knives and chew through the silver tape around my wrists. Bits of it get caught in and on my teeth. I spit them out and keep gnawing until the tape is split enough to pull apart, and I cuss when it rips my arm hairs out.

Looking around, reality sets in. In front of me is a cave. Behind me is the exit, showing that we're in the middle of a barren desert. If I run, I've got no place to hide. No bush, no tree, not one rock or a single cactus in sight. With nothing for miles but these two cars and a group of people digging my grave, I'll be spotted in no time. And then another thought comes to me: it doesn't seem smart, leaving me unattended in the car.

My heart races with excitement as it hits me that there might be keys in one of these cars, and I silently thank Charlie for teaching me how to drive in Toronto—one of his first bonding attempts. I don't risk turning on the interior lights by opening the doors again. Instead, with a deep breath, I rise to a crouch and listen closely. When I'm sure no one is paying any attention or coming my way, I stick my arm through the open window, awkwardly feeling around the underside of the steering wheel for keys, careful not to touch the horn or signals. My heart leaps when my hand bumps into them, dangling from the ignition. *Bingo!*

I retreat and slouch down the side of the car, working up the nerve to get back in, start the engine, and get out of here. I suck in a chest full of cool air, ball my hands tight, then shake them out to get rid of my nervous energy. I count to three. Unbending at the knees, I hunch over and rise. But when I reach for the door handle, I chicken out, remembering the interior lights. Instead, I pout and crawl through the open window; my belly barely makes the cut. I've put on a few pounds since becoming Marc: old Marc, the sporty thrill-seeker, was fit and never ate meat.

Once inside, I peek at the group still digging in the spotlight. No one has even glanced in my direction. Relieved and proud of my stealthy manoeuvring, I climb over the middle console and squeeze my way into the driver's seat.

My elbow makes contact with the horn. *Shit!*

I should be moving at the speed of a majestic, fluid cheetah to get the car started now that the group is running toward me. Instead, I'm frozen in fear one second and the next, I'm fumbling the keys as if instead of fingers, I have camel hooves. At long last, my hooves find the key and turn it in the ignition. The music comes on, but not the car. Confused, I stare at the lights on the dashboard, and then I turn the key back and over again and repeat.

Still nothing—again.

What the fuck? My heart thrusts through my ribcage, my chest on fire.

"C'mon!" I yell.

I glance between the kidnappers running toward me and the dashboard with little icons all lit up, and I slam my fists on the steering wheel, smashing the horn angrily. How can this be? No revving, no choking, nothing! My captors are fast approaching and I realize I can't keep trying to start this stupid shit car and am going to have to make a run for it.

I fling the door open, the interior lights blare, and I stumble out of the vehicle. My captors are a couple of hundred feet away from me at best. I should run like my life depends on it, since it probably does, but I decide to try my luck in the other car. I yank the door open and pray to find the keys in the ignition, leaving the door ajar for the light. I spot the keys right where I want them to be and turn.

My heart sinks into my gut.

"No! No! No!" I cry out.

Why won't these cars start? I abandon the vehicle and break out in a sprint, glancing over my shoulder just in time to see someone leaping through the air and tackling me to the ground.

The wind knocked out of me, I struggle to twist around and fight.

"Tie him back up!" Jordan yells to whoever is trying to secure my arms. "Marc, it'll be much easier if you stop fighting," he promises.

My face is pressed into the dirt. I spit out rock and sand. There is an eight-hundred-pound man sitting on my back with octopus-like limbs controlling my arms and movements.

I reluctantly stop struggling—if not for anything, I need oxygen.

The man gets off me and lifts me off the ground by my arms without any effort, like I'm a stuffed teddy bear.

When I'm standing, a woman walks up to me and my jaw hits the ground.

"Morgan Bell?" I blurt out, bewildered.

Jordan hands his hot so-called *lawyer* something and she stabs me in the abdomen with it. I don't have a second to react to the sting because my muscles instantly turn to mush and my neck gives out. If it weren't for the ogre's giant hands under my pits, I'd be a heap of slop at their feet. My lids, they're so heavy, too heavy, but they stay open long enough to see Jordan shrug.

The last thing to go is my hearing. I catch Jordan saying, "Sorry, Marc." My name hits my ears like it's travelled a thousand years through a dark abyss, and then I hear Jordan giving someone an order: "Hurry up and bury the body."

CHAPTER 20 - GRACE

Kay and I are meeting Charlie at one of the bars at Caesars Palace, our old hotel. When we arrive, he greets us both with a kiss on the cheek, lingering longer on Kay's, same as her hand does on his bicep when she gives it a wee squeeze.

"Sorry we're late. I had to get out of my bunny slippers," Kay says as we all take our seats. She omits the part about the long shower, blow-drying her hair, and stopping at the taxi driver's favourite restaurant for a spicy burrito. At least she filled me in on what Charlie said on the phone. It seems Adalia has had other visitors, and Charlie managed to sneak a peek at the guestbook.

"Anywho, ask me why we're also freaking out," Kay says to Charlie.

He glances between us, clearly noticing that only one of us is freaking out: her. The other one of us—me—is on the brink of a mental breakdown. "OK, what's up?"

Kay does all the talking while I throw shots back like I'm training for a drinking marathon. She recaps the storage room, the newspaper clippings, the note between Jordan and Dr. Messie... I tune out right about there, my brain not able to absorb two things at once, and if I have to choose between information and alcohol, alcohol wins.

Then the conversation stops and they stare at me. I think they're waiting for me to speak.

"Huh?" I ask.

"Marc. Where is he?" My brother throws pity glances my way while Kay answers for me. She tells him Marc and I fought, leaving out the sex part, and then tells him about the note.

"He left you? With a note? Oh, Gracie," Charlie says, and then apologizes like it's somehow his fault. "What did the note say?"

I reply by downing another mouthful of tequila and denying myself a chaser. Marc leaving me is exactly what I had coming to me. I don't deserve to be soothed.

After an awkward silence, Charlie takes the hint and steers the conversation away from the most mortifying experience of my life.

Turns out, the people on the nursing home's visitor log were no help. While Charlie waited for us, he looked them up and called them, spoke to each of them, and determined they were either Adalia's neighbours or her old friends. Charlie and Kay exchange dialogue back and forth: Yes, he asked if they'd ever heard of Dr. Messie, and did they know where to find Adalia's brother. All visitors answered the same thing: they didn't know she had a brother, dead or alive.

"What about the one you said had just left for a run when you called?" Kay asks.

"I called him back. Same thing."

"Gee, you had time to do all that while you waited for us?" Kay asks, flipping her blow-dried hair to the side.

"So what's the plan?" I slur. I'm tipsy, feeling bold. "Kay? You're the smart one. How do we find out if Messie is dead or alive?"

"Talk to Jordan again." She shrugs.

"Is that the best you got?"

"Shh. Grace, you're shouting," she says.

"No I'm not!" I am. I'm shouting. "Sorry."

Charlie pushes his water to me. "Drink this. Sober up. I might have an idea."

"An idea?"

"Shhhh!" they both say.

"I think your guys' shushings are far louder than my talkings."

"Let Charlie speak," Kay scolds.

My fingers zip my lips with a pretend zipper key.

The waitress returns carrying a giant nacho plate. I'm salivating. Unlike Kay, I didn't eat a burrito the size of a newborn on the taxi ride over here. Charlie also ordered a concoction of watermelon and liqueur topped with a maraschino cherry for Kay. She beams like a child when the waitress sets it down in front of her.

"Adalia said you two weren't the first to travel back, remember?" Charlie asks.

Great. We're back to Adalia. "Don't you think we've over-rung that bell?"

"What does that mean?" Kay asks. "I think you mean—"

"Oh, forget it!" Sure, when *she* misuses idioms, it's funny. But when I try one…

"As I was saying," Charlie says, raising his voice. Look who's shouting now. "I don't believe it was a coincidence that her family owned the funeral home. The first time you two came here, she orchestrated running into you there. I'll bet my stack of money she did the same with other life-travellers. It would make sense that the funeral home was a meeting place. We should pay a visit there to speak with… what was her name?"

We all exchange a blank look, trying to remember.

Charlie shakes his head. "Her name isn't important. You know who I mean, that employee." Then he looks at me. "Gracie, Kay's right. We need to confront Jordan about Dr. Messie, persuade him to tell us what he knows. We can't dismiss anything until we do. In person would be better."

"A road trip," Kay says, suppressing a smile.

CHAPTER 21 - MARC

Am I dying or am I dead? I don't feel anything, as if I'm floating. A whirring sound fades in and out: *whir whir whir.*

"Leo?" someone asks from up above. He has a thick, whispery voice, like an old man.

Something pricks the soft spot in the crook of my arm and icy fingers are holding my wrist where a pulse should be. My elbow is resting on a hard surface. No, I'm not floating, but I might be dead because beneath me is a steel table, I'm sure of it. I'm lying on a gurney at a morgue, aren't I? *Whir whir.*

"This isn't working," a familiar voice says.

"Patience, Jordan," says the old man. "He'll wake into Leo in a moment."

Jordan? I know him. And I also recognize the old man's voice and search my memory. Where have I met him?

A rubber tourniquet snaps off my arm.

Jordan speaks, "And if it doesn't work?"

"Then we discard him in the desert, bury him like the others," the old man replies.

"But he isn't like the others," Jordan protests.

My eyelids flutter. I don't want to be an "other" in the desert, buried alone. A voice in my head asks Rachel, "So when you die, who do you want to be buried next to?"

"Excuse me?" she replies.

"Just answer the question."

"I refuse to answer such a ridiculous question." And yet, she just has. Any way you slice it, I'll be buried alone.

Rachel's voice fades away and black turns to white. I let my lashes shade the light and search for the talking people.

"What am I sensing in you, Jordan—is that doubt?" the old man asks. His tone implies doubt isn't permitted.

Jordan clears his throat. "Course not. I just think he'd be more useful alive than as a dead specimen."

"Patience, Jordan," the old man repeats.

Through the tiniest slit in my lids, behind a curtain of dark lashes, my eyes find the kid. He's leaning on a white cloud like some kind of cartoon angel. But that kid is no angel, and if heaven is a real place, then so is hell, which is where people like me go after we run out of lives.

"Marc?" Jordan calls my name, lifting off the cloud and floating to my side. "Can you hear me?"

"Leo?" asks the old man.

My eyes, still mostly closed, move to find the old man. His voice is closest to me and I see his wide frame, but I can't see his face. It seems blanketed in fog. And then a feather tickles my nose and whatever it's doused in torches my nostrils. I jolt and thrash and were it not for whatever is restraining me, I'd catapult off this steel slab. Chlorine-flavoured snot runs down the back of my throat and burns like I've snorted cocaine laced in wasabi, sending me into a fit of coughs. My eyes snap open and water the second time the feather grazes my nose.

The old man who's hovering over me comes in close for a good look at me, his dark eyes searching mine, pulling me in like I'm staring into a black hole. Then he asks whether I'm Leo or Marc.

The wakefulness lasts only a few seconds. It's just long enough for me to discern from Jordan's expression that he's worried, and to put a name to the old man's face: Dr. Messie. *Hello, old friend.*

CHAPTER 22 - GRACE

For the last two days, Kay and I have been staying at Jordan's condo, hoping he'll come home so we can ambush him. Meanwhile, Charlie has been carrying out the other part of his plan, the stupid part that I agreed to while turbocharged on tequila.

To Kay's disappointment, there was no road trip to Utah, Jordan's current worksite. Before we arrived at the bar at Caesars Palace, Charlie had all the time in the world. He not only called and spoke to all of Adalia's nursing home visitors, but he also called Jordan's workplace and determined he was on a leave of absence. Charlie even called the funeral home to speak with what's-her-face, but had to leave a message. The funeral home voicemail informed callers it would be closed for repairs for four days.

It's now three in the morning, heading into day three of no Jordan, and I can't sleep—again. Kay is quietly snoring away in the spare bedroom. I'm lying wide awake on the couch, staring at the ceiling, turning Charlie's stupid plan around in my head.

"I left my number for the funeral home to call me back," he said. "In the meantime, you two wait at Jordan's condo, and I'll camp out at the shuttle site where we landed. We still need to find a way home. I know the shuttles were supposed to end six years ago, but how can we know for sure without seeing for ourselves? No harm in checking."

I watched Kay, waiting for her to say something. She was sipping her watermelon cherry drink down to the last drop, until the twisty straw made that sucking sound against the ice. Then she slid her glass aside and folded her hands in front of her, quiet. Even positive Kay couldn't find a way to spin Charlie's idea. She wore a mask of skepticism and did that thing she always does when she can't say something nice: purses her lips, refrains from blinking.

I was so drunk by then that I more than made up for Kay's awkwardness. I slapped my brother's back and declared him a hero. "Great idea, Charlie-o! Why didn't we think of that earlier, right, Kay? Kay? Hello, Kay?"

Now that I'm sober and have been turning this plan around in my head for the last two wasted days, I realize how dumb it all sounds. I don't have a better idea, though, and the fact that Kay is going along with it means neither does she. For two days, she hasn't breathed a word about Charlie's plan to me. In fact, no-negative Kay has allowed me to live in blissful ignorance. She hasn't even brought up Jordan or Marc.

I don't know what time I finally fall asleep, but when the sound of the elevator wakes me, the clock reads five in the morning. Kay must be using the bathroom. In the elevator. Wait... *elevator?* What the...?

I snap my eyes wide open just in time to catch a man leaving the condo. Shit! Was that Jordan?

I run into the bedroom and flip on the light. "Kay! We have to go!"

"I don't want any helicopters," she mumbles and turns over, pulls the blanket over her head.

Forget her. There's no time to waste. I rush out of the condo to catch up to the man I hope is Jordan.

When I get out onto the street, I watch as he hails a cab. It's definitely him. Then I hail one of my own. "Follow that taxi," I tell my driver and slam the door quick to keep out the cold. I'm wearing sweatpants and a t-shirt, having run out without my jacket. Damn it! My cell phone is in my jacket pocket.

"Really follow?" he asks in an accent I don't recognize, the car still in park.

"Ya, really!" I shout.

"I don't play stalking games, lady. Tell me where you wanna go and I take you."

"This isn't a game! I have money to pay. Drive!" I command, irritated as the taillights of Jordan's cab disappear around a corner and I fear losing him before even starting. I'm pushing my foot on the floor of the car like that will make it go.

The driver doesn't move and narrows his eyes at me in his rear-view mirror.

"Look, Ivan," I say more calmly, reading his name off a laminated paper strapped to the back of his headrest, trying to channel my inner Kay. "I need to know where he's going. I'm not a stalker. I'm a worried mother. Please," I beg, desperate not to lose both my temper and this perfect opportunity to see where my son is going. Obviously, I would've preferred a face-to-face, but this is the next best thing.

Ivan relents and pursues Jordan's taxi. I sit back with relief and try to relax. We catch up pretty fast. Thankfully, we weren't that far behind and there are very few cars on the road at this hour.

"Stay back a bit, so we're not noticed, please?" I frame my demand as a friendly suggestion, with puppy eyes in the rear-view mirror.

Ivan grunts in affirmation.

My mind ping-pongs between the two people I love the most in the world: Jordan and Marc. Outwardly, I've been either drunk or quiet since Marc left. But my heart hurts so bad I wish I could shut it off. The first time I lost Marc, it was because I had pushed him away. I hid behind a wall to protect myself from feeling anything when Dad committed suicide. I lost Marc again when I saved Jordan's life. Then I had a chance at redemption with new Marc and I broke the wall down, brick by brick; I apologized, I let myself be seen at my worst. But I lost him anyway. And it all circles back to Jordan. I gave up everything to save his life and he's becoming the bane of my existence. Just like new Marc, Jordan is secretive, mean, and spiteful. But the pill I'm having the hardest time swallowing is the letter he wrote to Dr. Messie, offering a truce. I dread finding out where my son is leading me to at five in the morning. All I can say is that I hope I'm right, that Jordan was luring Dr. Messie. The alternative would be the end of me.

"Forty-four dollars," the driver grumbles at me, snapping me out of my trance. I wasn't paying attention to where we were going, so when I look out the window and see that we're at Jordan's condo, I'm shocked.

"What are we doing back here?" I ask, looking around for Jordan's taxi. It's not here.

"You say 'follow,' I follow. You say 'not close,' I fall back. You women can never make up your minds! Why you no say what you want?" he shouts at his rear-view.

"You *lost* him?" I accuse.

Ivan turns right around to look at me through his middle console.

"You just like my ex-wife! I listen to you and do what you say and you angry for something that is your fault! You a trouble-making lady and I no like trouble." His breath smells of spearmint and stale cigarette and he's pointing a stubby finger in my face. I have to press my back into the seat to avoid his touch. "Now pay and get out!"

"Pay you?" I spit the question at him, outraged. "Here's something else I bet your ex-wife did!" I jump out of the cab without paying—I've also just realized my money's in my jacket pocket, anyway—and I slam the door shut as he yells obscenities at me.

Ivan calls me by her name, Alyona, using it as an adjective for all that is evil in me. "Witch woman! You have to pay money. Life is no free! *Alyonaaa!*"

I don't look back. My inner Kay is gone.

I ride the elevator up, seething, and peek at my watch. It's nearing six. We've been circling for almost an hour. What a colossal waste of time. Now I'll never know where Jordan was off to. I waited two days for him to show up and when he finally does… Who knows if I'll get another chance like this?

Defeated and frustrated, I'm dying to crawl under the covers on the couch and wallow in misery. But when I enter the condo, there's evidence that Kay has been up and about. My best friend is as tidy as a hurricane when she passes through a room. Bunny slippers are strewn left and right near the couch. Her jacket, which was previously hanging on the back of the chair, has been replaced by her pyjama top. A half glass of orange juice sits on the counter next to a half-eaten muffin and a hairbrush. Gross.

"Kay?" I call out as I search the condo. But I already know she's left. Her shoes are gone. Where would she go at this hour? I take my phone out of my jacket pocket to call her, and I notice a missed call, and a text message full of exclamation points—typical Kay.

I don't see the keys anywhere! Angry face! Did you go to the storage unit again?! Why didn't you wake me?! I would've come with! Anywho, Charlie called. He has big news!!! Call us when you're back, babe! Also, you left without your cell phone! I tried calling you and your jacket pocket was ringing. Arrrgh!

I did leave my cell phone. And I will call Kay and Charlie to find out what this big news is. But first things first… I didn't take the keys with me. I'm one-hundred-percent positive that they were on the counter. So if she couldn't find them and I don't have them… That must have been what Jordan came here for. When he offered us his condo, I'll bet he meant for us to have only the elevator key, not giving much thought to what else was on the keychain. Let's hope he's at the storage unit now.

CHAPTER 23 - GRACE

Charlie and Kay have already eaten, but they ordered me break-fast, which arrives just as I'm sliding into the Mustang booth across from them. It's in a takeout bag, though.

"Why can't I eat it now?" I pout, my mouth watering.

"Our ride will be here any minute," Charlie explains, then immediately starts grilling me about Jordan.

"When I realized he took the keys, I went to the storage unit, hoping that was where he went," I say.

"And?" they both press at the same time.

"And that's it. Jordan wasn't there. I already told you all this over the phone."

"Any word from Marc?" Charlie asks, cautiously.

I shake my head. My brother's been asking me this flipping question each time we speak, as if he is also obsessing over Marc. There is no way Charlie's imagining what I am, though. Vegas is the perfect place to be when you've just dumped your wife. I'm convinced Marc is partying, hopping around from nightclub to concert hall to strip joint. But he wouldn't be alone, would he? No. Not in my mind. I picture Marc with a woman. I imagine high-heeled shoes behind his ears, his hands groping breasts, her nails clawing his back, him asking if she wants him, and her screaming *yes, yes, yes.*

We sit silently as if mourning a death, but *this* Marc's not dead—he left me—and I'm done grieving. I stick my hand into the takeout bag and retrieve the first thing my fingers touch, a hash-brown patty, and I take a greedy bite. I chew through the awkward moment, swallow, and then state, "I don't want to talk about my *ex*-husband." The ease with which that familiar title slips past my lips is unexpected. "I want to kill Dr. Messie, if he isn't already dead, then I want to go home. Now, what is it that you two couldn't tell me over the phone?" I ask as I devour another yummy hash-brown, the best I've ever tasted.

"First, I didn't find anything at the shuttle location," says Charlie. "I spent two nights in a tent for good measure."

Kay touches Charlie's hand and they exchange a look, the kind that couples do. "Your brother's lucky to be alive. He found an Arizona bark scorpion one morning. Those are the most venomous. Remember, Grace?" She's addressing me but looking at Charlie like he's her celebrity crush.

What were these two discussing before I arrived—their honeymoon? I have no idea what a bark scorpion is, but it rings a bell, so I assume we learned about it the last time we were in Vegas, probably on that tour of the Great Basin caves.

Charlie blushes and takes her hand in his and my opinion on the matter of them wavers between cute and gross. He looks at me and says, "But I was right about the funeral home. Amy called me back."

"And Jessica should be picking us up any minute now, so we can meet her face to face. Charlie set everything up," Kay says, googly-eyed.

I give them both a blank stare. "Who are these people?" I ask as I start on a fried-egg sandwich from the bag.

"Amy was the attendant we met at the funeral home," Charlie replies. "She gave me Jessica's contact information. I spoke to her on the phone. Remember Walt?"

I don't obsess over Walt, but from time to time I do think of him. We were all fond of him. He was the big brother Jordan never had. I can still picture him teaching Jordan how to play chess. He died of Metagenesis shortly after I returned from Vegas.

It seems disrespectful to eat while speaking of the dead. I set my sandwich down on its wrapper and wipe my face with a napkin. "Of course I remember him. Why?"

Just then, a woman approaches our booth, looking down at us. She has a hard face, cold strong eyes like she has lived through each circle of hell. I furrow my brows.

The mystery woman says, "I'm Jessica, Walt's mother." As soon as she says it, it becomes obvious.

A sudden ache grips my chest and I lose my appetite. This was the dark-haired woman standing next to Walt in the framed holo-gram he kept on his bedside shelf. They had the same almond-shaped eyes. I placed that hologram across her son's chest before they buried him, wondering why his mother had abandoned him in his final days. And now his mother is standing in front of me. Only now her eyes are weathered like they've cried too many tears and slept too few nights. Her hair has gone mostly grey, and the crow's feet are deeper than they should be for a woman her age.

"Sanjeet is waiting in the van. Let's go," she says and then walks away.

Charlie pulls a few bills out of his money clip, leaving them on the table. I salvage the half-eaten sandwich and tuck it back into the bag, and take the to-go coffee with me.

We follow Jessica out to a white van waiting across the street. Kay tugs at my sleeve, hinting at me to fall back to let Charlie and Jessica have a head start.

"Sanjeet is her subject, her soulmate," Kay whispers, even though Charlie and Jessica are now on the other side of the street. Then she gives me a bit of info as we wait for another opening in the traffic to cross. "Jessica was sent here to clone his soul to re-pair and save her son's, same as you, except she went back to the nineties. But she was intercepted—by the hitman, of all people. It wasn't Mister, though. It was another hitman. He was quitting, said he wasn't going to work for Dr. Messie anymore. That's who warned her that once injected, the subject would have to be killed for the cloning to work. He told her that if she found the subject, Sanjeet, she'd have to kill him herself. Can you imagine?"

I almost snap at her, *Yes, I can! Umm, Leo?* but I stop myself when I catch the wide-eyed, regretful innocence all over her face.

"Sorry, I didn't mean…"

There's an opening in the traffic and I go for it.

Kay runs behind me and concludes. "Anyway, she said she considered it, but ultimately decided against it."

"Where are they taking us?" I ask.

"Their headquarters."

"What's that? Whose headquarters? What happens there?"

Kay responds with a shrug just as we reach the van.

Jessica lets us climb in and slides the door closed behind us. Charlie is already in the back row, allowing Kay and me to take the middle row. Jessica gets in on the passenger side next to the driver, who introduces himself as Sanjeet. He puts the van in gear as soon as we're buckled in and then we drive away.

Jessica flips down her visor, using her mirror to watch us as she speaks. "Before we get down to business, let me clear up something for you both. As I already told Charlie, yes, we knew your son was here. But we barely interacted with each other." She suggests that she's addressing Kay and me, but I'm the only mom back here, and her gaze is fixed on me. "Your son... he wanted to be left alone after the big trial, and we respected that." The way she lingers on the words "your son," it's as if she's angry with me, or jealous. She and I were once cornered in the same dilemma. The only difference is—and it's a big one—my son is alive and hers is dead.

"But understand this. Jordan is using your desperation to go home as bait, and I have zero guesses what for. I've been back in time for almost ten years. There is no way home. Those shuttles ended six years ago. Period. The sooner you accept you are all stuck here, the better off you'll be."

"Stuck here?" I blurt. "There must be a way home. I have a...." I stop myself from finishing my sentence—that I have a son at home waiting, because Jessica does not.

"The good news," Jessica continues, turning around in her seat to look at us through the middle console, "is that a very old Dr. Messie is also stuck here, alive, in Vegas. Welcome to our team and mission: Operation Messie. I'll give you one guess what our main objective is."

"Stop-stop Dr. Messie," Kay says.

Sanjeet laughs. "Stop-stop? Are we in a PG movie?"

Jessica's cold face melts into a smile when he laughs, as if the sound is music to her ears. I'm the jealous one. "Sure, Kay. Stop-stop," she says, then turns back around to face forward. "You can put it that way if it makes you feel better."

"How?" I speak for the first time.

No one responds for a good chunk of time. We merge onto a freeway.

Then Jessica addresses us via the visor's mirror again. "We've been looking for Dr. Messie for a long time. Six years, to be precise. Sanjeet and I were living in New York City when I saw that picture of Dr. Messie in the paper and we came back straight away. It was pure luck that Leo was the head of a Fortune 500 company and his death made the news. Many life-travellers saw the article, and we all united with one common goal. We came close once, tracking Dr. Messie down to Henderson, a city not far from Vegas. He got away, though not without a fight. A lot of good people lost their lives that day." She pauses, allowing a respectful moment of silence for her fallen team.

I use the moment to calm myself. Charlie and Kay don't say much about Leo in my presence. To hear Jessica speak so openly about him is making my palms sweat on my paper coffee cup. I shouldn't have brought it along. I haven't taken one sip and probably won't. My heart is racing enough without help from the caffeine.

"After Henderson, we never came close again. Until now." She watches only me in her mirror again. "You're probably wondering why your son was interested in Leo. Rest assured, I put one of my people on it right after Charlie informed me. We are all wondering why. Specifically, we want to know how it is connected to Dr. Messie, and why your son became involved. These answers could lead us to finally… stop-stop Dr. Messie." She glances at Sanjeet and they exchange a smile.

"My son isn't *involved* with Dr. Messie. He was probably luring him, setting a trap. If you haven't seen Dr. Messie since Henderson, how do you know he isn't already dead?" I ask, hopelessly defending Jordan. Not even I believe what I'm saying. But more importantly, no one has answered my question about how we will find Dr. Messie, and it's making me more anxious.

I glance around the van, first at Kay, who is staring out her window with her hands folded tautly in her lap, and then over my shoulder at Charlie, who meets my gaze but is holding his breath. It hits me that I'm the only one who doesn't understand something very important.

"Grace, I have many guesses as to why your son, who knew we wanted Dr. Messie dead, didn't tell us about the correspondence between them. None of my guesses include Jordan doing our job for us, and then letting us continue our mission knowing it was already done. Additionally, recent developments have given us reasonable hope that Dr. Messie *is* alive."

Kay turns her attention to me. "Maybe now isn't the best time to talk about this," she suggests. She notices that I'm clutching my coffee cup for dear life and offers to take it. I let her, and she gives my fingers a supportive squeeze.

"Go ahead, Jessica," I say, trying to control the tremor in my voice. My throat is beginning to close in on itself.

"Around the time you all arrived, we believe Dr. Messie once again began experimenting on humans. Those seniors who have been turning up dead—have you heard of them?"

"I don't think so?" I question.

"The missing palliative-care patients," Jessica clarifies.

Then Kay adds in a soft voice, "Remember Randy, the taxi driver, telling us about those seniors who ran away from their hospice?"

"Randy said a lot of things," I say, but it's jogging my memory.

"We joked they went skydiving? Randy told us about his cousin Lexi who worked in the morgue?"

Lexi was his cat's name, I recall. But I let Kay throw clues at me until one sticks, and I fully remember.

"They were poisoned?" I confirm.

Kay nods.

Jessica continues. "I'll give you one guess what the poison was."

She allows time for me to answer. I'm getting tired of her guessing games and wait her out.

"Copper," she says. "Do you know what the key ingredient is in that vial Adalia gave you?"

I shake my head.

"Also copper." Then she adjusts her mirror to look right at me. "Are you aware your son works at a mine?"

"A copper mine," Kay whispers, making me instantly sickened. Whatever Jessica is sharing, Kay and Charlie have already heard and are seemingly on board with it.

"Dr. Messie has never worked alone," Jessica says. "He has always had a partner. I have a good guess who that is. Do I need to tell you?"

"Please don't," I manage to say through the lump in my throat.

We remain silent as Sanjeet merges into the exit lane, taking us off the freeway and turning into a cookie-cutter neighbourhood.

"Jessica, the copper connections you've made seem far-fetched," I say, defending Jordan again. "Yes, he works at a copper mine. So what?"

"You're right," she says, catching me by surprise by agreeing with me. "It's all circumstantial," she adds, unconcerned. But when she turns around in her seat to look me right in the eye, I know our concurrence ends there. "And yet, you believe I'm right, don't you? You've had a gut feeling all along about your son. Even you, his mother, can't ignore these coincidences. A mother is always right."

"That's enough for now," Charlie cuts in.

Jessica looks over my shoulder at him, but she doesn't obey. "Your brother told me about your initial plan, stopping Hitler and Dr. Messie. Ambitious. But have you ever considered—"

"I said that's enough," Charlie's voice booms, making Kay and I jump.

"You can't protect her from this one, Charlie. At some point, she must know our plan whether or not she is to participate in it."

"I'll decide when that is," he sneers at her.

I'm being handled again. Everyone knows what's happening except me. They've all decided how to deal with me, how much information I should have, and when. Part of me wants to defy my brother and insist on hearing whatever he is protecting me from. What could be worse than facing the possibility that my son is experimenting on humans alongside Dr. Messie? But Charlie knows me best. He knows that sometimes I prefer ignorance. Oblivion is my survival tool. So when Jessica looks at me, waiting for me to insist that she continue, I don't. I opt to let my brother protect me, like always.

CHAPTER 24 - MARC

A woman speaks to me in the darkness, "I wish you wouldn't ask me that."

I can't tell if it's Rachel or Grace, and I can't tell which version of me she's speaking to: Marc, Cyrus, or Leo. Everything is black. I'm in nothingness. There's no gravity, or maybe I have no body. Is this a dream or a memory?

"Yes, sometimes I wonder what my life would've been like if Darius were still here," she says.

I remember these exact words, how they're said, and who says them. Rachel. I wish I could see her face. Is she floating with me now? "Do you think about him all the time?"

"I can't help it."

"What about when we're together? Do you think about him then, too?" I never asked Rachel that question. I didn't want to know the answer. I ask it now, into the black void that is my subconscious hell—the place where the memory of Rachel lives. Is this the beginning of another code 33, where flashbacks of the last moments of my past lives will torment me?

"Who? When *who* is together? What is your name?" a voice intrudes. It's Dr. Messie's—I think. But he knows my name. Why is he asking?

"You can start over. Just tell me what I need to know," Dr. Messie says.

It's not the first time he's tried to strike a bargain with me. Last time, he told me he'd let Rachel go if I'd travel back to kill Grace. I said I would. I was desperate and would've agreed to anything. But when I arrived in Grace's life, I came to the realization Dr. Messie was never going to hold up his end of the bargain. That day, I learned a lesson I should've learned long before: never dance with the devil.

Rachel speaks again, pulling me back under. "I came home one day and Darius was gone. I don't know how long he'd been gone for. I don't even remember if he kissed me goodbye. I think about that part a lot."

She isn't crying yet. But she will when I say all those horrible things I wish I never had. I break her heart and she leaves me for the last time. I don't try to win her back. She's better off without me.

Then another voice cuts in. Jordan's. "What are you doing?" he asks. He doesn't sound happy.

"Jordan. How nice of you to join. I hear Jessica is back in the picture."

A long silence follows.

"I'll take care of it," Jordan says.

CHAPTER 25 - GRACE

Over the last six days, Charlie, Kay, and I have been living at Jordan's condo while splitting our days between headquarters and surveillance at the places that Jessica's team has discovered Jordan frequents. We no longer have the storage room key, but Oscar still has elevator keys. If Jordan returns, we are to behave as if nothing has changed, and allow him to believe that we are still relying on him to get us home. "We'll take it from there," Jessica said. Whatever that means.

Charlie and Kay have been reluctant to leave me alone. But I insist on it. Every day. Frankly, I'm getting tired of these two. They're smothering me.

"You sure you don't want company?" Kay asks as she reverses out of Jessica's driveway.

Kay asks me this every time. I know she thinks I'm torturing myself. She doesn't understand that being at a blackjack table brings me comfort, even if it reminds me of all the people I've loved, pushed away, killed, and lost.

"Nope. I'm good." I'm sitting in the backseat but I still catch the look between her and Charlie in the front, as if they're my concerned parents. I've become distant and aloof since Jessica told me my son is working with a mass murderer, and it's weirdly peaceful in my head. Coldness is how I cope with the impossible, though I know I've been making my friend and brother anxious.

"Let us at least pick you up?" Charlie asks.

"No thanks," I reply. I already told them I'd take a taxi to meet them at the condo after dinner. I prefer to eat alone.

Something smashes next to us, crumbling beneath the tire and weight of the van. Kay has backed into something. "Dang it! Why is that hobbit thing right there?"

The better question is: why are we letting Kay drive? Charlie is more experienced, having driven Dad's antiques on those deserted back roads all the time. Jessica taught us all how to drive what she called a "stick shift," telling us it was important to be able to go anywhere at a moment's notice, though I think the purpose was to distract me from joining their Operation Messie meetings. It seems everyone is waiting for Charlie to deem it the right time to include me. In any case, even I'm better than Kay behind the wheel. But I keep quiet and hang tight as Kay abandons the fallen garden gnome and drives off.

Six days ago, when we arrived at The Ridge, a quiet gated community in a suburb a good thirty minutes from Vegas, I thought it was a big joke. Jessica's home, which serves as head-quarters, is a homey bungalow with a blue door and fenced-in yard. Flowerpots and kitschy ceramic characters (minus one gnome) line the walkway, and a cheery mat at the front door reads *Welcome*. Inside, it has furniture suited to a knitting group of grandmothers, not an organized brood of rebels planning an assas-sination.

However, if the home was decorated by someone's dear old aunt Ethel, she didn't get to the backyard shed. From the outside, the shed is just a shed. Inside, it looks like the control centre for a war against alien invaders. There's even tinfoil on the only win-dow, blocking out the nosy neighbours. Lining the walls are news-papers, whiteboards, diagrams, maps, shorthand notes, and photo-graphs, and none of it makes any sense to me. If I hadn't seen Dr. Messie in that newspaper article the same as they all had, I'd think these people were a crazy cult.

People come in and out of Jessica's house regularly and it's hard to remember their names, but I try. Only three are life-trav-ellers: Sunny, Ethan, and Daniel. A few are subjects who were spared, like Sanjeet. Most of the group are people Jessica reached out to for their skills and discretion. Every one of them has the same goal: stop Dr. Messie. As for how, they don't all agree.

Sanjeet, Jessica's long-time boyfriend and soulmate, doesn't like me. He looks at me as if I'm a stray pet his girlfriend brought in off the street, unsure if I'll eventually bite my rescuers. Sanjeet wants to kill Messie.

Then there are former agents Sanchez and Batista. They've been tasked with digging into anything and everything about Jordan: his hangouts, friends, job and, most importantly, his interest in Leo. These two are not life-travellers; they used to be from some other group called the FBI. Until meeting them, I hadn't a clue what that stood for, but these two walk around like they own the place. It makes me laugh. They don't hold a candle to the Worldwide Law Enforcement from my era. The WLE are ruthless, acting as judge, jury, and literal executioner. In any event, if I had to pick one of these FBIs to be my new friend, it would be Batista. She's not so bad. They want Dr. Messie brought to justice, which translates to the death penalty.

The youngest and most likeable member is Amy, who works at the funeral home. It's funny, I remember thinking she had such a forgettable name for a forgettable face. No, she's not a life-traveller, but she was someone's subject who was spared. She started working at the funeral home, hoping to intercept others and educate them, but no one ever came. The shuttles had already ended. Amy is a bit dumb (in my opinion) and Kay has taken a liking to her, probably because Amy is in the minority of those who want Dr. Messie behind bars for life. Amy doesn't believe in an eye for an eye.

Jessica, the founder and leader of this group, has made it clear she wants to gouge Dr. Messie's eyes right out of his head, fry them up with hot sauce, and force-feed them to him. "How's that for an eye for an eye?" she asked me with a cackle and a knee-slap one night while we were sharing a few beers. "I'll give you one guess what'll come next. I'm going to pull him apart one piece at a time. What about you, Grace? What do you want?"

"Dead," I said, cautiously. I think Jessica is nuts.

"Would you rip his eyes out?" She was practically drooling for an affirmative answer; it sickened me.

"I'll give you one guess," I said, which she took to mean yes, and she laughed so hard it was awkward.

But now that we're constantly talking about it, it's getting too real for me. People think if you've committed murder once, it'll be easier the next time. I believe that statement is true for psychopaths and dentists—those who feel no empathy when inflicting pain on others. Now that I know how it feels to end someone's life, I know I'll never do it again. Even if Dr. Messie deserves it. Even if it will save lives. Yes, I want him dead, and unlike Adalia, who pleaded for kindness, I don't care how it's done. I just don't want to do it myself and lucky for me, there's a whole clan here who will.

The radio in the van is broken, so Charlie and Kay's chattering accompanies my thoughts the whole drive to the Vegas strip. They giggle and swap stories like a new couple. It's nice to be ignored, but a bit strange. All my life, Charlie has spent his energy solely on me. At first, I couldn't decide if I was happy for him or jealous of Kay. But I warmed up to the idea each time I caught the sparkle in Charlie's eyes. I've decided that I'm happy for both of them.

When they drop me off at the casino, they try once more to talk me into letting one of them stay with me.

"No. I have a phone. I'll call you guys if I get so emotional that I simply can't survive another second without you," I tell them in the same tone I use when asking someone to please pass the salt. Again, they exchange glances. "I know you're worried about me. I've gone cold but I'm not reverting to the old me. I just need time. Love you both." And with that, I slip out of the car and enter the casino.

I lose a hundred bucks at a twenty-dollar blackjack table before deciding to zone out at a slot machine instead. I hardly play these—there is no skill involved. But lately, something about not having to use my brain has appealed to me, and these money-sucking slots have become part of my ritual.

I feed the machine a ten-dollar bill. I'm a few spins in when I feel someone standing behind me. It's probably one of those machine hoarders waiting to claim my spot, and I should leave because if I'm right, they won't. But I refuse to give in. I'm in a shitty mood. "Lose your money elsewhere. This one's taken."

Then, with an audacity I've never before seen, the machine hoarder drags a chair over from a neighbouring slot machine and sits beside me.

I look over and snap, "Are you deaf? I said—"

I stop cold. It's like someone has kicked me in the gut. While the rest of Jessica's crew are staking out Jordan's known places—his condo, workplace, favourite bars and restaurants, lawyer's office, storage facility—he's sitting right beside me.

"Hi, Grace." He waves.

CHAPTER 26 - MARC

'm no longer in the void of zero gravity. It's not black anymore, either. This scene comes alive in Technicolor. I taste bourbon on my tongue. I feel linen under my ass and someone's hands on my hips. I smell a damp towel in a pile of laundry I never wash mixed with the scent of cheap, acrid perfume. It's the most vivid of my hallucinations, so much so that I wonder if it's a memory or if I'm reliving it. I'm right there. In fact, I'm almost *there* and I clench my butt cheeks to get me there faster. I block Rachel out of my thoughts while at the same time wishing it was her mouth on me and not this other woman—this lady of the night.

"Rachel," I think her name in my head at the same time this woman says it out loud in a low, raspy voice.

"What?" I say. Hearing Rachel's name momentarily distracts me from my pleasure, forcing one eye open.

The hooker repeats her question. "Is this how Rachel did it?"

"*What?*" I feel myself become limp, flopping around like a salmon in her mouth, and I crab-crawl backward on all fours en route to the headboard.

"Come on, baby. Just relax," she says as she slinks toward me, her hands ice cold on my inner thighs. "I can do it another way if you'd like." She throws me a naughty sideways glance as she wags her butt in the air and then goes back down on me.

"Relax?" I yell, my mood ruined. Any chance at an orgasm is gone like a cigarette puff in a breeze. I haven't had one in months—an orgasm, that is. "Get off my dick!" I command the hooker whose name I don't even remember, so I improvise, "Whore!"

This changes everything. She shoves off me, pushing off my chest like it's a springboard, and leaps away from me. "What'd you call me?"

"Get out! Get your shit and get out!" I grab a handful of her clothes beside me and toss them at her.

She reaches for and misses most of them, catching only her red bra. The rest of her stuff falls to the ground in a pile at her feet. She puts her bra back over her big tits. Then I hear the front door push open and the flames in the fireplace beside me dance from the air seeping under the gap of my bedroom door. It trembles in its jamb from the gush of wind.

"Cyrus?"

It's Rachel. I panic. We're not together, haven't been in more than two years, unless you count the odd moments of weakness (angry sex), but she's still my wife. The lady of the night cackles and I shoot her a shut-the-fuck-up look, which she promptly ignores by laughing louder. Before she can take her revenge on me by shouting out to give me away, I lunge across the bed and cup my hand over her lipstick-smeared mouth. I look down at myself and see the same shade on the band of my boxers.

"Shit!" I mutter under my breath at the same time the whore bites the beefy part of my hand. "Shit!" I grit my teeth and wince. "I am going to take my hand off your mouth and I swear to God if you breathe a word, I will end your life, you whore."

I give her the scariest face I can manage but she rolls her eyes, revealing that she's not afraid of me. "Not only will you not get paid, but I'll make sure no one ever hires you again." She's still not convinced and so I add, "I'll tell everyone you gave me crabs!"

Now I've made an impression on her, because she sighs through her nostrils, then nods cooperation.

I put my finger over my lips, shushing and keeping eye contact with the hooker, then change out of my underwear into a pair of clean boxers. Rachel's footsteps approach the bedroom and my heartbeat speeds up to that of a marathon runner in full sprint. I point to the window to insinuate that the hooker is to use it as an exit. She folds her arms across her chest, shaking her head with a firm no, leaving me no choice but to intercept Rachel in my boxers. I run out of the room and confront my estranged wife.

"Hey," I greet her in my living room with a frown. The room is frigid from the brief moment it took for Rachel to boldly let herself in, as if she still has the right to do so.

"Hey," she says back, just as lively.

I walk past her to throw another log on the fire.

"I knocked, but I guess you were otherwise occupied."

I steal a glance at her. She has removed her hood but not her cloak. Her dark hair falls around her delicate face, her cheeks red from the cruel outdoors. There is no denying that Rachel is beautiful. She catches me watching her; I feel completely naked in my boxers, and I look away sheepishly. We haven't been together-together in… I try to draw up the memory of the last time and can't. It was too long ago. I miss her. When we first split, she used to let me sleep with her occasionally, to fill a mutual need. But not lately.

"How wonderful of you to stop in. To what do I owe the pleasure of your visit?" I ask sarcastically. It's neither wonderful nor pleasurable and her timing is terrible, given the hooker in my bed.

I grab my fur coat and put it on. It instantly warms me, having been sitting next to the fire. Rachel looks at me and I can't read her expression. I have no idea what she wants or needs or even if she's angry or sad. As usual, she shows no real emotion on her face. I don't even know if she's noticed the pair of red patent leather shoes sitting near the small table. They match the hooker's bra and I mentally kick myself, vowing to get Rachel out of here as soon as possible.

"What do you want, Rachel?" I ask, coldly. The last dozen times she came here, it was to tell me she was dying. It's her new thing, ever since she started seeing that doctor. The quack claimed he could help her overcome her grief once and for all, but it's only gotten worse. Now Rachel has horrible dreams of burning alive. She lives in fear of dying every day, working herself up until her heart rate is at the brink of failure. Simply put, she fears dying from her fear of dying. No one dies of their fears. But Rachel always thinks she will be the first. It's completely irrational, although so is being jealous of a dead husband, so who am I to judge?

Rachel stares blankly at me, but I'm eager to get rid of her, so I beat her to the punch. "So when will you be dead? Soon, I hope?"

There are days I wish she would just quietly die so I could finally be free of her. She doesn't look shocked by my attitude toward her. She shouldn't be. To say that we don't get along is like saying that angels and demons have a small difference in opinion. It's a complete understatement. We no longer live together, but she's still always over here, seeking something I can never seem to give her, and I don't know what or why. Closure, maybe? But I'm not the husband who died. I'm the one she left.

"I'm dying?" she asks with a clueless expression. She removes her fur gloves, puts her thin fingers on her trembling lips, then looks at her hands like she's afraid they might disappear.

I tilt my head at her, confused. Is this an escalation of her fears? Is she losing her mind? "Cut the crap, Rachel. You're always dying," I say in a voice that is part mean, part concerned. If I don't keep up my usual coldness toward her, she may mistake my concern for something else. Like love, or a broken heart.

She looks me up and down like she's coming out of a trance and is just now noticing I'm near nude under my fur coat in the middle of the afternoon. She's usually ranting at this point about some conspiracy.

She purses her lips and stares hard at me. "I need your help," she says in a small voice.

"My help?" I scrunch my face at her.

She has a crazy look in her eye and I'm suddenly more worried about my hooker seeing my wife like this than I am about my wife meeting my hooker.

"Someone's been following me," she says, her tone urgent.

I force an eye-roll. "Oh, c'mon, Rach." If I didn't still care about her, love her, I wouldn't let her do this to me over and over again. Play twisted head games and suck me into her elaborate tales, brought on by one dream or another. She loves to punish me. I wish she'd fire that doctor. But something seems different about her today, and I can't put my finger on it.

"I mean it, Cyrus. I have to leave this place. But I don't want to go alone and..." She hesitates, considering her next words. "You're the only soul in the world I trust."

That's when I hear a crash coming from the bedroom and wonder if the hooker has changed her mind about exiting through the window or about keeping quiet. The subsequent *thump thump* tells me she's considering the latter.

Rachel looks toward the bedroom. "Are you alone?" she asks, looking around the room curiously.

She probably doesn't even care that there might be someone in there. I'm flattering myself to think she does. But I answer in the affirmative.

"Ya, of course I'm alone." I'm anxious to get her out of my house before the hooker comes out of my room, and so I put on my nice voice and say, "Rach, why don't we talk about this tomorrow? Meet me at the lighthouse, noon."

I usher her out. She sees the shoes, I know she does, but she doesn't say anything.

And that was the last time I ever saw Rachel. Just like her first husband, I didn't even kiss her goodbye before I left to be Marc. I don't even know if she knows the truth about why Dr. Messie took her from me. No good deed goes unpunished.

CHAPTER 27 - GRACE

"I know Uncle Charlie, Kay, and you joined that clan," Jordan says. "I've been watching you watching me, so I also know you always come here alone. Give me your cell phone."

"What? No," I reply.

Then he lifts his sweater above his waistband, revealing the butt of a gun. "Please?"

My gaze goes from his expressionless face to the gun and back to his face. Words lodge in my throat. We're in public, in a casino. Should I scream? Run?

"Is it in your jacket?" he asks.

I nod once.

"Let me," he says as he approaches me.

Then it hits me that he's planning on helping himself to my pockets. I snap out of my shock and fumble to protect my phone. He also goes for it, trying to snatch it out of my hand, missing by a hair. There's a glass of water next to me and I'll drop the phone in there before I let him have it. But when I reach out to toss it in the cup, he grabs my wrist and pries it out of my grip with little effort.

He flips the phone open, punches away at some buttons, and then spends a minute scrolling through it. "I wish you'd stayed out of it," he says with a frown as he reads the exchanges between me and the others. Most of the messages are from Jessica, asking if Jordan has come home, and me replying that he hasn't. Occasionally she texts things like, "Dr. Messie will be eating eyeballs for dinner in no time" and "I'm sorry Jordan is working for Dr. Messie. If you ever want to talk…"

With a sigh, Jordan snaps the phone shut, removes the battery, which he puts in his pocket, and then drops the phone back into mine. He sits back down. "I told you to stay out of sight. You never listen to me."

I just stare at him. He's so calm and collected. The attitude he had toward me at the café is gone. Is it because we're face to face? Is it the gun in his waistband? Why isn't he denying that he's working for Dr. Messie? I want him to. I need him to offer me another explanation, lie to me, tell me the gods made him do it, anything.

"Why have you come here?" I ask, finally finding my voice.

"Two reasons, actually. First, if the three of you still want to go home, I wasn't bluffing when I said I might have a way. I just texted Oscar from your phone, so now he has your number. I should have things figured out in the next few days and when I do, he'll pass it on to you. Don't waste your time interrogating him, by the way. Oscar is just a concierge. He thinks my travel agent is booking you a flight home to Toronto."

"And your second reason?"

He takes a deep breath. "A message."

He's staring me dead in the eye, but whatever he's about to say is making him nervous. I can sense it. As for me, I'm terrified and my blood is thumping in my eardrums.

"I know it may not seem like it, but I'm on your side," he says.

"That's your message?"

He shakes his head and then takes another deep breath, blowing it out slowly. "Tell Jessica I'll have him delivered to her as soon as possible. This doesn't have to end like it did in Henderson. But right now, we're working on something that cannot be interrupted and she has to back off. I need him."

"You need who?" I ask. My mouth is suddenly dry like I've been sipping on sawdust; I'm barely able to get the words out. I don't want to hear the response, not really. It's my last bit of hope that he'll say someone else. He needs John or Mary or Spiderman. Anyone other than…

"I think you know." He doesn't want to say his name to my face, like he's nine years old again and afraid of getting in trouble. Then, without another word, he gets up to leave.

"Wait," I say, and he obeys. But I don't know what more can be said. I can't ask him to tell me where Dr. Messie is. He won't tell me. I can't ask him why he needs Dr. Messie. He won't tell me. I can't demand that he deliver Dr. Messie to me now. He won't. But Jordan is standing in front of me and it may be the only chance I get to ask him anything ever again. "Why are you interested in Leo?"

His jaw clenches, then he turns around and starts walking away. I guess even that won't elicit a response. I don't follow right away, afraid my knees may buckle. But then something hits me.

"What about Marc?" I shout.

He stops in his tracks but doesn't turn around, like he's deciding if he should bother. I find the willpower to rise and go toward him. "You said you could get the three of us home: me, Charlie, Kay. Why didn't you mention Marc?"

"I meant all of you," he says over his shoulder, unconvincingly.

"But you didn't mention him at all. Why not? Have you already spoken to him?"

"Of course not," he says, and then he leaves.

A feeling deep down in my gut tells me he's lying. And a mother's always right.

I'm sitting in Jessica's backyard without Charlie and Kay. When Kay told me, "We're at the condo. Let me just get out of my bunny slippers and we'll be on our way," I knew I'd be in for a long wait. Last time, getting out of her bunny slippers meant having a mini spa day and a stop at a burrito joint.

Phone booths are harder to come by in 2006. And when I finally found one, it took me a few tries to get Kay's number right from memory, calling and hanging up on three random people. On the fourth attempt, I got the right combination of numbers and my call was answered on the first ring. "Thank goodness it's you!" She covered the phone and announced, "It's Grace—she's OK."

"Why wouldn't I be?" I said. It wasn't like I'd opened the conversation by telling her about Jordan. As far as they knew, I'd been blissfully engaged in a blackjack game. She replied that they'd been calling and calling and a machine kept saying I was unreachable. It seems I'd been gone for hours. I'd been so tired of apologizing to the world that the "sorry" I gave came out sounding as if I were sleepwalking. I grimaced when she reprimanded me, saying that she and my brother had been worried sick. It was like she'd taken on the role of my big brother's wife, and I'd become her honorary little sister rather than her best friend.

Now, it's dark out, and I'm sitting on a lawn chair facing Jessica's backyard fire pit, repeating the same information I gave Kay on the phone to Jessica as she joins me with ham sandwiches. Yes, I'm OK. No, I don't know where Jordan went. And then I ended with: "I didn't follow him because without a phone battery I had no way to call any of you, and he had a gun."

"A gun?" Jessica is much calmer than Kay was. Kay had shouted, "Holy dang, a gun?" so loudly in my ear I nearly dropped the receiver.

Sanjeet approaches, carrying two beers and handing them to Jessica and me. "Thanks, Sanj," Jessica says, and he leaves us again. We finish our sandwiches and sip quietly on our beers.

"Have Batista and Sanchez learned anything about Leo?" I ask as I swallow my last bite.

"Mostly stuff about his research—board members piecing off assets to giant corporations in Russia, China, Germany. And..." She pauses to take a swig of beer. "A lot of conspiracies surrounding his murder. But we don't have to guess as to the merit of those, since we all know you're the one who killed Leo."

Jessica is the bluntest of the group, in an indirect sort of way. I like her and hate her for it at the same time. I throw back a third of my beer and then stare into the fire in front of me, mesmerized by it. I feel like throwing myself into those flames right now. Instead, I flick a tidbit of bark and watch it crackle and disintegrate before it reaches the flames.

"What do you make of Jordan's claim about getting us home?" I ask as I start to peel the label from my bottle, challenging myself to pull it off in one piece.

"False."

"And about Marc?"

"Marc went to the lawyer's office to speak to Jordan without you. I'm sure Charlie told you why?"

"Charlie?" I ask.

"I guess he didn't." Jessica shakes her head. "Marc wanted to find out if it was possible to go back to his own time. That's why he wanted to be alone with Jordan."

"Oh," I say. I should've expected this from Marc, and I don't blame him. We never belonged to each other. But what I didn't expect was my brother keeping this conversation with Marc from me.

"My guess is that Jordan and your ex are still in contact. I'll have someone look for Marc, too. Just because he left you doesn't mean my team can't persuade him to answer a few questions."

First, she casually mentions me killing Leo, then discloses a conversation I'm sure my brother doesn't want me to know about, and now openly touches on Marc leaving me. None of these topics seem like a big deal to her. And strangely, they don't affect me, either. That's why I decide to go for it. "I want to hear the rest," I say plainly. "I want to hear what you were going to say to me in the van the other day."

Jessica looks at me. "Your brother—"

"Never mind my brother!" I snap, glaring at her. "Sorry, I'm just tired." I sigh. "I'm tired of him and Kay, of the secrecy, of being protected, of half-truths. You're a no-bullshit kind of person. Please, tell me everything."

"Fair enough. Did you ever ask yourself what would've happened if your plan to kill Hitler had been successful?" she asks.

I focus back on my beer, tearing the label off in one piece with success. Then I take a long swig, readying myself for Jessica's indirect way of giving information.

"Hitler wasn't a lone wolf, Grace. Anyone could've taken his place. Charlie worried that the outcome could've been worse. Didn't you?"

"Yes, I did," I admit out loud for the first time. "Charlie?" I ask again, meeting her eyes.

"We discussed it at length. The plan was ambitious, but it was enormously flawed, and he knew it."

I look away, staring into the fire, and start balling bits of the perfect beer label between my fingers. One by one, I flick tiny paper balls into the fire, while processing. She and my brother spoke at length about worries he never once mentioned to me. It would've been nice if he had, since I had felt the same.

"I don't think he wanted to hurt you. Charlie is deeply protective of you," she says as if reading my thoughts. "He seems overbearing, even for a big brother, if you don't mind me saying."

"I do mind," I reply. "But you're right."

Jessica laughs. "You said no bullshit." She pauses again, studying me. "Just like Hitler, Dr. Messie was a tyrant, but not a lone wolf. If we kill Dr. Messie, it's our guess that someone else will take his place. That is why we have to eliminate all of them. Do you understand?"

I don't reply. She always answers her own questions anyway.

"What I'm hinting at is this: Dr. Messie's entire team must be killed. I'm afraid that includes your son, Jordan."

CHAPTER 28 - MARC

Consciousness always remains seconds out of my reach. When I try to grasp it, to let go of Rachel, it vanishes like a hallucination and I'm back to her. And then she's gone again, and then back again, gone, back. I've lost track of how long I've been here on this slab—could be days, could be months. In the moments of wakefulness—if you can even call them that—over and over I'm asked what my name is, about my life in the future, the year I was born, what city I come from. I'm also grilled about the Halation, my life in the past, about my research. Occasionally I hear my voice giving replies, but I'm never sure if I'm talking out loud or if it's all in my head and my lips are flapping soundlessly like a fish's.

I'm never alone. All day, someone occupies a white chair against the clouds, which I now believe may be a wall—of clouds. When it's Tweedle-Dee, he sits in the chair and flips through a magazine; not reading, just flipping. And he's either underwater or I am because the pages seem buoyant and make no sound. Tweedle-Dum, the ogre who wrestled me to the ground, sleeps the few minutes he visits, a newspaper propped on his giant heap of a belly. Morgan, that lawyer bitch, checks my vitals every other second. I've tried to talk to her—or I think I have—but she never pays me any attention. She treats me like I'm a corpse and I still believe that's a possibility—maybe I am dead. Others have come and gone as well, no one I recognize, and they never engage with me. But I save my energy for Dr. Messie and Jordan. I do all I can to keep awake when they come into the room together.

Sometimes they're in a good mood. Dr. Messie treats Jordan differently from everyone. I've heard him offer Jordan advice on the best way to cook chicken thighs, tell him to drive safe when he's leaving for the day, and even reminisce about the time Jordan's pet bird flew away and Dr. Messie replaced it with a lookalike.

"I had a hunch it wasn't Sammy," Jordan said. "The new bird was too chatty. But then the real Sammy came back..." He laughed.

Dr. Messie also laughed, a hearty deep-from-the-gut, genuine laugh I hadn't thought him capable of. "Who ever heard of a fly-away bird returning?" he said.

One time, Dr. Messie encouraged Jordan to soften his approach with people. "You'll push people away, Jordan. Life is long. Don't you want to share it with someone special?" But what really shocked me was when Jordan replied that he didn't have time for dating, and Dr. Messie calmly said, "When all this is over, you must live your life. It's not too late for you. You're a good man, Jordan, and you deserve happiness. I want that for you."

But usually, they're not in a good mood. Usually, they're arguing like they are now.

"This is a waste of time and resources," Jordan says. He's been singing this song for days. Always insisting that they should wake me, that whatever they're doing would work better if I were a willing participant.

"You're right," Dr. Messie replies.

"I am?" Jordan asks, surprised.

I'm also surprised. Usually, this argument leads to Dr. Messie telling him to be patient in that patronizing tone of his.

"Yes. It's time to cut our losses and euthanize him. I'll have the crew get rid of him tomorrow."

CHAPTER 29 - GRACE

A couple of things happened last night after Jessica told me they planned on killing my son. First of all, it didn't sink in right away (and still hasn't). I sort of laughed it off, which confused Jessica into silence. Charlie and Kay arrived moments later with a giant shrimp ring, chips and dip, and a cold-cut platter. Getting out of bunny slippers had included a supermarket pit stop, this time. For some reason, I decided not to bring Jordan up to them, and neither did Jessica. It was like we had made a pact to let Charlie think I was still living in the dark. The next thing that happened is the reason Kay is at the condo alone with a bellyache, and Charlie and I are now sitting on a park bench across from the nursing home at 8 a.m. The shrimp made Kay sick, and it turns out there was something to Adalia's babbling after all.

Sanjeet and Amy had joined us around the fire, bringing a twelve-pack of beer with them. Amy brought up the topic of service dogs and it was obvious, by Jessica's and Sanjeet's reactions, that it wasn't the first time she'd asked about getting one. Amy went on about how dogs can be trained to do anything, and pretty please, can they get one to join the team. Given that Amy's would-be service animal already had a name, Georgie, it was clear she just wanted a pet. "Dogs can sniff out drugs and weapons, detect seizures, and they smell fear, which means..." She paused as if this next point would be the one she'd win. "Dr. Messie is afraid of dogs, and our Georgie would sniff him right out!"

Charlie nudged Kay in the rib and they both started laughing. "Georgie would need a disguise," Kay said to him.

"Angel wings," Charlie replied, and Kay nearly choked on a shrimp. In an attempt to explain their inside joke, he said, "Dr. Messie is in heaven, where they don't allow dogs." Only no one understood except me, and I was too numb to appreciate the joke. Amid her laughter, Kay, who was well on her way to polishing off the shrimp ring entirely on her own, explained Adalia's babbling about Dr. Messie at Heaven's Gate.

"Heaven's Gate?" Jessica repeated and bolted upright in her seat. Amy was in her usual state of cluelessness, but Sanjeet caught on and he and Jessica stared at each other, speechless. Finally, Jessica let us in on whatever she and Sanjeet knew. "That's the name of a gated community."

And so, Jessica has spread the team even thinner than it already was by sending Charlie and me to stake out the nursing home, while she and Sanjeet watch Heaven's Gate. Kay preferred to stay at the condo, rubbing her tummy and blaming the quality of the shrimp as the culprit of her troubles, and not the fact that she ate the whole thing on her own. Trying to sound helpful, she said it'd be good for someone to stay behind in case Jordan came back, however unlikely that was.

Charlie offers me an apple. I accept it and start shining it on my shirt. We watch silently as more employees exit the home with lunch bags and purses in hand. It's a shift change. A few of them are gathered and smoking together in the parking lot while others leave right away. When we first arrived, I tried to give one of them Adalia's rock carving to return to her, but they wouldn't accept it. There's a whole procedure for dropping things off for patients; a ward clerk has to label them and enter them as part of her belongings, and so it can only be done during visiting hours. I could've told them that it was already part of her inventory, but I decided it'd be easier to wait for visiting hours than explain the fiasco about why I had it. If Kay were here, she would've talked her way in there. But it's just me and Charlie.

We've been quiet toward each other. It's partly because spending time together without Kay is no longer the norm, but mostly, it's because his kid-gloved handling of me has created a barrier between us.

"What do you think motivates Dr. Messie?" I finally speak, still thinking of Adalia's rock. "I mean, is it greed? Money and fame? Was he born that way? Or did something... happen?"

"All of the above," he replies. "Including option D: something happened. No one is born bad."

"But what if he was? What if he was predisposed..." I hesitate, trying to phrase my thoughts. "Was he genetically destined to be evil because he was Hitler in his last life?"

"No. He had a choice," Charlie replies, but he looks like he's still considering my question, and after a long pause, he elaborates. "Ever seen two kids cut from the same cloth, raised by the same shitty parents, and wonder why one repeats the cycle and the other breaks it? Predisposed, genetics, call it whatever. But Dr. Messie could've made decisions in spite of his last life rather than repeating the cycle because of it. He knew better."

We fall silent again and eat our apples. I mull over Charlie's response, right down to the last bite. What Dr. Messie wrote to Adalia on the rock keepsake was sweet. But he also said, *It's too late for me, but not for you.* That makes me believe there was a turning point, a fork in the road where he took the wrong turn and she did not. They were cut from the same cloth. Evil isn't something he was born with, it's what he became over time. I suddenly feel Adalia's pain. She knew what he was like before they reached the fork.

"This is a dead end," I say after I check my watch. "How much longer are we going to sit here and do nothing? Even the FBI screened the people on Adalia's visitor's list. They're all neighbours and old friends, like you said."

Charlie takes a deep breath and then blurts, "I knew Marc was going to leave you and I did nothing to stop him."

I snap my head around and look at him.

"In fact, I encouraged it. I told him not to stay if he couldn't get over what had happened, and that I wouldn't hold it against him if he left."

He rolls his shoulders as if a heavy boulder has just been lifted off them. Then he watches me and waits. He doesn't look sorry for his actions; he just looks worried that I won't take it well. Even if this were a punishable offence, Charlie's punished himself enough. My brother is hard on himself and has always taken the task of looking out for me far more seriously than any sibling should.

"I'm not mad. You were right to say that to Marc. Don't feel bad, Charlie."

He gives me a weak smile. "Thanks," he says. "Now, to segue back to what you were saying. Damn right, this is a dead end. I requested we take on the nursing home because I figured it'd be the safest place for you."

"Charlie…" I blow out a frustrated sigh.

"I know, I know," he says, putting his hands up in surrender. "But you did say you wanted to return that rock to Adalia. Kill two birds, one stone. Get it?" He laughs nervously.

"When are you going to stop babying me?"

"Probably never." His phone rings and he pulls it out of his pocket and checks the display like he's debating whether to answer. It rings a few times and he presses a button to silence it. "There's something else," he says, then meets my eyes again. "They're planning on killing Jordan."

"So they say."

He scrunches his forehead. "You already knew?"

I nod. "Jessica."

He shakes his head, chewing his lip, likely making a mental note to chastise her later for this betrayal. "I want Dr. Messie gone, but not at the price of my nephew's life."

This is exactly the moment when the barrier between us comes down and the ice in my heart melts away, and what Jessica said—about killing my son—finally sinks in as fast as a holey canoe in an angry ocean. A sob escapes my lips. "But she's right, Charlie." And I begin to cry.

"Maybe. Maybe not."

"So what are we doing here? Why are we going along with this, this *cult*?" I spit the word out and sob, not caring that the smoking nurses are glancing our way.

Charlie places a strong hand on my shoulder, tilting his chin down to look at me in that big-brother way he always does. I'm wailing like a baby and I want my big brother to fix this but I know he can't and it's killing me. "Gracie, we came here to stop Dr. Messie. We found like-minded people to get the job done. Once he's dead, or behind bars, or without eyeballs—whatever— hopefully Jordan wasn't completely full of shit and we can return home. As far as Jordan goes, he's a big boy and will have to take care of himself; change his name, go into hiding, do whatever it is that people do when they're being hunted by a crazy cult."

"But that doesn't solve anything, Charlie." Sob, hiccup, sob, sob. "What does Jordan need from Dr. Messie? Why are they working together? Is Jordan experimenting on humans, too? What if Jessica's right? What if we let him go, then he steps in and takes Dr. Messie's place? What if—"

"We cannot control the outcome, Gracie. We can only control our actions. And why do you always go to the worst what-if? What if someone better steps in instead? Look..." He pauses, takes in a deep breath, and gives me a knee squeeze. "I'll be honest with you: whether or not it was worth the risk, I never liked the Germany plan." Even when Charlie is expressing disagreement with me, his voice soothes me, his face is gentle and kind. No one will ever understand and care for me the way he does. But I wish he'd stop living his life worrying for me.

"I wish you'd said so before we left." I wipe my face and nose on my sleeve, trying to rein in my desperation and fears. If I'm calm, he will feel better. And he's right: I'd never considered a good what-if scenario.

"Me too." Charlie's phone rings again and this time when he checks the display, he takes the call. "What's up, Kay-Kay?... Are they sure?... How?" Then he gives me an apologetic glance and walks away so I can't listen. Here he goes again, protecting me.

When Charlie comes back moments later, his face is drained of colour. "They have news. About Dr. Messie, and also..." He hesitates; the ball in this throat bobs. "...About Marc."

CHAPTER 30 - GRACE

I set aside everything Charlie said to me about what Kay told him over the phone—Marc's note, Jordan's note, and finding Dr. Messie—in favour of the least important thing: Kay's invasion of my privacy. I made Charlie call her back immediately so I could yell at her. She called me jejune and then hung up on me.

So when I spot Kay waiting outside Jordan's condo as we arrive to pick her up, I roll my window down, unwilling to hold back. I resume my tantrum exactly where I left off on the phone. "What the hell is jejune?"

"Immature. Childish. Petty. Take your pick!" she yells back at me, stomping toward the van.

"How dare you go through my stuff without asking?"

"They found Dr. Messie. I was looking for the vial!"

"And you think I'd leave something that important in my backpack? I would never go through your personal belongings without your permission." I take the vial out of my pocket and whip it at her. "Here it is!"

She doesn't catch it and it bounces off her and hits the sidewalk.

"So important that you're catapulting it at my head? What the hell is wrong with you, Grace?" She plucks the vial off the ground and flings it back at me. It's a good thing it's not breakable.

"Why didn't you call me and ask?"

"I did better than that! First I called *you*, but you obviously haven't replaced your battery yet—and then I called *Charlie*, but he *ignored* my call!" She gives my brother the death stare as she climbs in behind us, taking the middle seat.

"Enough!" Charlie says, putting the van in gear and driving off before the door is even closed. He's had to endure my complaints the whole way here and he commented about both of us overreacting over silliness.

I tuck the vial back into my pocket and pull out my phone to check it. Sure enough, four missed calls. I had replaced the battery but unintentionally left it on silent. I'll never get used to these archaic devices.

"What's the update, Kay?" Charlie asks, calmer.

"As I said on the phone, after the umpteenth time of being ignored—"

"Knock it off, Kay. I said I was sorry," Charlie says, eyeing her in the rear-view. I think I'm witnessing their first fight.

"But you didn't mean it."

"Because letting one call go to voicemail isn't a big deal. Now, what's the update?"

I hear Kay let out a sigh behind me. She apologizes to Charlie, telling him she's being snappy because I've gotten her all riled up, not because of anything he's done. It's like I'm not even in the van. Now who's being jejune? Of course, I keep my comment to myself.

A calmer Kay gives us the update. "They found Dr. Messie somewhere in Utah. Something about an abandoned copper mine. Jessica's team should be halfway there by now. They're going to set a trap for Messie and his team. She asked that we wait at this truck stop," Kay reaches through the middle and hands me a map with a big X marking the spot, "and to bring the vial. That's all I know."

"Messie and his team?" I swallow my fear, thinking of Jessica's promise to kill them all, including my son. This is the real reason I'm flipping out on Kay for going through my things. Avoidance.

Kay pops her head between the front seats to ask Charlie, "Does she know?"

He nods.

Kay looks at me. "I asked if Jordan was also there. Jessica didn't know, but she's not an idiot and I'm sure she knows we only want to stop-stop Dr. Messie, not Jordan. She might not have answered honestly. We didn't even know they had a lead on Dr. Messie, and now magically they've tracked him down to an exact location. We're not truly part of their group, you know?"

"Can we go to the mine directly? Try and warn Jordan?"

"Gracie… we shouldn't warn him," Charlie says in a sad voice. "He and Dr. Messie will vanish into thin air if we do."

I'd known it was a selfish suggestion before I even made it. But keeping Jordan safe is my default setting, no matter what he's done. I'm his mother.

"There are tons of abandoned copper mines in Utah and Jessica never said which one. Besides, they've had a big head start. We'd never beat them to it even if we did know," Kay says, patting me on the shoulder. "But I have an idea and also a backup idea and even a backup to *that* idea. First, I already left a message with Oscar. If Jordan checks in with him, he'll get my urgent request to call one of us."

"Why not get Jordan's number from Oscar?" Charlie asks.

"I did. And I already called, but it's no longer in service. Jordan must've changed his number, so he can call Oscar, but not the other way around. Sneaky and clever like his mom," Kay says and it's meant to be a joke, but I'm not in a joking mood. "Idea two is Jordan's claim that he can get us home. I told Jessica we had to at least speak to him before she does anything at all, in case he was telling the truth."

So far, her ideas suck. I hold my breath waiting for the third and final one, hoping she's saved the best for last.

"And my backup to my backup is the vial. We have it, and they want it. We offer an exchange: the vial for Jordan's life."

"That's a great plan, Kay," Charlie says, but it's not. It's a mediocre plan and we all know it.

"Would it be OK if we didn't talk about this anymore? I need to blank out for a bit. Please." I lean my head on the window.

They obey my wish and Kay rests back in her seat. A working radio would be nice right about now. I try to numb my mind and not think about Jordan. Instead, I think about the bizarre revelation Kay made to Charlie over the phone about Marc's note, and wonder what it all means. "I don't think Marc wrote that note,"

Kay had told him. "I'm no graphologist, but I'd say it's the same handwriting on the note Jordan wrote to Dr. Messie."

I told Charlie that maybe Jordan and Marc had the same handwriting, suggesting that even though they are strangers, they are physically father and son. Charlie didn't burst my bubble in any way. He let me believe that Marc left me that note instead of letting me wonder why Jordan would've forged it.

Kay's phone buzzes, breaking the silence. "They've arrived at the mine," she announces. "They're setting the trap now."

"What's the trap?" I ask, realizing Kay never explained this.

"They're bombing the entry points," she replies.

"They're what?" I say, snapping my head around to look at her. Then I glance over at Charlie and immediately know they already talked about this. "But if they bomb the entry points, no one will get out. Everyone will be trapped inside, no?" Charlie and Kay don't respond. "Jessica said she'd let us speak to Jordan first. And I have the vial for Dr. Messie. Kay, you said—"

"I said I'd asked Jessica to let us speak to Jordan first. I never said she'd agreed," Kay replies from the back in a little voice. "But I believe she will, for the vial. I'm sure they'll grab Jordan and Dr. Messie before sealing off the exits. I'm sure." She sounds anything but sure.

CHAPTER 31 - MARC

When I wake again, I'm convinced it's tomorrow, the day they'll be getting rid of me. White, bright lights. "Turn them off," I try to say but can't. My mouth is like sandpaper.

At first, a cold hand pats my face, gently, but then a bigger, more impatient hand takes over and instead of patting, it's smacking my cheeks.

"Marc, open your damn eyes!" Jordan commands. "Wake him up, now!"

"I'm trying, sir," someone says. It's a woman.

I moan to let them know I'm awake so they'll stop touching me. Then something stings my arm, sending an icy fluid through my veins to my heart, making it race as fast as a hummingbird's. But it's the wasabi cotton ball under my nose that makes my eyes snap open. For a split second, I'm alert. I don't want to be, I've given up, and so I fight it, squeezing my eyes shut.

"Give him another shot."

"Sir, I strongly advise against that."

"Did I ask you for your counsel, Morgan?"

"No, sir. But even a lawyer can see that if you wish for him to die pain free, then—"

I find my voice: "I'm alive?" This is the most awake I've been in... how long have I been here?

"Marc?" Jordan says, then grabs my chin and gives it a shake.

I identify those fingers as the same ones that were just smacking me. "Fuck off," I groan.

"Hand me that syringe and leave us," he says to Morgan.

Afraid of being jabbed with whatever is in that syringe, I force my eyes open. Morgan hasn't left. She's standing beside Jordan. He seems irritated by her.

"Where am I?" I moan.

"Marc, we need Leo's memories," Jordan says.

"So go dig him up." I roll my eyes and regret it right away, wincing in pain. "Can you turn off the lights, kid?" I blink and squint, trying to acclimatize to the brightness.

Morgan says, "Sir, we should let him go in his sleep, peacefully."

He ignores her. "Did you hear me? We need Leo."

"Lights. Off."

Jordan sighs, but turns to do as I've asked. When his back is to me, I try to get up and catch him off guard. Morgan flinches, but I quickly realize my torso and legs are strapped down and I don't get far. Even my wrists have white rubber straps around them, with barely enough slack to scratch my nut sack. Now that the lights are dimmed and I'm fully alert, I lift my thousand-pound head for a look around.

"Jordan, what the white fuck? Am I in an asylum?" A white padded room—not clouds—eight by eight, no windows, no vents. I don't know how he turned down the lights because I don't see even a wall switch. My neck gives out and my head drops back down onto the cold slab beneath me. The ceiling doesn't have individual lights; the whole thing is one sheet of light, which would explain the level of brightness. A small camera mounted in the upper corner seems to be the only permanent fixture in the room and is the source of the whirring sounds the clouds were making. Even now, the camera zooms in and out, as if following every micro-movement. Next to me, a tray is set up with nothing but a syringe. There's a chair—also white—where everyone took a turn babysitting me.

"I'll do anything for the Halation, so I suggest you start listening to us and open your mind. Cooperate." Jordan raises his brows and tips his head to the tray where the syringe sits. Again, he asks Morgan to leave, but she doesn't, telling him the doctor wouldn't approve.

"Anything? How about you let me out of here?" I shake my head, which is throbbing something fierce. I try to bring my hands up to cover my face but I can't. "How does someone cooperate while strapped down like a lamb to slaughter?"

Jordan picks up the syringe. "We need you to be Leo."

He comes closer to me, but not close enough for me to grab him—I try and fail. Frustrated, I yank at the straps over and over, throwing a tantrum like a toddler while cussing like a trucker, spittle flying from my mouth. I pull and tug until I'm spent, which takes a mere few seconds, then I try in vain to turn my head away from them so they can't see the tears pooling.

Jordan moves to the other side of me, so I have to choose between looking at him, at Morgan, and at the ceiling. I'd close my eyes, but I want to stay alert now. I'm afraid if I blink for too long, the fog will return and suck me back under its spell, back to Rachel, and closer to death. They're looking for Leo, but they won't find him through me. I stare at the ceiling, where I can watch them both from the edge of my vision but give neither the satisfaction of direct eye contact.

"I want one more shot at this. Alone. Morgan, leave us."

"Sir, I can't do that. Dr. Messie would—"

"You work for me—not Dr. Messie! Now get the fuck out!" Jordan screams without looking at her.

She has a pale complexion and it turns fire-engine red at being scolded. She hesitates only a second and then leaves. As far as I know, this is the first time Jordan has been alone in this room with me since they snatched me off the streets.

Jordan stalls for a minute before approaching me. He whispers, "Look at me."

Of course, I refuse.

"This is gonna hurt. Sorry."

Before I get to ask what's going to hurt, he's got a hand over my mouth to muffle my agony and yanks out a catheter I didn't know I was wearing until this hellish moment. My body jerks on the table and I bite Jordan's hand, yelping into it. Then he continues talking to me like he didn't just try to turn my dick inside out. He's tugging at my wrist straps.

"Marc, please. We don't have much time before Morgan comes back."

I turn my face to Jordan, and I scrunch my eyebrows when I realize he's undoing my straps. He's watching me intently. I'm about to speak but he puts a finger to his lips, urgent, his eyes full of fear.

"Look, I meant what I said about doing anything for the Halation—but not like this. If I get caught letting you go, they're going to kill me, which means you're as good as dead, too. So pay attention. Can you run?"

Is this a trick?

"*Can you run?*" he repeats.

I don't think I can, yet I nod yes.

"I'm going to leave the door unlocked, but I can't turn off the camera. I'll create a distraction for security, but you have to be quick." He slips something into my hand. It's a watch. "Wait exactly five minutes and then run. Keep to the right. Your life depends on it. Please, please trust me."

"How far?" I ask, afraid I won't make it five feet. My limbs are weak and if I've been lying here drugged for days, weeks, or perhaps months, how will my body react to a sudden change?

"It's a sixty-second jaunt and you'll have ten seconds before they notice the empty bed on the security camera and ring the alarms. Run or die."

CHAPTER 32 - MARC

This has been the longest four minutes of my life. I've been slipping in and out of a vivid nightmare where I'm being buried alive, and then I wake up suffocating on my tongue. Now, with only sixty seconds left on the countdown, the camera in the corner stops zooming in and out, and I wonder if I should stick to Jordan's instruction to wait exactly five minutes. This is when the watch's hands seem to move at Mach 1 speed and panic pumps my heart into overdrive. I spent the first four minutes forcing myself to stay awake and now the last trying not to go into cardiac arrest.

At the last tick of the second hand, I get off the metal slab—or rather, fall off. It's impossible to ignore dizziness and my legs are even number than my hands. I can't crawl, let alone run like Jordan told me to do. Instead, I do my best to snake like a cobra across the cold white floor to the door. My legs feel as though they're wrapped in Styrofoam; I rely on my toes to grip the concrete and inch me forward. I imagine I resemble more a half-dead worm than a killer serpent.

Just when I think I'm closing the distance toward freedom, the padded door swings open. It's over. My heart sinks and I let my eyes shut, resting my face on the cold floor, giving up. I don't fight the hands that grab me under my pits—I haven't got the energy. I've been caught before making it a foot from the edge of the metal bed and I can't do a thing about it, not even yell. A pathetic croak escapes my throat as whoever begins to drag and pull me.

"You said you could run, idiot!"

My heavy lids flutter open and I glance up, fighting back tears of joy when I see Jordan. I must be infected with Stockholm Syndrome because I hate this kid and I never thought I'd be happy to see him. He yanks me up, wraps his arm around my waist, and throws my arm behind his neck and over his shoulder. Hugging me to his hip, he hobbles with me out through the door. I manage a small smile of thanks, but he doesn't see. His eyes are darting around, scanning the hall, his face twisted in fear.

Once out of the white room, we run—Jordan runs and I try to contribute by bending my knees—down an all-white corridor. When we skirt around the corner, the decor switches abruptly from heavenly white to rocky hell. Gone are the white, sterile padded walls; we're now running in near darkness through a tunnel of rugged rock. A string of naked bulbs hangs from a chain above our heads, illuminating only a few feet at a time. Jordan drags me along as if I'm a corpse who can't feel my toes grinding into rock. I swear my nails have filed off: stones are now cutting in under the meat. I don't doubt that we're leaving a trail of my blood like bread crumbs for someone to follow and I helplessly try to lift my feet. I might as well be a dead body. Keeping up the pace is impossible and I'm on the verge of tears when, at last, the kid throws me into a hole in the stone wall and climbs in behind me.

Jordan shakes his head at my state, then grabs me by both arms and props me up against a jagged wall. Something cuts into my back but I don't care; it's a good distraction from my throbbing toes. The kid's practically sitting on top of me in this cramped space suited for a person the size of a possum, not two grown men. I stink like a possum, though, and wish I had the energy to hold my breath so I wouldn't have to smell me and whatever the other odour is that's coming out of the walls. Instead, I'm panting as if I was the one expending all effort to lug Jordan to freedom and not the other way around.

"Where are we?" I ask.

"A cave."

"No shit, smartass. I mean geographically, where are we?"

"Abandoned copper mines, in Utah."

"*Copper mines? Utah?*"

"Shhh!"

Now that I know where we are, logic tells me the dank odour mixing with my stink is copper from the sweating walls; nonetheless, I taste blood when I breathe it in and cough when it reaches my esophagus. Again Jordan shushes me and I stick my face inside my white cotton hospital gown. It doesn't do anything to muffle the fit, but it appeases him that I'm making an effort.

We huddle for a solid few minutes, and all the while Jordan watches me. He is waiting for me to gain strength. I manage to control my breathing and go to work on my legs, massaging them. The palms of my hands are pins and needles and my thighs feel like cardboard.

"One more minute," I whisper.

Jordan nods, but his expression says, *we don't have one more minute.* Then a loud blast, like an explosion, sends a tremble throughout, shaking the walls around us. Rock and dust sprinkle onto my face and lap.

"What was that?" I ask. The stunned horror on Jordan's face tells me he wasn't expecting it. Another blast goes off. "I thought you said this was an abandoned mine?"

"It is. I don't know what that was." I believe him. He's terrified.

Scuffling feet run past our hideout and he cusses under his breath a second before sirens go off, blaring in my ear. There must be a speaker right above our heads.

He stares hard at me, regaining his courage, and shouts, "We have to go!"

I shake my head. "I can't." I don't think Jordan hears me and I haven't got the strength to repeat it any louder, but the anguish on my face must say it all. He's chewing his cheek like he's recalculating.

He leans in to shout into my ear. "Change of plans. I'm going out there to help them look for you, get them off in the other direction. Don't go until you're able to run. As soon as you can, continue down the same hallway, go through the great room, and you'll eventually hit a parking lot. There's a dark blue car, licence plate 304ZEE. Get in the trunk and wait for me. There's a body in there—ignore him."

Should I care that I'm being asked to snuggle in the trunk with a dead body?

"304ZEE—got it?" he repeats.

I nod and he hands me car keys, instructing me to leave them in the ignition for him. He hops out of the hole, and then a second later, pops his head back in.

"And Marc?" he shouts. "It's a standard transmission. Don't try to drive it like you did on your last attempted escape. *Capiche?*" And he's gone.

I bonk the back of my head against rock, finally understanding why I couldn't start those cars. Standard transmission. Why hadn't Charlie taught me in one of those?

"Don't go until I'm able to run" is a terrible plan. I'll never be ready. So I go when I think I'm capable of walking, even if it's on a tilt while holding onto the cave walls for balance. It's the best chance I have of getting to that trunk. I emerge from the hole and the sirens are still blaring, only now they're bouncing inside my skull as well as off the walls. What's more troubling are the explosions, which seem to be getting closer. With each bang, bigger pieces of rock break off and hit me. I'm convinced the next explosion will have me buried alive under rocks and rubble, just like in my nightmare. I wish I could cover my ears but I need my hands to keep me upright. I squeeze my eyes into a squint as if that will help drown out the noise, but it only makes my head hurt in a different way.

I stumble like a drunk through the tunnel. It's like I'm on that turbulent plane again, bumping through a stormy sky, trying to keep my balance. Jordan said that eventually I'd hit a parking lot, but he didn't give me an idea of how long "eventually" would be and I'm regretting not waiting until I could run. My legs behave as if they're moving through sludge. I already need a break. And the explosions are messing with my equilibrium. When I notice a literal light at the end of the tunnel, I make a deal with myself: if I can make it to the light, then I can rest. Anyhow, it's not like I have a choice. It's either keep going or return to the hole I just climbed out of, get caught and strapped back down to a table, and then put to sleep like an animal.

In ten more excruciating baby steps, I reach the end of the hall and enter what must be the great room. The alarm is even louder in here, like I'm standing in the heart of it. I blink to adjust to the sudden change in light. My eyes survey a room the size of a royal family banquet hall as it comes into focus. How will I find the energy to get to the other side? This is no ordinary copper mine.

As I move further into the great room, I see the outline of large shelving units with stray books. My eyes are drawn upward, amazed at the height of the shelves, which extend to the rock ceiling—at least fifty feet, to never-never land. In front of me lies a long table stretching lengthwise with no end in sight, either. Artifacts are strewn on the table as if they were in the midst of being logged into the books beside them, before they were abandoned.

Just as I think I might take that rest I promised myself, to my horror, I hear yelling from inside this room, coming toward me, forcing me to back up. If they can be heard over the wailing sirens and booming, they're too close. My heart thumps in my ears, creating a bass drum to accompany the alarms.

I panic and turn back to the rock hallway, where there are nooks and crannies in the walls. I do my best to fit into one of them and disappear.

My weak knees bang together when I make out what's being said: "I'll check the parking lot; you check the labs! And what the fuck is that blasting?"

I don't recognize the voice. I close my eyes and pray for a miracle. I suck my gut in, desperate for the wall to swallow me, but I can't do anything about my feet, which jut out into the hall. Hell, my nose juts out into the hall and if I turn my face, my ears will. This is the worst hiding spot. I'd do just as well sitting in the centre of the hall dressed in a monkey costume, smashing cymbals together.

"Hi, Marc."

I peek at the speaker. He has eyes that protrude like a pug's and he's as little as a mosquito. I have to look down at him to meet his eyes. I'm sure he'd lose a fight against Minnie Mouse, and in any other physical state, I'd beat my way past him with ease. Today, I'd bet against myself, and I'm not a gambling man.

Mosquito man knows it because he smiles and uses just an index finger to hook me like a halibut by the collar, reeling me out of the crook in the wall.

I don't fight. I couldn't even if I tried. But I smile when over his shoulder, Jordan appears and throws a plastic bag over the mosquito man's head, pulls it taut around his little neck, and begins the dirty job of suffocating him.

"Run, for fuck's sake!" Jordan yells at me.

Finally, I do. I run.

CHAPTER 33 - GRACE

We've been at the truck stop an hour, sitting at a picnic table by a green patch for road trippers and truck drivers to stretch their legs, when Kay gets the text. She reads it aloud: "They sealed the exits, but not before a couple of cars slipped out." She looks across the table at me and delivers her opinion carefully. "That must mean everyone's trapped inside except for whoever was in those cars."

"So they don't know who was in the car?" I ask, my voice cracking. "They blasted the place without trying to find my son first? Or without the vial? These people don't give a damn what happens to my son—he could be trapped in there! We have to call for help!"

Kay and Charlie exchange a look and I completely lose it. "Stop looking at each other!" I shout at them. "Stop deciding whose turn it is to take care of me. I'm not a chore to be divided between you. And you," I lean across the table and narrow in on Kay. "You're my best friend. Stop behaving as if you share in Charlie's self-proclaimed responsibility to take care of me. Understood? Now call someone on that little phone of yours to let them know there are people trapped inside an abandoned mine."

"But we don't know which one?" Kay says.

"Just do it!" I slam my fists down on the picnic table, garnering some attention from the few people walking their dogs nearby. Then I get up to go grab my phone out of the van. Forget her. I'll do it myself.

"OK, OK. Calm down. Sit, I'll call." But before she makes the call, another text comes through. "Wait. She just messaged to say there was no sign of Jordan or Dr. Messie before they sealed the final exit. They assume that's who was in the cars."

"*Assume?*" I say through gritted teeth.

"Why don't I call her for clarification?" Kay offers and leaves the picnic table, walking away from us to make the call.

"Grace, I know you're upset, but logic says they wouldn't have blasted the place shut if they thought Dr. Messie was in there. They won't kill him without that vial. If they believe he and Jordan were the ones in either of the cars, we have no reason to doubt them."

"But Kay said they assume—"

"Kay's doing her best and you're being a jerk to her. She's just the messenger."

He's right. I take a deep breath and drop it.

When Kay returns, we apologize to each other. She apologizes for handling me like a child instead of a friend and promises to be on Team Grace from now on, giving Charlie a shrug. I apologize for snapping at her and for being a pain.

She bats a hand. "Water under the bridge. You're worried about Jordan, I get it." We give each other a best-friend bear hug before she dives into what Jessica said on the phone. "They did a full search of the place, sealing off one area at a time as they went, and for sure there was no Messie or Jordan inside. So she doesn't know if they were in those cars or not—she just knows they weren't in the mine. But she confirmed that there was some kind of room set up for a patient, like a lab of some sort, with high-tech monitoring stuff. Its use was likely for…" She pauses, glances at Charlie for approval.

"Human experiments." I finish her sentence. "Team Grace, remember?"

"On the bright side, they're not planning on letting those people die in there. They trapped them, but also called the authorities. Said everything in the mine should be enough to charge those people with a hundred different things. Maybe Jessica's crew isn't so bad."

This calms me down. A bit. "Maybe," I say. "What's next?"

"They're splitting back up to stake out all the usual places. She asked us to go directly to Dr. Messie's since we'll get there the fastest. They believe it's the most likely place where he or Jordan will turn up. Ethan is still there but without a vehicle."

After Jordan intercepted me at the casino, they've been banking on Dr. Messie's place, believing that Jordan wouldn't risk showing up somewhere he knows we know about. He has no reason to think we'd have Dr. Messie's home address, which is why one of Jessica's crew, Ethan, broke in and has been squatting there for days.

"Can I drive?" Kay asks as I follow her back to the van.

Charlie turns to throw her the keys, hesitates when he sees me behind her, shaking my head and mouthing, "No," but he replies, "Of course," and ultimately hands her the keys.

"Sorry," he whispers in my ear as I pass him to climb in the back, giving him the passenger seat.

CHAPTER 34 - MARC

Thankfully, the body I'm lying next to is wrapped in a giant black blanket so I'm not snuggling with it, though I'm tempted to. I'm wearing only a thin hospital gown and I think my teeth are going to chatter right out of my mouth. Knowing there's a rotting corpse beside me, combined with the bumpy ride, is enough to make my stomach seize. I manage to hold my barf until Jordan lets me out of the trunk after fifteen minutes, as he promised.

It feels like I've been at sea for weeks and as soon as I reach land, I'm on all fours—my bare ass in the air—retching. There's nothing in my stomach but bile and it burns like bleach, making me heave uncontrollably, coming up through my nostrils. After a good long fit, I manage to control it and catch my breath, my eyes watering. I give my head a shake. Everything is still foggy and I'm not satisfied that whatever they've drugged me with is gone. Determined, I stick my fingers down my throat and go at it again.

Once I've had a good enough bout, Jordan, who's standing over me, hands me a bottle labelled "spring water." Instantly cured of my Stockholm episode, I'm back to distrusting the kid and I look from the bottle to him.

"It's water, I promise," he tells me.

I take it but don't drink, just in case. Instead, I gargle, rinse, spit, repeat. It does taste like water, and it kills me to waste it instead of quenching my thirst. Before I'm tempted to swallow some, I pour the rest over my head. The sun is doing nothing to warm the air; it's cold out here. But I'm clammy and gross, and this is the next best thing to a real shower even if it brings on the shivers.

Jordan sets a backpack down in front of me. "Clothes," he says.

Eager to get out of the hospital gown, I dress without a word while taking in my surroundings. Even with blurry vision, I can see that I'm screwed. There's desert ahead of us, mountains behind us. Able or not, I'd have nowhere to run to.

"I hate to rush you, but someone'll be after us." Jordan walks over to the passenger side and opens the door for me.

I don't follow him.

"Marc, you're not my prisoner. You're free to leave. But you're safer with me than you are without me. Besides, we're five hours away from civilization."

Five *hours*? What other choice do I have? I ease into the front seat. There's a small care pack on the middle console, with snacks and more drinks, which he tells me to help myself to. Even if I wasn't worried they'd be laced with poison, my stomach isn't ready to accept one crumb.

I pay close attention to Jordan as he drives, amazed at how the car behaves each time he shifts the stick in the middle. He catches me watching and offers a meek smile. "I gotta say, you're tougher than I thought. And you look pretty good considering..." He clears his throat. "Those, uh, drugs you were on... They make you hyper focus."

I avert my gaze, catching on that I must be staring at him. Then a few minutes later, he says, "It's standard transmission. I can teach you?" and I realize I'm staring again. Fuck. If I had an ounce of wind in me, I'd spend it on teaching *him* a lesson by putting his face through the window.

"I understand if you don't want to talk..." He trails off and watches me from the corner of his eye. "Will you listen?"

Asshole! I want to scream at him for setting me up. I manage a grunting sound and a screwface. I say "go ahead" with my eyes. The truth is, I want to hear everything.

"I don't know how much you know about the history of life-travelling..." He pauses like he's expecting me to recite everything I know. "Before it was possible to travel to past lives, there was a way to watch snippets of it, like movie clips. Though, it often resembled more a nightmare on acid than a coherent clip." He pauses again, adjusts his grip on the steering wheel. "We were trying to make you recall Leo's life, to learn about the Halation. But with only today's technology, Dr. Messie and I had different ideas on how. He wanted to induce a code 33, which meant bringing you near death. For me, that was the last resort. I wanted to try things naturally—hypnosis, meditation—to induce a trance, not a near-death experience. I never should've gone along with him." Jordan peeks at me. I suppose that was an apology. "This whole project was mine. I'm the one who was trying to learn what I could about Leo. *Messie* worked for *me*, not the other way around. And you were supposed to be the answer to everything. I never thought he'd treat you like—"

"The others—dead, buried?" I ask, my voice coming out barely over a whisper. I'm desperate to ask questions, frustrated that I'm unable to form a complete sentence. I bet Dr. Messie was after much more than he let on. Because whenever Dr. Messie was alone with me, he only wanted to hear about my future life, not my past one.

I clear my throat and repeat my question, curiously recalling Dr. Messie's order to discard me in the desert like *the others*, which also makes it obvious to me that Jordan's confused—Dr. Messie is the one who is in charge.

Jordan sighs but doesn't answer me. I get the feeling he's telling me more than he thought he'd have to. He seems nervous—afraid, even.

"Dead guy in the trunk?" I ask.

"He's sedated, not dead."

I widen my eyes, waiting for an explanation. When none comes, I ask, "Little man, big eyes, plastic bag. You kill him?"

"I hope not."

"Answer me about the others."

He blows out a breath and rolls his shoulders. "They were at death's door and gave us their consent in exchange for compensation for their families."

"How do you justify killing people for compensa—" I cough and hack, almost bring up a lung with the effort of raising my voice. Jordan passes me an airsick bag and I smack it out of his hand.

It's amazing how people will find ways to justify almost anything. Dr. Messie discovered it was possible to travel to your past lives like a tourist, but when travelling to past lives caused people in the future to lose their souls—Metagenesis—he didn't stop; he tried to fix it. Then Grace made it worse by saving her son. And now her son, Jordan, is killing old people to fix her mistake. Even me, what I did because of Rachel.

"You know, I'm risking a lot by helping you. I'm as good as dead now that you're free. I'll have to hide and start all over again. All of you showing up here ruined everything. And you know what, Marc? I was the one keeping you alive in that copper mine. Dr. Messie would've killed you." He stresses this part like I should be grateful he didn't let his worker bees have their way with me after he baited me into their nest.

"Fuck you, kid."

A long time passes and neither of us speaks and eventually I fall asleep. I don't know how long I'm out for. When I wake, I finally eat a granola bar, throw up into the care pack, and I sleep some more. I repeat the pattern twice over. Sleeping is what has the most impact on my brain fog. Each time I wake, Jordan picks up where he left off, till I doze again. He tells me about the group that Grace, Charlie, and Kay joined. He explains where we're going; first to the storage room for a rainy-day bag of money, then to loot Dr. Messie's home for the same. He also tells me, "Then I'm going to meet with the guy who will get you home."

I sit up straight, feeling alert for the first time. "Home? You should've started with that."

He side-glances at me. "Home, home. Like, back to your wife."

My chest tightens and I stare at him.

He chews his bottom lip, then adds, "If that's what you want."

I've kept quiet about my life all this time, so I don't know why I suddenly admit it, and to Jordan of all people: "She wouldn't want me back."

He turns his head to look at me and we lock eyes for too long. He should be watching the road, not me. "I'm sorry." He sounds like he means it. "You were, uh, saying stuff while you were under.

I figured as much, but…" He stops then, saves me the shame of letting me in on how much he knows. "What about my mom?"

"I messed that up, too." I rest back in my seat.

"In more ways than you know," he mumbles. Then he tells me he left her a goodbye sticky note and signed it from me.

"A *sticky note?*" Shit. She must hate me.

Vegas appears in the distance, jutting out from the flat desert landscape, a spotlight from the pyramid hotel shooting up like a lighthouse guiding a spaceship to safety.

"So you're a rocket scientist?" I make small talk, for no reason other than to steer Jordan away from asking me anything else. I'm afraid I may answer honestly again, as if these drugs double as a truth serum.

"Hasn't done me a lot of good here." He shakes his head, disappointed in himself.

"So where does Dr. Messie live?" I ask to keep him talking.

"Heaven's Gate."

I laugh. "Holy shit, are you serious?"

"It's a gated community," he clarifies. "What's so funny?"

"No dogs allowed, right?" It hurts to laugh but there's no stopping now.

"I don't know. Why?"

"Do you believe in miracles, kid?"

He scrunches his face. "Huh?"

"Let me tell you what your problem is. You're suffering from a messiah complex. You think it's your job to cleanse the world from Dr. Messie's sins. But listen here, kid—you're gonna need more than a miracle if channelling Leo is the Halation's only hope. What you need is divine intervention, like in those Greek tragedies I used to suffer through—Deus Ex Machina!" I'm on a roll now, thinking myself a comedian. "Then again, a chariot could ascend from the sky with the word 'Halation' written on it and you wouldn't know what to do with it, you're so blinded by Dr. Messie."

"Marc, you're a dick."

"I'm not a dick, I'm Greek! You know, from former Greece? Or rather, I was…" I'm amazed at how easy it is to tell him something else about me as Cyrus and relieved that he doesn't

185

seem to already know it. Maybe while drugged, I didn't yell out as much as I thought I did. But again, I keep babbling out truths that I would rather keep to myself, and I realize the trick to me shutting up is to keep him answering questions.

"Hey kid, tell me something. You were trying to get me to remember Leo. What were you doing with the 'others'? What do those human experiments have to do with the Halation?"

"We weren't *experimenting* on humans."

I want to hurdle over the middle console and jam my fist in his ear, my playful mood gone out the window in an instant. "Yes, you were!" I point out the obvious by snapping my arm out straight and slapping two fingers at the bruised crook like an addict in search of a vein. "Inducing a code 33 is an experiment and I am a human!"

Jordan shifts gears in a way that makes a grinding sound, the car jerks, and the seat belt cuts into my collarbone. I swear he did that on purpose.

"They were practice subjects."

"Pardon?"

"As soon as I learned you were here, my lawyer organized volunteers to test out our methods of recalling past lives. They were from the palliative care home." He glances at me, swallows hard when he sees my expression of utter disgust.

"I'm having a heck of a time deciding if you're dumb or naive."

"Desperate," he admits. "For six years, the world's most qualified minds, including a few who came here from a time when Halation was still in its history, have been gathered here in Vegas. We've been trying to make heads or tails out of what little research Leo did. Those who came from a time when Halation was in its history, like me, didn't know the ins and outs of it, so it wasn't like we could've worked backward. And then you arrived and we saw an opportunity, and then… The majority decided that inducing a code 33 would be the quickest way to reach our end point."

"You weren't worried you'd kill me along the way, like those 'others'?"

"As I said, they were already at death's door. They were dying, frail, immune systems compromised. You were perfectly healthy. It should've worked."

"According to whom? Dr. Messie, your friendly neighbour-hood psychopath?"

He slams his hands on the steering wheel, the start of one of his temper tantrums. "I know. I know. I know! OK? I get it! But he is brilliant. I need him, and we usually work well together. Besides, what good would killing him do? He's not the first person to mess around with life-travelling, so why do you assume he'll be the last? Removing someone from a timeline doesn't mean you've removed their ideas. An imprint of them is left behind, like a ghost. And he never worked alone, so at any moment, anyone can pick up where he left off."

"Like who?"

He ignores my question, assuming it was rhetorical. It wasn't. I'm genuinely curious.

"Why not use him to get what I need?"

"He is the one using you, Jordan," I tell him calmly. By his expression, I can tell deep down he already knows he's another one of Dr. Messie's tools. I'm not bringing anything to light that Jordan hasn't already thought of. It's a moot point. But he is right that Dr. Messie never worked alone.

We pull onto a street and Jordan slams on the brakes. "Shit! Those people are still here."

"What people?"

"The ones who almost killed us all in the mines. I needed that cash." He curses over and over under his breath, before giving up and turning around, mumbling about how he thought for sure they would've abandoned this place in favour of the mine.

We pull onto a freeway. The kid looks nervous as hell. I only care because he suggested a way home for me and I hope the money had nothing to do with it. "So what now?" I ask.

"Take my chances at Heaven's Gate. Then make good on my promise and get you all home."

I ask him why he didn't loot Dr. Messie's place before breaking me out. He gives me some wishy-washy answer about not wanting to lead those people there since they've been on his tail.

"In other words, you were protecting him," I say.

He shakes his head, flexes his jaw, but he doesn't bite.

"And the Halation?" I ask because I am genuinely concerned. Despite how misguided he is, his intentions are good.

"Start over again."

"Thought you said you can't do anything without Dr. Messie?"

"Who do you think is in the trunk?"

CHAPTER 35 - GRACE

On the drive to Dr. Messie's house, I made it clear to Charlie and Kay that if given the chance, I would risk losing Dr. Messie to save my son from Jessica. But Jordan isn't making it easy if he won't even check in with Oscar, with whom Kay left the message to call us urgently.

When the three of us arrive at Dr. Messie's house, Kay switches places with Ethan inside. He wants fresh air and human contact, and she still has a bit of a tummy ache and prefers to be near a real toilet. A good hour or so later, Jessica and Sanjeet show up, but still no Dr. Messie. Jessica is disappointed but doesn't want to detour from the plan.

"This is a million-dollar home," she says. "My guess is Dr. Messie isn't going to simply abandon it. Where else would he and Jordan go?" Then she looks at me, as if reading my mind, but more likely because of what Kay must've said to her over the phone. "I will not harm one hair on your son's head without letting you all speak to him first." She assures me, promises me, swears on her life. But this is what I read between the lines: she will harm him, just not until after I've spoken to him to say my goodbyes.

We divide up, Jessica and Ethan go inside, and Sanjeet remains with Charlie and me in our van, parked down the street. It seems strategic, not leaving me and my brother alone. Charlie is in the front passenger seat and Sanjeet has taken the driver's seat. We all have binoculars and there's one walkie-talkie between us so we can chitter-chatter.

"I knew he was a germaphobe like Hitler, but wow," Kay comments. "He has hand-sanitizer dispensers at the entrance to every room of his own house, and I'm convinced his bathroom hand soap is medical grade. I swear I've washed off layers of skin." She also can't stop oohing and ahhing over Dr. Messie's toilet: "With all the sprays and nozzles and the warm air dryer, mamma mia." She moans and we all get a good chuckle. "It's like a spa for my under-parts."

As the day turns to night, the banter between us and the household stops, and we're beginning to feel like we are at another dead end. With Sanjeet in the van, it's impossible to strategize with my brother about how to warn Jordan without spooking Dr. Messie away. Other than the occasional "pass me a cookie," the three of us barely speak. There isn't even music to entertain us, since the radio is broken.

So after a particularly long silence in the van, Charlie and I jolt up as if tasered when Sanjeet lets out a gasp.

"That's him!" he declares as he glances from his binoculars to a note in his hand, and then points at a blue car entering the gated community.

"How do you know? I can't make out the passengers through the tinted windows. It's too dark," Charlie says, squinting through his binoculars.

"That's one of the cars from the mines," he says, waving his list at us. "We noted all the plate numbers."

Sanjeet speaks into the walkie-talkie: "Incoming. Make like a turtle."

"Ten-four," Jessica's crackled-up voice responds a second later.

We all collectively hold our breaths and wait in near silence. The only noise is the tippy-tappy of Charlie typing out a text message. He's alerting those sitting outside Morgan's law office (Sanchez is leading that crew), those sitting outside Jordan's condo (Batista's team), and Sunny's group, who are in the parking lot across from Adalia's nursing home. We're so close to catching Dr. Messie that pre-victory is pumping through my veins and making my hands tremble, so it's a good thing Charlie's in charge of the texting. Besides, my shaky fingers are occupied: they're playing with the vial in my pocket like a leprechaun with a nugget of gold.

After the longest fifteen minutes of my life, the walkie-talkie chirps back to life. Jessica comes through. "It's not Messie. It's Jordan."

We all release a breath like a bunch of balloons deflating.

"Alone?" Sanjeet asks.

"Affirmative."

"And?"

"He ran in, emptied that safe we couldn't open, the one in the master bedroom, then left. Should be coming back out any second."

"Do you want us to intercept?" asks Sanjeet.

"Negative. He might warn Dr. Messie. Can't risk it."

"What should we do?"

I can't help my eye-roll. This man is Jessica's puppet. He never makes a decision without her first yanking his strings left and right. He's much younger than her, and he obeys her like he's her child, his personality fitting her bossy nature like a glove.

"Pursue Jordan," Jessica instructs.

"Ten-four," Sanjeet, the puppet, replies.

Sanjeet keeps a few cars between us and Jordan. We drive and drive for hours in silence. Between my anxiousness over Jordan and excitement at finding Messie, I don't know how it's possible, but somehow, I rest my eyes and fall half asleep.

I allow myself to have one of those dreams I love: the kind where you know you're dreaming and can control your actions and influence the actions of your co-stars. Dr. Messie is trapped in a glass room at the back of a plane, only we didn't give him the foggy drink. So when the floor shatters away from his feet, he's going to plummet and splat-land on concrete like a bug on a windshield. The best part is that he knows it. His palms are spread against the walls and he's stammering a plea for his life while we all look in on him: me, Charlie, Jessica, Sanjeet, and Amy. I even allowed Batista and jerk-face Sanchez into my dream.

Where's Kay? Oh, there she is—wearing one of those curled white wigs and a judge's black robe, lacy frills around the collar. She's holding a gavel and proclaiming Dr. Messie "Guilty! Guilty!

Guilt*yyyy*!" She drags out the final judgment call while swinging the gavel up and down like a lumberjack would an axe to a tree. I let out a wicked laugh as she does it, but then she gets this crazy look in her eye. She starts shouting, "Feed him! Feed him!"

This is where the dream becomes confusing, the way dreams do. Ethan and the others join in and chant like brainwashed cult members: "Feed him! Feed him!" Pitchforks appear in their hands and they're stomping them and their feet in unison. "Feed him!"

"Feed him what?" I ask. I'm sinking deeper into dreamland, where I can control what I do, but not my co-conspirators. They're taking over the scene and aren't listening to my subconscious demands.

"Where's Sanjeet?" I ask Jessica but she ignores me.

She's holding a giant metal t-bar with strings, pulling at it this way and that way, her attention focused on Dr. Messie. "Feed him!"

Suddenly realizing I no longer hear Dr. Messie's pleading, I look back at him. He's still behind the glass, but now leather straps are binding him into an electric chair. There's a wet sponge tied atop his head and water dribbles from it, down from his hairline, and seeps into the two black holes under his brows. Why's he so quiet? And where are his eyes? Oh no. A wave of nausea washes over me when it dawns on me that he isn't speaking on account of the fried eyeballs stuffed into his mouth. Sanjeet is beside him, large pliers in his hand, strings tied to his arms and legs.

"Stop!" I plead. Why aren't they listening to me? "This isn't what I wanted."

At Jessica's command, the strings move Sanjeet's arms and legs. "Pluck him apart and feed him! Feed him! Feed him!"

"*No*!" I scream, my stomach in my throat.

Sanjeet secures the pliers around Dr. Messie's fingers, who's writhing in the metal seat and gagging on his own body parts.

"Stop! Please stop!" The yelling is pointless. I can't be heard over the crowd that has suddenly grown into a village behind Jessica's main crew. I hear a loud crunch coming from the glass room. Has the floor shattered away? No such luck. A few of Dr. Messie's fingers are now hanging out of his mouth and I watch in horror as Sanjeet snaps the rest off, one by one—crunch, crack, pop. Then Sanjeet starts offering to feed me the extra fingers, his hands reaching to me, strings tangling with my hair.

"Get off me! Get away!" I squeeze my eyes shut, cover my ears with my hands, but when I do, Dr. Messie's fingers find their way into my mouth. I gag and rip them out and each time I succeed, a new one takes its place.

"Isn't this what you wanted, Gracie?" Charlie asks from right beside me.

When I turn to tell Charlie, no, this isn't what I wanted, a young Adalia, dressed in a neatly pressed white pantsuit, is there instead of him. She leans in and whispers in my ear, "Be kind."

"Wake up, Grace!" I shriek my name, spitting rotting body parts out of my mouth, my teeth falling out as I do it. "Wake up!"

"Gracie!" Charlie grabs my thigh, shakes me good and hard, right out of my dream and back into the van.

My eyes dart around like a wild animal in a cramped cage. Cold sweat is running down my spine, my temples are throbbing and I'm panting. Then I swear on my life I feel a tickle in my ear and I hear Adalia's whisper reaching for me from dreamland—*be kind*. I scrub the itch away and shudder.

"Gracie, you all right?" Charlie asks. He's staring at me through the middle console and Sanjeet eyes me in the rear-view.

"Bad dream," I say and take Charlie up on his offer of a fresh bottle of water. I chug. What the hell am I going to do when we find Dr. Messie? I can't kill him, and it seems I'm not OK with anyone else doing it, either.

"Is that the radio?" I ask, noticing a rhythmic thudding. "Could you turn it down some? I've got a headache." I squint and massage my temples.

"Radio's broken," Sanjeet reminds me.

"Where's that music coming from?" I look out the window, suddenly realizing we're not in a city anymore. We're out in the desert on a two-lane road with no streetlights. The cars on the opposite side lower their high beams as they approach, a country road courtesy we learned from the last time we were in Vegas. How long did I sleep? The clock under the broken radio reads three-thirty in the morning.

"It's the festival," Charlie calls out from the front.

"Are you sure you're still behind the right car?" I question, sliding my bum to the edge of my seat for a better view.

"Yes, ma'am," Sanjeet replies.

"Jordan's going to a party?" I ask.

No one answers. Instead, they tell me we're almost out of gas, driving on fumes, and we have been for a long while. The other concern is that the closer we get to the strobe lights and sound of electronic music, the thicker the traffic becomes. There are more than just a few cars between us and Jordan now—it couldn't be helped.

When at last Jordan pulls into one of the parking areas, the attendant closes the gate after him, and declares the lot full with an orange sign that matches the bright crisscross on her vest. We watch as Jordan's car drives away, far away.

There's no time to think. If we don't react, we'll lose him.

"Stop the van. I'm getting out," I say and slide the back door open. Charlie jumps out as well, leaving Sanjeet in the van.

"I'll text you when I park!" Sanjeet shouts behind us.

My brother and I run to catch up to Jordan's car in the parking lot. It's not a proper lot, it's a field of dust lined with parked cars. At least it's lit enough to spot the back of Jordan's head getting lost in a crowd.

CHAPTER 36 - GRACE

At nearly four in the morning, this music festival is still pumping, so it's easy to hide among the attendees but just as easy to lose Jordan. Charlie and I carefully balance remaining a safe distance to keep an eye on Jordan with not letting the crowd get too thick between us. It helps that Jordan doesn't fit in. I overheard someone call this festival an all-night rave and he's dressed neatly in dark jeans and a black bomber jacket. Normally, someone in plain clothes wouldn't stand out, but against the backdrop of these sparkly clothed ravers, Jordan-spotting isn't so bad. Every so often we're separated by mobs of girls in glittery outfits and guys sporting colourful headpieces that look to me like clown wigs, but then ordinary-Jordan reappears.

After an hour of following Jordan, weaving around crowds, Charlie checks his phone and reports that Sanjeet has finally found parking in a far-away lot. "What should I tell Sanjeet?" he asks.

"It's a zoo in here. It's better if he waits, I guess?" I shrug. "What the hell is Jordan doing here?" I wonder out loud.

Charlie and I exchange a wary look. He has dark circles under his red-rimmed eyes, reminding me he hasn't slept. I, at least, had a nightmarish snooze in the van.

"Beats me, Gracie."

Jordan hasn't partaken in any festivities, hasn't stopped for a drink, and doesn't seem to be enjoying himself. Other than stopping to ask one of the promoters for directions, he also hasn't met up with or spoken to anyone. My stomach started speaking when we walked past food stalls with mouth-watering aromas of smoked meat and burned sugar. Apples and cookies haven't been cutting it. We've passed bandshells with thousands of dancing drunks singing off key and now we're in the amusement park area with an enormous lit-up Ferris wheel as the centrepiece.

Someone screams from above and I duck and shield myself, expecting a human to fall on my head. Charlie pulls me close to protect me, out of habit. I look up through my fingers and see a giant swing ride in motion. Feet dangle, some with no shoes. It's freezing out here—how can they be barefoot? An argument breaks out. From what I can gather, someone spilled their drink on the screamer. When I turn my attention back to Jordan, he's gone. I've lost him.

"Shit! Where'd he go?" Charlie says.

Correction—*we* have lost him.

Charlie stands in the same spot, scanning the area while I run through the crowd in the general direction Jordan seemed to be heading. Nothing.

"Damn it!" I scream out, stomping my feet in the dust and grabbing fistfuls of my curls. "*Where is he?*"

Someone taps me on my shoulder. "Hay girrrl," she says, or he says, I'm not sure. "Your beau went that way." A long, curled, sparkly fingernail points to a red-brick building behind the swings. Eyes with long, multicoloured lashes look me up and down. I guess I stand out by not standing out as well.

"Thank you!" I squeal, Kay-style, and I almost hug the tall, brown, beautiful stranger.

"One love!" they say and give me a peace sign. "Let me know if you need a hand with him, he's sweet." Long lashes wink, shimmery pink on the lids.

I laugh. "You'll be the first to know," I reply with a playful smile. I wave Charlie over, jumping on my tiptoes.

No one would guess we were falling to pieces from fatigue by the speed at which we run toward our target. A barbed-wire fence encloses the building, giving it a small dirt yard. It looks like a prison yard and doesn't appear to be part of the festival. No one is on the other side of the fence and the gate is padlocked. A rusted sign warns *Employees only*. How did Jordan get in?

"There, he must've crawled under," Charlie says, pointing at a breach in the fence. He grabs my arm. "Wait here, I'll check it out."

I twist out of his grip and go.

"Gracie," he hisses my name like an adult warning a four-year-old that the stove is hot.

I look around to make sure no one is paying attention before snaking on my belly under the fence. Charlie huffs, curses, and then follows.

Inside, remnants of an indoor event space under refurbishment are illuminated by fluorescent lighting. It's a big exhibition area with vacant vendor spots on one side and tarps as far as the eye can see, on the other. Either the walls have been taken down to the cement, or industrial is the look they're going for. Sounds echo. It seems Jordan came here to meet with someone—we hear faint voices escalating from the other end of the building.

I know one of the voices is Jordan's because we followed him here, but we're too far to recognize the other. We can't make out what they're saying, either, which makes our snooping expedition pointless. My heart hammers against my chest, paranoid about being seen and messing up another opportunity. I'm sure he doesn't suspect we're here, but we remain as cautious as a couple of cat burglars as we tiptoe run toward the voices. Or at least, we try to.

As we get close enough to identify Jordan's voice one hundred percent, my foot snags on something—a wire?—and I tumble over. The fall isn't my worry. It's the loud clang that follows from whatever is attached to the wire. I share the horror on Charlie's face as he grabs me, pulls me to my feet, and then we slide behind a cement pillar. The voices stop as abruptly as my breathing. Other than my pounding heart, there isn't a sound to be heard. Doesn't this place have a fan, an air-conditioner, anything to mask my mistake? If we were able to hear Jordan, then he just heard us.

CHAPTER 37 - GRACE

I don't know what that clang was; some sort of tool, I assume. Charlie and I stand behind the cement pillar, mimicking its still-ness for a good while, as we wait to see if Jordan will investigate the source of the noise. He was shouting at someone but paused, as if expecting the noise to repeat, or for someone to interrupt. Finally, and to our relief, whoever Jordan must've been shouting at did something to refocus his attention.

"Where do you think you're going? Stop!" he shouts.

"Why are you doing this?" someone replies.

Charlie and I exchange puzzled looks. Neither of us recognizes the other voice. But it's a man's, and there's a whine to it, like he's pleading. Who is it? Tucked behind this pillar, we can hear, but we can't see. Realizing we might need help, I mouth to Charlie, "*Text Sanjeet*," and he nods.

"I have no choice!" says Jordan.

"You do! Just walk away—it's not too late," the man replies.

"I can't do that."

"Yes you can. Disappear as I have. Please, leave us alone."

"You have to go back!" Jordan shouts so loud his voice shakes.

"I can't! Please, I've started a life, a family. You can do the same!" I can feel terror in the man's tone.

"I'm sorry," Jordan says more calmly. Then I hear a woman crying. Someone else is there.

"No! No! No! Please!" the man begs. "All right, I'll go. OK? Just, just, let my wife get back to our kids, please. It's me Dr.

Messie wants to punish. I'm the one who betrayed him." Who the hell is he arguing with? Wife and kids? Jordan is punishing someone for betraying Dr. Messie?

"Remind me, where will you be and when? Say it!" Jordan demands.

I crawl around the corner to peek, my brother at my heels. I clench my fists—damn it, I still can't see. There's another cement post a few feet away. We should run over and tuck in behind it to get a better view, but I'm afraid to move and be seen. Charlie mustn't be because he darts out in front of me and goes for it. *Damn it!*

"I'll be there, I promise. Meet me at the shuttle with the others who need to go back, no fuss. My family is innocent," the man says.

"Spell it out for me, Eddie! Where? *Where?*"

Eddie? I know an Eddie. I make eye contact with Charlie; he's terrified and confused.

"I want to make sure you haven't forgotten the location like you've forgotten your loyalty to your job," Jordan says.

I make a run for it, to join Charlie at the other post, and crouch down. My heart pounds hard in my ears. I wait a few seconds before talking myself into taking a peek. What I see astonishes me and explains Charlie's expression—but he doesn't know the young couple the way I do. They're on their knees. Jordan's back is to us, but I clearly see Eddie, dressed in a security guard uniform, with his arm around a crying woman's shoulders: Camilla, our waitress. They have kids, according to Eddie, innocent ones who should be freed. What is happening?

"You'll let me say bye to Charlie and Gracie first?" My hand flies to my mouth at the sound of our names and Charlie squeezes my arm. My brother calls me Gracie, just like Dad used to.

"I'm sorry, but your kids have to go home with you," Jordan says. His kids, *Charlie and Gracie?*

"What? Why?" Eddie asks.

"I'm sorry," Jordan says, his voice cracking. "Now, tell me where the damn shuttle leaves from, Eddie!"

Dad's name was Edward.

"Please, don't let Dr. Messie and his society dictate what you have to do." Eddie tries to reason. "Don't be a casualty of society! They're wrong, don't you see?"

My heart stops at this statement. I've heard it before, that exact phrasing about being a casualty of society. Dad told us that, on a car ride, the night before he hung himself.

"Mimi will take the kids back to New York. They'll disappear."

My dad proposed to my mom at the Statue of Liberty. He rarely spoke of my mom but when he did, he used his pet name for her, Mimi. I'd thought her name was Maria. Jesus Christ, I'm staring at my parents when they were a young couple. How can this be?

Jordan drops his hands to his side then, and that's when I see the gun in his right hand. My blood pressure goes through the roof. He must've been pointing it at Camilla and Eddie. Why?

"Your wife became a casualty the day she met you. Now I'm growing tired, Eddie. Where's the shuttle?" Jordan raises his gun again and aims it at Camilla.

"Bob's Future Skydiving! Midnight. Every Tuesday!" Eddie finally gives in.

"I'm sorry," Jordan says.

I suddenly understand, and so must Charlie. The realization cements me to my spot and propels Charlie from his.

Charlie bolts out and crashes into Jordan from behind, knocking him over. The two are a pile of arms and legs as they struggle for the gun. Terror grips me and I watch, helpless and frozen, a scream caught in my throat. Eddie and Camilla scramble to their feet, preparing to run, but then it goes off—the gun. *Crack!*

A red-black stain blooms in the centre of my mother's sunny yellow shirt. I go deaf a flash second after hearing my father's bloodcurdling scream. The crack rings and pulsates in my head, turning my vision fuzzy. But the sound doubles as a spark, igniting me like a live wire and launches me into action. I screech, clambering like a rabid animal toward Camilla, my mother; toward Eddie, my father. Then I spot the gun a few feet away from them and I make a split-second decision.

Jordan frees himself from Charlie long enough to see me swooping in for the gun. "Shit!" he shouts. He scrambles to his feet and dives for me, tackling me at my knees, and I'm down.

I yank one foot out from the bear grip he has around my calves and plant it hard on his face, kicking the expression of shock and terror right off of it. He tucks his chin down and clings tighter instead of releasing me, and I keep jamming my foot at his head until he does. Charlie is back on him then—where is the gun?—giving me the break I need to try to get to our parents.

When I see my mother, her face slack, her limbs flopped lifeless on the ground, a terrifying thought runs through my mind: is she going to make it? She *has* to, please! But I don't get anywhere near them. A hand cuffs my mouth and stifles my screams. An arm around my torso grabs me and pulls me into a warm body. It's not Charlie or Jordan. They're still on the ground, struggling again for the gun, which is just out of Jordan's reach.

I scream into the hand and squirm, trying to break free from the arm so I can be with my parents. I'm lifted off the ground and carried kicking backward. I struggle with the arm, try to wriggle my way out, desperate to be with my mother. A man is whispering in my ear but I can't hear what he's saying through the roaring ocean of confusion in my head. I'm being dragged backward away from the scene, through a hallway into another room entirely. No, don't take me away!

Lips in my ear shush me. I bite the hand on my mouth and it becomes firmer but doesn't let go. The thumb blocks the airway to my nose. Stars appear in my vision from lack of air. I don't stop fighting, I can't, I won't. But against my will and despite my best efforts, my body betrays me and weakens, my struggle slows. My heels scrape the floor as I'm dragged farther away, and the hand loosens a bit, allowing me to suck in air through fingers. Then I hear the voice that's whispering to me and realize it's Marc's.

"Shhh, it's OK, it's OK. You're safe. I got you," he breathes in my ear on repeat.

I go limp in Marc's arms until he loosens his hold enough for me to do what I need. I stomp my heel down hard on his foot, break free and flee.

My mother's still on the ground, my father huddled over her, and Charlie and Jordan are still grappling a few feet away from them.

Again Marc grabs at me. "Stop screaming. You'll scare the kids, please," he says, but it makes no sense to me. What kids?

"Let me go!" I shout. This time, I don't let his hand get over my mouth and I thrash, whipping my head around this way and that way. "Daddy!"

Marc's arm wraps around my neck and pulls, choking me so I can't scream again. Eddie, consumed by grief, either doesn't hear me or doesn't care. But Jordan does. He's managed to win the gun away from Charlie, who's slowly picking himself off the floor with a hand on his ribs. Even from this distance, I can see Jordan's features contort into shock when he glances over his shoulder at Camilla and he sees what he's done. When he looks back at me, I see him say "fuck" and he rakes his free hand over his head.

Marc drags me back down the hall. He's no longer trying to quiet me, it's too late for that, but he's still holding me so I can't run to Eddie. To get to him I'd have to get past Jordan, who is closing the gap between us, and who, with torment on his face, is aiming the barrel of his gun at my chest.

CHAPTER 38 - GRACE

Jordan rounds up Charlie and Eddie to join Marc and me. Whatever command he is screaming gets scrambled by the ringing in my ears. But his gun, swinging between our chests, directing us to keep moving, is loud and clear. I'm no longer struggling against Marc. My body has gone limp, my knees have buckled. His arm is around my back, under an armpit, and he half carries, half drags me backward, obeying Jordan. He manages to show Jordan his hands, awkwardly, under my pits, palms turned up.

Slowly, the fog in my head lifts and I hear Marc say, "Take it easy, kid. Take it easy." He's right beside me but it's like his voice is coming from Jupiter. My father's cries and incoherent mumbling are also coming from a million miles away, but he is right here, too, next to Charlie. Charlie is stone-cold silent, like me. Does he understand what's happened? I'm beginning to, but not how nor why. Why is my young father here in Vegas, 2006? In what capacity did he and Dr. Messie work together? And Jordan... did he mean to kill my mother? He brought the gun. He aimed it at her... Yes, I believe he meant to.

"Back up! To the office! Now!" Jordan demands. The hand holding the gun is shaking and his face is red under a layer of perspiration.

"Yes, OK, we're doing as you ask," Marc says, pulling me in closer to him, his lips brushing my ear. His tone is calm and controlled, betraying his steady heart pounding through his chest into my back.

We stop the backward walk at gunpoint when we reach a small security room. Jordan closes the door behind him, enclosing all five of us in the cramped quarters. Marc eases me down onto a low, creaky chair and gently moves my hair off my face. I watch my father as he immediately goes to a folded-out futon against one wall, and rifles through a pile of patterned blankets. I notice colourful ponies on one and race cars on another. They're not only child-like, but familiar. Above the futon mounted on the wall, multiple TVs are screening different areas of the festival in black and white: the fairgrounds, parking lots, food stalls, and inside of each building. One TV shows Camilla, alone, lying in a pool of her blood. My breath catches and I have to look away.

Eddie is done sifting through the blankets. Strangled in his grip is a floppy-limbed stuffed monkey wearing a yellow pointy hat. I've never seen that monkey before, but those blankets… the purple ponies were my favourite. Dad always brought us to work with him when we were little; that is, until Charlie was old enough to babysit me.

With a trembling chin, my dad begins to plead with Jordan, begs him to let him go find his family. "They need me," he whimpers, his gaze flickering to Charlie and me long enough to make me wonder if he knows that we're his family. Maybe that's why he hasn't bothered to ask who we are.

"Empty your pockets," Jordan says, forcing Eddie to hand over his cell phone, a giant ring full of keys, and a walkie-talkie, and then he lets him go. I'm filled with rage as Eddie profusely thanks his wife's killer on his way out, rambling repeated gratitude. I want to yell at him that he's making a fool of himself, to blame him for not doing enough to protect my mother, for leaving us years later when he commits suicide, for not explaining why he did… for being a coward. But I'm just like him, or worse, because I can't even speak.

"I know where the kids are," Charlie says once Eddie leaves, slicing the tension in the room. "They're hiding and he'll never find them without me. Let me go help." Bewildered, I look at my brother. He's staring tunnel-visioned at Jordan as if I'm not in the room.

Jordan hesitates but then says, "Keep your distance and don't touch them. You can't."

Charlie nods, understanding the cryptic warning, as do I. I didn't see them, but Marc and Charlie must have. There are children somewhere in this building—us—and it's dangerous to encounter yourself when life-travelling. But how does Charlie know where they're hiding?

"Leave your cell phone," Jordan tells him.

Rather than putting it down delicately, Charlie holds it up high above his head, then lets it drop. Pieces of it break off when it bangs onto the ground. He didn't beg when he asked to leave, nor does he express gratitude when he does.

Jordan demands that I also hand over my cell phone. My limbs are like jelly and I don't immediately obey, prompting Marc to crouch down to speak to me.

"It's OK, everything will be OK." He gently takes my phone out of my pocket and slides it on the floor toward Jordan. Then he places a steady hand on my numb ones, squeezes my fingers. Then to Jordan, he calmly says, "What's your plan, kid?"

"Why couldn't you just trust me?" Jordan shouts at Marc. His gun moves frantically back and forth between the two of us, and so does his yelling. "What the fuck are you and Charlie doing here?" Jordan directs at me, his voice breaking, then back at Marc: "And you—I told you to wait in the car!"

"I *was* waiting. But then I saw your mom and uncle, so I followed them."

"For God's sake, *why?*"

My mind is spinning in circles. Is he asking *me* why Charlie and I followed him, or is he asking Marc why *he* followed *us?* A wave of dizziness washes over me when what he said about the car sinks in. I bow my head, keep my eyes on my lap, and try to breathe through it. Marc was with Jordan, together in a car... I pull my hand away from his. I trust no one.

And though my throat feels like it's been subjected to a thousand paper cuts, I finally speak. My voice comes out in a low rasp. "I should've let you die."

"*What?*" Jordan says.

"Calm down. No need for anyone to get hurt," Marc says. He stands slowly, his hands out in front of him in the universal symbol for "we come in peace."

My eyes are still on my lap, but in my peripheral vision, I see Jordan looking at his hand as if he only now realizes he's holding a loaded gun. He lowers it to his side. "I'm not going to hurt you," he spits out as if disgusted that we think him capable of this. Then he looks at me; his eyes search my face like he's questioning if I really said what I said.

My heart has turned to stone.

I raise my gaze to fixate on Jordan and muster up the will to repeat it loud enough. I don't want him to have any doubts. "I should've let you die." Marc touches my shoulder. I shake him off. "Did you hear me? I should've let you *die*." I don't break eye contact with Jordan. I don't blink, I don't cry.

Jordan's brows knit together. "You're incredible," he replies in a low voice, shaking his head in awe. He draws an exasperated breath. "I presume you heard Eddie, which means you know where to catch the shuttle. Now that you got what you needed from me, go the fuck home, and don't ever come back," he says, his eyes brimming.

He looks at the TV screens. I don't know what he's looking for but whatever he sees satisfies him. He collects our discarded things into a bag—cell phones, walkie-talkie, keys—tucks his gun into his waistband, and then he leaves.

I watch as Jordan walks down the hall, thinking this will be the last time I ever see him. I hate myself for hating my child and a part of me is now dead because of it. My hatred bubbles over and I scream, "I should've let you die!" I take my shoe off and whip it at him. It smacks him in the back, then bounces off a wall and hits the floor.

Marc says something, but I don't hear what over the boiling rage in my ears. He tries to hold me back when I leap off my seat but I twist out of his grip. I grab whatever I can from the desk behind me: a stapler, a hole puncher, keyboard, pens, and start whipping them out of the room, hurling them at my son while screaming, "I should've let you die I should've let you die I should've let you die."

Jordan turns back, batting the flying objects away before they hit him, his face red as a hot pepper. "Why didn't you?" he screams back at me as he re-enters the office.

Marc places himself between Jordan and me, but we're not having it. I step to the side, and so does Jordan; we're almost nose to nose. Marc doesn't give up: his arms act like pliers prying the two of us apart.

"You're my son," I screech, pushing against Marc's arm. "I saved your life at the cost of millions of others and you thank me by murdering my mother? Why do you hate me?"

Jordan throws his head back and laughs. "Why do *I* hate *you*? *You* keep leaving me. You left me on my deathbed when I was nine. You came back in time for my recovery, then left again when I was eleven by setting that fire in the labs. You died," he shouts, then points to his burn scar. "Do you see this?" He slaps his face, leaving finger marks. "And then I come to Vegas looking for you, I tell you—warn you—about what would happen if you went ahead with Dr. Messie's stupid, faulty, ethically irresponsible plan, and you not only ignored my wishes and wasted my sacrifice, but you left me again! You had two days before catching that last shuttle. Why didn't you come find me? Didn't I deserve to know what you'd done in my name? Or at least say goodbye instead of leaving me to clean up your Halation mess? And now you're asking me why I hate you? You of all people should understand what it's like to be left by your parents."

Marc unsuccessfully tries again to get between us. "Calm down," he keeps saying.

"I left you so I could save you," I yell, shoving Marc aside.

Jordan grabs my wrist. His hand is hot and sweaty and he is trembling like a volcano.

"Let her go, kid." Marc's voice is stern as he guides Jordan back a foot or two with a firm push.

Before releasing me, Jordan shoves something into my hand, heavy and imbalanced. It's his gun. "If you want me dead, then do it," he growls.

Marc steps out of the way when he realizes what Jordan has given me. "Kid, I think you should leave," he warns, probably sensing that I might use it. Part of me wants to. I hear Jessica's voice in my head, reminding me that Dr. Messie didn't work alone. That someone worse could take his place. That his whole team must be eliminated.

"Pull the trigger and be done with me, Mom. It's what you really want, isn't it?" He clutches the barrel and pulls it to the centre of his chest. "Do it."

"Jordan, please," Marc says, then to me, "Grace?"

I clench the handle and he isn't letting go. Jordan digs the barrel between his ribs, ramming it over and over so hard I'm sure it's bruising. But it's my chest that aches. Rage and sorrow have gnawed at my heart for too long, and soon it'll eat what's left of my soul.

Marc places both of his hands on the gun, over Jordan's and my hands. "Kid, it's time to leave. Please. Go." He delicately peels Jordan's hand from mine.

Jordan doesn't object, but he takes the gun with him, tucking it back into his waistband. He leaves.

I allow Jordan enough time for a head start, so I can follow him again without being seen. As dead as I feel, I haven't forgotten that I came here to find Dr. Messie and I'm not leaving until I do. But when I'm satisfied and ready to pursue Jordan, Marc closes us in the room and barricades the door.

"What the fuck are you doing?"

"Protecting you," he replies.

"Protecting me? Get out of my way!" I try to force him out of the way. When pushing and shoving have no effect, I kick his shins. It's no use. Marc's a brick wall. I glower at him and he reaches a hand out to soothe me. I slap it away and rise to my tippy toes so I can yell in his face. "Never. Touch. Me. Again."

He puts both hands out in front of him, palms out. "I—I'm sorry, I didn't mean to…" He trails off.

I examine him from head to toe. He looks like death—sacs under his eyes, his complexion pale—but he's dressed like he belongs on the cover of a fashion magazine. I don't recognize the clothes—was he out on a shopping spree? Starting a new life as a Vegas party guy with his new friend, Jordan? He even looks like he's lost a few pounds. Is he on a diet or party drugs?

"Where have you been?" I ask.

He bites his lip.

"Never mind," I say, remembering that I don't give a shit. "I need to catch up to Jordan before he leaves. I don't need or want your protection. Move out of my way."

"He's not going anywhere," Marc takes a set of keys out of his pocket, "without these." Then he nods to the TVs. "Besides, he's heading to the wrong parking lot."

I scan the TVs until I spot the right one. Jordan's car is in lot 17, not 7, where he is heading. The signage he's following has been painted over, making it look like a 17, so it's an easy mistake if you're flustered, one I won't make now that I see the error. The TV screens are labelled correctly.

"Let me out, Marc. I have to find Dr. Messie. I have to, or everything, all of this, you, me, Leo, everything I've done and sacrificed... I *killed*..." My voice cracks. "...And it will be for nothing."

He chews his lip, thinking far too long and far too hard. "You don't need to follow Jordan to find Dr. Messie." He holds the car keys out to me. "You just need to get to his car before he does. Check the trunk."

CHAPTER 39 - MARC

I regret it now. Like an idiot, I stepped aside and opened the door for Grace. Based on the way she eyed Jordan's car keys, as if they were a hit of her favourite drug and she an addict, I knew she wouldn't leave without them. I put on my most sincere expression when I explained I was going to give her the keys. "Before I do, I just want you to know I'm doing this as a sign of trust. I'm on your side," I assured her, keeping my eyes wide and innocent.

She screwed her face up in a way that'd make you think I'd admitted to wanking off on public buses in my spare time. Then, as if by magic, she breezed past me and snatched the keys out of my hand so fast I didn't even feel it.

Now I've been following Grace, hoping we'll beat Jordan to his car, but also afraid that when we reach it, I'll have to fight my way into it. I tread a few feet behind, weaving through the crowd to keep up. The festival is a whole different vibe now that the sun is rising. The crowd looks hungover and over-partied, but subdued and happy. Guys with bloodshot eyes stand alongside ladies with smudged makeup and watch the sunrise. I don't know how they can ignore the grounds littered with empty liquor bottles, cigarette butts, shiny condom rappers, and hairpieces. Some party this was.

When I declined Jordan's offer (begging) to drop me off at the Four Seasons, where he'd booked me a room, he told me we were going to an all-night rave. He said, "The man who can get you home is freelancing there tonight." I don't know why, but I thought he meant a DJ. By the time we got there, I was cranky and pissed off at myself—why hadn't I gone to the Four Seasons?—so I didn't give a shit as to why the kid didn't want me to go with him to meet some DJ. Besides, there was the little problem of the body in the trunk. Jordan did inject Dr. Messie with I-don't-know-what right after letting him out to take a whiz in a corner of his garage. Dr. Messie was having the sleep of the dead in the trunk. Still, the kid asked me to stand guard and wait in the car, and I stupidly agreed. Now I know it was because he didn't want me to get in the way.

If I had known that my way back to Rachel was to kill Grace and Charlie's mother... If I hadn't been concerned about only me... I hate myself right now. Things couldn't have gone worse if Satan himself had planned them.

My body has yet to recover and every so often, I'm hit with a dizzy spell. One hits me now, and I bump into a couple.

They glower at me and I get a warning from the smaller one. "Watch where you're going, buddy."

I offer the apologetic smile-and-nod, bumping into another couple in the process. *Shit.*

"Grace, slow down," I call out, keeping the whine out of my voice. In response, she doubles her speed like we're playing the opposite game. We're almost at the parking lot—thank my lucky stars—but I don't have it in me to fight her for the keys, so I try another make-nice approach. "I'm sorry about Camilla."

"Sure, Marc. Whatever," she shouts over her shoulder.

"I care about you, Grace. I'll answer any question you have," I say, hoping this will be my golden ticket into the car. She's always wanted to learn about me, and I'm finally ready to tell her. I know this is not the best time, but when will it ever be? In addition to giving her my truth, I believe she should know about where I've been and why. Does she know about the Halation? The kid yelled something about it at her back there and she didn't flinch.

Grace stops walking, turns around to face me, and lets me catch up to her. I'm so grateful I could kiss her feet. "You care about me, you just don't love me," she says as calm as I've ever seen her, like it's no big deal and she's relieved. "Listen, Marc. You're off the hook. We're done, and if I never see you again, I'm OK with that."

"Grace, I'm sorry."

"For *what?*" she asks, the real her almost cracking through the cold façade, but then she shakes her head. "I gotta pee." She leaves me to enter the ladies' side of a trailer of portable washrooms.

I wait.

And wait.

I pace back and forth, kicking up dirt and cussing at myself, my stomach in knots. I replay the moments before it all went to hell. As Charlie was running out from behind the pillar, he glanced back. I thought he'd spotted me. But when I looked back too, I saw them: a boy and a girl with the tightest curls you've ever seen. The boy looked to be about four or five, the girl was maybe two. She had a thumb in her mouth and was clinging to her brother who stood tall, partly shielding her. The struggle brought my attention back to what was happening and I had to make a decision: protect those children or join Charlie. I swear I turned away only long enough to blink, but when I looked for the children, they were gone.

I like Charlie. Maybe that's why I sided with him, doing what he would've wanted: dragging Grace away to protect her. But I should've jumped in to help Charlie instead. I could've saved Camilla.

I smack my head with both hands when that damn dizziness runs its course through my system. *Not now!* I might pass out, the stress is doing me in, so I stop pacing to lean my hands on my knees and slow my breaths.

A chubby redhead leaving the bathroom trailer bumps into me, nearly knocking me over, and offers a weak apology.

"Stupid cow," I mutter under my breath at her back, prompting her to spin around and glare at me. She wears a multicoloured sweatband across her forehead, her mascara is smudged, and there's yellow-black gunk in the corner of her eyes. I try not to recoil.

"Well, that explains it," she says with a smirk as recognition crosses her face. "No wonder she left your sorry-ass."

"What?" I snap up.

Her grin widens and she takes great pleasure in telling me, "Your missus went out the back door a long while ago."

"Shit!"

I rush past her as she calls out a sarcastic "good luck." I take the stairs into the bathroom trailer two at a time, and bust open the door. It slams against the wall, startling the few ladies in front of the mirror. Grace couldn't have left. Please, *no*.

"Hey man! You can't go in there!" someone yells from behind.

"Grace!" I push each door and stick my head under the ones that don't open. Women yell at me, feet kick at me.

"Get out, pervert!" Someone swings a purse at me, it hits me square in the face. "Fuckin' pig!"

I shoulder-slam through the back door and perform a frantic search for Grace. No such luck. She's gone. I don't have a hope in hell of catching up to her. There goes my chance to smooth things over, and probably even my ride.

I leave the festival feeling defeated and so very stupid. As for Jordan's car? It's as gone as Grace is. I wait at least an hour, sort of hoping my kidnapper comes back for me so I have somewhere to go. When he doesn't, and I can't find a taxi (not that I have money to pay for one), I hitch a ride with a group of partygoers in their twenties: four hungover guys, and one pretty and also hungover girl who stares at me like I'm her next meal. I tell them where I'm heading and they look me up and down.

"Four Seasons? Wow, that's a real nice resort. What are you, some kinda big shot businessman?" asks the girl with a sideways grin.

I could tell her I'm suffering from an acute case of Stockholm Syndrome and beg them to take me someplace safe instead. But I imagine that that hotel has plush beds, room service, and showers with a hundred nozzles spouting glorious clean water.

"You don't look the type to be here," she adds, eyeing me from head to toe, then nods at my jeans. "Gucci?"

"You can have them if you take me to my hotel."

"Hop in, man, but it's a tight squeeze back there," says the driver. "And you can keep the pants."

The tight squeeze means I have to endure the three-hour ride with the flirty girl on my lap.

Minutes into the ride, the driver lights up something and passes it around to the other passengers. No one bothers to crack a window open and I'm OK with that. I recognize the calming aroma. No one talks. Music blares. Vi, the girl who keeps deliberately rubbing her ass on my lap with each bump in the road, takes a few puffs before offering it to me with a naughty glance. I grab it to take my mind off her swaying hips. Not only am I not interested, but I also don't want to be thrown out of the vehicle, since it's obvious by the way they call each other "snookums" that the driver is her boyfriend. So I suck in a few drags, then pass the joint back.

Another is lit after the first one makes a few more rounds. Under normal circumstances, I'd keep up. But I'm tired and still under the influence of Dr. Messie's poison, so I don't take any more, at least not directly. I still have to breathe while in the boxy little car. With each breath I take, the music slows and the lyrics disappear. Is it me or is that tune stuck on repeat? I feel like an infant unable to hold the weight of my head, so I rest it back. I can't even gather the strength to close my mouth. Vi shuffles and grins at me, seemingly pleased and misreading the reason why I'm cock-eyed and drooling. My heavy eyelids surrender as she blows smoke in my face. I might choke on my saliva and should cough but I haven't the energy.

We arrive at the Four Seasons and a cloud of smoke follows me out of the car. Fresh air strikes my face and when I stand, the high swarms me, travels through my body and rushes to my head so I'm floating. How the hell I make my way through the lobby then up to the room is a blur. I vaguely recall passing Jordan on my way to doing a faceplant onto the bed. The little energy I have left is spent on raising my head just enough to turn it to the side, to prevent the pillow from smothering me.

"Marc! You came back. Thank you, thank you, thank you. Please tell me you have my car?"

"Mmm?"

"Did you take it? Say yes, please."

I let out a sound that's supposed to be a laugh. He knows damn well I don't know how to drive his car.

"This is important—holy fuck, answer me."

Answer him? Ha! I'm too busy trying to keep my eyes from rolling back in my head like marbles.

"Marc? What's wrong with you?" I hear him ask. And then moments later, "Dad? You OK?"

"Ya, ya, kid," I say with the last bit of breath in me, and then pass out.

CHAPTER 40 - GRACE

I drive until Jordan's GPS brings me to an acceptable truck stop so I can check the trunk. By acceptable, I mean someplace where I won't call attention to myself, far from the festival and void of people because I'm driving a stolen car. I still can't believe I did it. Not wanting to give Jordan (or Marc) time to catch up, when I reached the car, I hopped in without a second thought. I hee-hawed a big *"thank-you-Jessica"* when I realized it was stick shift, threw it into first gear, and then hightailed it out of there.

As soon as Marc had said I could find Dr. Messie with what-ever was in the trunk, every other worry slid off my shoulders, leaving me light on my toes like I'd previously been balancing a basket of rocks on my head. I imagine a treasure map with a giant red X marking the spot to Dr. Messie's secret lair. I'll deliver it to Jessica, drop it on her doorstep for her to find Dr. Messie and feed him his eyeballs. I'll have to watch, of course, to know that it's been done. I want him dead. That hasn't changed. Then I'll run for the shuttle. Because in the end, I want nothing more than to get back to my son in the future, who is still nine years old. Things don't have to be this way...

I should be in the early stages of post-traumatic stress disorder after witnessing my mother's death at the hands of my son, but my mind is doing that thing it always does: focuses on the less impor-tant thing to distract me—nine-year-old Jordan, in this case. Something inside me believes I can change today's outcome by raising him differently. It's like I've been given a crystal ball, so instead of torturing myself over what has happened, I'm banking on the chance to change the future. Or would it be the past?

But first things first: find Dr. Messie and stop-stop him. It's finally time to see what gift awaits me. My eager fingers feel around the dash and sides of my seat for a lever to pop the trunk. When they find none, I jump out, clutching the key, happy as a birthday girl, and practically skip to the back of the car. I jam the key in and jiggle until it unlatches.

"Holy fucking shit!" I scream at the top of my lungs. I slam the lid and leap back, stumbling over my feet and land flat on my ass. I rise and brush off my backside, looking around, afraid someone saw my gift—I mean, *prisoner*—wrapped in a blanket.

By the state of the truck stop, I'm not surprised there's only one other car here. I assume it belongs to the wholesome-looking family wearing sensible shoes, trying to open the door to the building and discovering it's closed, just like the big sign says it is. I thought the main point of a twenty-four-hour truck stop (as per the bigger sign) was twenty-four-hour convenience. It's early in the morning, but not *that* early.

Suddenly parched, I crack open a bottle of water that was in the front seat, and I pace along the back of the car. Oh, the state of the car... candy wrappers, half-eaten fruit, and a hospital gown in the backseat. What was *that* about? And I had to drive with the windows open because of a stale urine odour. I make an ick-face when I think of it. And when I think about my gift, and what Jessica will do to it—to *him*... My heart is slamming against my chest, thump-thump-thumping in my ears. Is it from disgust? Excitement? Wait, is that thumping from my heart, or is it...? *Crap!* It's coming from the trunk.

"Stop kicking, you piece of shit!" I shout to the trunk and slap the hood. The father of the family going back to their car gives me a look of distaste. When I'm satisfied he's shaking his head because he's appalled at my language and not because I'm yelling at a possible something alive that is kicking in my trunk, I offer an excuse. "I forgot my umbrella." It's the first thing that comes to my mind and makes zero sense, I know.

He steers away a young boy looking in my direction as they head back to their car. "Darn rain," I add, half laughing. It hasn't started raining yet and I know I look crazy, but I can't stop myself from slapping the car and yapping, trying to cover up Dr. Messie's kicking. "It's sure gonna come down! When it rains it pours, they say!" Slap, slap.

I put on a show of strolling to the driver's side and easing into the front seat. Revving the engine is a good sound buffer, and I swear Dr. Messie kicks harder when I do it. I squeal out of the lot, and gravel spits up and dings the car. In the rear-view, I see the family collectively shaking their heads. So long as they weren't writing down my plate number, I don't give a good damn.

For twenty minutes I drive, sticking to more deserted roads. I want to avoid people and cars and law enforcement. I beg the rain to start so it can cover up the ruckus coming from the back. I need gas but can't risk stopping for it. Dr. Messie has been kicking the whole time and with each thwack, my blood heats a degree closer to its boiling point. In my rear-view, the seat bucks one too many times and I've had enough. That last kick just about broke through the backseat.

I jerk the wheel to the right, skid off the road, and slam on the brakes, swinging the door open before the car comes to a complete stop.

Seconds later, I'm at the back, glaring down at him. "Stop it!"

He's wearing his usual white attire, and it's filthy. His back is to me. Somehow he's unwrapped himself out of the blanket and twisted his big body around so he can better position himself to pummel away at the seat from behind. It's come loose; there's a gap at the top, letting in light. Another few kicks and the seat would likely be right down, giving him access to crawl through and fight me for his freedom.

He's trying to talk, his voice muffled by duct tape. I reach over and yank the gag off his mouth. I cringe at the flecks of his skin glued to the tape, then frantically hop around and shake it off my fingertips, afraid of catching the cooties.

"I need the washroom, Grace!" he yells.

"Shouldn't you be begging for your life instead of a bathroom break?"

"Please, Grace?" he whines and begins the tricky process of flipping himself over.

"You know I'm going to kill you, right?" I say, mostly to remind myself he must die. It's a much different feeling to know you want someone dead when you're eye to eye.

When he flops over to face me, I'm sickened over the pieces of skin that tore off with the tape; my stomach turns, knowing I did that—and what's wrong with his neck? But I'm also surprised to see how old he is. He's not the same Dr. Messie I remember. He looks a good ten to fifteen years older. He also has a nasty gash over his eye. Dried blood is crusted into his eyebrow. When he swings his feet over the side, I jolt back and am disgusted with myself for how nervous I am at his proximity to me. He's tied at the wrists and ankles, but I don't have a weapon and by the time it hits me that I would have to put my hands on him to force him to stay in the trunk, he's already out.

Dr. Messie hobbles and then trips over his feet, which are strapped together by a belt; his own, I presume. His jeans are loose and he has to hold them up while he awkwardly gets back up and shuffles to the other side of the car for privacy. With his back to me, he relieves himself. I turn away, squeeze my eyes shut, and shove my fingers in my ears to drown out the sound of piss hitting dust. I'm gagging. How am I going to watch him die if I can't even endure urine sounds?

When he's done, he totters back and leans against the side of the car. He won't look at me, but I can't stop looking at him. It's amazing how much smaller he seems, his shoulders slumped and his cheeks sunken. His hair is thinner than when I last knew him. How *old* is he? He's still overweight, but somehow deflated like a balloon without enough air, and his skin is dried out like leather in the sun.

The rain starts and neither of us moves even though we're in the middle of nowhere. But I need gas, I'm getting wet, and he has to die. Why didn't I call Kay from that truck stop?

"Get back in the trunk."

"No."

"Get back in the trunk," I command, gritting my teeth.

"No," he repeats and finally glares at me, his eyes defiant and his lips pursed, determined to retain some dignity. The rain comes down harder, pelting his face, and he doesn't shield himself. His blood-crusted brows dampen and pink droplets coat his eyelashes. He blinks them away.

"Fine. Have it your way," I say and go around the opposite side of the car to avoid crossing paths with him. I'll just drive off and leave him here. Maybe I'll run him over with the car and be done with it. Wait! I have to inject the serum into him first. So I'll just hit him with the car to disable him, and then stab him with the vial before he succumbs to his injuries.

I get back in the car and so does he—in the backseat.

"Oh no you don't!" I threaten into the rear-view. My voice cracks. "Get out!"

"*No!*" And then he bends over out of my view.

Instantly I realize what the clinking sound is. He's undoing the buckle of the belt looped around his feet now that he has room. That belt could be taut around my neck in a few short seconds. A rage-filled fear comes over me.

I'm back out of the vehicle at his door, whipping it open and grabbing him by his collar, dragging him out of the car. He lands with a thud on his ass, knocking me backward, my legs momentarily trapped underneath him. He's still messing with the belt and I break free and kick him in the head repeatedly. His hands are still tied together, but his feet are now loose, and I wrestle and tug the belt out of his grip. He's disoriented from the blows to his head. I take advantage and pounce on top of him.

"You son of a bitch!" I scream like a crazed maniac, spittle flying out of my mouth. My hands are around his neck before I can think about what I'm doing.

Everything he has done, the things he has made me do, the life I should've had, Jordan, my mother: these are what motivate me to squeeze. Things crush under my thumbs and his face reddens. Red lines zigzag the whites of his eyes. His arms and hands try to push me off, desperate, but all my weight is on his throat, squashing it.

His legs flail behind me, but to my bitter frustration, I can't do it! I can't take his life.

"AHHHH!" I screech and spring off him.

My vision is blurry, the vein in my temple bursting from a hatred I've never experienced. I want to rip my hair out, to punish me for my fear and weakness. Instead, I rise and begin horsewhipping him with his belt, lashing at him, screaming my fear in the form of red-hot rage. I crack the belt with fury and each time the strap connects to his flesh, I feel a worse kind of better.

And so I beat harder and faster until I'm lashing so fiercely my arms could spin out of their sockets, like propellers. Blood and rain splash with each hit, staining his shirt a deep blood brown. I whip and whip with madness and glee until he curls into the fetal position and I can no longer breathe from the cardio of it. I collapse, panting with exertion. The rain is coming down hard now and I swear there's steam evaporating off the top of my head.

I'm instantly hit with strange guilt over how good it felt to whip a super-old someone to within an inch of his life. And that's the other problem. The bastard still has an inch of life left. He is still breathing.

"Why won't you die?" I cry-scream, but what I want to know is, why can't I just kill him?

I crawl over to him. He's shielding his face with his forearms and doesn't fight me as I strap the belt around his already-tied wrists. I should stab him with the syringe right now, tie him to the bumper, and drag him until he's dead. I should beat or choke him until he's dead. *I should make him dead.* But I can't kill again.

"Get in the trunk," I say breathlessly, but not yet defeated. This present is more suited to Jessica. I'm re-gifting it.

CHAPTER 41 - GRACE

Dr. Messie refuses to get back into the trunk and I can't make him. He keeps bitching that he isn't feeling well, like I'm supposed to care. But he knows I'm not going to leave without him. So the only way to get him to cooperate is to give him something in return. Hence, I let him sit behind the front passenger seat and fix my mirror on him. To ease my paranoia, I loop the belt from around his wrists up through the ceiling grab handle. He sits with his arms uncomfortably raised over his head, but he doesn't argue with me. Other than asking me to crack open a window, complaining that he's hot, he doesn't say much of anything. The rain has stopped but it's overcast and cool, so screw him and his hot flash.

About an hour into the ride, he clues in to the location on the GPS, sits up tall, and breaks the silence. "Are you taking me to that group?"

I glance in the rear-view at him and he waits like he thinks I'll respond.

"You're taking quite the circuitous route," he adds with a raised eyebrow. He's right. It's after eleven, broad daylight, and so as to not call attention to the man tied up in the backseat of my stolen car, I've stuck to back desert roads. I find it weird that he not only knows the best route to get to Jessica's but, given what the group's mission is, it's weirder that he hasn't done anything about it.

"Operation Messie," he says with a dry, cocky laugh.

Now I get it. He's been confident they'll never succeed.

He stares in the mirror at me and I do my best to ignore him. His face is red and covered in sweat, though it isn't as beaten up as the rest of him; he did a good job of shielding it. But his bloody forearms with exposed flesh are hard to look at. I think that's why he let me tie his arms up like that, so I can see what I've done. Every so often he shifts around, forcing me to look at him and see the damage I inflicted. And his neck: whatever was wrong with it before has been exacerbated by my failed attempt to strangle the life out of him; there are indentations from my rings in it, or worse—maybe nail marks? I shudder at the thought of his skin under my nails, and immediately start picking them clean over the steering wheel.

"Imagine that—a whole group named after me. Like followers. Christianity started like that."

Did he just compare himself to Jesus Christ? I shake my head.

"Where's your—" His face breaks into a spasm, his upper lip and cheek contract and relax like a rubber band, and fresh sweat dribbles down from his hairline. I remember that he had a habit of dabbing off his forehead. This face-twitch must be a nervous tic in the absence of his precious white handkerchief. "Where's *your* group, Grace? Why are you all alone? Where are your followers?" Another pause while his face muscles jerk. "Grace's apocalypse." Again, he lets out that sarcastic laugh.

I narrow my eyes at him. What is he insinuating?

"Oh, you didn't think I knew about that?" He smirks, carrying on the one-sided conversation, and wrongly assumes I know what he's talking about. "Or didn't Jordan tell you who Leo was about to become?"

I crank the fan to the highest so it's harder to hear him.

"I'm a scientist like your son," he says, raising his voice. "I came back here with good intentions: to help Jordan with Leo's research to save the Halation." A drop of blood appears under his nostril and he twitches his nose, scrunches his face. "For God's sake, Grace. Lower the window! I can't breathe."

I turn on the radio instead. "Can't hear you!" I shout, exaggerated.

Dr. Messie says something else and I turn the radio up as he does. I point to my ears and shrug. He shouts louder in response and I still hear nothing. I force a smile, but inside, dread bubbles into panic as what he said finally burns into my mind like hot lava. Back at the festival, Jordan screamed about fixing my mess. Mid-tantrum, he blurted something about the Halation, but his words didn't register. Until now. The name Leonardo Abruzzo hits me like a steel-toed boot in the gut, leaving me so winded that I'm the one who can't breathe. I feel like I've lost a contest to Dr. Messie when I have to crack open the window for much-needed air. Grace's apocalypse? Adalia was not insane. *The world is ending, ice and fire*, she said. She's been speaking a truth no one has bothered to decipher. She knew everything, from Dr. Messie to Leo. The answer to Jordan's obsession has been right under our noses.

I grip the steering wheel with such force, my knuckles go white. The music is blaring, the window is down, and the fan has been on full blast for a long while. But not long enough. Just as I feared, we run out of gas.

I slam my hands onto the dashboard and cuss under my breath. The GPS says we still have another forty-five miles until we arrive at our destination. The radio is giving me a headache and hasn't drowned out the discussion in my head, but as soon as I turn it off, Dr. Messie speaks.

"I tried to warn you, Grace. Blasting the fan like that drains fuel." His wet face twitches into a smug smile. I don't know how he's still sweating.

I snap the GPS out of its holder and get out of the car, then pop the trunk and look for something resembling a weapon. I grab a tire iron and give the tool a good whack in my hand. That'll do. I come around to his side and open the door. His bloodshot eyes make me shudder, and when I reach over to untie the belt from the coat hook, he flinches. Seems neither of us can tolerate the other.

"What are you going to do, Grace?"

"Get out. We're walking the rest of the way."

"Have you gone mad?" he protests.

I hold the door open, refuse to budge on the matter. Left with a choice between a beating in the face with my metal bar and co-operating, he obeys. But of course, we won't hike forty-five miles. We'll stop when we hit a gas station.

We stick to the shoulder and I fret someone will notice the car we abandoned, catch up to us, and offer a ride. I have a weapon in one hand and Dr. Messie's belt in the other, using it to pull him along. How would I explain the man on a leash? But for that to happen, we'd need a vehicle to pass us, and none have. We're really out in the middle of nowhere and I'm relieved, but also worried the gas station on my GPS is as real as a mirage in the desert, and we'll arrive only to find it boarded up and abandoned.

Dr. Messie's been mostly quiet, complaining here and there about his sore legs, and as soon as the sun breaks free from the dark clouds, he complains of a headache. The twitching seems to have gotten worse, and his face and neck are swollen, his cheeks red as tomatoes. But I don't care about his comfort and refuse to stop for a break until I'm good and ready. We walk until *my* feet ache, until *I'm* sweating from the blazing midday sun, until *I* wish for a passing vehicle to flag down, even if it'd mean explaining my prisoner.

We sit under a small tree, facing each other. I examine the GPS to distract myself from having to look at him while he refuses to look away from me. I hate to admit that he's making me self-conscious.

"That guilt gnawing at you, it makes you hesitant to embrace even the smallest pleasures, doesn't it?" He pauses, measuring my expression like he's expecting even a slight change—*dream on, Messie.* "You're punishing yourself, aren't you, Grace? It's why you—" Face spasm, twitch, twitch. "It's why you always end up alone. Even those closest to you, whom you nurtured and loved…"

He trails off and at first I think he's still waiting for me to reply, but when I steal a glimpse at him, I decide he isn't even talking to me or about me. His eyes are downcast and he's picking hard at the cuticle around his thumb. He's talking to himself.

"If you're smart enough, you distance yourself before any damage is done. Of course there are the ones who slip past your defences, and you believe they're worth the risk, so you let them; you embrace it, even, hoping this time will be different. But they betray you in the end. It's comes with the part, unfortunately." His thumb starts to bleed and he leaves it, then looks back up at me.

I keep a solid stone face and study the GPS like I'm cramming for an exam.

"I know how you feel, Grace, and I can tell you from experience, the best antidote for guilt is the passage of time. This will pass. All things do."

Dr. Messie talks less when we're walking, so I'm eager to get moving again. According to the GPS, we've made it four miles. Frustration sets in. We're only halfway to the gas station and it's unrealistic that we will make it there and back on foot. What was I thinking?

"Grace, I'm not a stupid man, I'm aware of what people think of me, but Metagenesis was an accident. I felt deep guilt when I realized the repercussions of my research, and my team and I worked diligently to rectify the problem. That's how it all began. We weren't trying to harm people—we were trying to save them. And we were this close." He uses his index fingers to show me what an inch looks like. "I always knew there would be a butterfly effect should someone important be killed; I just didn't think…" He throws his head back and laughs. "The inventor of the Halation? What are the odds?"

"Shut up," I whisper through my teeth, feeling that gut punch again.

It's impossible to ignore him when he's the only sound in the desert for what looks like miles in all directions. Even the wind has stopped blowing. And why is he saying "we"? *He* was the only one responsible for Metagenesis.

"What is it, Grace? Do I remind you of yourself? You weren't trying to hurt anyone when you killed Leo. You were trying to save Jordan. And now here you are, back to fix your mistake, out of guilt. What year were you trying to land in, by the way? Please, I'm curious. You know, it became impossible to travel to a time before Leo's death. And Jordan, he's a good boy. Smart, but not smart enough to create the Halation by himself. He needs me, always has."

I push buttons on the GPS, resisting the urge to throw it at Dr. Messie's head. I need the GPS. It's my only lifeline since my *good boy* took my cell phone.

"You shouldn't play with that device. It'll run out of battery as the car did fuel. Maybe this time you'll heed my warning, Grace."

Each time he says my name, I want to reach into his mouth and rip out his tongue.

I lean forward and force myself to lock eyes with him. "Just so we're clear," I say through gritted teeth, "I'm not buying your good-intention fiction. You have no redeeming qualities. You're a psychopath. I'm delivering you to that cult and I don't care what they do with you. My son is a scientist, as you pointed out, and my guess is he's a better one than you. The fact that you were in the trunk of his car like a load of garbage tells me he no longer needed your services. I have faith that he will fix what you call my mistake but we both know is yours." I give him an evil little smile. "There's a gas station four miles up the road, according to this icon. But if we head that way," I point to the open desert behind him, "we'll cut our time in half. Let's go, Messie."

CHAPTER 42 - MARC

When I open my eyes, Jordan is shaking me awake with one hand and holding a bottle of water in the other. What's his urgency?

"Marc?" he says with puppy eyes, then takes a seat beside me.

My mouth is dry like I fell asleep licking salt off a dried-up sea floor. My body is desperate for a glass of water, a drop of water, anything. Hell, I'd suck on a sandcastle because that would have more moisture than my mouth can produce.

I stretch across and snatch the bottle out of Jordan's hands and before even sitting up, I slurp it back greedily, squeezing the bottle to siphon the liquid into my mouth faster. The curtains are drawn, but through the crack it's daylight.

"What time is it?" I could sleep another hundred years.

"Noon. I gave you a solid five hours."

I prop myself up and look down. I'm fully clothed on top of the bed, shoes on. The memory of what Grace said to me earlier is crystal clear: "we're done and I'm OK with that," though not much more. I remember where I am but not how I got here. I look at Jordan and he bows his head, eyes to the ground.

"I still can't believe you made Grace think I left her. With a note." My voice comes out sounding like a chain smoker.

Jordan shrugs.

"I guess telling her the truth—that you kidnapped and almost killed me—would be awkward?"

"About as awkward as you telling her that your future wife hates your guts." He keeps his head down but leaves the snark in his tone.

I want to punch him for throwing it in my face: the one personal thing I willingly shared with him. "You're a little prick," I shoot back at him and then cough and cough. I make like a gorilla and pound a fist on my cramped chest to loosen phlegm, dislodging my lungs from my windpipe.

"Dr. Messie was in the trunk of my car. Do you know where it is or not?"

"Not." *Cough cough.*

He slumps in his chair. He looks so dejected that I feel a little sorry for him.

"If he isn't dead already, he will be soon," I say when I catch my breath. "I gave Grace the keys to your car. You're welcome."

"You did *what?*"

"Kid, you keep telling yourself you need Dr. Messie. Can't you see he's brainwashed you into thinking that without him, you're too stupid to figure out the Halation?"

"I'm a rocket scientist, not an environmentalist. And if I can't tap into your more intelligent past lives, he's got me by my balls."

I thump my head on the wall behind me. Tap into my *past* lives. What a joke. All that experiment did was bring me back to my *next* life. I don't need a shuttle to take me home—just pump me full of drugs and I'll relive my failures in my head, thank you very much. The thought of the shuttle unlocks the part of my brain that was blocking out what happened at the festival. I look at him. "The reason we know where the shuttle to go home is... I ran into Grace because I followed her and Charlie to that building where... You shot Camilla."

Jordan drops his head in his hands, his elbows on his knees. If I didn't think he was a heartless asshole, I'd swear he was crying.

"It was an accident. Will you hear me out?" His voice is muffled, but I can tell he's choking back dragon tears.

"Ya, kid. I'll hear you out." He's not the only one in need of a second chance.

CHAPTER 43 - GRACE

Once we abandon the shoulder for our two-mile desert hike, it becomes clear that Dr. Messie is not the outdoor type. At one point, we have to wade through tall grass and his voice comes out shaky and high pitched when he says we could run into hidden snakes. I agree, which is why I make him take the lead.

"What if I get bit, Grace?" he whines as he takes longer strides on his tiptoes to decrease the odds.

"If only I could be so lucky," I murmur. What a relief it would be if he just died all on his own.

The longer we walk, the more I honestly think he *could* keel over and die. His pace slows down to a snail's, his face gets puffier, and he develops a rash on his neck where I strangled him, like he's sensitive to my costume jewellery. At first, I'm delighted. I picture myself returning Adalia's carved stone and reporting to her that her brother died of natural causes. But when he starts to wheeze, it makes me remember Walt, how he must've gasped for air while Metagenesis ripped his soul from his body in his final days, alone. Yes, it'd be easier if Dr. Messie died naturally, but it wouldn't be fair to Jessica. She wants to face the man responsible for her son's death, and I believe she's earned it. I'll have to let Dr. Messie rest if Jessica is to get her chance. Besides, when it comes down to it, I'd rather his death be on her hands, not mine. And so, as soon as the gas station is in sight, I decide to go it alone. I find a tree and use Dr. Messie's belt to tie his hands around a low branch, and leave him. I bet he's wishing he never wore a belt.

The first thing I do at the gas station is look for a pay phone. Kay's number is the only one I know by heart, and the ideal scenario would be her coming to get me (and my prisoner), then I could abandon the stolen vehicle in the desert. I almost cry when I see the phone receiver dangling off its cable, broken. Knowing this is the only gas station for miles, I put on my Kay-inspired nice-face as I approach the counter to pay for a gas can, some energy bars, and a few bottles of water.

"May I please use your phone?" I ask the clerk who is propped up on a stool behind the counter, eating a bag of chips and flipping through a magazine. He's a chubby man, mid-fifties, balding. He wears an unbuttoned, faded plaid shirt cut off at the sleeves, and underneath that, he has on a thinned-out white undershirt, revealing perfect outlines of his nipples.

"Employees only," he responds without looking up from his magazine.

"Please, I've run out of gas. My car is miles away."

"I can call Triple A for ya."

"What's Triple A?" I guess that was a stupid question, based on the way he lifts his eyes to mine. "I mean, that won't be necessary," I say quickly, then dip my head down for maximum big-eye effect, and bat my lashes. "I can pay you for your phone."

He straightens his posture and looks awake for the first time. "How's about I give ya a lift?" He wags his eyebrows, completely over-reading my flirtation.

"HELL, NO!" I shout, repulsed. I don't want to pay the way he suggests, but my reaction is also about him noticing the old man tied to the tree.

"Well." He shrugs, brushing off the crumbs from his shirt and missing most of them. "Can't help ya, then. Phone is for employees only, and *you* ain't an em-ploy-ee."

So much for my Kay-inspired niceness. At least the attendant lets me buy the gross mop propped up in a bucket next to a wet floor sign. It's funny that the mop looks overused, yet it seems like the floor hasn't been washed since the time before time. The *Wet floor* sign isn't fooling anyone. I untwist the handle and discard the mop head in the bucket. The stick is to scare off potential snakes on our return hike.

From a distance, I notice Dr. Messie is slumped over, his head at a weird angle. I hope he's asleep and not dead. When I reach him, I gasp, unable to hide my shock at what I see, and he startles awake.

"That bad, huh?" he asks, squinting at me through swollen, purple eyelids.

It's true that I can't stand to look at him, to see what I've done. But that's not all that's making me squirm. His rash—which I no longer believe is from my rings or nails—has spread in all directions, and his neck is so swollen on the one side, his jawline is nonexistent. I try my best not to touch him as I untie the belt. All I can think is, what if he's contagious? and I scram as soon as the belt is loose enough for his hands to slip out.

He shakes his hands out, rubs them together, and tries to clench them, but his fingers won't bend. What is wrong with him? He licks his cracked lips, which are also purple, and watches the bottle of water in my hand. "I'll keep up better if I'm hydrated."

I throw my half-empty bottle at him. I not only miss, but it lands on the ground. He scrambles for it before the water drains but it's too late. I sigh and open another bottle, stepping barely close enough to hand it to him.

"Thank you, Grace. Why don't you take a rest before we head back?" he suggests, but the rest is for him, not me. Who is he kidding? He's in no shape to walk.

"Please, Grace. I still have much to tell you."

I hate how desperate he looks, how powerless. Sick or not, I know deep down he is manipulating me, trying to get me to feel for him so I'll change my mind. I wish it wasn't so obvious, so I could be more engaged, because God knows I am curious.

If we don't get moving, we'll never make it back before nightfall. Ever since Dr. Messie mentioned snakes, I haven't stopped thinking about Charlie's run-in with a scorpion when he camped out in the desert. The last thing I want is to be stuck out here in the dark, with no shelter from critters. But looking at my prisoner, what choice do I have? I cave and throw him an energy bar, then park myself two metres away from him.

Dr. Messie inhales the energy bar and a whole bottle of water before he inevitably breaks the silence. First, he complains again of a headache, says he thinks he has a fever and asks if I have any Tylenol. I honestly wish I did. I need him well enough to get going. But then he brings up my son, and my desire for him to hurry up and die comes back in a flash.

"If it's any consolation, I treated Jordan like a son after you died. I care deeply about what happens to him."

I don't know why he thinks this would bring me comfort. It infuriates me.

"He is *my* son," I seethe.

"He is. But that group doesn't care for him like you and I do. They are not going to spare him, Grace. All those years, I was the only one they were after: I kept Jordan out of it, safe, because I cared about him—can't you see that? When you exposed him, and I know you didn't mean to, it's as if you signed his death warrant. And if I'm not around to protect him… They believe anyone I work with is evil, and if they find him…" He lets the unfinished thoughts linger in the air while he sucks in a few deep breaths and rubs his arms. He's shivering. "Well, I must say, you were right about what you said," he admits and then chooses that moment to shut up.

I sigh, annoyed with my curiosity. What's the harm? "Right about what?"

"I didn't have good intentions in travelling back here."

I raise my eyebrows at him.

"I made a lot of enemies. You were just one of many families encouraged to participate in our clinical trials."

"No kidding?" I scoff.

"It's too bad about Walt. What a waste." He shakes his head as if Walt was a waste of time, not a human whose life ended because of Dr. Messie. "His mother chose not to save him," he says quietly, like it's an afterthought. I bet he's repeated this lie to himself often enough to believe it. I think he's done, but he's only pausing long enough to catch his breath and for his cheek to stop twitching. "I came here to hide, though I was aiming for another decade. No better place than Vegas to hide."

"Everyone keeps saying that," I mutter. And yet, they keep getting found: Camilla, Jordan, even Dr. Messie.

"Pardon me?"

"Nothing," I say. I shouldn't engage in a conversation with someone I'm conspiring to kill. I glance between my watch and the GPS, and I fret at the daylight slipping away and the distance left to go with a sick old man.

"I missed the eighties by a long shot," he continues. "I was stunned when I landed in the same spot you had just taken off from. Thank you for leaving me Leo's car, by the way. What I wouldn't do for one now..." He trails off.

I should shut up now that he has, but my curiosity gets the better of me. "Who were you hiding from? Why'd you run?" I ask and he gladly elaborates, satisfied that he's piqued my interest. I make a promise to myself that this is my last question.

"The first time I ran was because of Jordan. After he left, things began to unravel, information leaking. A mole. My assistant—"

"Adalia," I interject on her behalf, wanting him to acknowledge her by name.

"Yes, Adalia, my sister." He clears his throat. "She left a trail of bread crumbs leading suspicion in my direction, and Jordan picked up on it. I never liked the climate in Toronto, anyhow, so I relocated."

"To Vegas," I say.

"No, no. That came much, much later. Did you know you can travel to the future as well? Not just backward? But it's far more complicated, in every respect. Travelling ahead was where it all went wrong for me. I upset someone I considered a good friend. I asked him for a favour, but I may have gone about it the wrong way. He was going through a crisis, and instead of empathizing with his situation, I used it against him, demanded cooperation, pushed the boundaries of the truth for my selfish goal of—" He stops and stares at me.

I realize I have a smile on my face and I let out a chuckle. He's describing the actions of a textbook narcissist and doesn't even know it.

"What is it?" he asks, his face twitching again.

"Nothing. Carry on."

"You know, Grace, I'm telling you things I've not told a soul," he says with a hint of irritation. "Even Jordan. He knows little of my journey to get here, where or when I was just before my arrival, who I worked with."

I give him a "so what?" shrug.

He continues, reluctantly at first, defending himself by saying, "It's not like he didn't know what he was getting into." When I keep a straight face, he gets comfortable again and elaborates, telling me his so-called friend fled to another life after the disagreement, but not before exposing Dr. Messie, which left him no choice but to flee as well. "Were I in his spot, I'd have done the same. Lucky for me, his method of travel opened up portals that had been shut for decades, making my trip much smoother than his." He laughs at an irony I don't get. "That's when I came here. And I'm quite certain you would not like to hear more of that story."

I want to slap that smile off his face. I know he is hoping I'll ask him to tell me more.

"Anyhow, I came here to hide and start over. Simple as that. When I landed in 2006 instead of the 1980s, I was baffled and wanted to understand what had gone awry. The best person to answer this was someone with in-depth knowledge of Metagenesis: your son." He doesn't look at me when he says this. Instead, he stares down at his hands, flexes and shakes them, still trying to bring life back into his swollen, blueish fingers. "I searched for Jordan, though once I found him, I feared the reunion might not go well, given how we'd left things off, so I didn't approach him. It was he who came to me. He informed me about Leo and the Halation, enlisting my assistance. You see, each time someone is removed from the past, the future is modified. Sometimes the modifications are minimal, and other times not. In both circumstances, they go unnoticed by those living in the future. Having been in the future when Leo was removed, I had never heard of him or his earth-saving invention. To my recollection, the climate had been spiralling out of control since my childhood. Though we experienced long periods of reprieve, sometimes years at a time, it would inevitably revert to chaos. And so, Jordan and I had an opportunity to rewrite history. A good man he is, your son. He was willing to set our differences aside for the greater good. I did the same. I came here to hide as I said, but Jordan gave me a new purpose."

Something is missing from his logic, though, because I have no trouble remembering the Halation. And the weather had been crazy for weeks, not decades as he recalls it. We don't remember things the same way. Why? He glances at me now and I realize by his smile that I'm furrowing my brows, and I reset my face to neutral.

"It's because you were here when Leo was removed," he says. "That's why you remember the Halation. You're recalling an invention that will not be created unless—" He pauses, grinning at the shock on my face, then says, "No, I'm not a mind reader, Grace. I know you better than you think." He clears his throat before continuing. "You're recalling an invention that will not exist unless I rewrite history with my new partner, Jordan."

"And take credit for the invention of Halation as if it were your own?"

He laughs. "Touché. However, you are overreaching. I simply want to undo a wrong the only way I know how. Can you not relate to that?"

A few moments pass and I can't take his staring at me. It's like his eyes are boring into my mind, and he is indeed reading my most private, guilty thoughts. "You've been here a long time," I say, preferring he remains distracted.

"Yes, Grace. And I've changed, I'm rehabilitated. If you kill me, it will be out of revenge, for who I was then and not who I am now," he says, giving me his sales pitch at last.

It's interesting how he leaves out the human experiments he's been conducting. The missing seniors haven't come up once during the lead-up to his "let me go" speech. "I told you, I'm not killing you. What they do with you is their business. So long as they stab you with that syringe, I don't give a damn what happens."

He cocks his head.

"So you'll never be reincarnated again. Time isn't the antidote to my guilt. Justice is," I explain, enjoying the worried creases my words bring to his inflated face.

Now that I've dumped the news about his fate on him, he falls silent and expressionless, other than the occasional spasm. I wanted nothing more than to shut him up but now that I have, it worries me. I take it as a sign that he's given up trying to relate to me, being submissive, and admitting fault, which means he must be plotting his final effort: a hostile takeover.

CHAPTER 44 - MARC

Jordan has promised to confess all but says I smell skunky and insists I shower first. When I come out of the bathroom, there's a pile of clean clothes neatly folded on the bed and no sign of him. I recognize the outfit as another one of Jordan's. We have the same physique, so everything fits like a glove.

I find a resort pamphlet tucked into one of my shoes. The Four Seasons is secluded, the only resort for miles, according to the little map. I thought he was short on cash. Why'd he pick this paradise? One of the resort bars is circled on the pamphlet with a *Meet me here* scribbled next to it. This kid better be there with a stiff drink to take the edge off. I'm awake but I'm cranky.

I ride the elevator down and examine my reflection in the mirror. Jordan and I also have the same square jaw, cheekbones, and the same-shaped eyes, hazel in colour. Except for his hair, which he inherited from Grace's side, we could be brothers. No matter what I do or where I go, I will always be reminded of him when I look at myself in the mirror. But when I take the time to really focus on my eyes, I see each dot of amber, the shades of greens, and each tiny speckle of brown. They are identical in every detail to Leo's, and Cyrus's. Indistinguishable. My eyes staring back at me are the only things that connect me to my soul and ultimately remind me I existed, and I don't know how to feel about that. The more time I've spent as Marc, the less I want to be Cyrus.

I reach the bar and spot Jordan. He sits with his back to me and his shoulders hunched, in a booth in the far corner. I pause and take a deep breath before approaching, gathering energy and patience to deal with whatever he has to say. When I sit across from him, he signals the waiter and orders a carafe of coffee. His eyes are wet, the lids puffy. I don't think he got any sleep.

"I'm really sorry," he begins. A tissue is clutched in his hand and he nervously wipes his nose. Then he clears his throat and starts rambling some deep-thought bullshit, half of which my hungover brain has trouble grasping. "...Which means time is intertwined. It's not linear. It's an illusion and happens all at once. It isn't just the past that influences the future. The future also influences the past. They aren't independent from—"

I wince and massage my temples. "Cut to the main event, kid."

Jordan laughs suddenly. "Do you want to hear something funny?"

"Not really, but I bet you're gonna tell me." I can't imagine what he could be finding humour in right now and I frankly don't care. Where's that coffee?

He blurts it out, "My dad used to call me 'kid.' Did you know that?"

I open my mouth to say something, but can't think of what to say. I don't need to tell him that I didn't know. He can see it on my face.

He laughs again and fresh tears wet his eyes. He scrubs them away. "You can't know what's it's like to be an orphan for over a decade, then actually run into your parents again, only to have them crush the image you had painted of them as good, kind, loving people." He sobs, then adds, "I wish I'd never met you two again."

I'm speechless.

He gathers himself, discards his tissue on top of a small, snotty pile in the corner, then pulls another napkin from the dispenser on the table. A waiter comes by—*finally*—and drops off two glasses of water, coffee cups, and the beloved carafe of glorious coffee. Jordan thanks him with a nod. He gives me a minute to pour and sip the heavenly liquid and then retrieves a folded-up piece of paper from his pocket.

"Read this. It's the beginning," he says and slides it across to me with a stiff hand. His eyes say *go on, take it.*

I unfold the paper with care. It's a letter. The creases are nearly torn with age and it's so soft it no longer resembles paper. It's from Eddie. As I read, Jordan sits quietly, switching between fidgeting with his tissue and stabbing at the ice in his glass with a straw.

The letter is interesting, to say the least, and would shock Grace to the core, I'm sure. Her father was one of Dr. Messie's hitmen and it seems he didn't commit suicide. He must've pissed Dr. Messie off, because that's who was somehow responsible for Eddie's death, according to the letter. It's probably a good thing Grace arrived a minute too late, or she would've run into Eddie's killer. I reread the section I assume is the reason Jordan is showing it to me:

Dr. Messie sent someone back to find and retrieve me... He had the new hitman execute your mother right in front of me. He called her a casualty of society. I had a choice to come back to Toronto present-day with my children or to die with your mother in Las Vegas...

I fold the letter and look up at Jordan, who is watching and waiting for a reaction.

"This is why you did what you did to Camilla?" I don't want to use the words "kill" or "murder" or "shoot," afraid it will deter him from talking.

"I wanted Eddie to tell me the shuttle location and then I was going to let them both go, I swear." Jordan puts a hand over his heart, his wet eyes wide and innocent. "Eddie wouldn't disclose anything, acting like he had no idea what I was talking about, even after I showed him my gun. I had no intention of shooting anyone." His voice wavers and he pauses to control it. "It was a threat, nothing more. I was using the same words as whoever actually killed Camilla, so I could get what I needed from Eddie. I had an idea of when the shuttles would be, based on how old my mom and uncle were when they came to live in Toronto. That's how I figured there still had to be a way out of here. But then Charlie tackled me and the gun went off... and then Camilla..." He pulls out another napkin, blows his nose.

My heart breaks for Grace and Charlie. They believe so much of who they are is a result of Eddie's death. It must've been easier to blame him since he had been the only parent present in their lives. But it was the loss of their mother that shaped how Eddie raised them. And then there's Camilla... I never knew her, but she was an innocent bystander who never should've been mixed up with Eddie. But what's weird is, although it shouldn't, this explanation also makes me feel sorry for Jordan.

"Why didn't you say something when it happened?"

"What would've been the point?" His voice breaks into a sob as he says it.

I almost want to hug him. Almost. "You didn't intend for Camilla to die. It's a good point."

He laughs. "What I mean is, would anyone have believed me? I know what you all think of me." He hesitates, playing with his glass of water, his chin quivering. "And how would my uncle feel? If he hadn't jumped in, Camilla would still be... the gun never would've..."

Jordan lets the thought hang in the air. I am starting to understand him better. When I first met him, I never would've guessed he had any good conscience in him. But when he came to his senses, he helped me escape, and now he's protecting Charlie from lifelong guilt. Jordan's a rotten decision-maker, and he could use a little practice fixing his mistakes since he always seems to screw up, but somewhere beneath his roughness is someone who wants to do right.

"You know what makes me sick?" His voice cracks and he's wagging a finger at the letter, holding back new tears. "Eddie wrote his family's destiny. *He* did that. And like it or not, I carried it out. It's what I was trying to tell you—the future influences the past, too. History or fate or whatever it is, it repeats and plays out one way or another, because it's actually happening at the same time. This isn't how I wanted it. You gotta believe me." He searches my face like a child looking for validation from a parent.

"Kid, I wish you had trusted me from the start." I realize it's a stupid thing to say. If I was the one plotting to pretend-murder my grandmother, I wouldn't tell my dad about it either. Especially if I'd also kidnapped and performed near-death experiments on my dad, against his will.

"Trust you?" He says it as if the idea is absurd, leaning across the table and looking at my face like there's monkey shit on it.

"You mean the way my uncle trusted you with the 'one-minute mistake' and you spilled the beans in less than a day? Telling *me*, no less? You told *me*, the one person no one else trusted." He sits back and rips out more fresh napkins, emptying the dispenser. He scrubs his face with them, drying up tears that aren't there yet. "Shit, I'm only telling you now because I'm balls deep in trouble and don't have anyone left to turn to. I've even lost Dr. Messie." He half laughs, like losing Dr. Messie is the same as losing your stuffed teddy bear in a parking lot. "I'm all alone. I was hoping somewhere in that head of yours, in your soul—Leo, *Dad*, whoever you are would've been able to help me." He hiccups, and blows his nose.

"Cyrus," I say.

"What?"

"The 'whoever' I am," I say quietly. "No more secrets, kid."

He blows his nose, honking away, and murmurs a weak "nice to meet you."

I watch his face, study him to see if my name seems familiar to him, trying to gauge how much of myself I revealed while I was under. He appears clueless, thank God.

CHAPTER 45 - MARC

"If I promise not to kill you, will you stick around a bit and help me?" Jordan asks, then stammers, "I mean, I'll help you get home—if possible—whether or not you say yes. No obligation."

I top up my coffee and then narrow my eyes at him. "If possible?"

"No secrets, right?" he says, more to himself, then rolls his shoulders and meets my gaze. "You exist here and now but if the Halation is never created, the world will probably end before Cyrus is born. There may not be a world to go home to."

"You said you could help get me back to my life," I say, though oddly, I'm not entirely disappointed. It's nice having the decision made for me. I relax in my seat, studying my coffee cup as the idea sinks in. "Are you saying Cyrus, me, myself, and I never existed?"

"I'm sorry." He misreads my shocked relief for sadness. "But in a way, your memories of that life exist and are real. What you're remembering is a future that may never happen, like false memories; remnants of an old timeline, if that makes any sense. I'm sorry if you never get a chance to make things right with your wife... tell her bye—uh... or whatever."

I cringe. *Or whatever?* I wish he'd quit hinting at things I yelled while in a drug-induced coma. It's humiliating.

"So will you?"

"Will I what?"

"Stay a while, help me."

I set my coffee down and lean my elbows on the table. "Listen, kid. Even though I want to help you about as bad as I want to slam my dick in a door—" Jordan breaks out with genuine laughter, a rare occurrence. He's growing on me. "Even though I want to," I continue, "don't you realize all that stuff your people injected me with only brought me back to my future life, not my past ones?"

He nods hesitantly like he's embarrassed for me. I must've been wailing, begging and whimpering for my wife like a big loser. "It would be naturally this time," he says. "My way, and on your terms."

"Like voodoo or yoga or whatever?" I can't believe I'm considering it.

"I had something else in mind, but yes, along those lines," he says, watching me and holding his breath.

"Two conditions," I say and stick up two fingers like bunny ears. "One, you swear not to kill me." I lower my index finger, leaving the middle one upright and turning my hand so the gesture is aimed at Jordan. He laughs again, his face relaxing. "Two, if I change my mind at any moment, we part ways and you let me live, no questions asked."

Jordan reaches out his hand to me for a shake. "Agreed. Should I call you Cyrus?"

"I prefer you call me Marc," I tell him, as we shake on our terms. But Jordan doesn't seem to like my answer. "Uh... would you rather call me 'Dad'?" Please say no.

Jordan barks out a laugh. "Hell no!" Then he gets quiet and starts to fidget with his straw, his gaze fixed on the empty glass. "I don't mind you calling me 'kid' the way he used to, but I never liked you using his name. It doesn't sit well with me."

I consider what he says and can't say I blame him. Though I'm relieved he's permitted me to keep calling him "kid" (I don't think I'd be able to break the habit), I no longer want to be Cyrus. Finding out I can't get home may be a blessing in disguise and I want to rid myself of him like a snake sheds its skin.

Suddenly, Jordan's face lights up. "What if we chose new names? Those people will be after me, so I'll need a new identity if

I want to stay alive, anyway. I have a few connections and can have new documents made up. Would that be OK?"

My heart warms at the idea and I smile from cheek to cheek. "Sure, kid. You know what? I'll let you christen me with a new name. You choose."

He loves the idea and promises to give me the perfect name, then, rising from his seat, he tells me we should get moving.

"Are you going to tell me where we're going?"

"I'd rather show you. Part of the voodoo experience," he says, winking at me. He drops money to pay for our coffee with a very generous tip, then grabs his jacket. "You coming?"

Jordan didn't tell me where we were going. Well, he told me where, a town called Kayenta, just not the specific location, but he did say why (sort of). "Step one is to see if memories from your other life surface without prompting," he said. Whatever that means.

The taxi driver had refused to take us, saying it was too far. "You're better off renting a car. Ain't nobody gonna take you there," he added with an apologetic smile, forcing us to turn back to our resort.

Now we're waiting our turn in the front desk's rent-a-car line. There's a short wait, only one set of customers at the counter, a young couple. They wear matching white shirts with *Just married* scrolled across the back in silver cursive. She picks at her pale-pink nail polish while he signs on each X the rental employee points to. A TV is mounted behind the employee's head, showing the weather forecast. They're predicting heavy rain starting soon and continuing through the night.

Jordan complains, worried about driving back on dark, un-marked roads in the rain.

"We could leave in the morning," I offer.

"I want to capitalize on those hyper-focusing drugs that might still be in your system," Jordan says, checking his watch again. "So I'd rather get there tonight."

"Get where?" I casually ask. Maybe he'll slip up and give a better answer.

"Kayenta," he replies, then, noticing my nervous stare, he adds, "It's not a copper mine. I swear. No more drugs, either."

However absurd the idea of letting Jordan take me somewhere far and secluded, it isn't what's making my palms sweat. It's the thought of letting him into my head and literally baring my soul to him with whatever natural plan he has in mind.

Jordan lets me drive. It's fun, and it also makes conversation flow easily since I have to keep focused on the road instead of him. Fluffy information is exchanged between us: we both like theatre, we both like cats (so did Leo, I learn), we both grew up without parents (his died, I left mine). I ask him if he's thought of a new name for me and he tells me not yet, but says he will pick something Greek, as an ode to my future past. And then things get serious when I ask about Dr. Messie.

"Why do you care what happens to him?"

Jordan chews his lip and watches me.

"No more secrets, kid," I warn him, quickly meeting his gaze. Another thing we have in common: we don't like to talk about ourselves.

He sighs. "To you, he's the creator of Metagenesis. To me, he was something else. He treated me..." He hesitates; from the corner of my eye, I see his cheeks flush. "It's stupid."

"It's not stupid. Tell me."

"Adalia looked out for me, always checking in on me, giving me advice. But Dr. Messie, he treated me like a son. Once he even applied to have me live with him, to take me out of the group home. I hated it there, but the system wouldn't allow it, said he worked too much. He would've taken me into his home despite his illness."

"The lupus," I add.

Jordan gives me a curious look. "I meant his OCD. His house is as sterile as his lab, if you can believe it. How'd you know he has lupus?"

"Everyone knows," I say with conviction.

My response satisfies Jordan and he returns to staring straight ahead. His hands are clasped on his lap, fingers tensely threaded together. I keep my eyes on the road and pretend I don't notice how nervous he is.

"Still, much of his free time was spent with me. He'd pick me up, then his kids, and off we'd go. We'd take trips, go to museums, or just hang out. If his kids were busy—they were older than me and had their own lives—he'd still come for me. He taught me everything I know, and even paid for my education."

"Dr. Messie has kids?" I feign shock.

"Two daughters. Lived with their mother. It was pretty impressive, the lengths he went through to keep them out of the public eye. He was amazing to them... to me. Dr. Messie didn't become a monster until..." He trails off, starts cracking his knuckles.

"Until you discovered the truth?"

Jordan nods. "On one hand, Dr. Messie saved my life. On the other, he's the reason I needed saving. But then, he took an interest in me after my parents died. He didn't have to. None of it mattered, though. When I found out, it was like I'd flipped a switch, and overnight, he went from being my role model to wanting me dead. The fucked-up thing is that *I'm* the one who feels guilty about doing nothing to help him now."

"You grew up knowing another side of Dr. Messie and then he betrayed you. How confusing it must've been for you, kid. But make no mistake, he deserves what's coming to him."

Jordan brings his hands together again and stares out the passenger-side window, his head turned so I can't see his expression. "If I thought getting rid of Dr. Messie would be the best solution, I'd have been more inclined to hand him over. But he had a partner. Remove Dr. Messie and someone else will take his place." He pauses and looks at me. "Better the devil you know than the devil you don't."

"Even if you're right about a partner, there is no devil worse than Dr. Messie," I assure him. "Who was his partner, anyway?" I ask, casually.

"He never disclosed it," he replies, still watching me. "I asked after we started working together, thinking I'd earned his trust back. He denied everything."

"Dr. Messie was the only face of his company. You're probably being paranoid."

"He was a narcissist and preferred to have all attention on him—it came naturally. But like I said, I spent a lot of time with

Dr. Messie and he was less careful around me. He used to spend hours in his office on hologram-chats. He'd let me stay to learn about the company, but then he'd kick me out whenever his golf buddy called."

"So?"

"Dr. Messie didn't golf."

I smirk. "Ya, he doesn't strike me as the type. He sweats just stretching. Ever wonder why his white suits never turn yellow with sweat stains?"

"It's all the hand sanitizer. I wouldn't be surprised if he bathed in it." Jordan chuckles. "You know, he even wore white when he took us camping."

"He went *camping*?" We both burst into laughter.

Then Jordan keeps the Dr. Messie-wears-white jokes coming fast and furious. Though they're not actual jokes, they're just places and activities, and I think Jordan is only laughing because I can't stop. Dr. Messie wore white to funerals and weddings, and on those camping trips while fishing and canoeing—Jesus Christ, *fishing? Canoeing?*—and did I know that he wears only pink socks? And when Jordan, who can barely speak through his laughter, tells me that he'd bet his bottom dollar that OCD Dr. Messie was the type of guy who kept those pink socks on while shagging his wife, I just about die. "Picture it, I bet they're toe-socks!" I blabber through snorts. That visual sends both of us over the edge and we laugh until tears spring from our eyes. I can hardly see straight and at one point, Jordan grabs the wheel so I don't drive us into a ditch.

Dr. Messie having a golf buddy is hardly reason to think he had a partner, so I decide to drop it and we don't bring him up again the rest of the drive. Why spoil the kid's good mood?

Two hours later, we arrive at our destination. It a rickety old trailer home parked in the middle of nowhere. I wouldn't be too concerned were it not for the twenty-foot barbed-wire fence surrounding the property. There's no driveway and we have to leave the car on the dirt road. I give Jordan a cautious look before taking my seat belt off.

"Don't worry, I've been here before," he offers and then hops out of the car.

We approach the fence, which is electric. A green light at the top of one of the posts tells us it's on. Half a dozen dogs greet us at the gate, clambering over one another to be the first to attack. They're smart dogs, knowing better than to come in contact with the gate so they don't get electrocuted. They bark and growl and one is foaming at the mouth like his diet is made up entirely of intruders. As if the fear of electric shock or killer dogs wasn't enough to deter visitors, there is a variety of signs scattered all over the fence. *No Solicitors, Beware of Dog, Private Property*, and my personal favourite, *Go Away, Asshole.* The most worrisome is the rusted sign hanging at an angle on a post, which reads *Trespassers will be shot. Survivors will be shot again.* There's a bullet hole in the post—a real one.

There's a call button and a video camera at the gate. Jordan presses the button. It takes a few attempts until finally, a little light on the camera turns on. We're live.

"Hello?" Jordan shouts toward the camera. If someone replies, we don't hear it over the pack of dogs. Jordan repeats himself, sticking his face close to the camera, then turning his ear to listen. This time, someone speaks and then moments later, the barking subsides.

"Cool it, pups," the voice says until the barking fades into a baritone of growls. It's a woman. To us she asks, "Hey idiots, can't you read the sign?"

"Which one?" I mumble to myself.

Jordan replies, "We've met before, and I was hoping we could talk. I'm Jordan, this is…" He glances at me, studying me for a moment. "Darius."

What the *fuck*? My eyes grow wide as saucers, and I shoot Jordan a murderous look. What would possess him to use *that* name? Of all the things I was yelling in my coma… my wife's first husband's name?

"*Who?*" she asks.

"We knew your husband."

What is this kid up to?

There's a long pause on the other end. Jordan speaks again. "Are you there? Hello?"

And then the green light turns off and the gate buzzes open.

"Why'd in the world did you pick *Darius*?"

"It's Greek. Thought you'd like it." He seems genuinely confused. Then he slowly pulls open the gate and steps through.

"Holy shit, kid. We gotta walk past these wolves? This better be worth it."

Jordan licks his lips nervously. "Show them your hands, walk slowly."

I cuss again, at Jordan, suck in a breath and follow his lead. We eye the dogs as we tiptoe across the dusty yard toward the trailer. Jordan holds his palms out in an "I'm unarmed" sort of way, but I don't trust these K9s and I cup my hands over my nuts instead. The alpha dog gives us a wary look while the others growl quietly and wait for their leader to make the first move.

When we're ten feet from the trailer, a door swings open. There's a woman in the entrance, aiming a shotgun at us. At first, I see only the barrel and my heart cramps like a vice has seized around it. Have I fallen for another of Jordan's traps?

And then I focus on the woman's face and the vice squeezes so hard my vision blurs and I stop breathing.

"Rachel?" I blurt.

CHAPTER 46 - MARC

"You two know each other?" Jordan asks, wide eyed.

Rachel and I answer simultaneously. I say, "Yes," while she says, "No." Both of us tilt our heads, confused at the other's reply, and our eyes meet. Hers are dark as midnight—just like Grace's, just like my Rachel's. Suddenly it hits me that she wouldn't know me as Marc. Then I study her face, and I realize she wouldn't know me as Cyrus, either. This Rachel has smooth and youthful skin, not one wrinkle, and her cheekbones aren't as pronounced as I remember because her face is fuller. Her eyebrows are thicker, her lips softer, and her hair is a natural hue of mahogany without a strand of grey. I'd put her in her mid-twenties, not her late thirties, which is when I knew her (or will know her?).

"Sorry," I manage, then stammer out an excuse, "I feel like we've met before?" I want to reach out and touch her, make sure she's real, and without meaning to, I take a step toward her.

This younger version of Rachel, my wife, tightens her grip on the shotgun and says, "One more step, and I blow your head off." But then she takes a step forward, and I can't help but inch closer. I'm desperate to touch her, run my thumb along her jawline, across her lips.

Her eyes move over my face, making my heart accelerate. "Don't think so," she replies.

"My mistake," I say, concentrating on keeping my expression cool and my voice neutral, though it must be obvious that I'm not blinking—I'm afraid she'll disappear if I do.

"Who are you?" she asks me.

Jordan, who's still glancing between the two of us in astonishment, replies because I can't. My throat just closed up. "I'm Jordan. He's Darius," he says, pointing a thumb at his chest and a finger in my direction.

Again, I want to kill him for the name. But then I wonder, has Rachel met *her* Darius yet? I remember they married young—or rather, she was young. I don't know about him. My heart hammers hard enough to be heard by them. I'm dizzy and my legs tingle like they did when I was drugged.

"We knew your husband, Leo. Do you remember me? I visited you a few years back."

"*Ex-boyfriend.*" She corrects him before I can even process what he said. "As I told you before, that obit was wrong." Then she relaxes her grip on the shotgun. "Ya, I remember you. You're that rude scientist. Is this your brother?"

"We're family." A prideful smile spreads across Jordan's face. "Can we come in?"

Rachel's eyes widen as if to say, *Why? What do you want?*

Jordan looks from me to her, shifting from one foot to the other. I sense he doesn't want to say something to influence the flood of memories he hopes I'm having. He probably thinks his plan is working, introducing me to people in Leo's life to make me recall memories. I can't wait to see his expression when I tell him how and why I really know Rachel.

"Do you still have that box?" he asks her.

Rachel groans. "I told you the last time you asked me for Leo's shit: if you want it, you have to pay for it. The stuff is vintage."

"We only want to look through it, not keep it."

Rachel squints at him and I smile at her. Seems her paranoid habit of trusting no one started way before she met me. She has killer dogs guarding her place, and the way she holds her shotgun is hot.

"Why are you looking at me like that?" she says, meeting my dreamy gaze.

I smother my smile. Rachel lowers the weapon all the way and closes the distance between us. My stomach flips as she searches my face again. Is it recognition? It takes the brute force needed to stop a runaway train not to pull her into my arms, bury my face in her neck, and lose myself in her strawberry-scented hair.

She backs up again, returning the shotgun to its position and her attention to Jordan. "It's a box of Leo's childhood toys. Why do you care?" she asks.

Jordan pulls out a wad of money. "If it's just a box of childhood toys, why do *you* care, Rachel? Why cling to a box of junk belonging to your dead *ex-boyfriend?*"

"I told you—vintage."

"Vintage junk. But I'll give you fifty bucks for the lot." Then he looks around at her yard. "I'm sure you can use the money."

Rachel's face changes in an instant, as if Jordan has just kicked one of her dogs. He has got to learn the art of buying people without making them feel, you know, *bought*.

I hold my breath when her grip stiffens on the shotgun, and even though I haven't said a thing, the weapon is still aimed in my direction. I'm afraid she's going to blow a hole in the centre of my chest, purposely or accidentally.

"Two thousand bucks," she says.

Jordan lets out an incredulous laugh. "Are you on crack? No way is that box worth anything more than the shit-tickets it used to hold. A hundred bucks, final offer." Then he waves his cash around, clearly way more than he's offered, like a pimp.

She spins on her heels to leave.

"Fuck," Jordan utters, then ups his offer. "Two hundred? Three? Four? C'mon, Rachel. Be reasonable."

"How much you got in your hand right now?"

They barter back and forth and I laugh when they settle on a number: two thousand bucks. It isn't Jordan who's a sucker, it's my Rachel who's feisty. Persistent. A little nutty. Tough as nails. I've missed her.

She tucks her new money into her back pocket, thrusts her chin up, and in a haughty tone says, "Wait here."

"Kid, she hates you," I say the second Rachel closes the door.

"We didn't get off on the right foot the first time we met."

"And you're still not on the right foot. Impressions matter. You can't just wave cash around at women like you're at a strip club. *Looks like you can use the money.* What are you, stupid?"

"Speaking of impressions," he says, looking at me like I'm a magical unicorn, "you obviously feel something."

"It's not what you think" is all I manage to sneak in before Rachel reopens the door. She no longer holds a shotgun. In its place, she cradles a beat-up box the size of a medium-sized suitcase. It's tan in colour with a name brand in cursive black writing, and a family of bears is depicted on one side, each holding a roll of toilet paper. Ancient water stains travel from the bears to the bottom of the box. It's an interesting way to store valuable vintage items and I stifle the urge to laugh.

At first, Rachel seems to be holding the toilet-paper box with such care, as if its irreplaceable contents are her most cherished mementoes. I instinctively step forward to help her with the box, show respect for her late ex-boyfriend, but as I stretch out my arms to take it, she heaves it. I duck in the nick of time and it grazes my hair as it flies over our heads. It lands with a poof, busting open like a piñata. Was she aiming to hit us?

"What the fuck, Rachel?" Jordan shouts.

"Take it and fuck right off!"

"Charming woman," Jordan says after she slams the door behind her.

Rachel's alpha dog rises from his spot on the other side of the yard like he's waiting for a command from his owner. When none comes, Jordan and I drop to the ground on all fours and rummage through the scattered contents. I feel stupid doing this out here, steps from Rachel's front door. I bet she's watching us through a window like we're rodents scavenging through her trash on garbage day. Any second now, I predict she's going to hose us down to scare us away.

"Hey kid," I whisper. "She said to take it and leave."

"I know, but we need to capitalize on this moment, of... whatever you're feeling. Stop looking at me and look at the stuff in front of you, Marc. Anything?" he asks, desperation in his voice.

"Call me Darius," I say, no longer hating the name. "But the dogs. One of them looks ready to eat us."

"Just... start touching stuff!" he demands through clenched teeth.

For Jordan's sake, I give it a try, my eyes moving from one item to the next. My guess is none of this stuff is worth anywhere near the two thousand Jordan paid. I should've stopped him from buying essentially a bunch of childhood toys: mini cars, mini spaceships, mini army men. There are also a few old photographs of a kid, whom I assume is an eight- or nine-year-old Leo, strewn in with some old artwork probably made by the same Leo. His name is printed in uneven block letters in blue crayon across the bottom. He loved spacecraft and planets, apparently.

"I know you're hoping I'm going to have an epiphany but if—"

"Touch the stuff if you have to, for God's sake. Put some effort in, *Darius!*"

"Why don't you tell me what you want?" I whisper-yell.

Jordan exhales deeply. He gets up, dusts off his knees, then his shirt, leaving behind dusty red prints. "You're right. I'm rushing you and getting ahead of myself." He offers me an apologetic half smile. "Let's pack this stuff up and get out of here before Rachel sics her dogs on us." He nods to the scraps of what was once a sturdy box. "I'll see if there's a bag or something we can use in the trunk."

Jordan leaves me and I glance at the trailer's window, secretly hoping Rachel is watching me, and that she sensed that I loved her at first sight. The window is filthy; an inch of reddish-brown dust covers it, so I can't tell if she's there or not. I smile, just in case, then busy myself with gathering the toys and pictures and drawings into one pile. Leo's a stranger to me, but it seems we had things in common. There's this pamphlet with old tickets to a play, for example...

"Do you like Greek tragedies?" It's Rachel, leaning in her doorframe.

I watch her for a second and she shifts her feet, uncrossing then crossing them again. I think I've made her uncomfortable.

"I hate them."

"Then why are you smiling?"

I look back at the pamphlet in my hand. "I've seen this one. Also, I hate sushi."

"What?" she laughs, and it has the same effect on me as water to a wilting plant.

"If I ever take you to dinner, you should know that I hate sushi."

"Take me to dinner?"

"Are you asking me?"

"What?" Again she laughs, but she also averts her gaze and I swear she's blushing. "Why don't I get you a bag?" she offers, then disappears into her trailer.

I turn back to the pieces of Leo's life.

Jordan returns. "Nothing in the trunk. We'll have to make do with what's left of that toilet-paper box," he says, just as I pick up a yellow, postcard-sized folder. "Hello? Earth to Darius?"

The folder doesn't capture my attention because I'm having a flashback. It captures my attention because of what's written on it: *Grandma Addy's. Trust me*, she'd said and held my gaze longer than everyone else's.

I sit on my feet and open the flap using my fingertips because my hands are dirty. Inside is a bunch of party pictures. The first one shows Leo wearing a birthday hat. He's eight. The candle on the cake he stands behind confirms it.

"Rachel's getting us a bag," I say, sorting through the photographs.

"She is?" Jordan asks as he watches me.

"I'm going to marry her one day. That's why I know her." I state it as a fact.

Jordan makes a face at me. Then I pause on a picture of little Leo, smiling from ear to ear. He and his Grandma Addy hold his recently unwrapped gift, bits of wrapping paper stuck to the bottom, and display it for the photographer. The gift from his grandmother is a spaceship. "What was it that you said before? Remnants of a timeline... the past and future intertwined..." I scrunch my brows and hand the picture to Jordan. "Check this out."

"What am I looking at?" Jordan asks, crouching down to join me. He takes the photo from me, turning it over as if expecting to read a full explanation on the back.

I recite what Jordan told me that day in the car: "Removing someone from a timeline doesn't mean you've removed their ideas. An imprint is left behind, like a ghost, and at any moment..."

"What's your point?"

I stare right at him and start laughing. Hard. Loud. Like a lunatic, I laugh. Jordan shifts uncomfortably. And when I don't stop—can't stop—his expression tells me he's going to hit me. "Look closely at the spaceship Grandma Addy gave him," I sputter out between snort-inducing laughter.

Jordan squints at it and then gasps.

"It's your chariot, kid!" I blurt out. "Deus Ex Machina!"

Leo's spaceship has the word "Halation" scrolled down the side of it and Jordan doesn't know what to do with it—just like I said he wouldn't.

"I don't get it," he says in a daze.

"Jordan, you're a rocket scientist! Doesn't that mean you design spacecraft?"

"Get to the point," he shouts.

"If only you knew someone to help you build a physical setting for life on a spacecraft." This whole time, the kid's been trying to reinvent the Halation the way Leo had intended, when all he had to do was build a spaceship resembling a planet. "The Halation was never a permanent solution. Getting the human race off the planet *is*. I'm an urban designer, kid. I shape how cities look and function, sustainably, which means with as few resources as possible. Adalia *did* send us here for a reason, even if she didn't know what that reason was. It was fate! She wrote her own fate! Don't you get it? If you design a spacecraft built to last, I can turn it into a planet."

And that's when Jordan punches me, in the shoulder thankfully, and I tip over flat on my ass. I instantly stop laughing, shocked. I'm about to call him a colourful name and then I see he's wearing a smirk. The kid gets it.

CHAPTER 47 - GRACE

When I tell Dr. Messie our break is over, that it's time to go, he waves me off. I repeat my demand, whacking the mop handle in my hand to show him I mean business.

"You're not going to kill me, Grace," he says and meets my gaze with a lopsided grin.

"I already told you, I'm taking you to some very nice people who will."

"Which means, you don't have it in you to do it yourself." He fakes pity, tilts his head, and sticks his lower lip out. "Listen, Grace. I've reached my exercise limit. So either kill me now or go get the car and come back to collect me." He curls up as if readying for a nap, then adds, "Oh, and bring me that blanket from the trunk, would you? I'm feverish."

I think I surprise him when I agree. I'm halfway done strapping his belt back around the branch when he clues in that I've surrendered. It's then that he starts to plead with me to leave him as is. "Where will I go, Grace? I can barely move my fingers, never mind walk."

I ignore him. But I do leave him the last bottle of water. My hands are full, anyway. I abandoned the tire iron with the nasty mop head at the gas station but now have a jug of gas and mop handle to juggle. After I leave him, I laugh and laugh when it dawns on me that he won't be able to reach the water bottle to his mouth with his arms strapped around the branch.

Dr. Messie was right that he never would've been able to keep up, which makes the hike back to the car quicker without him, but not peaceful. When I'm not on alert for an attack, and when I don't have to put forth the effort to drown out his constant chatter, I have nothing but my thoughts to occupy me. To break the usual cycle of guilt over all those I've hurt and lost, I obsess over my decision to leave Dr. Messie tied to the tree. What if he gets out of his restraints? Did I leave anything behind that he could use as a weapon? Was he faking his fragility? Maybe he *can* get to the gas station, and when he does, the attendant won't hold tight to his employees-only phone policy in the face of a sick old man. I'll get back to the tree and there'll be nothing left of Dr. Messie but his belt dangling from a branch.

Worry keeps me going at a steady pace, but I'm still beat. My arms are ready to fall out from carrying the gas can which, with each step, has gotten as heavy as the car it's meant to fuel. My legs are rubbery and I'm certain there's a giant, fully formed, ready-to-burst blister on my left heel. Yet, the instant I spot the car, I'm struck with lightning-bolt energy and I sprint the rest of the way. Eager to get back to where I left Dr. Messie, I fuel up, jump in, plop the GPS back into its holder, and take off like a race-car driver on cocaine. I half expect to spot Dr. Messie hobbling down the desert road and flagging down a vehicle. I promise myself that if I do, his fate will be to die in a hit-and-run accident.

I arrive at the gas station without running into, or over, Dr. Messie. I also don't see any police cars, or rushing ambulances, or even another vehicle, so there's a good chance he is still where I left him. This car isn't meant for off road, so while I fill up the rest of the tank, I consider leaving it here while I hike the ten minutes it'll take to get to the tree.

"You need to pre-pay," a voice says behind me, and I jump.

It's the pig-clerk, standing over me.

Confused, I look at the gas metre. The gauge hasn't budged. I quietly curse, then force a smile. "Right. I forgot," I say.

He gives me what I bet he thinks is a smouldering, sexy smile and I instantly change my mind about leaving the car behind. If I do, he'll call that Triple A he mentioned before. Instead, I pre-pay, pump gas, don't go back for my change, then drive away. Once

I'm far enough from the station, I do a quick check to make sure the coast is clear before I take the car off road to cut through the desert.

The bumpity-bumps force me to drive slowly, grinding the gears as I do, and I hope I won't burn the clutch like Jessica warned when teaching us to drive stick. My panic subsides as soon as I see the tree and, thankfully, Dr. Messie under it, and I whisper a silent "thank you" to the universe.

I pull up beside him and kill the engine so as not to waste precious fuel. As soon as I get out of the car, I can hear he is wheezing. Why's he out of breath? I'm cautious as I approach, mop stick in hand, in case he's gotten out of his restraints and has fashioned a weapon out of rocks.

My hand flies to my chest when I get a closer look at him. "Dr. Messie? What the...?"

He's frothing at the mouth like a rabid animal and there's dried blood under his nose. His face and neck have ballooned so much I wouldn't be surprised to discover a family of tapeworm aliens oozing from either.

"Grace," he whispers. "Thank goodness. I, I..." His face spasms and he coughs. "I'm c-cold." It's then I realize how tense he is from trying not to tremble.

I hesitate only a moment and then bend down to untie him. "Get in the car. It's warmer in there," I say, still crouching in front of him.

He meets my gaze; his eyes tiny poke holes in his doughy face. He's panting, and bile rises in the back of my throat when I catch a whiff of his breath, which smells strangely sweet, but also like cat urine. I don't think he can get up on his own, and so even though it makes me gag, I clasp his pudgy hand and forearm to pull him up.

"C'mon, I won't let you die. Not yet." I can't believe I'm saying this. "I'll... I'll get you help." The crazy thing is, I mean it. I want to deliver him to Jessica, alive and well—or at least alive.

He shakes his head, then his body goes into convulsions. Startled, I stagger and fall onto my backside, scatter away from him.

"Cold," he repeats when he's settled.

Watching him struggle to breathe should bring me joy after everything this madman has done. Instead, my lungs tighten as if I'm the one fighting to stay alive, and all that crosses my mind is his sister, the only person who knew him from the beginning, who thinks he deserves kindness. I let out a long sigh to think straight.

"OK," I say. "Let's get you warmed up a bit first. Then to the car. Deal?"

He gives me a purple, swollen thumbs-up.

But it's clear he isn't going anywhere. He's dying. And when I grab the blanket from the trunk and give it a little shake, I discover of what. Likely relieved to be back on dirt, Dr. Messie's killer scurries off, but not before I identify its snappy claws and pointy stingers. A black scorpion. I look over at Dr. Messie and know that he saw it, too. He closes his eyes as if in defeat, then curls up in the fetal position.

I bring him the scorpion-free blanket and tuck it around him. Then I sit a few feet back, and with the syringe in my hand and my heart hammering in my chest, I watch and wait. For the serum to work, the subject must die soon after it hits the bloodstream, not hours later. How close to death is he?

"Grace, I have a family. Two daughters. A grandson." He doesn't stutter or convulse or twitch once.

Maybe he's not dying quite yet. Maybe the blanket is doing the trick and I can still take him to Jessica. I'll get him in the car, drive fast, find a pharmacy, get help. I don't want to watch him die.

"I won't make it," he says as if reading my mind.

I scrunch my brows and tilt my head at him. "Then why are you still talking?"

He looks at my hand, and then I get it. He's spotted the vial and wants mercy for his future lives. He's misjudged me if he thinks I give a shit.

But then he says, "So you won't leave," and I don't know what to make of his response. Does he really not want to die alone or is this just another manipulation strategy?

He coughs, sputters pink fluid, which tells me he's bleeding internally, and it makes him cough more. I'm sitting too close for comfort and so I slide back and to the side, out of the line of fire.

My stomach churns as he tries and fails to clear his throat. It's becoming very real that he's dying right in front of me.

"I'll tell you my partner's name if…" He trails off, struggles to take in a breath, and when he does it's more like a gurgle, as if he's drowning in his own body.

"If I destroy this," I finish his sentence and make a screwface, then look down at my open palm to study the vial. I think about Kay and me acting like stupid kids, throwing it at each other. It's unbreakable. I could stomp on it, try to crush it with a rock, throw it under a moving train, and it wouldn't crack. When Adalia gave me a vial the first time I came to Vegas, she told me to keep it safe, but she only meant for me not to lose it. Dr. Messie would know this. So why would he use this as a bargaining tool?

But he shakes his head. That's not what he wanted to say. When he doesn't offer to finish his thought, I try to speak on his behalf again. "If I promise not to stab you with this?"

He lets out a laugh that brings on a coughing fit, and he manages to hork out pink phlegm, darker than before. Then tears, real tears, run down his face. Looks like we both know that before he dies, of course he's getting a dose of his own medicine, no matter what I promise to do or not do. It's my duty, the reason for this whole mission, to make sure he never walks the earth again. His life cycle will end; this reincarnation is his last.

When he's ready, he finally voices his terms. "I'll tell you my partner's name if you stay." He gurgles on the last word, then meets my stare, and his eyes water all over again.

I try to decode his words, looking to read the lie between the lines, but I don't find the lie. All I see is desperation and fear. What does it say about me that I don't care, that if he didn't have collateral to make me stay, I wouldn't? I'd happily let him die alone. I hate to say it, but all I feel is annoyance. There is a human being in front of me, drowning in his own snot and blood and whatever other bodily fluids as his lungs disintegrate from poison, and I'm… annoyed. I'm annoyed that he's found a reason to make me stay, that my curiosity has gotten the better of me, and that if he doesn't give me the name of his partner, if this isn't a deathbed confession and he's bluffing, then he's suckered me into staying till his last breath and he's somehow won. I'm annoyed that asking me to stay is a cruel final wish, like he knows that if I grant it, his dying image will live in my nightmares and fester in my subconscious, like his final *fuck you.*

My hand tightens on the vial. I don't want Dr. Messie to win and it's go-time, I'm sure of it. I'm surprised that he doesn't fight me when I place the vial against his squashy, swollen neck, and dispense the serum. But his eyes meet mine, a question in his expression, he mouths the word *stay*. I could leave—I *should* leave right now, let the poison of both the vial and the scorpion finish him. He's bluffing, right? Probably. Maybe. Then I think of the woman who gave me the vial, Adalia. *Be kind.* I still have the carved stone in my jacket pocket and I suddenly realize why she fought so hard not to take it back when I tried: she didn't want me to have it—she wanted me to give it to him.

I think about the inscription again and my heart breaks for her. Her life has been one huge sacrifice. I remember how I thought that she was lucky to start over. But what a way to live, hunting down her big brother, someone she had probably looked up to and respected once, so she could kill him and stop his reincarnation cycle for good. She left everything she knew for this one mission. Sure, she married, had a son, a grandson. But I killed him.

I go to the car and take Adalia's gift for her brother out of my jacket and I bring it back and show it to him. He recognizes it right away and his facial expression moves from low to high, like a symphony. He probably realizes she's the one who supplied the vial to end his reincarnation cycle; that explains the bit of anger I see. But then the corners of his lips lift and pride sweeps over his face, and he sobs out her name, "Addy." This also annoys me, but still, I hand him the stone. I don't do it for him. I do it for Adalia.

At least five minutes go by without speaking. He clutches that rock to his heart like it's the only thing giving him strength. But he struggles to breathe, sometimes stops for seconds at a time, then he sucks in a gurgling breath. As I watch him breathe and stop, breathe and stop, I tell myself that even if he discloses no name, I'm doing the right thing by staying with him, not for anything, but to be sure he dies in minutes, not hours on account of the serum's expiry. If this takes much longer, I'll have no choice but to help things along and the thought turns my skin to gooseflesh.

For five hours—or likely, another five minutes—I watch as his breaths become shorter and shorter, and I repeat the question, "Who's your partner?"

I hold my breath each time he lets his out, and count how long it takes for him to repeat the chore. He's barely breathing, but there's still life in his stare—and defiance. The son of a bitch is playing me. So I stand up to leave, deciding that his motive is to make me stay, not to divulge a name, and he doesn't need my help to die. He has minutes, not hours. He follows me with his eyes, and I ask him one more time, "Your partner?"

But then his eyes go blank and I realize it's too late.

When I imagined this moment, I predicted he'd writhe and squirm, gag and gurgle. I expected his tongue to hang from his mouth and his eyes to bulge out of his head, and that he'd bleed from his ears. But he doesn't. He just falls asleep and… dies. I'm seeing stars from holding my breath and I release it, instantly filled with rage. He got his way, he won. I stayed to the bitter end.

"Asshole!" I scream at the dead body and kick up dirt like an angry child.

As if waking from a deep sleep, Dr. Messie gasps.

He isn't dead? We lock eyes.

"My partner was," he says, then sucks in his final breath to speak a name: "Cyrus."

EPILOGUE – CHARLIE
THREE MONTHS LATER

It's a hot Vegas evening and Charlie's sweating. His refusal to hail a cab, like Kay wanted to do when they left their place, isn't just about saving face because it was his idea to walk. He finds it easier to deliver uncomfortable information when walking side by side rather than sitting across from each other at a restaurant, and he hopes to get it out of the way before they get there. The two agree on most topics, but when Grace comes up in conversation, Charlie always uses his big-brother card to trump Kay's best-friend card and they end up like a deadlocked jury.

"As I was saying, my sister's Germany plan was far-fetched and downright reckless," Charlie says. He started by confessing that when Grace first presented it to him, he supported it—enthusiastically, even. Supporting and protecting her had been his self-imposed duty since that night he'd done nothing to save their mother. Unbeknown to Grace, he'd never planned to go through with Germany. "So yes, Adalia screwed us over, but it was at my request. I'd proposed a better plan: stop Gracie from killing Leo. Adalia was supposed to take us to the early 2000s." He steals a glance at Kay for a reaction and notices she's clenching her jaw. "We were going to ditch you all for an hour or two to kidnap Leo. We'd snatch him up at his dad's funeral and then let him loose as soon as it was safe. So I wasn't exactly shocked when we landed in Vegas." He pauses, remembering how he panicked when Adalia had stepped out of and then locked them in the glass room. She had the vial, which wasn't actually the serum for Dr. Messie, but rather a roofie to slip into Leo's drink. Once they landed, at first Charlie had laughed to himself. They were in Vegas, where a plethora of drugs would be at his fingertips. Then he silently cursed Adalia for not only abandoning him, but for dropping them off directly in front of the *Welcome* sign. He remembers thinking: could she not have dropped them in a more discreet or, at minimum, a more convenient location? Say… at an airport where they could've caught a taxi?

"Anyway," Charlie concludes. "It wasn't until I saw Leo's grave that I realized the jig was up. At least it all worked out in the end: Dr. Messie has been stop-stopped." He never uses the word "killed" so as not to elicit a bad reaction from Kay. Now he watches her from his peripheral vision, waiting for her to have any kind of reaction.

"Huh," Kay says. Then she asks, "Is my eyeliner all smudged? I feel like it is."

"You look beautiful," Charlie replies without missing a beat. He knows this is a stall tactic to avoid talking about Grace, but he also knows better than to answer the question honestly. Kay spent hours getting ready only to have the Vegas heat undo it all in a matter of minutes. She looks like a beautiful racoon.

They're on their way to their favourite restaurant, a popular spot Oscar recommended they try, which has now become their regular place: The Cheesecake Factory. It isn't just the mango key-lime cheesecake or the Cajun jambalaya penne that has kept them coming back these three months. It's become *their* restaurant, in the same way a couple has a song, or share inside couple-jokes. Three months ago, Charlie and Kay were waiting for a table here when Kay told him she'd decided to stay in 2006. She said this decade had far more to offer than theirs, notably the weather and food, and especially the desserts. "Besides, I have no one to go home to, Charlie," she'd said, trying to keep a brave face, but her eyes were damp, as she no doubt thought about her late brother, Peter. To be clear, she wasn't asking Charlie for his opinion or approval. It was an FYI. Kay had always been independent and spontaneous and her decision to live in 2006 was no exception. The only predictable thing about her is her unpredictability. It's what he loves about her. Charlie, on the other hand, is as predict-able as a peanut-butter sandwich.

Now, the restaurant is in view, which means his window of op-portunity is closing and he still has a bigger bomb to drop on her. "Are you mad?" he asks.

"About making me walk on the hottest night of the year in high heels, or about lying to me that my makeup isn't melting off my face? I must look like a cheap hooker."

"I wouldn't call you cheap," Charlie says. He means it as a joke but she shoots him a side-glare and her lips purse. He puts his hands up in surrender. "I'm kidding, Kay."

She sighs and replies to his real question. "You're a good man, Charlie," she says, which isn't an answer at all. And then she falls silent again, and a silent Kay means she has nothing nice to say, which is basically the same as being mad.

"You know, it wasn't an easy decision to lie to her," Charlie says, his tone defensive. "But Gracie never would've gone along with the idea because it would've meant letting Jordan die. As much as losing my nephew would've pained me, it would've been the right thing to do."

"But you told her before she went home to the 2080s, right?" Kay asks in that tone she uses when she already knows the answer. Of course, Charlie didn't tell Grace. Now, when he thinks of the last conversation he had with his sister, he believes she would've seen reason and even forgiven him. The night before the shuttle home, he broke the news to her that he was staying behind with Kay. He had expected backlash; a dispute, some pleading, guilt, and sadness. He imagined she'd throw that argument in his face about the butterfly effect, that his presence would disrupt history. He had the perfect rebuttal prepared: he'd tell her he had been born in this decade to Camilla, which meant he was a citizen of both eras. But in the end, he didn't need a speech. Grace smiled and said: "If I didn't have nine-year-old Jordan waiting, I'd stay too." It was like she was dismissing him of his unspoken duty to protect her.

They embraced, long and tight. He was about to tell her about his longest-kept secret when she whispered, "It wasn't your fault, Charlie. But thank you, for everything." A giant weight he'd been carrying on his shoulders since that fateful night when he was five and she was three, when he saw the two men shoot his mother and he did nothing, not even call for help like he'd been taught to, was suddenly lifted. Grace had already figured it out. And that was that. The next morning, she went home without them and he never told her about his and Adalia's botched plan, not wanting to give her a reason to be disappointed in him when he knew they'd never see each other again.

They're almost at the restaurant and Charlie wants this over and done with, so he asks, "What are you thinking, Kay?"

"Like I said, you're a good man. You protected Grace from the truth. A *classic* Charlie thing to do," she says.

"And?"

"And I think I'll try the pot pie this time," she says.

"*Pot pie?*" Charlie repeats, frustrated with her idioms and analogies. He hates it when she avoids tough conversations like this.

"Boring, but it's a *classic.*"

He sighs heavily. Why does he get the feeling she's comparing him to pot pie?

In their teens, Grace once compared him to a maple tree, strong and reliable. She had meant it as a compliment, but it left him thinking about that saying, the one where if a tree falls and no one is there to hear it, does it make a sound? He was thinking about that when Kay told him she was staying in 2006. They were in the lobby of The Cheesecake Factory, waiting for their table, and he replied, "I'm staying with you." She'd pounced on him like a lottery winner. She threw her arms around his neck, squealed in his ear while jumping up and down. His heart filled with joy. He laughed, even as she trampled on and bruised his toes, and they lost their balance and toppled to the ground in a heap of arms and legs in the middle of the restaurant's busy lobby. Customers assumed he had proposed marriage, applauding the happy couple and snapping pictures. Though not for marriage, it was a proposal of sorts. He could've said *I'm staying too*, or *I'm not going back either*, but he made a point of asserting himself by telling her—not asking—that he was staying *with her*. Kay had a way of making him feel important. He never felt invisible around her, like that fallen, lonely maple tree.

"So I'm a fucking pot pie?" Swearing always gets an instant re-action out of Kay, which is one reason he does it. The other rea-son is that he is a person who swears and she'll have to get over it. Period.

Kay stops mid-stride and spins to face him. "What do you want me to say?" She waits a moment with her hands on her hips.

Charlie has a hard time holding her gaze when he's upset her, but he forces himself to do it. This argument must happen because he needs to get to the next thing he's withheld from her, the whole Cyrus thing, before dinner. Charlie waits; he knows she'll eventu-ally burst.

Finally, Kay blabs, "When it comes to *Gracieee*—" he knows she's imitating him but he's pretty sure that's not how he sounds when he says her name, "—you're a predictable jerk, Charlie! My little sister this, and my little sister that, I did it for Gracie, Gracie needed me, I was defending her, protecting her, fixing her, making sure she blah blah blahhh!" She drags out the final *blah* until she's out of breath and red in the face. "You should've told her. She's not a child and she deserved to know. And it's been three dog-gone months since she left and you didn't even tell *me*! I thought we were a team! So I hope you're satisfied because yes, I'm mad. Is there anything else you haven't told me?"

When he doesn't immediately answer, Kay's eyes grow to dou-ble their size and she crosses her arms over her chest. "Hurry up and spit it out, Charlie. My feet hurt and I'm hungry."

"I confronted Marc and—" Charlie starts but is immediately interrupted by Kay's giant gasp. Her hand flies to her open mouth and she bombards him with questions.

"How did you even find him? What about Jordan? Please don't tell me you're working with that crazy Jessica bunch. Even Grace said to let it go! It's not our place to—" She places a hand over her heart like she's going into cardiac arrest. "What have you done?"

When Charlie's sure she's finished the interrogation, he draws a deep breath and tells her the rest. First, he conclusively clarifies for her that he would never do anything that may hurt Jordan. "He's my nephew, Kay." She relaxes when he says this, but only a bit. "As for Marc…" Charlie runs a hand over his head. "I honestly thought about killing him," he says and then waits for a reaction from Kay. When none comes, he then explains why he changed his mind.

When Marc had said to him, "I'm building a spaceship planet with Jordan," Charlie laughed. Not a funny laugh, but an are-you-fucking-kidding-me laugh. Then Marc gave him a picture of Adalia and eight-year-old Leo holding that spaceship with the word *Halation* scrolled on it, and Charlie understood in an instant. Now, he shows the picture to a silent, stunned Kay. She takes it but is staring at Charlie like she's star-struck, and not at the picture.

"If Grace hadn't already told us about the Halation, and Jessica—crazy or not—hadn't confirmed its existence, I might've felt differently," he says. "Seeing the picture made me remember that thing Jordan had said about the future influencing the past. It made me think about how I literally watched my mother die twice even though it only happened once." Charlie clears the lump forming in his throat. "The first time I saw her die, I was a child who did nothing to stop it. The second time, I was one of the men who caused it to happen." Kay's face softens as he takes a moment to fight back tears. "Marc told me Cyrus no longer existed, that he was no longer that person, that he was sorry he ever was, and I believed him. And so instead of doing something stupid, like setting off another deadly chain reaction, I accepted his apology and then asked him if there was anything we could do to help. I figured he'd tell me to f-off given how we'd started: like I said, I wanted to kill him. But he surprised me by saying yes, so long as we were no longer associated with Jessica, which we're not. Anyway, I suggested we talk about it over dinner."

Kay raises a questioning eyebrow.

Charlie replies, "Tonight."

As unpredictable as always, Kay throws her arms around Charlie's neck, same as she had that day in the restaurant when he told her—not asked—that he was staying *with* her.

"Oh, Charlie," she says. "What you did, confronting and forgiving him, that's brave and bold. I'm sorry I ever called you a chicken pot pie."

And he knows, once and for all, that he's done being Grace's reliable maple tree.

ACKNOWLEDGMENTS

Writing a book isn't all about creativity. It takes buckets of enthusiasm and focus, and if those are lacking, a whole damn village is needed. Without the following (pushy) village people, *Deus Ex Machina* would be resting in my laptop's recycle bin instead of in readers' hands.

From that proverbial village, Emina, you were the one holding a pitchfork at the front, and every so often, Jill would take a turn. You both ~~nagged~~ inquired about my progress enough to keep me going, but not so much that I wanted to write you into the story for the sole purpose of killing you off. But above all, encouragement, inspiration, friendship: *these* are the things I'm most thankful for.

Don Olson, my fellow writer-beta friend, as someone who hadn't yet read *Hamartia*, thank you for helping me pepper in the right amount of back-story to orient those who read books out of order. (Attention non-*Hamartia* readers: if you don't understand what is happening, blame this guy.)

I owe a huge thank you to Scott Pinkowski, a kick-ass writer, beta, and friend. The changes I made based on your feedback were so many that you won't even recognize the final product. THAT'S how much you helped me. But rest assured, Jordan is still a twat (your words, not mine) and Grace is still insufferable (my words, not yours).

Katie and Melissa, the final but just-as-important beta readers, I don't know how you did it, but thank you for finding inconsistencies no one else had (ahem, Emina and Jill?).

Vicky, my editor extraordinaire, you fixed everything from my passive voice habits to my awkward sentences without ever compromising my sometimes humorous, oftentimes psychopathic style. Thank you for your patience and insight and for always going the extra mile.

Greg, the guy who sleeps with me: no matter how many times I told you I was done—even though I'd barely scratched the surface—you always celebrated with me as if you were hearing me proclaim it for the first time. You high-fived me, jumped up and down for joy with me, and even threw me one-person parties. I love you, and if, like Grace, I had to kill you to save our children's lives, it'd be a real toss-up.

To Gregory and Liam, said children mentioned in the above paragraph and to whom I dedicate this book, don't worry, I'd choose you. Probably. Te amo. ;)

A PLEA TO YOU, READER

Grace has lived in my head since I started this series in 2012. That's right, TWO. THOUSAND. TWELVE. Ironically, that number probably also represents how many rewrites of each book I did to get the finished copies in your hands. And I don't even like Grace. She's an insufferable, frustrating woman who whined about her problems to me, never took my advice, yet insisted I tell her story without prejudice. So, I'm not begging, but if you've enjoyed either book, would you mind leaving me a review? Please?

ABOUT THE AUTHOR

© Christine Albee

Raquel Rich loves to travel, suntan, walk her dog, and is obsessed with all things Beauty & the Beast. She despises cold weather, balloons, and writing about herself in the third person but noticed all the real authors do that. Born and raised in Canada to Brazilian parents, she lives in the Toronto area with her family. She's married to the guy she's been with since she was fifteen (her baby daddy) and her superpowers include being a mom to their two awesome grown-ass boys and one fur baby.

Connect with the author
www.raquelrich.com
Facebook @AuthorRaquelRich
Twitter @Raquelriosrich
Instagram @rich-raquel

www.ingramcontent.com/pod-product-compliance
Lightning Source LLC
Chambersburg PA
CBHW030810210726
48290CB00002B/516